One Taste of Scandal

Also by Heather Hiestand

The Marquess of Cake

One Taste of Scandal

His Wicked Smile
(coming soon)

Published by Kensington Publishing Corporation

One Taste of Scandal

HEATHER HIESTAND

KENSINGTON BOOKS
Kensington Publishing Corp.
http://www.kensingtonbooks.com

KENSINGTON BOOKS are published by

Kensington Publishing Corp.
119 West 40th Street
New York, NY 10018

All Kensington titles, imprints, and distributed lines are available at special quantity discounts for bulk purchases for sales promotion, premiums, fund-raising, educational, or institutional use.

Special book excerpts or customized printings can also be created to fit specific needs. For details, write or phone the office of the Kensington Special Sales Manager: Attn. Special Sales Department. Kensington Publishing Corp., 119 West 40th Street, New York, NY 10018. Phone: 1-800-221-2647.

Kensington and the K logo Reg. U.S. Pat. & TM Off.

eISBN-13: 978-1-60183-112-5
eISBN-10: 1-60183-112-9
First Electronic Edition: December 2013

ISBN-13: 978-1-60183-138-5
ISBN-10: 1-60183-138-2
First Print Edition: December 2013

Printed in the United States of America

For the community of Romance Reader at Heart,
especially Web mistress Nancy Davis

Acknowledgments

My critique partners and beta readers are the unsung heroes of this book! Thank you to Eilis Flynn, Mary Jo Hiestand, Delle Jacobs, Judy Laik, and Jacquie Rogers for your thoughts and support. Thank you to Uzma Khan and the Guha ladies, Rupa and Jayasri, for being sounding boards regarding India.

Chapter One

August 1887

"Penny daily, sir, penny daily! Latest edition!" the newsboy called, his pointed chin thrust upward as he shouted.

The sun shone hotly over the tarmacadam surfaces of Trafalgar Square as Judah Shield, hearing the lad's call, strode to the base of Nelson's Column to buy a newspaper. He had an hour before his meeting at Redcake's Tea Shop and Emporium, only a mile away, and was desperate to look at the employment notices. Never was a man more in need of a position than when he'd bet nearly all his army pay on an Indian gem shipment that wouldn't arrive in England for another two months.

"Latest scandal in the navy! Trouble at Osborne House!" The boy thrust a paper into the hands of an elderly dandy and tucked away the penny.

As the man tottered away, clutching his paper and cane, Judah reached for the newsboy's next paper. His hand collided with someone's wrist.

"My apologies," Judah said, taking the paper and tossing the boy a penny.

"Eddy Jackson at your service, milord." He grinned and slipped the penny into his pocket.

"No milording for me," Judah told him, thinking his years in the army should have knocked the aristocratic polish off him. His civilian clothes were years out of date for London.

Next to him, the lady whose wrist he had touched raised a delicate eyebrow. Or rather, a forceful eyebrow, as the damsel in question had formidable dark brows over a pair of piercing blue eyes. They created a sharp contrast to her blond hair, giving her the appearance of off-kilter strength.

She wore a gray-blue dress that didn't appear to be stylish, though he couldn't know for sure, being only a week off the boat from India, but her slim-fingered hands were genteel, though perhaps more reddened than they should be. A lady whose household could only afford a maid-of-all-work?

He doffed his bowler and held out the paper to the fetching miss.

"Oh, I couldn't," she said, clutching her reticule.

"I insist, please." He thrust it at her and pulled another coin from his pocket, tossing it to Eddy, who handed him a second paper.

Turning with military precision, he strode across the Square, still perturbed by being called "my lord." He no longer wanted to use his courtesy title. Truly, even "captain" seemed wrong, since he'd left the army.

His mother had not served him well upon her deathbed earlier this year. She had written him after surgery, perhaps thinking there would be time to explain, though a massive infection had robbed them of that time. How could she have sent a letter informing him he was not the late Marquess of Hatbrook's true son, but a bastard?

Even worse, she had not informed him of his true father's name. She'd set him loose from the birthright he'd thought was his own.

Until he had seen his brother, the current Marquess of Hatbrook, he hadn't known Hatbrook did not care. In fact, he admitted he had been the one to accidentally uncover their mother's sordid past. Still, Judah felt cut adrift from family life, in a way similar to how he'd felt when he'd joined the army then had been posted to India seven years before.

Oh, it had been exciting, true, but he had missed England. Funny that he would arrive back during the heat of summer when what he remembered was the fog, wind, and cold.

"Are you following me, sir?" said a voice at his elbow.

He discovered the young miss was directly next to him, clutching her paper. "Not at all. I am on my way to an appointment."

"It is coincidence, then," she said, matching his stride.

"Why would you think I would follow you?"

Her shoulders lifted and fell, a graceful movement that somehow drew his attention to her full bosom, hidden under sprigged muslin. He felt a spark of interest, though his attentions were best focused elsewhere until he had secured his future, one that did not involve taking money from his brother.

"I have an appointment at Redcake's." He attempted to keep his tone cool, though his blood ran warmly through his veins and risked the consequence of tightening his already snug lower garments.

"Why, so do I," she said. "It is a coincidence for certain."

He wondered why the lady seemed so paranoid. A strict father? Or lover? It didn't matter to him. He had no time to chase potential mistresses and he wasn't wife hunting either. His brother had chosen to restore the family fortunes by hard work. Hatbrook's recent marriage to a woman from a wealthy family had been a love match. Judah could do no less than follow the example and make his own fortune.

So, he had rented a small house on Adelaide Street with a valet and housemaid, both new to their present positions and related to long-term retainers of Hatbrook House. He'd eat meals out and look for employment.

The woman smiled tentatively at him. "I apologize, but you cannot be too careful on the streets around here. It has been rough going this summer."

Realizing the lady walked quickly in an attempt to keep up with him, he smiled vaguely in her direction. Had the ladies of London become so forward in the last seven years? Or had she decided he was now her protection from street ruffians?

"What kind of a place is Redcake's?" he asked. "I have never been there."

"It's quite nice, the first perfect place for ladies to relax. Not that gentlemen are unwelcome, but the atmosphere is most genteel. What is unusual is that a woman is at the helm. A marchioness, no less."

His own sister-in-law, Alys, who was born a Redcake. He had not yet met her. She had been raised to be a baker, not an aristocrat, and his curiosity about her was intense.

"Ah. I am meeting a lady there."

"Not for a tryst, I hope," she said sharply. "It is not that kind of establishment."

My, but the lady had an impetuous tongue. What business was it of hers? "I am astonished you would find me such a danger to your sensibilities."

She stopped dead on busy Regent Street, allowing others to stream around her as she stared at him. Carriages and carts passed by slowly, the scent of fresh bread and horse manure wafting through the warming air.

What did she see? He had no visible scars. He'd shaved off his military mustache on the ship. He knew his thick brown hair was neatly trimmed, his sideburns in check, his attire appropriate. His gaze had been called piercing, but never alarming. Perhaps it was his military bearing that had alarmed her gentle femininity.

"Why are you grinning?" she demanded, gathering curious stares from passing gentlemen.

"I'm grinning at you," he replied, resuming his walk. "Really, you'd think I was a Thuggee."

She trotted to keep up. "I can see the parallel, though you did buy me the newspaper."

"Women don't usually read the news," he observed.

"My cousin is very often late for appointments," she told him. "I thought the paper would amuse me."

"Ah. You are soon to find out if she has surprised you, as I believe we are nearly at the tea shop." He nodded to her. "Good day to you."

She stopped again, perhaps to gape at him. He passed through the iron gates that led to a small, neatly cobbled courtyard outside the building proper, observing the window display of pastry his brother had written about in his letters, somewhat plaintively, as he had an illness of digestion that prevented him from enjoying the goods he so loved.

Once inside, Judah found himself in a wide entryway. The polished wood floor gleamed and the ceiling hung verdantly with ferns. Most palpable was the scent of fresh baking, the best possible advertisement for such a place. To the left he could see the tearoom, lit by large windows facing the street. Ladies in fashionable garments were dotted around the room at small tables, though he did see two with gentlemen. On the right bustled a bakery with glass cases full of cakes, pies, and other items. People of all ages moved past him carrying distinctive white boxes, embossed in gold and tied with red ribbon.

The enterprise was comprised of these two parts, plus a delivery service, sales to businesses such as hotels, and a party service, for which cakes were the calling cards. All of this he had learned from a clipping his brother had sent him from a business paper, about Sir Bartley Redcake selling his flagship to the Marquess of Hatbrook just before he married Sir Bartley's oldest daughter.

What Judah did not know was why his sister-in-law had requested an interview with him here. He had promised to visit the family in Sussex when he had time as he did not intend to be a complete stranger to the extended family, who might not know of his shameful secret.

"Lord Judah?"

He turned, frowning at the name, and saw a pretty full-figured girl in a black uniform smiling at him. "Yes?"

"Goodness, I thought it was you. You have the same mouth and chin as the marquess." She studied him most impertinently. "But your eyes are a completely different color. And you are so tall!"

He tilted his head. "Are you a friend of the family?"

"I'm Betsy Popham. I make cakes with Alys, that is to say, her ladyship." Her smile became sheepish. "I've known her for nearly three years."

"I understand, and 'Captain' or 'Mr. Shield' is good enough for me."

She looked confused, and for the first time he realized his discomfort with the courtesy title might cause him some trouble outside the family. After all, his late mother had a well-tarnished reputation, but no one actually knew he was not his father's son.

"Never mind." He folded his hands together behind his back.

"Oh, I understand. You were a military man, and no doubt quite proud of being a captain."

He chuckled. That was a good explanation. He liked this girl, whom he judged to be in her late teens. Sharp like the slightly older lady from Trafalgar Square, but without the paranoid edges. "How did you come to work here?"

"My father has been with the company since before the Redcakes left Bristol. We moved when Sir Bartley set up here and he promoted my father to bakery manager. I've worked here since the day it opened."

A door opened in front of them, apparently one that led into back rooms. A tall, curvaceous redhead dressed in a striped gray and lilac gown stepped into the entryway.

"There she is," Betsy said, waving at the lady.

The Marchioness of Hatbrook smiled and held out her hand. "Captain Shield, I would have recognized you anywhere."

Once Judah's brother stepped out from behind the lady, he recognized her too. Then he moved closer and took her hand. The scent of cake and oranges filled his nostrils. Now this was the Alys his brother had described to him in letters. Ambrosial Alys, he had called her.

He couldn't hold back his smile. "Such a pleasure to finally meet you."

"All settled in?" the marquess asked.

Hatbrook had met him at the docks when he first arrived, and tried to persuade him to live at Hatbrook House in Belgravia, but his wife hadn't been feeling well at the time and had remained in Heathfield. At least she was in the full bloom of health now.

"The private dining room is free," Betsy said.

"Excellent," the marquess said, rubbing his hands together. "We have business to discuss."

"I was surprised you didn't want to live at Hatbrook House," the marchioness said to him as they traversed the dining room. "It is so large, and we are not always there."

Judah waited to respond until they were seated at an intimate dining table for four. The room was as well appointed as any at a club, with upholstered chairs, an ornate fireplace, and a cage filled with stuffed birds. A gasolier hung over the dining table and sconces were spaced along the walls for excellent lighting.

"Cousin Lewis wants Alys to upgrade to electricity," the marquess said.

Judah raised a brow.

The marchioness smiled. "Michael gifted this business to me after our marriage. Lewis is my cousin, not yours, if you were uncertain."

He was certain of very little regarding his relations now. "Quite a gift, my lady."

She smiled. "Indeed, but circumstances continue to change. Please, do call me Alys. We are family now."

Family. She said the word so easily, a lady sure of her place in the world. He had once had the same certainty, but no more.

Young women wearing the same black dress uniform as Betsy stepped in, carrying trays with tea, scones, and eggs. Judah watched without comment as his brother took an egg instead of a scone, something he never would have done as a child. He did wonder how much one could truly know a person by letters, however. His brother had gone off to school when Judah was five. When he joined the army at seventeen, his brother was still at school. They hadn't seen each other for more than holiday visits in over twenty years. At least they had been faithful correspondents.

"Are you planning to sell the establishment?" Judah inquired.

"No, no," she said hastily, buttering a scone. "It has been such a successful year. We did a brisk line in Golden Jubilee cakes. Our retail line of Victoria serving ware was very profitable too. I have learned more this year than in any other, I can assure you."

"You have been managing the entire enterprise?"

"We had one gentleman for three months, but his behavior toward the cakies was inexcusable." She colored at the memory. "But I can no longer shoulder the burden."

He looked more closely at his sister-in-law.

His brother cleared his throat. "We have expectations, at the beginning of spring."

Judah lifted his teacup. So he was to be an uncle. "Congratulations to the both of you."

The marchioness blushed and nodded.

"I understand now. At some point the work will simply become too much."

"Yes, and the air is much more pleasant at Hatbrook Farm. London in late autumn and winter is not so nice."

"What about the social whirl?"

"I do not know if you are acquainted with my personal history, but Society was never an interest of mine."

"Nor my brother's, I understand."

"Exactly. We are happier down at the Farm at this moment. What do you say, Judah?"

Confused and startled, he set down his teacup. "What are you asking?"

"That you manage Redcake's," Alys said, sweeping an arm around the room. "All of it. The supply piece is the easiest, since most of our goods come from my father's mills and factories. Except the porcelain, which was an innovation of that manager we had so briefly."

His breath stilled. Could finding a position be as simple as this? Wasn't this taking money from his brother something he'd promised himself not to do? "I have no experience," he countered.

"You have insisted to me that you want employment, instead of taking your rightful place in Society," Hatbrook said.

"That is true, but managing such a place as this is not a position for someone just starting in London. Should I not work on accounts or supplies or some such, and earn the manager position?" He didn't want to take anything from the family that he didn't earn, desperate as he was for work. The coal bill needed paying, and he must have new clothes. The rent on the house would send him to the workhouse soon enough, not to mention the servants' wages.

Alys smiled. "I like you, Judah. I really do. If you would simply agree to come in every day while we are gone, I promise to teach you everything I know during September and October, before we retire to the Farm for the winter."

"You are leaving?" Yet another shock.

His brother smiled. "Off to France on the first train tomorrow. Alys needs to rest and I have some research to do in the Loire Valley."

"This feels like a sneak attack," Judah said.

His brother's smile widened. "You wanted employment, Judah. I recognize your reasons for not taking an allowance from the estates, even though you are entitled and welcome to it. Legally, you are not a bastard, no matter what Mother did."

"I didn't mean for you to offer me a position. I didn't want to take anything from you."

"I am well aware of that, as much as I wish you felt differently. Alys made this decision. She said she would know what to do as soon as she saw you."

He glanced at the lady, who was frowning at one of the scones. He noticed the minutest speck of black in the dough. "A problem?"

She glanced up. "We pride ourselves on unadulterated flour. Or, I should say, the mills do. This is probably just a random bit of bug, but it is something to keep an eye on."

"You have a detailed eye on this venture."

"I am very, very proud of it. What do you think?"

He heard the note of steel in her voice. Family or not, she would be an exacting employer. He made a quick decision, as it was in everyone's best interest. "It is a fine establishment, and I shall do my best while you are away. I do not want you to worry during this time of joy for you both."

Hatbrook clapped him on the shoulder. "I am glad for all of us."

"We'll pay a fair wage as well," Alys assured him, naming a figure. "That is what the previous manager accepted. He was very qualified, if not of the moral character I had hoped."

"Then that is too high a wage."

"Stop that," his brother said. "You are an experienced leader of men. That is the most important factor. We have written to Alys's brother Gawain, who promised to come in from Bristol this week and give you some advice. He still works for his father in addition to managing his own concern."

"That is Sergeant Redcake, correct?" Their army service had overlapped by some years, though it must have been about three years since their paths crossed. The distance between officers and enlisted men was vast, but Gawain had a wealthy family and was very intelligent, which set him apart.

"Yes, the same man you knew."

"Did he work here?"

"Yes. He learned the accounting side before Father sold the business to Michael," Alys said. "But he didn't love it."

"He worked with supplies when I knew him," Judah mused. "I think he liked his army duties well enough. In a small station you get to know the men."

"You are exactly right. He enjoyed dealing with the traders and not doing the same thing every day, the way he did here. But he will advise you properly."

"I do agree. He was wounded. Has he recovered completely?"

Alys's lips tightened. "No, he still limps. That does not seem to trouble him much, but he suffers greatly with his eye."

"Did he lose it?" Judah winced.

"No, just the vision. He is almost blind on one side and scarred, but he can still see light and dark and is convinced that he can find a cure."

"Indian medicine is so different from our own. I expect he remembers the variety of herbal remedies and wonders if some cure might be found."

She folded her hands on the table. "Do you know, that is exactly his way of thinking. That is probably the main reason why he has gone into business for himself, to interact with traders."

"Gawain is making good money with his imports," Hatbrook said. "Plenty of money to be made still in Indian trading."

Judah tilted his head. "You have been considering my future."

Hatbrook regarded him closely. "I've been worried about you. You cannot imagine the strain we felt when we were told you were dead."

Alys's eyes were suddenly bright and Judah wondered if she might cry. He understood expectant ladies could be emotional. He thought it best to end the interview before it became maudlin.

Pushing his chair back from the table a couple of inches, he tapped his fingers on his thighs. "I know our time together is short. Would you give me a tour?"

Magdalene Cross found Lady Bricker on the far end of the tearoom and hurried over to her. Her cousin, formerly known as Lady Lillian, now married to yet another cousin, was a newlywed. She had been banished to Yorkshire over some naughty bit of gossip and was forced to marry her elderly spouse a year or two ahead of schedule. Now, she had returned to London within a month of her marriage to consult on her wardrobe.

Magdalene suspected Lady Bricker's father, Earl Gerrick, had only allowed her to come here now because the time of year was rather unfashionable. The Season was down to its final moments and many people had already left Town. After all, if Lady Bricker had been here in November as the government sort began to return, her plump cousin would not waste time on a poor Cross girl when there were far more prominent friends or relatives to enjoy. People who had the funds for new ball gowns and time to pay afternoon calls.

Nonetheless, Lady Bricker's dark sausage curls vibrated excitedly as she stood, brushing crumbs from her bosom. She squealed and embraced Magdalene, burying her cousin's nose in her scented neck. "Oh, I have so missed the Town gossip!" She squealed again.

Magdalene coughed away the scent of strong powder and gently removed her much slighter person from her cousin's ample form.

"I am sorry, but I arrived a bit early and was simply famished. I am always hungry when I'm out and about at an unfashionable hour."

This was exactly when Magdalene liked to leave home. Things the ton must never see her do would pass unnoticed, such as shopping for food. No one knew they were down to one maid-of-all-work at her brother George's home. She did her best to hide their circumstances so she could still cling to her tenuous place in the fashionable world.

"I am glad to hear I'm not late." She had been forced to learn to cook since her sister-in-law was so ill, and she had made breakfast for the household before she left. Her brother tutored his two sons. Privately, she thought he should look for employment, to supplement his meager trust fund, but she knew he hated to leave his wife for long.

"No, no, and even if you were, I'd expect you were tending to poor sweet Nancy. The dear lady."

Then there was their youngest brother, Manfred, walking trouble in trousers. He was nineteen now, and longed to be part of the usual male pursuits. But they could scarcely afford to keep up George's one club membership. Manfred would have to make his own way but he needed to learn discipline first. When Lady Lillian, as she was known then, shared the delicious gossip from New Year's Eve about Manfred and his sordid exploits with Lord and Lady Mews, Magdalene had never wanted to show her face in public again. But Manfred? He thought his erotic adventures were the height of entertainment.

No wonder they were known as the Scandalous Crosses. She could not remember the last time she'd gone to a party and not had inappropriate offers from gentlemen.

"Nancy is as well as can be expected."

"The doctors offer hope?" Lady Bricker buttered another bit of scone as a cakie, as the female waitstaff were called here, approached them.

She placed a tariff in front of Magdalene.

Her cousin must have seen her hesitation. "Go on, Maggie, anything you like, my treat."

Magdalene had sacrificed her bacon to George and her oatmeal to the boys, so this was welcome news. She perused the menu and ordered eggs, toast, and tea.

"I am not surprised you keep that slim figure with a diet like that," Lady Bricker observed. "Don't you want a cake or something?"

"Maybe from the bakery when we leave," she demurred.

"Oh yes, all those boys. Cakie," Lady Bricker said. "Can you box up a dozen of those petits fours with the Queen's face on them? We'll take it when we leave."

"The boys will adore you," Magdalene exclaimed as the cakie nodded and left the table.

"I'm glad I can make someone happy."

"Your father is still upset with you?"

Her cousin leaned forward. "You have heard the rumors about Matilda Redcake, haven't you? I assure you they are all true. And I am to be blamed for it all, as if the conception was immaculate and not the fault of that Theodore Bliven."

Magdalene didn't dare glance around to make sure no one heard, just in case that drew attention to their table. "When is the unhappy event expected?"

"Just before Christmas, I think. There is still time to find Mr. Bliven and make him come up to snuff, but not much. I wonder if your brother Mark has run across him in India. He's still there, isn't he?"

Magdalene bit her lip. They'd had word he resigned his commission, and expected him to be on the boat with a couple others in the regiment, like Captain Judah Shield, who by all accounts was his best friend and partner in troublesome exploits. But Mark hadn't returned, and they'd had no word in months. "India is a very large country."

"No word then?" Lady Bricker tutted. "I hope he isn't dead."

Chapter Two

"Oh no, not dead. We'd have had word." Magdalene spread her napkin across her lap to hide the shaking in her fingers at the idea Mark could be gone from this world.

"Not if he's left the army. Who would tell you?" Lady Bricker toyed with a loop of pearls.

Magdalene laced her fingers together tightly. "He had friends. One of them arrived in England last week, though I'm not sure of his current address. He is the brother of the Marquess of Hatbrook."

"You mean Lord Judah? Why, Magdalene, he just walked past us with the marquess and marchioness!"

"Are they in the room? I didn't see them." She wished she didn't have her back to everyone. Not surprisingly, Lady Bricker had taken the seat that allowed her to peruse the comings and goings of everyone in the tearoom.

"No, I believe they went into the private dining room. It's a new space designed for ladies' clubs to meet."

Magdalene drummed her fingers on her napkin. "How rude would it be to knock on the door and inquire after my brother, do you think?"

Lady Bricker wrinkled her nose. "Very rude, I suspect. After all, this might be their first reunion. I am no longer welcome around that family, you understand, so I am not privy to the latest news."

Magdalene wanted to stamp her feet with frustration. Judah Shield was only a few feet away. She had to take action. "Do you have any paper, Lillian?"

Her cousin dug in her reticule and found a small notebook. Magdalene tore off a couple of sheets and hunted in her own shabby bag for a pencil, then wrote a note.

As soon as she saw their cakie, she waved her down. "Please, could you take this to Lord Judah Shield?"

"I will see what I can do," the cakie said, taking the note.

"A woman of action," Lady Bricker approved. "But then your side of the family always was impulsive."

Magdalene raised an eyebrow.

"Oh, don't look at me like that. I know you are all tamped fires and scathing propriety. Now, tell me all about your family. Letters are simply not enough. I do hope I can persuade my husband to take a house in Town for the winter. Yorkshire is not the place to spend the end of the year."

"I wonder," Magdalene said. "Do you remember Constance Lively? She is our age and lived near my parents' house."

"She was your close companion, I believe. Almost albino, correct?"

"Pale, certainly, but her hair and eyes did darken later. When I last saw her three years ago, she'd become rather striking."

"What happened to her? As I recall, the father lost all his money and the mother wasted away on laudanum," her cousin said sardonically.

"She became a lady's companion. In Harrogate, with a widow who lives with her married son. Lady Varney."

"Lady Varney," Lady Bricker said thoughtfully. She poked at one of her curls and pushed it back over her shoulder. "I shall ask my husband to introduce us. I need to make calls when I return and increase my friendships in the neighborhood."

"It is too bad Constance is in such a different position. She could be a good friend to you."

"Perhaps I can hire her away to be my companion. The heavens know I am isolated. My husband is a dear man, of course, but there is such a difference between twenty-two and fifty-two." She stabbed her fork into a berry.

"I have missed you, Lillian," Magdalene said, impulsively pressing her hand. "It is so enjoyable to speak frankly with someone."

"What about Aunt Amelia March?" She chewed thoughtfully. "She's a very frank lady."

"Yes, but she's not my generation."

"I suppose she is nearly as old as my husband," Lady Bricker said with a sigh. "I remember her as much more dashing."

"She does appear younger than her age. She pays a call every fortnight or so, but she's very busy with political matters these days. An abundant number of causes."

"Ha, is that what she tells you? All of that lovemaking keeps her young, I suppose. Plus no rigors of childbirth. Perhaps she only receives calls from Members of Parliament these days."

Magdalene pressed a hand to her mouth. Lillian really did go too far sometimes, fun as she was. "I should be getting back. Nancy might need me."

"I understand, my dear, though I had hoped you would come to my dressmaker's with me."

How she wished she could go. "Another day? When I can make arrangements with someone to sit with her?"

"Of course."

The cakie returned and bent to Magdalene. "I brought in your note, miss, and his lordship said for you to come into the private dining room."

"What about me?" demanded Lady Bricker.

"I didn't mention you, my lady."

Lady Bricker forked up her last berry. "Better not chance it, then. Run along, Maggie. I shall send around a note this afternoon to remind you of our plans."

Magdalene stood with alacrity, kissed her cousin's cheek, and thanked her for breakfast before following the cakie out of the tearoom and down a short hall decorated with tinted photographs of fancy cakes.

When her father had been alive, she had had one Season on a minor scale and had seen how Society entertained. She'd always imagined having a cake like one of these at a party in her honor. Now that she was cooking, she wondered if she could learn to bake as well. It wouldn't be so bad if cake was the end result.

The cakie opened a paneled wood door at one side of the hallway and ushered Magdalene in. She stood in the doorway, clutching her reticule as the cakie closed the door behind her.

Two men rose to their feet to greet her. One was the Marquess of Hatbrook, whom she recognized as being a premier nobleman. He had visited her family early in the year during that time when the War Office had claimed her brother was dead. The other man was taller, a darker shade of handsome—and the man who had bought her a newspaper this morning!

"Lord Judah?" She faltered, as his unusual amber eyes focused in her direction.

"Captain Judah Shield." He bowed slightly. "I should have introduced myself earlier."

"Did you know who I was? A Cross, I mean?"

"No, no." He shook his head. "My mind was on other things."

"It sounds like there is a tale here," the marchioness said.

"We reached for a paper at the same time and ended up walking here together," Captain Shield said. "Nothing more exciting than that."

The marchioness nodded and introduced herself to Magdalene with an informality that reminded her of her brothers.

When Magdalene was seated, Captain Shield said, "You inquired about Lieutenant Cross?"

"Yes. Of course there was all that business last winter about your deaths, and then being disciplined for being in Lahore. Then you both resigned your commissions?"

Captain Shield frowned. "He had not resigned when I left."

"No?"

He shook his head. "I am afraid you know more than I do if that is the case."

"But you were close friends, were you not?"

"I have not received a letter from him since I arrived." He turned to his brother. "Nothing came to the Farm or Hatbrook House?"

"Not that I'm aware of."

"I will send letters to a couple of places that might reach him," he offered. "And send you word of the results."

Magdalene tried to smile. "My family would appreciate that. You can contact my brother George directly if you prefer." She pulled a second piece of paper from her reticule, on which she'd written the address.

He accepted the paper and smiled, a dashing tilt of the lips that exposed a wry sensibility and even, white teeth. "I much prefer to communicate directly with beautiful ladies. Forgive me if my years in India have taken the polish from my manners."

"Directness is common in military men, I believe," she replied.

"How did you discover who I was?" he asked.

"Lady Bricker mentioned you were here."

The marquess and marchioness both frowned.

"Even I have heard the lady is a viper," Captain Shield remarked.

"She is my cousin, my lord." She could see that whatever her cousin's dealings had been with Matilda Redcake, the wound was still fresh among her relatives. "Thank you for seeing me."

The men rose. The marchioness extended her hand and Magdalene took it, and then left the room. Outside, the cakie rushed up with a white box tied with exquisite ribbon.

"Her ladyship said to give this to you."

"My petits fours," Magdalene said with pleasure. "How kind of her to remember."

She left Redcake's and hurried for home, hoping her sister-in-law would have the energy to eat at least one cake.

At eight a.m. the next day, Judah left Adelaide Street for his first day of work. The bakery opened at nine a.m. after a busy early morning of deliveries. The tearoom opened at ten. He wanted to do a thorough job and prove to Alys that her trust, so easily given, was not misplaced. On the way, he turned into Trafalgar Square to buy himself a paper as he hadn't asked his valet to order subscriptions yet.

"Penny daily, penny daily! Latest edition!" Eddy Jackson shouted.

The lad had impressive lungs. Twelve or so, he was tall for a street urchin, and his stocking-covered ankles could be seen under the ragged hem of his trousers. His jacket, in contrast, was three sizes too large. With so much time out in the sun, his sharp nose had become coated with a thick layer of freckles and his light brown hair had a distinct dusting of auburn. He had worn a cap the day before but today his head was bare.

When Judah came closer to reach for a paper, he saw the boy's eye had been blackened and his jaw was bruised. "Been in a fight?"

Eddy's mouth closed mid-yell. "Hello, guvnor. One paper or two today?"

"You remember me, do you?"

"I remember all my regulars. You're going to be one, right?"

Judah grinned. "I like your spirit. Just one today, thank you." He pulled out a penny and exchanged it for a paper. "What happened to your face?"

Eddy shrugged. "Bit of a dustup at the station last night. Some lads from an anarchist paper were yelling nonsense at an old gentleman."

"Rescued him, did you?"

" 'e needed it." The boy hitched up his pants defiantly. "They took his cane. It were a nice one, worth good money at a pawnshop, but 'e couldn't walk without it."

"You're a brave lad."

"So 'e said." Eddy grinned. " 'e bought me a steak for my trouble. Told me to put it on my eye, but I ate it instead. Might be why it's swollen shut now."

"I don't know about that, but I'd say you deserve another steak." He reached into a pocket, pulled out a shilling, and flipped it to the boy. "Mind you don't mix that in with your newspaper money."

"Yes, sir!" His face scrunched. "Might I put it toward a hat?"

"Lost it in the scuffle?"

The boy nodded.

Judah didn't know if he was being taken, but he tossed him a couple more shillings. "That should do you, in honor of the old gentleman."

"And then some. Thank you!" Eddy tucked it away hastily, then, after giving him a sharp look, as if afraid Judah would change his mind, began calling out the news again.

Judah nodded, eager to be on his way to Redcake's, though he couldn't quite keep from craning his neck around the Square, looking for a certain attractive young lady. Of course, he was here at a different time of day, so there was no reason to think Miss Cross would be out. He had her address, after all, so if he wanted to call he could. But he didn't. He was rebuilding his life, and it wasn't as if his brother hadn't shared a few tales of the Scandalous Crosses with him when they'd dined. It sounded as if Cross women were more mistress material than wife, something to keep in mind for the future.

Instead of going around the front of Redcake's, he headed into the alley behind the shops, discovering a bustling world all of its own. Shopgirls in tidy dresses rushed to their places of employment, chattering like exotic birds. Carts full of bread rumbled over the cobblestones, pushed by tired-looking men scraping their boots on the ground. The occasional pile of malodorous horse droppings told him larger deliveries had passed by not long before.

He saw casks piled up behind the back door of the bakery, in front of the loading dock. A wagon was being filled with wheeled trays of white boxes and he saw horses coming up the alley from the opposite direction. He nodded to the workers and ducked in the door at the side.

"Captain Shield?" A middle-aged man with graying brown hair bustled up, his mustache twitching in irritation.

"Yes, and you are?"

"Ralph Popham, bakery manager. Behind me is Simon Hellman, in charge of deliveries."

Another man, about the same age, lifted his hand as he dashed by, out to the loading dock.

"Glad to have you on board, Captain." Popham pulled a white handkerchief from a pocket and wiped his forehead. "You had better see Alfred Melville right away."

"And he is?"

"In charge of the kitchens. It's a mess down there, I'm afraid."

"I should see what Ewan Hales has for me." He'd met the manager's secretary yesterday and he seemed a competent man.

"You can do as you wish, Captain, but the action is below." Popham pointed to a set of doors. Someone called for him and he rushed off in the direction of the bakery.

Judah put his hands on his hips and surveyed the frantic faces of people moving about. He didn't know any of them yet, but he suspected he'd better investigate below.

Opening the doors revealed steps leading down to the basement kitchens. He'd noted his brother's comment yesterday that this would be the first place to be electrified, since there was no outer light coming in. Of course, there was a freight elevator to move goods, but a lot of people came through this staircase.

When he reached the base of the stairs, he pointed at the first man he saw. "Mr. Melville, please?"

The man, clad all in white, including a dusting of flour in his hair, pointed to the left. "Back by the kneading machines. But you ought not to be here."

"I'm Captain Shield, the temporary manager."

The man's face opened into a bucktoothed smile. "Ah, well then. Pleased to meet you. I'm Tom Mumford, a baker. If you don't mind, I need to meet a load of bread at the elevator."

"Go on then; thank you for the direction." Judah walked swiftly down the hall, since he heard loud cursing coming toward him.

He pushed open double doors and saw a group of four or five men with towels, swearing as they wiped flour from their faces. As he drew closer, the sound of clanking machinery overwhelmed the human noises. He saw a man in a checkered waistcoat turning dials and pushing switches behind a large machine that appeared to be mixing dough. A little farther into the room, a fog of floury particulate matter coated the air.

The dough mixer stopped abruptly and he heard coughing as the flour fog spread.

"Mr. Melville?" He called in a loud firm voice that had gotten him what he needed even in the midst of battle.

The man in the checkered waistcoat turned. Half of his face had been splattered with dough. His nose was disfigured with the stuff, making it appear twice as long as it was.

"I'm not hiring today. Who let you down here?" The man stomped forward, taking the towel someone offered him and wiping his face.

Judah stood his ground. "I am the new temporary manager."

"Eh? You are, are you? Some lordling, right?"

"I am Captain Judah Shield, recently of the Royal Sussex Regiment," he said evenly.

Melville rubbed the towel against his nose. The hook the dough had created disappeared, leaving a blob. "Well, Mister Captain Judah Shield, recently of the Royal Sussex Regiment, you can take yourself up to the offices where you belong. Ask Hales to send a note around to Lewis Noble, will you? We're going to need him to fix this."

"I hope you didn't speak to the marchioness in this condescending manner."

"Who, Alys? Why, she's one of us. She'd be the first person at the controls, trying to shut down her cousin's blasted machine."

"I'd understood these machines were the wonder of the baking community."

"Aye, we have the best conditions for bakers in London, when they are working. But as you can see, they are not. We've patched these bloody machines together as best we could for months."

"Why patched?"

"Because Lewis fell out with his uncle, and I suspect there is more to the story than that, because Alys wouldn't call on him either. But you're a stranger to them, and you'll pay him a fair wage, right? We can't keep on like this."

"I thought the bread had been baked by this time of day," Judah said. "The marchioness gave me a timetable."

"The bread went fine. This is the scone dough for the tearoom."

"Any idea what happened? Sabotage?"

"Now you're thinking like a military campaigner. This isn't some outpost with tribal Indians about; it's just a business, with machines that break. If you can't get me Lewis Noble, then you're no good to me."

"I'm the man who signs your paycheck," Judah warned. "I would think about that and adjust your attitude accordingly."

The man rubbed at his nose again. "I am never my best during times of disaster, and for that I apologize." He sneezed.

Judah regarded him for a moment. The clanking and cursing and thumping as someone slid on flour and toppled onto his backside fell away. "We'll let this go then, but I am not as informal a manager as the marchioness apparently was."

Melville sneezed again.

Judah stalked out and went in search of Hales, who he could only hope had Lewis Noble's direction.

"They can't fix the machinery without him?" Ewan Hales, an urbane man in his mid-twenties, asked as they stood in the outer room of the manager's office, where his desk was located.

"They say not. Sounds as if it's been held together with bits, bobs, and a prayer for months now."

Hales rubbed his nose. It seemed the flour cloud had permeated the building now. Judah could feel it too, tickling his nostrils, but he'd ignored worse physical discomforts.

"I think it would be best if you wrote a personal entreaty," Hales said, "mentioning you are the new manager. Say nothing about being temporary, but do say that you'll pay a fair wage."

"Wouldn't that be expected?"

"No, Captain; he's family. Grew up with the Redcakes after his parents died. Sir Bartley never paid him much of anything for his work."

"Are we sure he'll remember how to fix the machines?"

"He's moved on to some kind of horseless carriage project now, but it is all machinery, correct?"

He doubted Lewis Noble saw it that way. "I'll write the note immediately."

"I'll send someone with it straightaway when it is ready."

Judah went into the office he'd only seen for the first time yesterday and sat down at the desk. He found a fountain pen and unscrewed the cap carefully, in case ink had dribbled from the pen, and found himself rewarded for his caution. After he wiped up the ink, he pulled out a piece of paper and wrote a short note, then took it out to Hales.

This note had better do the job properly. He was not going to be a failure his first day.

A boy waited in the anteroom and Hales handed him the note as soon as he'd scribbled the address. After the boy left, Judah asked, "Can we open the tearoom today?"

"The bakers will have to do the sifting and kneading by hand. It will slow them down but they'll get something made."

Judah checked his pocket watch. He'd already lost nearly an hour and the bakery would be opening any minute. "I believe I'll go downstairs and observe the bakery."

"If you would, Captain, I have a dozen or so papers that need your signature. Requisitions and the like."

"Didn't the marchioness handle all that before she left?"

"That was yesterday."

He sighed. At least Alys must have told the staff here not to call him "my lord." He still felt a shudder every time someone called him that. Until his brother arrived home from his vacation though, he wouldn't be able to dig into old family history and attempt to discover who his father really was. For now, he resolved to learn the business he'd been thrust into.

Lewis Noble was not at his workroom when the boy called, but the next morning, as Judah was walking up to the loading dock at eight a.m., he heard a couple of shouts, then saw a small, open carriage moving toward him, without horses. Steam billowed into a nimbus behind and above as the wheels crackled over the pavement.

He grinned. He'd heard of the existence of such things but had never seen a horseless carriage. Lewis Noble was a man he wanted to meet. What an imagination he must have, and such ability. Men scattered with alarmed cries as the contraption came through, belching smoke. It stopped between the back door of Redcake's and the loading dock.

One man stepped down from behind the wheel he'd been piloting and ran to the back to kick down a step. Another man opened the rear door and stepped to the ground. Steam dispersed as an engine shut down.

Simon Hellman jumped down from the loading dock. "I say! Lewis Noble and Gawain Redcake! What a sight for sore eyes you two lads are!"

Judah would have recognized that long, hawkish nose anywhere, though the eye patch and scar running down the left cheek were new. The other man had the same blond hair, and roughly the same build and height, but moved more easily. His hands had ground-in lines of black, probably from oil. Redcake, on the other hand, was well-dressed. Hat, gloves, and cane. You'd never know he'd once lived and worked in the harsh conditions of the Black Mountains of India, though the limp might tell you he'd been through a few serious scuffles.

Judah moved forward, unable to contain his grin at the sight of an old soldier. "Sergeant Redcake!" He lifted his arm to clap his hand to the other man's shoulder.

Redcake glanced in his direction, his good eye narrowed. No sign of good will. "Before my cousin steps foot in that establishment, I want his fee made clear. He will not be cheated in future."

Judah lowered his arm and frowned. "When have you ever not known me to be a fair man?"

"I do not know what orders you are under."

"None in particular, other than to keep this establishment from failing in the next couple of weeks while my brother and his wife are vacationing. Don't you trust your own sister? I found her delightful."

"Leave off, Gawain," said Lewis Noble, coming toward them now that he'd finished fiddling with his machine. He held a large toolbox. The muscles of his forearm corded with sinew, and his bicep bunched under his striped linen shirt. "It was only Uncle Bartley who didn't pay fairly."

"And Alys."

"Alys did not call me for help, not once. We never discussed my fee. I imagined she had found someone else to fix the appliances."

"Wonderful machine, old man," Judah said. "I hope you will explain it to me when our immediate crisis here is averted."

Meanwhile, all the workers nearby had moved away, clearly concerned that the horseless carriage would blow up. He wondered if that said something for Lewis Noble's other inventions.

Noble grinned and stuck out a grimy hand. "You've made yourself a friend, Captain Shield."

"Good man. First, I know I need to get the bakery machines fixed. What do you think is a fair fee for this visit?"

Redcake set his jaw. "Eight shillings."

"Done," Judah said, fishing in his pocket. "I've got two half crowns—no wait, three. And a few pennies here."

Noble sighed and took the money. "I am sorry for this embarrassment. My cousin is very money minded."

"It is only fair. I'm sure we have a petty cash box somewhere. I'll get you the rest."

"This is close enough," he said, his cheeks flushed with embarrassment. "You're mixed up in an old problem and I'm sorry for it."

"So am I, but we'll pay you fairly. I don't want to lose the business while the family is gone."

Noble shook his head and turned away. Judah frowned. He didn't know much about the family but knew he was missing some details that were important to running this business.

"The marchioness seemed a fair-minded lady," he said to Redcake.

"She's as flinty as Father ever was," Redcake retorted. "And given that Lewis was in love with her for years, she could have used him just as shamefully."

Ah, now he thought he understood. "But she did not."

"No, but I have to say she has no other model than Father."

"I can understand why you do not trust her with your cousin, but I assure you I will care for him as tenderly as a mother tends her infant. I need that equipment fixed."

"You do not want to play the fool for your brother."

Judah laughed harshly. "Not any more than I have to. He's a sharp businessman, these days."

Redcake snorted. "I understand you received some shocking news upon your return."

So the sergeant had become a gossip? He lowered his voice, refusing to be shamed, but not about to share his news with the world, either. "No, I received it when I was still in India. That is why I returned, but I was only chasing bones."

Redcake looked away. "I am sorry for the loss of your mother."

"Neither she nor my father were ever much a part of my life. Now I know why."

"I am sorry. You had more nobility in you than most officers." He cleared his throat. "I was most surprised to hear the rumors about you and Lieutenant Cross. Well, less so about him, given his proclivities."

"We were doing reconnaissance. I cannot imagine how we were reported dead."

Redcake nodded. "The army never admits they'll use men as spies."

"I wish I knew what happened to Cross since. Met his sister yesterday and she said the family has heard nothing from him."

Redcake tapped his cane on a cobblestone. "I have a trader associate, Zahir Khan, who ran across him again recently. If you want to know about Cross, I can tell you."

"Come inside," Judah said. "We had better speak about this privately."

Upstairs, they traversed Ewan Hales's territory, heading to the office. Redcake took off his bowler and flung it into the air. Despite his having only one good eye, it fell directly upon the hook on a stand and vibrated against it. With a smirk at Hales, he stomped toward the office.

"Not a fan of the secretary?" Judah said, when they were settled in the inner sanctum.

"He wants your job."

"I don't know if *I* want my job. We'll see how I feel when the family returns."

"You'll want it," Redcake said. "Never a dull moment here. Too many employees, too much action. Alys loves changing things and you'll be welcome to innovate. You're not the man to be shut up in a counting office, or law office, doing repetitive tasks. This will suit you, unless there's some estate you can manage."

"I understand from my brother that he is in funds rather more so than when my father died, but I do not know if there are estates. I have been gone too long to have good contacts in the land-owning families, but my brother might."

"He's a good man, though his choice of friends is execrable. But we were speaking of Cross family scandals, of which there are many, not my own family."

Judah smiled, thinking of the straightforward Miss Cross. "They are a scandalous bunch, so my brother said. Mark never spoke much about his family, but I know whenever he received a letter he read it many times."

"They are a notoriously licentious bunch, going back generations, and terrible with money. The Scandalous Crosses, they are called. Not received in better society, unless their own family is involved, like the Gerricks, Brickers, and the like." He made a face. "Lady Bricker, now there's another bad one. She led my sister Matilda down a ruinous path."

He didn't need to hear the gossip again. "But we were speaking of Mark Cross."

"Yes, and my friend Khan. He trades in the markets, saw you and Cross in Lahore. That's how we knew you weren't dead after all."

"I did not know how the truth was discovered. I have you to thank for the family's peace of mind."

"Sheer luck." Gawain lifted a hand into the air. "There's a long-established trader in Jaipur, well known for his herbs. I sent Khan there because I'm trying to track down a rare herb that I believe might help my vision."

"Of course."

"He saw Cross there with the trader, acting the part of one of his boys, laid out like a harem girl on the carpets. Now, you and I know that's just Cross's line. I don't know if he's on a mission or just found a more congenial way to live, but that's where he was recently."

Judah rubbed the space between his eyes. "That is not going to be fun to share with his family."

Redcake shrugged. "They must know his habits. I cannot imagine he came by that fey manner after he joined the army."

"No, I suppose you are right."

He tapped his cane on the floor. "I understand from Alys that you want instruction on the books."

"I need to understand the money going in and out."

"Of course. We'll have to pull the books for you. Unless you have further questions about Mark Cross."

Judah shook his head. "Just ask your friend to keep you updated with any news."

"I will." He stood and led Judah out.

Chapter Three

The Redcake's drama settled down. Lewis spent a day repairing the kneading machines that allowed the bakers to nap an extra hour in the middle of the night, and then another day fixing a broken bank of ovens. He had to go back to his shop to fabricate replacement parts for the mixers after that, but assured Judah he would return soon.

Alfred Melville had explained that these and other Lewis Noble inventions were what allowed him to hire the best bakers in London. Without them they were just another bakery, and most bakers didn't live to be old because the work was so demanding. Since they didn't work them so hard at Redcake's, they had more experienced men.

Judah had seen the look of relief on the men's faces as Lewis put away his tools late on Wednesday, and could well believe Melville. While his army experience had taught him not to be a big believer in leisure time that didn't revolve around hunting parties, given the trouble men could get into, he did understand the value of adequate sleep.

Gawain Redcake had given him a day of his time, imparting a lot of details about the finances of Redcake's, though nothing more about Mark Cross. He spoke a great deal about the health benefits of ingesting Indian herbs. Judah found him to be a more commanding character than he remembered. His battle wounds had brought out an acerbic part of his personality.

On Friday, Judah decided to visit the Cross family in the midafternoon, after having sent a note in the morning post to warn them he might do so. After verifying with Ewan Hales that it was safe for him to be out of the office for part of the afternoon, he set off on the half hour walk to the Cross home. He found the house on a failing court, on the other side of the Strand from his own comfortable cottage.

The Crosses needed fresh paint and a new roof soon. The niceties had been tended however, in a clean step and a pot of violets next to the door. Had this area ever been good enough for gentry? The Cross family were related to earls. Someone must have gambled away their funds. Or squandered the money in other ways.

He knocked on the door. A maid-of-all-work opened it, still holding her feather duster next to her dirty apron.

"Can I 'elp you, please, sir?"

"Captain Judah Shield to see Miss Magdalene Cross." He held out his new card, a replacement for the ones with his courtesy title.

She placed it on a little silver tray that was well polished, though the plating had worn off on the handles, and wandered down the hall to the back of the house, leaving him to stand in the entryway. *They must not receive many visitors here.*

Above his head he heard running footsteps and the high-pitched laughter of children. A male voice admonished them to be quiet, then called, "Did I hear the door?"

Judah looked up the staircase. "It is Judah Shield, to see Miss Cross."

"Hatbrook's brother?"

"Yes." His gaze wandered the walls. Three ink drawings of horses caught his eye. He stepped closer, noted the individual characteristics of each beast. A talented artist had done the work.

The voice held a hint of amusement. "Well, I'll be. Just a minute."

Judah heard whispers ordering the children into the bedroom to play quietly, then shoes clattered on the steps. He saw long thin legs first, then the rest of the man, who approached with his hand outstretched.

"I suppose it is visiting hours, isn't it? We don't entertain much with my wife ill." George Cross was a pleasant-looking fellow, with hair that desperately needed trimming. Judah wondered how his peccadilloes fit into the Scandalous Crosses.

"I am sorry. I only meant to convey some sensitive information to your sister."

"Oh?"

"She asked me about Lieutenant Cross when I saw her earlier in the week."

"I see. Very kind of you to offer us some comfort." He glanced at the wall. "Like those drawings, do you? My sister did them—horses we owned when we were young."

"Very nice." Judah saw Miss Cross come into the hall. Her knuckles were shiny red from some kind of kitchen work. He thought he saw a burn on one wrist and could see a pearl of water by her temple. He wondered how long this girl of strikingly fresh looks could stay so pretty with what seemed to be a hard life for a lady of her class. Why had she not married instead of being an unpaid servant to her brother?

"Captain Shield," she breathed, holding out her hand. "How kind of you to visit. Hetty is bringing us tea. George, will you join us?"

"Of course. Ought to have some kind of chaperone."

Miss Cross's lips upturned in an amused smile. "This house is too small for any real privacy."

George pushed open the paneled door at the right of the hall, exposing the parlor. "You can set your hat right there, my lord, on that rack."

"He prefers 'Captain Shield' now," Miss Cross murmured.

"Oh, I see. Very good. 'Captain Shield' it is." George walked into the parlor.

Judah tossed his hat on one of the open hooks and followed his host. Everything looked secondhand and out of date, but clean enough. The best feature of the room was more pen and ink drawings, plus two watercolors, one of a snowy moor, and the other of Mark Cross, looking ethereal yet competent, an angelic soldier. Judah sat on a faded red velvet chair after Miss Cross perched at the edge of a sofa. Her brother took the other side. A rough-hewn handmade table rested upon a threadbare carpet, and on that was a wooden birdcage, empty.

"How did you learn anything so quickly?" Miss Cross inquired, folding her hands over her lap. "Did another officer return from India?"

"No, but I had occasion to speak to Sergeant Redcake, who served with us until he was injured and discharged."

"That must be a relation of yours now. You know your brother and I were at school together," George said.

In some distant past when they had money. "Yes, my brother married the sergeant's twin. He is an importer now, and a connection of his saw your brother in Jaipur, probably a couple of months ago."

The maid brought in a tray with a teapot and cups and placed it next to the birdcage. While Miss Cross poured, Judah acquainted them with the Indian landscape.

"Why do you think he was there? On assignment?" George asked.

Judah decided to take the most liberal interpretation of what this Khan fellow had seen. After all, they really had no idea what was going on. "Have you ever heard the term 'a shooting holiday'?"

"Probably not in the way you are meaning it," Miss Cross said.

Judah took a sip of tea. It was light and fresh, probably the best the household had to offer. "It's what the army says when men are up to a bit of espionage, to put it bluntly."

She set down her cup, her large eyes wide. "My brother is on a shooting holiday?"

He could not help admiring her beauty, but in her brother's presence, stayed focused. "That is my interpretation. I do not know if he resigned his commission. You would have to contact his commanding officer."

George stroked his mustache. "I believe he hopes to become rich."

Miss Cross nodded.

Mark had always liked luxury and certainly their family coffers could no longer provide any. "He was staying with a trader so a great deal of money is exchanging hands around him. That provides opportunities."

Miss Cross bit her lip. "I hope he hasn't chosen too dangerous of a lifestyle."

He wanted to rub the small hurt away, but didn't allow himself to move. "It depends on what kind of information he comes across."

George frowned. "Do you know much about this trader?"

"No." Judah wasn't about to bring up their brother's sexual leaning. If they didn't already know, then they could guess without information from him. "But I do hope what little I've been able to share is a comfort to you."

"Oh, it is, very much so," said Miss Cross, biting her lip again.

Judah didn't believe her, but her lips were dewy, sensual red. He hadn't satisfied her at all. For himself, he felt physically uncomfortable as he reacted to her flushed appearance, but he had discharged his duty and could offer no more.

George asked after his brother and spent a pleasant ten minutes reminiscing about Eton. Judah's military training kept him from squirming under Miss Cross's continuing gaze, until a loud crash came from upstairs.

George glanced up. "That will be the children. I am sorry I cannot present my wife to you."

"Under the circumstances," murmured Judah.

"Indeed. I shall let my sister see you out, while I attend to that crashing." He nodded at Judah and walked out.

"This is a lively household?" Judah said, crossing his legs.

"Oh yes." Miss Cross smiled. "The boys are eight."

Her smile made her even more attractive. She was old enough to be past her first Season, but by how much? "I have never had much contact with children, but I look forward to the experience in the spring."

"Oh, how exciting. The marchioness?"

He nodded.

Miss Cross locked her fingers together, across her teacup. "I wanted to ask about last winter. Did you go on 'shooting holiday' as you put it, with my brother?"

"I am very good with languages," Judah said, remembering the creative uses to which he had put his skill over the years. "And there were questions about the current dispositions of villages near Lahore."

"Is my brother good with languages?"

"He can get by, but he has his own charms."

She tapped her fingers on the cup. He could sense her nervous energy.

"I knew your brother very well," he ventured, to let her know she could confide in him.

Her fingers tightened until they were white at the knuckles. "My family is a close one, especially with my parents gone. Tell me, Captain, will we ever see Mark again?"

"Not everyone returns from India. It is a lifestyle congenial to many."

"England is not kind to men like him," she said softly. "I'm glad he had a friend in you, and must hope he has found another in this trader, or at least a safe place to conduct his business."

"I hope you do not think I was that kind of friend." Judah puffed out his chest. Certainly he found the girl attractive, and not her brother!

Magdalene smiled. "I have no concerns on that matter, Captain." Her fingers relaxed.

"I am relieved to hear it." He uncrossed his legs and sat forward.

Her gentle laugh was a tinkle of bells he could listen to all day. Who would have thought such a sharp lady could make that delicate sound? "Did you know, in India, bells are used to invoke the gods, Miss Cross?"

"Oh?"

"Yes, your laugh, it reminds me of the sound that was once so familiar to me. I am pleased to find it here again in England."

Her lips pressed together, into a mischievous smile that broke dimples on her cheeks. "You will make me self-conscious, Captain."

"I didn't intend to. But on that note, I should take my leave. The sounds overhead are increasing, and I must return to Redcake's." Indeed, a screech, worse than any cat in battle, rose into the air.

"You may rethink spending time with children," she said, rising.

"Infants aren't this bad," he said uneasily.

"I hope you never discover the joys of colic, sir." She held out her hand to him.

Some instinct led him to kiss it, just the faint brush of his lips against her reddened flesh, but when he lifted his head again, she'd lost her look of ease. He had been too familiar.

"I will see you in Trafalgar Square, perhaps?" he said, stepping away.

"I always go to Eddy when we need a paper," she said.

"So do I. He's a charmer."

"Until then." She inclined her head.

He followed her into the hall and she handed him his hat, then before he knew it, he was on the front stoop, smelling violets. A cacophony of images and words spread across his mind. The Cross household was not a placid one, yet for that moment, when Magdalene Cross had laughed, it was as if he'd entered a holy place.

August passed swiftly. Judah never ceased learning at Redcake's. The enterprise was complex and an unending variety of special events—whether teas held in the private room, weddings catered in private homes, or religious events requiring celebration—took place. Construction on a larger private room in the building continued on as well, which rarely allowed Judah to spend time at his home. He did not see Magdalene Cross again, though he visited Eddy most mornings to pick up a *Times*. He had an abundance of pretty women to flirt with, but none of them compared favorably to her. Those dimples had him aching many a warm night.

On the final weekend of August, he caught a train south, as he'd received a note from his brother announcing their return. He had not been at Hatbrook Farm in many years and was not sure he wanted to visit, though he did want to see his sister, Lady Elizabeth, called Beth.

Traveling from London to Heathfield was a good deal easier than it had been when he left for India. The Cuckoo Line had placed train tracks so close to the Farm that he could have walked there. Since he had sent a telegram though, a carriage was waiting. Inside, he was surprised to find Great Aunt Shield, who he had thought had not left her bed in years.

"Aunt Mary," he exclaimed, kissing her soft, powdered cheek. "What a pleasure to see you so well!"

Instead of speaking, she gave him a long, sharp gaze. "I used to think you took after your grandfather, you know."

Judah pulled off his hat, crunching the brim in his fist. Outside, he heard the shouts of travelers calling for cabs and the thumps as cargo was tossed around. "I didn't know I wasn't the late marquess's natural son until recently."

"I know, dear. And I'll never tell. I must say I feel like I've come back to life since your mother passed. Dear Alys has been having the house redecorated. It's as if each time a chaise is re-covered in blue or cream one nail is removed from my coffin."

"Was the house still entirely rose?" His mother had been obsessed with the shade and ignored all fashion in favor of it.

Aunt Mary shuddered. "Dreadful, yes? I was only safe in my room. But now I am walking in the kitchen garden. I have taken up my embroidery hoop. Alys is teaching me how to decorate cakes, though I'm a bit too shaky to do it properly."

"You sound positively girlish. Next thing you know, you'll have a beau."

She grinned, exposing decaying teeth. "Now dear, you know I lost my heart long ago. I promised my late fiancé I'd never marry. A foolish thing to do perhaps, but I have been comfortable enough."

Judah felt the baggage being loaded, and then the carriage moved away from the station. He watched out the window, recognizing familiar landmarks while Aunt Mary sang the new marchioness's praises.

Pleasure flowed through him as he saw how well tended the grounds were. He was glad to see new stands of elms had been planted in place of the ones felled by a bad storm the winter before he left. His parents hadn't sent him to Eton as they had his brother. He'd had tutors on the estate. He no longer knew if it was because his father had gambled away the funds, or if they just hadn't cared about him. However, a major-general in the Indian Army had taken him under his wing. He had done well. The man, deceased now, had been some connection of his mother. Now, of course, he had to wonder what the connection was.

Soon, they rolled up the gravel drive to Hatbrook Farm, a three-story brick building covered in stucco to imitate stone, a design by the famed architect Henry Holland. He'd found architecture fascinating as a boy and dreamed of building his own stately home one day, after he cut his teeth improving the look of this one, by rebuilding the front entirely of stone in neoclassical style. He wondered where he thought he'd ever find the money. An heiress, he supposed. He'd always had an easy way with women.

"Rather a shock being home, isn't it, boy?"

He nodded. "There have been times when I didn't think I would make it back."

"I am glad those premonitions did not bear fruit," she said as the carriage door was opened by a footman.

Inside, Aunt Mary greeted the staff, all of whom were strangers to Judah. He allowed himself to be led to a room, and had a chuckle when he was put in a rose room, the best of the old marchioness's style. It must have been decorated not long before her death. A fresh rose bouquet toile covered the walls, curtains, and bed hangings, as well as the upholstered furniture. Though no real flowers were in the room, the prints were so vivid he felt he could smell actual flowers. At least he hadn't been returned to the nursery, where he had stayed until he went into the army.

The footman deposited his baggage and shifted his stance. "I'll be your valet while you are here, my lord. I'm Matthew."

" 'Captain,' if you please. If you would unpack? I'll be leaving on the early train Monday, so this will be a short trip."

"Very good, Captain Shield."

Judah washed his hands and face in the rose-patterned basin, after pouring water from the rose-patterned ewer, and then went to wander the house. He had arrived between lunch and tea so he decided it would be all right.

First, he visited the nursery, which he could see was just beginning a transformation. Rugs had been removed, leaving faded spots on the wood, and wallpaper was pulled up around the edges, exposing old paint. He wondered how many children would play here during this generation and hoped his brother would have a happier marriage than their father. At least he didn't seem ruled by the same demons.

Of course, he remembered, the marquess hadn't been his father at all. With that thought, he went down a hall, found a flight of stairs, crossed to another wing of the house, and entered his mother's rooms. Here, the walls were still decorated in rose-covered silk, a pure saturation of the color. He felt instantly unsettled by the intensity of the shade. The estate had lacked for funds during most of his mother's later years and he could see that here, in faded spots on the furniture and a discreetly mended curtain.

But, that was Alys's problem to correct, not his. He wanted knowledge. Would his mother have kept any evidence of her love affairs? Was it a passing fancy or a long relationship that had led to his birth? He found her desk in her sitting room and opened the scroll top. Papers abounded, so he sat on the rose cushion of the delicately feminine chair and began to look through them.

He found dressmakers' bills from the past two years as well as notes about medical appointments, communications from caterers, and menus for the household. A few invitations, both for here and in London. All of this material was entirely too new for his purposes.

Ten minutes later, he pushed the last drawer closed with a sigh and looked around the room. He spotted an old trunk against a wall that he'd seen in his childhood, so he knelt before that and lifted the lid.

After half an hour of searching, he decided this information was too old. He found miniatures of his mother's parents, and a sister who had died in childhood, as well as correspondence from her brother who had died in the Crimea. Newspaper clippings of death, birth, and marriage notices were present. Faded nosegays gave no hint of provenance.

"I wondered where you were hiding."

Judah turned to see a familiar face. "Hatbrook."

"Don't give me that," said his brother, coming to stand next to him. He wore a clean pair of shoes but his trousers had dusty hems.

"Been walking the estate?"

"Alys was restless. We missed you coming up the drive. She wanted to attack immediately and grill you about Redcake's."

Judah chuckled. "She's lucky the place hasn't fallen in on itself. I had no idea how hard it was to run a business. All that machinery failing randomly, customers demanding to see the manager, aristocrats wanting to talk to the senior man to arrange their parties."

Hatbrook brushed off his lapels. "Are you certain you want to be in business?"

"I like London. I realize, of course, that August is not November and the bad winter air will make life harder there, but I had a very rustic youth, so all this is new for me. The theater, the busy streets, the endless variety of people."

"That's true. You were very isolated as a child."

"The army was not so different. I spent a lot of time in small villages, but I certainly had fun."

"I envy you the hunting."

"Yes, both for food and sport. The animals are magnificent there." Judah came to his feet and shut the lid of the chest. "A lot of family history in this chest."

He nodded. "Mother suffered great losses when she was young."

"You think it prevented her from attaching to others when she was older? She certainly seemed to have her hooks into you."

"I was away at school, Judah. Beth, on the other hand, saw a great deal of her. Like you, she stayed home."

"I have received letters from her. One a week, just like when I was in India. Is she here? I thought I might see her at the station, but Aunt Mary came instead."

"She insisted. Wanted to let you know she still considered you family."

"Kind of her."

"And presumptuous, to think that anyone here might treat you otherwise." The marquess's voice took on an icy tone reminiscent of their mother's. "I would not have her planting that thought in your head. You are family. Legally and morally."

"Still, I hope your first child is a boy, so that there is never a concern about the title."

The skin around his brother's eyes tightened. "I hope I have several healthy children of both sexes, but not for that reason. The title would be far better served by you than it ever was by Father."

"Not concerned about protecting the bloodlines?" Judah inquired.

"Considering our parents?"

They both laughed.

"What about Beth? Any deathbed confessions regarding her? I expected she would have been presented by now, since she turned eighteen in May."

"No, no deathbed confessions. Beth could have been presented in mourning, but chose not to be. Her court presentation is in early December."

So the family would return to London. "Who is presenting her?"

"Aunt Mary, I think. She is quite excited by the idea since she has not seen Her Majesty since Prince Albert died."

"Good for her."

"Now, what were you looking for?" asked the marquess.

"Some evidence of my parentage," Judah said. "Obviously."

"And you've found?"

"Papers from the last couple years, and memorabilia from the eighteen-forties and fifties."

"So you need the sixties."

"Exactly. Any ideas?" Hatbrook could have asked him not to search, but Judah was pleased that his brother accepted his quest.

"There is another chest in her bedroom. And the attics, of course. Didn't she keep a journal when we were children?"

Judah's attention perked. "Did she? That could contain some very interesting information."

"Let's ransack the bedroom," the marquess said.

They spent an hour turning the room inside out, until they were interrupted by Beth.

"Judah! Oh, you are handsome!" Beth ran into the room, holding out her arms.

At eighteen, she was as lovely as a fawn. The marquess had often written of her sweet nature and certainly her letters had been endearing, but he hadn't seen her for nearly half her lifetime and the much younger sister hadn't interested him as a boy. They had never shared staff or rooms. He noted her hair had remained blond, unlike her brother's, whose hair had darkened in late childhood. She had the marquess's blue eyes, and their mother's angularity. All this was the impression of a moment, then she was flinging her arms around him.

Instinctively, he swung her around, her plain black gown twirling into a bell, before he placed her next to the marquess.

"I would have recognized you anywhere," she said, pressing her hands to her chest. "You still have tiger's eyes."

"I do?"

"Oh yes. I was always jealous of the way amber and brown swirled in your eyes and wanted them instead of my boring blue. But you look a great deal like Michael too. So I would have known you."

"I am trying to decide if I would have recognized you," Judah said.

She posed, with raised eyebrows.

"I expected your hair to darken, you see, but all three of us have the same shape to our eyes and noses and even cheeks."

"It is strange to meet after so long. Why didn't you ever return on holiday?"

"I didn't feel welcome, I suppose." He corrected himself swiftly. "I was very engaged in my work."

"I would have welcomed you."

"We hardly knew one another as children. But, I understand you are coming to London in a few months and we will spend a lot of time together then."

"I would like that. It would be so nice to have a friendly face at all the parties."

"I am a tradesman now, not a member of Society, but you can come and visit me at Redcake's any time you like and I'll give you tea and listen patiently to your amours."

Beth laughed and blushed. "Don't be silly. I am going to be an old spinster lady and knit by the fire."

"Does that mean you'll be staying?" the marquess asked, ignoring Beth but for a roll of his eyes.

Judah took a deep breath. "I thought the army was a challenge, but Redcake's is all consuming, so yes, if your wife will have me, I will stay."

"She will be delighted to hear it."

Judah arrived back in Town late Monday morning. He left his cases at his house, then rushed to Trafalgar Square to get a newspaper before heading up to Redcake's. The pleasure of interesting work that he was anxious to get on with was not lost on him.

Nor could he forget to enjoy the very end of August weather, with a bit of crisp in the air under a bright sun, though clouds were coming in. He should have brought his umbrella, but had done nothing more than change his coat and run out the door.

"So then the maid says," Eddy Jackson said loudly as Judah approached, "I never 'ad a follower."

"Tell me the rest?" said a woman's voice. Her back was to him, but he thought he recognized her.

Eddy tapped his cap when he saw Judah. "Well, don't you know it, but a couple a nights later, the mistress smells strong drink in the kitchen, so she comes in, and what does she find but a soldier in the kitchen!"

Judah stepped closer, to hear the rest of the joke. Eddy nodded to him as he fished in his pocket for a penny.

"Oh, dear," said the lady.

Judah took another step and saw Magdalene Cross's face, though he might not have known her, she seemed so pale.

"So then the mistress, she says, 'Who is this man?' And the maid says, 'You know I ain't got no followers, this 'ere bloke must a been left by the last maid!' "

Judah chuckled, sharing a smile with Miss Cross, and pulled another penny from his pocket.

"Two papers this morning, Captain?" Eddy asked, catching the coins.

"One for the lady," he agreed. "Going to Redcake's this morning, Miss Cross?"

She smoothed her jacket with red, graceful fingers, and Judah's attention was brought to her skirts—thin and definitely patched. He could see something was terribly wrong. It had been less than a month since he saw her, but she didn't seem like the same girl.

"How is your sister-in-law?" he asked. She wasn't wearing mourning clothes, but still, something had happened.

"Very bad." She sighed. "We nurse her around the clock. She's such a dear soul, we can do nothing less."

He wondered how long the woman had been an invalid. "Does she take medicine?"

"Yes, and we've had the doctor round three times a week. She sleeps a great deal, however, and does not eat much. I feel guilty, but I was desperate for a walk before the weather changed, and Eddy is always so cheerful."

"Aw, thank you, miss," Eddy said, grabbing a tossed coin out of the air and throwing a newspaper to the passerby. "You're a dear girl and no mistake."

"Can I send over a special treat from the bakery? A cake, or something she particularly enjoys? Even soup—we have a daily selection."

"You're too kind," she demurred. "Both of you."

He knew she was thinking of the cost. "As a friend of the family, it would be my pleasure."

"It is funny, I did so love seeing those pictures of fancy cakes outside the tearoom," she said, with a hint of wistfulness in her voice. "But I don't think she could manage more than a clear soup, and we can easily provide that."

"Perhaps she would enjoy looking at a cake? I could have Betsy make up something pretty, and then the rest of the family could eat it."

"Oh." A faint wash of color came over her cheeks. "That sounds very nice. For the children."

"Would you like to see how cakes are made?" He made a split-second decision. "You know, we really could use another set of hands in the cake decorating department, and I couldn't help noticing what a talented artist you were when I visited your home."

"Are you offering me employment?" She looked shocked, but intrigued.

He glanced at her skirt again. She was his friend's little sister. If she was interested, yes, he would offer her a position. "I suppose I am. Very privately, of course. And no more hours than you can manage."

She surprised them both with her answer. "I would love to decorate cakes. Yes, I would like it very much."

"Could you, then?" At least she could eat at the bakery and fill out her curves.

"Would I be paid?" she asked boldly.

"Very well," he assured her. "Cake decorating is a serious business."

She nodded. "Then I can hire a neighbor to come in a few hours a day. She and my sister-in-law are very good friends."

"Excellent. When can you start?"

She smiled, exposing those dimples that had haunted him these past few weeks. "In a week?"

"Done!"

"Good luck to you both, miss!" Eddy crowed. "You will need it."

Chapter Four

The next Monday, Magdalene arrived at Redcake's promptly at eight in the morning. The air around the tea shop and emporium already smelled delicious, of bread and pies and pastry, ready to be sampled.

Despite the sumptuous scents wafting by her nose, the iron gate in front of the shop was locked tight. She rattled the bars hopefully. Perhaps she should have been given the key? She glanced around her, looking for a familiar cakie uniform or a face she recognized, but all she saw were hawkers and carters and men in somber suits.

Then, in a flash, it made sense to her. For the first time in her life, she was meant to go in by the servants' entrance. She put her gloved palm to her forehead. How foolish of her not to realize it. This was employment, not a pastime. She had accepted that her brother George was displeased, but had claimed this position was a lark more than something that might deepen his coffers. But no one outside her family would see it that way.

Now, drat it, she was late. She wandered around the gate, but there was no egress. The placard indicated the bakery didn't open for another hour.

"They aren't open yet," said a friendly red-coated postman, walking by with his bag.

"Do you know where the employee entrance is?" she asked. "I'm supposed to start work today."

"It's in the alley, miss," he said, glancing over her attire curiously.

She looked down at her cheerful summer frock. Or at least it had been cheerful five years ago when it had been new. And made for her sister-in-law. "I don't have a uniform, yet."

He shook his head. "Never known them to be so disorganized. You go around back, find the loading dock. Just go up to the corner and turn. You'll find it."

"Thank you," she said gravely, knowing her cheeks were flushed with embarrassment.

Five minutes later, she trotted down the alleyway. A loading dock was in sight. Hopefully she wouldn't be too late. Men bustled around her, pushing carts and leading horses pulling wagons. She stepped to the side to clear the path, then tripped on a fragment of a wooden crate.

"Miss Cross?" A buxom young woman in a cakie's uniform dashed out the side door by the loading dock and ran toward her.

"Yes?"

"I'm Betsy Popham, and you're late!"

"I am so very sorry. I went to the front." She tried to smile. "I didn't realize the employee entrance was in the back."

"Oh?" Betsy Popham tucked her lower lip between her pearly front teeth.

"Not the best impression, I admit. I will not make the same mistake again."

Betsy sniffed. "You had best not. We've a busy day ahead of us. I've been behind ever since Alys, I mean her ladyship, left us. Thank heavens it isn't high season for weddings."

"When is that?"

"October to December, then April to June. We have a month to get your training managed, then it's off to the races!"

Fifteen minutes later, Magdalene possessed her own uniform.

"We wear them just in case we need to help in the tearoom or bakery," Betsy said. "Or if we take a special cake into the bakery when our customers are picking up rather than taking a delivery."

"Very good." She hoped she wouldn't have to do that, having promised George no one would learn of Redcake's. They still attended Society gatherings and at twenty-one, she wasn't too old to find an acceptable husband.

As she followed Betsy down a flight of steps into their suite of rooms in the basement, she recalled that Nancy, George's wife, didn't want her dependent on him, but set up in an establishment of her own. She had insisted Magdalene would have a happier life that way. Thankfully Nancy was too ill to know that George had spent everyone's capital. Being a maiden aunt did not hold much appeal, but it was still better than marrying someone who spent most nights out with other women, as George had until the money ran out. In her experience, that seemed the way of Society men. Marriages were only for the begetting of heirs, not for love. But she hadn't found love or marriage, only insulting propositions from men even baser than George.

The cakie uniform was easy to put on, once Betsy helped her with removing her dress, and as she tightened it at the waist using the cord provided, she wondered if any girl with a romantic heart ever won in the marriage mart. Frankly, a girl without a dowry didn't have much hope at all. A love match might be her only option, unlikely as that seemed.

"So, here I am." *Come down in the world.*

"Yes, you are," Betsy said with a bright smile. She opened a drawer and pulled out a pin, securing her curly hair. "Starting a new position is a bit frightening, I know, but it is very nice here. You'll have two uniforms, so you'll always be able to wash one out at home when it needs doing."

"I won't be changing here?"

"If you want to do that, you'll have to wear a simpler frock. No lady's maid here." Betsy smiled brightly again, but Magdalene took the meaning. They were equals at best; she might even be inferior. She had much to become used to in this world.

"I have simpler clothing," she assured Betsy. "Please be patient with me. I am new to employment."

"But you've baked?"

Magdalene felt her cheek begin to itch, just under her eye, always a sign she was nervous. She clasped her hands together to avoid unladylike scratching. "I've become a good plain cook."

"It's a good thing we don't need to do much baking at the moment, mostly decorating. But for now, I will handle the mixing and baking, though I will let you measure the ingredients. We shall mostly focus on decorating."

"I am looking forward to that."

Betsy walked over to a sheath of papers in cubbyholes at one end of a long counter. "These are our orders by day. We have room for a month of orders. Then we have a standard production schedule for inventory items."

"But this department is all specialty items?"

"It is mostly wedding cakes, but we do have a rough idea, from experience, of what we'll need. The marchioness started making wedding cakes as soon as Redcake's opened. She taught me over the spring."

"Now it is my turn."

"This sheet here with blue ink shows us what to make today for the inventory. Everything with black ink is a specific order, mostly for decorating. I think this morning, we'll make second best wedding cakes. They don't soak in brandy so we can't store them as long." She showed Magdalene the blue ink sheet.

"Who makes up all the sheets?"

"My father is the bakery manager and he gives them to us. There is an order book upstairs. Sometimes orders come in through other means, but in the end the payment has to be made at the bakery and then the order makes it to us."

Magdalene stared at the complicated order sheet, her stomach churning. "What should I do first?"

"Let's assemble what we need on a tray, then we'll take it to the mixing room. We don't have one of our own. This room is mostly for decorating." She took two trays labeled "Fancy" and handed them to Magdalene.

"We do keep our spice mix in here. Ladle a sixth of a cup out of that jar, would you?" She pointed to a large brown glass jar that had a paper "Wedding Cake Two" label glued to it.

Magdalene took a scoop and eyeballed the correct amount. Betsy nodded, then led her out of the room and down a long corridor.

"This is where we store ingredients. Eggs and butter are delivered fresh every day." She pulled a key from her apron pocket, unlocked the door, and pushed it open.

Inside was a neat variety of casks, racks, bottles, and other containers.

"On your tray, now. One block of butter, and an egg."

Magdalene complied while Betsy measured out sugar and flour. "Now for the fruit. For this we need currants, golden raisins, lemon and orange peel."

Magdalene continued to assemble from Betsy's list.

"Last, we'll need rum, but that is kept under lock and key for obvious reasons. I'll get you started, then ask Mr. Melville for the fourth of a cup we need."

She followed Betsy out of the room, each holding a tray. Betsy deftly relocked the door while balancing. They went down a couple of corridors, then they entered a nightmare.

Or so it seemed. So many men, so much machinery. The noise of gears made a dark musical beat straight from Hell, and steam heated the room to an unpleasant level that made her feel instantly damp.

"Now, you've seen hand-cranked egg beaters, correct?" Betsy did not seem perturbed by the cacophony.

"In a store, I think."

"Well, Lewis Noble did us better than that. He made us a motorized version. It saves so much time." She waved at a man with a long apron like they wore and he pointed them to a cabinet. On top of it was a large beater, screwed into some kind of mechanical device.

"It looks dangerous."

"You can make quite a mess," Betsy said cheerfully.

Magdalene bit her lip. "How do you use it?"

Betsy set her tray on one of the scrubbed wooden tables nearby, then took a sturdy bowl and knife from a stack inside the mixer cabinet. "Let's cream the butter and sugar."

Magdalene poured in her measure of sugar and added the block of butter.

"Cut the butter into chunks. It lessens the risk of disaster."

While she did that, Betsy pulled a lever on the side of the machine from "off" to "warm." A motor began to whirr behind the beaters. Then, she opened the cabinet and pulled out a flat wooden spoon.

A man, about her age, with a round, cheerful countenance and flour in his hair walked by, then stopped with a big grin that exposed his buckteeth when he saw Betsy bending into the cabinet. He lifted a finger to his mouth when he saw Magdalene.

She wasn't sure if she should obey, but Betsy seemed the type to like a bit of fun. While she went back to cutting, the man leaned over the mixer and shouted, "Ti Hi Tiddelly Hi!"

Betsy's body jerked and she heard the girl's head hit the top of the cabinet. She came out rubbing it with one hand, and a pair of egg beaters in the other. She brandished them at the man.

"Tom Mumford, you had better not walk down any dark halls when I'm about. I'll get you!"

He burst out laughing and gave her a bow. "Ti Hi Tiddelly Hi!"

"Off with you and your dance hall rubbish!"

He pretended to doff his hat, then made a comical face when he found the flour in his hair and rubbed it off, creating a little whirly fog in the air. Then, he capered off.

"Thinks he's a comedian, he does," Betsy said.

"Did you hurt your head?" she asked, anxious.

"No, I'm made of sturdier stuff than that."

"Is he a beau of yours?"

Betsy sniffed. "He'd like to be, that one, but I like a man with more businesslike prospects."

"I have the butter cut."

She glanced into the bowl. "You don't have to do it that fine next time. Now bring the bowl over and hold it under the beaters." After she showed Magdalene the correct placement, she pulled the lever up to "mix."

The engine sounds grew louder, but to Magdalene's amazement, the egg beaters began to churn in the bowl. She struggled to hold the bowl in place as the beaters churned. Betsy watched intently and used the wooden spoon to scrape down the sides of the bowl as needed. When she was satisfied, she reached for their egg and cracked it in one-handed. Slowly, she added in the rest of the ingredients while Magdalene held on to the bowl.

"I'm going to turn it off now. Take the bowl back to the Fancy while I get the rum."

"What about the beaters?"

A middle-aged man stepped forward. He had an odd cast to his face, as if his features moved more slowly than most people's.

"This is Benny. He'll take care of tidying. That is his job. Right, Benny?"

The man smiled, revealing a mouth full of broken teeth.

"This is Magdalene. She's new here."

The man made a garbled noise.

Magdalene smiled at him. "Thank you, Benny. I'll go back to our room now."

Betsy glanced at the bowl. "The mixing went well enough. When you get back, pull three times the measure of the spice mix and we'll start again."

She nodded and slowly stepped through the maze of corridors until she found the Fancy. The tray went on one of their wooden tables. She measured out the spice mix and put it on a new tray, then looked around while she waited for Betsy to appear.

In an alcove she discovered they had their own gas oven. A pocket door currently in the wall would close the alcove off. She expected that was to keep the heat away from the area where they iced the cakes.

When she opened cupboards, she found an amazing assortment of decorative supplies as well as the products they needed for icing. Soon this would become as familiar as the kitchen in George's home, but at this moment the materials intimidated her. She wondered if Captain Shield would make an appearance. After all, he had hired her.

Betsy came in with a half-filled bottle of rum and measured some into the prepared batter. "I'll finish up here. You practice getting out ingredients and mixing them. One step at a time, I think. And I need this batter in the oven. Irene came down to get something from her coat and said a lot of orders are coming in."

"When I triple everything, do I mix it all in one bowl?"

"Yes. That's the maximum you want to do at once. Here is my key. We'll have one made for you." Betsy took the correct key off her ring and handed it to her.

Magdalene thanked her and threaded her way back to the ingredients, holding her tray. She wondered how long it would take to build up her muscles. Somehow she had only thought of the artistic aspect of this job, yet that hadn't even been discussed. At least the money would pay for Nancy's beloved Mrs. Gortimer to visit every day. She hated to admit to the pleasure of being away from the sick-room.

In the ingredients room she gathered everything she needed, pounds of raw stuff that was hard to manage. No one saw when she had to put her tray on the floor to lock the door, but she nearly lost everything when Tom barreled by, and whistled almost directly into her ear.

He righted her, laughing. "I do apologize, miss."

"Cross," she said.

"Here, I'll carry that for you. You're a bit delicate?"

She stiffened. "Not at all, just new."

"You'll be tough soon enough, or you won't last," Tom said. "They insist on hiring ladies here, but baking is heavy work and no mistake."

"I was meant to do the decorating," she ventured.

"Ah. Maybe when you've learned the basics." He broke into a whistle.

"I expect so." She sighed, pointing him to the table in front of their mixer. Benny had taken away the dirty beaters as promised, so she opened the cabinet and pulled out a couple of bowls, a knife and a spoon, as well as new beaters. The mixer was still set to "warm" and she wished she had another set of hands to set the lever and scrape down the bowl but she managed well enough.

When the butter and eggs looked well creamed, even she had to admit the machine did its job very quickly. She had brought double what she needed, afraid she'd make a mistake, so she found another bowl and made a second batch. Betsy would be pleased to have twice as much since they had so many orders coming. She set her bowl of chopped butter and sugar under the beaters and used her elbow to set the machine to "mix."

This machine didn't drum too loudly, unlike others she could hear farther down the cavernous room. In fact, she picked up the beat and began to hum an old Arthur Lloyd tune as her gaze wandered.

One of the bakers caught her eye. He waggled his ears at her. She turned away, horrified, and saw her batter needed scraping down. Feeling quite competent, she balanced the bowl against her chest and managed the entire process without having to turn the mixer off. She started her tune again, tapping her foot against the floor.

When the creaming was done, she worked her way through the first batter, then the second, her arms starting to ache. Benny waddled by, glancing at her curiously. He probably did not appreciate her not very musical humming. If only she could remember the actual words to the song, but they'd lost the sheet music when they moved three years ago. The piano had been sold soon after.

Unexpectedly, her tune went funny. She tried to pick up the rhythm again as she rebalanced and pulled the wooden spoon from her pocket. Her song no longer fit. When she put the spoon into the bowl, she noticed the beaters had slowed down. She smelled burning, then a loud popping noise sounded and the machine jerked.

She glanced from side to side, wondering if she should run away. No one was watching. She pulled the bowl away, sidling back to the table, then, gathering her bravado when nothing else happened, went back to it, put her hand to the lever and shoved it all the way to "off." Sparks burst from between two panels.

She cried out and backed away as a lick of flame poked its way out of the top of the machine. The rude baker ran at her. She froze, terrified, but he went right past her and kicked open the back of the machine. The flame doused and smoke rose into the air. They both coughed.

"Good heavens, woman!" shouted a man in a checkered waistcoat, dashing down the room. "Who are you and what have you done?"

"I'm Miss Cross, new to the Fancy."

"Who is your supervisor?" he roared.

"Miss Popham?" she ventured.

He pointed a finger. "Go. Now."

She swallowed hard, doing her best to hold back tears, and grabbed her bowls, ignoring the trays and containers. At least she could rescue the cake batter. She crept away, sniffing, and expecting to be fired.

"We'll have to call in Lewis Noble," said the man who'd ordered her away. "Go tell Mr. Hales."

"Yes, sir," said the rude baker, rushing past her as she made her slow way down the hall with the heavy batter.

When she reached the Fancy, she had to set down the bowls to open the door. Betsy stared at her in the doorway.

"Your arms are shaking! Why do you have so much batter?"

"I thought I would help by doing double," she said, holding back a fresh wave of tears with great difficulty. "But I broke the machine. I saw fire! Oh, they are so angry."

Betsy's eyes rounded. "You can't overtax the mixers. They are fragile beasts. When we are working in volume we use multiple machines. But, fire?"

"I panicked when it started acting funny. So I turned the lever from 'mix' to 'off.' "

"Not 'warm' first? You have to take it down by degrees."

She sniffed again. "I didn't know, I'm sorry. I suppose I'll be sacked now."

Betsy patted her on the shoulder. "You were just trying to help. But you're like a baby. You don't know anything about how to do things around here, so don't assume."

She wiped her eyes and nodded. From now on she would follow instructions. Betsy sighed and measured rum into the bowls. For the rest of the morning, she showed Magdalene how to sand trays and lay down paper, then put cake rings on the paper and ladle in the batter. She learned how to operate the gas oven.

At one, Betsy sent her home, saying the cakes needed to cool before she could learn to decorate them. "Since no one has come to sack you, be here at eight—the back entrance, mind."

"I will not make the same mistake twice," Magdalene promised. She took off her apron and tied it around her dress, too tired to even consider taking off the cakie uniform. She wouldn't dare ask Betsy to help her change.

Slowly, she hobbled her way up the stairs to the employee door, hoping she wouldn't see Captain Shield in her bedraggled state. Her wish was granted and she made her slow way home through a light September drizzle, feeling both exalted and shamed by her first day as a working woman.

Judah heard laughter as he entered Redcake's basement late the next morning. Female laughter at that, not at all what he would expect in the male-dominated bakery. He had come to hand Lewis Noble his shillings, feeling honor-bound to provide immediate payment in the hopes of keeping relations cordial with the inventor. Apparently, making Noble happy wasn't a matter of prompt payment though; a pretty girl would do just as well.

The back of one of the mixers hung open, but Noble's wrench was slack in his hand as he chatted to a slim blonde in a cakie uniform.

"No, I haven't seen the paper this morning, but I can't believe His Royal Highness would do that," she said.

"This country can do better than its degraded nobility," Lewis said.

Odd talk for a flirtation. No wonder Alys had rejected him in favor of Hatbrook.

"There are many wonderful people with titles," said the cakie. "Why, this bakery is owned by one of them."

"My point exactly. Alys is only an aristocrat by marriage."

"I have numerous title-holders in my family tree," she said. "They aren't all bad people by any means."

"Miss Cross!" Judah interjected, startled as he realized who the blonde was. "Is this how you learn to decorate cakes?"

She turned in a flash, her cheeks reddening as she lost her flirtatious smile. And here he'd thought she found him of interest, but he and Lewis Noble were so different as to be separate species entirely.

"I broke the machine, Captain Shield. Betsy said I should learn from Mr. Noble what I did wrong."

Judah frowned. "What were you doing with a mixer?"

"Making a cake." She tucked her hands into her dress as if delighted to find pockets.

He supposed the kind of clothes she was used to wouldn't have pockets. She had a style of her own, not fashionable precisely, almost American, even, in the calico prints he'd seen her wear. "Err, making a cake? I hired you for your artistic talents."

"I believe Betsy thinks me hired as her assistant for all aspects of the Fancy."

"How do you feel about that?"

She smiled wanly. "I set the mixer on fire yesterday."

"Yet you are still employed. Betsy must see some promise in you."

"It was a series of misfortunes. I was trying to impress her."

"Perhaps you should keep your head down in the future and simply do your work." His tone was severe.

She glanced at Lewis. The lady was intelligent. She knew he was displeased to catch her flirting. "I believe Mr. Noble has explained my error. Perhaps Betsy will have some new task for me."

"I am certain that is so." Judah put his hands behind his back and inclined his head in her direction.

Lewis reached out and took her right hand in his filthy mitts. "A pleasure to meet you, Miss Cross."

"Very pleased to meet you, sir."

Judah suppressed a growl in the back of his throat as the chit simpered. He tossed shillings on the wooden table and stalked off. If Noble wanted to speak to him he could just come to the office.

He went down the hall and back up the steps. When he faced the steps up to the offices, he decided to go out to the loading dock instead to get some fresh air. He needed to decide if he was heading back to Heathfield to continue his search through his mother's things. This position was engrossing him during every waking hour, but he had his very identity at stake. He had to know if he was a gentleman's son or not.

When he reached the outdoors, he lost the sense of claws digging into his throat. Desperate for fresh air, he jumped off the loading dock and took a running step into the alley.

"Pardon me, guvnor!"

He felt a smaller body crash into his. Instinctively, he grabbed the windmilling arm and pulled the lad upright. His cap fell off and he recognized Eddy Jackson.

"Eddy! What are you doing skulking behind the bakeshop?"

The newsboy blinked. "Captain Shield?"

"Yes, I manage this establishment."

"You work?"

"Yes, I do."

Eddy tilted his head. "Toffs like you usually don't."

"I like to keep busy," Judah said, stiffening.

" 'spect you need the soft," he suggested.

"I expect I do."

He scratched his cheek. "I'm not skulking. It's just that sometimes they put out old bread from the bakery and it's fine stuff. Well, you knows that."

"A boy like you is earning his own way." Judah frowned. "Why do you need charity bread? Not developing bad habits, I hope?"

The boy shrugged. "Just a way to save the chink. I spends a lot on my clothes, you know. Got to look presentable in my line."

Judah smiled. "Indeed you do." He clapped the boy on the shoulder and led him toward the stairs.

"Why are you bringin' me in 'ere? It's too fancy for me."

"You're with me, Eddy. It will be all right."

With slow steps, acting as if he was on his way to his execution, Eddy followed him into the back of Redcake's. Judah led him into the corridor behind the bakery, where racks of fresh goods were kept ready to be placed on the counters.

"You there, Irene."

The salesgirl glanced over, her hands full of a tray of petits fours. "Yes, sir?"

"Can you put this loaf on my account, please? And this bit of shortbread?"

"Yes, sir."

Judah handed Eddy a large loaf of white bread and a round shortbread biscuit. "For you, lad. Enjoy."

Eddy blinked. "Are you sure, sir?"

"My pleasure." Judah leaned to Eddy's ear. "I get a discount."

Eddy grinned. "Thank you."

"I'll show you out."

As they walked toward the loading dock, Judah noticed a sensation of renewal. A conversation with Eddy was as good as a walk through one of the Indian markets that had refreshed him over his years of army service.

The door to the basement steps flew open and a girl dashed out, her apron covering her mouth. Magdalene, again? What was wrong now?

Chapter Five

"Miss Cross? That you?" Eddy inquired.

The girl put down her apron and sniffed. Judah didn't recognize the cakie after all. Though slim and blond, her features were much more delicate than Magdalene's. Eddy shrugged and looked at him.

"The loading dock is that way, Eddy. Enjoy your treat."

The boy nodded and touched a finger to his cap. "See you in the Square."

Judah turned to the girl. "Now, what's this all about?"

The girl took one look at him and promptly burst into tears again. Ralph Popham dashed down the corridor leading toward the tearoom and took the girl in hand.

"I'm sorry, sir. It's only that Effie heard bad tidings from her family yesterday."

"My mum died!" the girl shrieked.

"She shouldn't be at work," Judah said, taken aback. "My condolences."

"I can't afford the fare. I've only been here two months." This set off a fresh round of tears.

Judah turned to Popham. "Give her train fare to wherever her mother lived, and her job back when she returns."

"Sir?" Popham said.

"Quickly, now," Judah said. "This is a place of business. The customers might be able to hear the commotion."

Popham nodded, then touched his head to make sure the flap of hair covering his bald pate remained in place. "Excellent, sir. Come to my closet, Effie, we'll take care of this."

He led off the girl, sobbing more quietly now. Judah stomped to his office, wondering if the marchioness would have done the same. He'd have to write her a note and ask. A solution like this would not have worked in the army.

Thoughts of the army kept Judah tossing that night. When he left Redcake's the next evening he found himself walking a circuitous route, not quite ready to return home.

As he walked down a street with establishments not as fine as Redcake's, he saw a man with a ragged soldier's coat holding a gentleman's horse. When he passed by, the gentleman stepped out of a tailor's shop, threw the old soldier a coin, and mounted his horse. The soldier climbed the curb, balancing uneasily on what was evidently a false leg, and went back to his position in front of the tailor's shop.

"This a good spot for you, Private?" Judah asked, following him to the shop.

"Good enough," said the man. He had a long scar running down his cheek, pulling up his upper lip at one corner.

Judah was reminded of Sergeant Redcake's wounds. This man had similar injuries but of a more severe nature, and presumably this man did not have a wealthy family to aid him. Still, his uniform was clean, what was left of it, and his boots were polished. He had his pride, even if he did have spirits on his breath. "Where did you take those wounds?"

"Afghanistan."

"I just returned from India last month. Royal Sussex, Second Battalion."

"I was with the East Lancashire Regiment."

"What brought you down here?"

"Eh. Didn't want to go back to fishing."

"It is not for everyone," Judah agreed.

"You done all right for yourself," the soldier observed.

"Family found me work."

"Me wife's brother is the owner of this 'ere shop," the soldier said, jerking his chin at the tailor's sign. Then, seeing a barouche roll up, he stepped into the street to help the inhabitants down.

Judah returned to his walk, happy to hear he wasn't the only former soldier finding employment through family. Humble or grand, someone had to know where the work was and match men to it.

The next morning he felt jaunty in a new yellow waistcoat paid for with his Redcake's earnings. The sun still shone in a summer kind of way, though he had his umbrella since the wind was up and some grayish clouds skulked in the distance. He set out to the Square for his paper and chat with Eddy earlier than usual.

As he crossed to Nelson's Column, he saw Magdalene Cross talking with Eddy. She wore a gray wool shawl over her cakie uniform. He hesitated, not knowing if she'd want to speak to him after his reprimand two days earlier. But then she turned and he could see her lovely blue eyes, catching bright sun as they met his. She didn't smile, but didn't recoil either.

"On your way in, Miss Cross?" he said, giving Eddy a nod and tossing him a penny.

"Yes. Betsy has me at work from eight to one." She touched her flat straw hat as a gust of wind rushed through the Square.

"The hours are congenial for you?"

"Very much so. I appreciate being out at an unfashionable hour."

"Concerned that you might be seen?" He nodded to Eddy. She smiled and they walked off together in the direction of Regent Street.

"It is always on my mind. I have not quite given up my place in Society."

"Fashionable people keep late hours."

"That will be a concern for us both, but the Season hasn't started yet."

"I do not plan to socialize."

She smiled knowingly. "You may feel differently when the weather changes, Captain Shield. It is pleasant to visit luxurious houses and be amused when it is no longer so nice outside."

"I take your point." They stepped into a busy intersection full of carts and carriages.

"I must say I appreciate the shorter skirt of my uniform," she said as they dashed across. "The hem doesn't get so dirty."

He glanced down, hoping for a flash of her leg, but only saw her shoes. "My brother told me his wife hated to leave off her uniform for fashionable attire."

"I can already understand that." They brushed past a wagon before reaching the curb. "I was a convert on my second day."

"And here you are on your fourth, a veteran already."

She laughed. "I never thought I would enjoy it so. I expected to like the decorating but we have not even done that yet."

A policeman pushed by, holding the arm of a thin, greasy man with a vacant grin. He jostled Magdalene, dropping a rasher of bacon in the process. Judah took her elbow and towed her out of the way. Setting them into a doorway, he asked, "Are you well?"

She brushed at her shawl and frowned when she saw lard shining along her arm. "It will take some scrubbing, that's all." A ragged boy pushed underneath Miss Cross's arm. In a flash, he'd used a knife to cut her reticule strings and dashed off across the street, threading through the traffic.

"Blast it!" Judah yelled.

He glanced at Magdalene quickly, but didn't see any harm to her, so he sped after the boy. After narrowly missing a donkey cart, he stared down the street, sure the boy wouldn't head into the fashionable area. He was right. A pair of skinny legs headed south, back toward Trafalgar Square. Taking off at a run, Judah knocked off a woman's top hat and nearly somersaulted as he dived for it before it hit the ground. He threw it back to her, then kept going.

A network of small streets off Haymarket might have ruined the chase but the pounding of the small feet told him where to go. He followed the sounds to the end of a silent residential lane. Did he have the lad cornered in a dead end? The boy's eyes were wide as he glanced around the closed doors of tenements lining the mews.

"Just give me the reticule," Judah called. "You saw that policeman, same as I did. I won't take you to him if I get the lady's possessions."

"I'm armed," threatened the boy. His hand fisted in his pocket.

Judah smiled grimly and opened his topcoat. The handle of his Enfield revolver showed at the top of a specially made pocket. Having left the military so recently, he was not yet ready to go about unarmed.

The boy's eyes widened. "Cor, I don't want no trouble!" He

pulled the crocheted bag out from his shirt and tossed it at Judah. It landed on his foot. Then, the little thief ran into a doorway and disappeared. A door slammed shut.

This had been his escape route all along. Judah decided it was best to go before the lad's friends arrived. He picked up the gray woolen reticule and straightened his clothing, then retraced his steps to Miss Cross.

She had followed him and he found her a couple of blocks away, standing in the middle of the sidewalk, peering around passersby in search of him as she took slow steps forward.

"Miss Cross!" He held up his hand, showing her the reticule, and was gratified by the look of pleasure in her eyes.

"Are you okay? Did he hurt you?" She rushed toward him and put her hands on his upper arms.

"I'm fine. You look as if you're about to shake me."

A bit wild-eyed, she did just that, then attempted to pull him forward. When she couldn't move his hard bulk, she pressed herself to him and gave him a hug.

"On a public street, Miss Cross? Someone might see you." He couldn't suppress a grin at this warrior's welcome.

"You could have died!" She stamped her foot. "Oh, I could slap you. You know how poor I am. My reticule isn't worth anything."

He pulled her against a chandler's window and handed the small item to her. "It looks handmade. It matches your shawl."

She took it with a sigh. "Yes, yes, but it holds no sentimental value. I made them both."

The value might not be monetary, but the reward here was he could tell she'd worried about him. "It was just a boy."

"I know, but these cutpurses are often in gangs. It isn't worth the trouble."

She still clung to him and he took the hero's liberty of placing his hands at her back. "I thought it was."

She shook her head, giving him a rueful half smile. "I suppose I should expect such gallantry from a military man."

"That is not to say I wouldn't like a reward," he countered.

"Oh?" Proving she was in on the game, her eyelids fluttered flirtatiously.

He put a gloved finger to her cheek. "Fear and worry has put such a pretty flush into your skin."

Her skin burned hotter under his touch. Her voice was breathy when she responded, "What reward? I only have a few pennies. Why, I even forgot to buy a newspaper."

He patted his pocket, then realized he'd dropped his when he ran after the thief. "I've lost mine."

"You must be very sad about that," she whispered, pressing closer.

He imagined he could feel her breasts, round and heavy, under her clothing. "I need comforting as well as rewarding."

She bit her lower lip between her teeth.

He felt his body's response. She maddened him. "And now you have a wound on your mouth. We are a sorry pair."

"We should call a doctor," she agreed, touching her lip.

"I have a better idea." He leaned forward, pressing her lightly against the window behind them, forgetting the passersby, the carts and the carriages, the shouts and the smells of bread and horse and coal.

That lovely mouth opened in a round little moue as his intention became known. Her hands gripped his arms more tightly as he placed his palms on either side of her head and bent forward, pressing his lips into hers. She yielded to him with a gasp of surprise, her soft warmth tasting of fresh apples and cream. The tip of his tongue brushed against her lip, an instinct to smooth the small hurt there.

"Captain Shield," she gasped, finding his chest with her small hands. Her reticule bounced against his arm, though she didn't put any force behind her movement.

He tilted his head and deepened the kiss, closing his eyes to get the full sensation. An English girl in September, with blond hair, blue eyes, and full, pouting lips. He had spent many a day in India dreaming of such a thing.

But this was a girl who pulled his umbrella from his hand and rapped him smartly on the arm. "Sir!"

He drew back, and blinked at her.

"Don't you give me that heavy-lidded look, sir." She spoke with a schoolmistress-like authority.

Was she not affected? "You can't tell me you've ever been kissed like that in your life."

She colored. "I—I, well, not by a shop at Piccadilly Circus, no."

He glanced around. "So that's where we are."

"I have to go to work. The manager is a stickler for correct behavior."

He chuckled. "This has nothing to do with work."

"I know that. But I do not know you very well, and I feel my high spirits have led me astray yet again."

His interest perked again. "You let men kiss you?"

"No!" she exclaimed. "You do not know my family's reputation, having been away so long, but I've always tried very hard not to emulate my relatives in the, er, kissing realm."

He smiled. "But it is clear you share their hot blood."

"You are not a gentleman to mention it." She gave him his umbrella.

"Very well." He stepped back and straightened his coat, glad it fell to midthigh and covered his erection. "We shall forget this ever happened."

"I appreciate that."

He nodded, feeling surly. A kiss like that ought to lead to the lady's boudoir, not to a day at the emporium, but it couldn't be helped. He wasn't used to London life yet. Perhaps, these days, ladies tongue-kissed gentlemen at Piccadilly Circus every day, before heading to the shops. At least, a member of the well-known Scandalous Cross family.

How was it that he had found himself attracted to the Scandalous Cross who claimed to be different? Still, with her background, she had to know she ran the risk of being taken as a mistress rather than a wife.

He stared across the busy street, so different from the street life in the small villages in India. "After a battle there is often a heightened sense of excitement. We shall chalk it up to that, shall we?"

"Yes." She coughed slightly. "I do not mean to interrupt your reflections, Captain, but I must be on my way or Betsy will scold me."

"Of course, of course." He held out his arm to indicate she could begin walking and followed behind her. The cakie uniform was relatively shapeless, but the way she'd wrapped her shawl caused her skirt to bellow out over what seemed like a most shapely bottom, particularly the way she used it. How had he never noticed her long, pavement-eating glide of leg, or the way her hips rotated so smoothly under the skirt?

His erection was not subsiding at all and he found it hard to keep up his usual pace. "I had a thought, Miss Cross."

She peered at him as they moved across the street. "Are you well? Your face is a bit pale."

"Very fine, absolutely. My thought was that you should not walk to work unescorted if criminals are actively working on your route."

"Surely that was an isolated occurrence."

"We know it was not. First we were pushed into the doorway by the policeman escorting his prisoner, and then your reticule was taken."

"My brother is too busy to take me. I cannot afford a cab and we have no available servants for escort."

"I was volunteering myself, not the members of your overworked household, Miss Cross. I propose we meet by Eddy Jackson each morning."

"But you do not need to be in as early as I do."

"Why not? I am the manager."

"It will not be pleasant in another month," she worried.

"Then we shall share an umbrella."

"I just mean you could afford to take a cab from your house. Or even hire your own carriage."

"I am a soldier and like the outdoors and exercise," he proclaimed. "I am tough."

"You will eat those words, sir, when you are shivering under a London fog. You have never lived here. It's all been sunny Sussex or broiling India."

His eyes went to slits as he cast her a glance. The corners of her lips were uptilted. The chit was teasing him.

"I shall prove you wrong." He took her arm and steered her away from a fresh pile of manure.

"Very well. I shall meet you at Nelson's Column each morning."

"And take a cab home, paid for by Redcake's."

"Now, Captain," she said sharply, "I will not have you wasting your sister-in-law's money that way."

"Out of my personal income then. As you say, I can afford it."

"No," she said, lifting her chin. "At least, not unless I see more evidence of crime on these streets in broad daylight. You know I leave at one."

"Very well. But the offer stands." He stepped aside once again so she could enter the alley that led to the loading dock. They walked single file to avoid the carts.

Betsy waved from the other direction, meeting them at the employee door. "I was just thinking about you, Captain, and wondering how you were settling in." She blinked.

Magdalene noticed how long and sooty her eyelashes were, considering her hair was chestnut brown. The girl had blackened them with something, but it had the effect of making her eyes large and mysterious. The captain smiled instantly and she growled to herself.

"It has been one of the most fascinating months of my life," said he. "I hope Miss Cross has been a smart choice of employee?"

As Magdalene stared her down, the girl smiled sweetly. "She is learning, sir. A bit old to be starting, but I will get her there."

Magdalene balled her hands into fists. Her cousin, Lady Bricker, would have pulled Betsy's hair from her head for a smaller insult than this. But she would not behave like a hoyden.

"If you'd seen her artwork, you would understand why I chose her," Captain Shield said. "I hope she will be decorating cakes very soon?"

He'd turned the statement into a question that sounded more like a command and Magdalene was delighted to see Betsy's expression falter. Ha! He'd put the girl in her place.

"Of course, Captain, but she has no grasp of the basics. Alys always said to start at the beginning."

"Her ladyship trusts my judgment," he said. "After all, I am in charge."

Magdalene put her hand to her mouth, hiding her grin as Betsy's cheeks went red.

"I've always baked in the morning and decorated in the afternoon. Miss Cross only works in the morning."

"Switch it around, Miss Popham. It gives the flavors time to develop overnight and the cakes will be cool and ready for frosting in the morning." He nodded curtly and marched through the open door.

Magdalene was impressed by his exit and most effective end to the conversation.

"Well," Betsy huffed. "What does he expect us to do this morning?"

"We can organize," Magdalene said in her sweetest tone. "The cupboards are a bit cluttered, don't you think?"

Betsy's gaze could have been daggers slicing at her, so Magdalene nodded at the door. "After you, Miss Popham."

The girl's words came out staccato. "Thank you, Miss Cross. Thankfully Thursday is not so busy. I am sure the captain would not want us ruining our clients' parties on his whim. Perhaps you should return home for the day. I don't think I need you."

Magdalene didn't think whims came into the captain's desires. He seemed much too forceful for mere whims. "Then I shall go to his office and see if he finds it acceptable for me to leave."

"You report to me." Betsy's eyes were blazing now.

"He never told me so. I might report to Mr. Melville. I shall go and ask." She smiled toothily and marched indoors, opening the door and starting up the stairs to the offices without looking back.

"Wait!" Betsy said. "I did think of one or two little things."

Magdalene turned. "Then I shall wait to speak to the captain." Little did the girl know she'd be seeing him every morning from now on—plenty of opportunity to head off any petty malice. Or flirtation. She couldn't help noticing the flirtation, and didn't like it one bit.

Had Magdalene claimed ownership of the man in the depth of her own heart? No, she could never have him. A man like him needed a rich wife, or he could never take a place in the fashionable world, as a second son who her brother said had no private income or inheritance from relatives. As he well knew, she would never be rich. All she had to offer was her position and family.

Clearly, the kiss had been a mistake. She closed her eyes, stumbling on the basement stairs as she relived the moment where the captain's warm, overpowering lips had met hers. That kiss had sunk into her bones, fanning her depths into flame. Her heated Cross blood might make her fall yet, despite her resolve to be different.

On Friday afternoon, Judah received a summons to Hatbrook House for dinner. He frowned at the note, wondering who was in Town.

The last he'd heard from his family was the weekly letter from Beth, which had arrived Wednesday. So, instead of walking home, he called for a cab, then bathed and changed into evening dress while it waited outside for the drive to Belgravia.

The season was descending into fall, as the streets were dark much earlier than they had been a month ago. He watched as gas lamps passed by, hoping everything was well with Alys. Surely they'd have sent specific word if anything was wrong. He'd have to make it clear to Hatbrook that he desired not to be spared any family details in future. Heathfield was not far away. The ever expanding railroad continued to compress travel times to almost nothing.

The hansom cab drove to the large white stucco mansion that was the Marquess of Hatbrook's London home. Judah could not remember ever spending a night in the house. His parents had frequently been in residence, but he'd been left at the Farm with servants.

He paid the driver and told him not to wait, then went up the front steps. A footman opened the front door.

"I have a letter of invitation," Judah said.

"Captain Shield," said the man smoothly. "I would recognize you as family anywhere."

"I do look something like the marquess," he said, stepping inside and taking off his hat. Hatbrook must have mentioned he preferred to be known by his military title.

"Your portrait is in the Grand Rose Salon," said the footman. "Also a painting of you and the marquess as boys is in a place of honor in the ladies' withdrawing room."

He frowned. "I never sat for such a portrait."

"I believe it is signed by Lady Elizabeth."

Beth had painted him? "Must have been a schoolroom exercise."

The footman inclined his head, then took his hat. "His lordship is in the library, Captain. If you would be so kind."

Judah followed the footman across the diamond-paned white and tan marble floor, amazed by the perfection of the surroundings. The house didn't look the least bit run down. He supposed Hatbrook had been quite honest about his success in restoring the family fortunes, even before he married into wealth.

Why was Hatbrook here? He wondered again about a family drama of some kind as the footman took him down a corridor illuminated by gaslit sconces. No money being spared on the gas bill here.

The footman knocked on a thick door and opened it a moment later, gesturing Judah inside. He stepped in, tugging at his collar. His evening suit was pre-army and much too tight now. He'd have to order something new when he was paid again.

Hatbrook turned, a book open in his hand. "Judah! You look nervous."

Judah laughed. "Old clothes. My neck has grown."

Hatbrook frowned. "I'd lend you something of mine, but you're taller than me now."

"And more muscular," Judah pointed out.

His brother smirked. "That won't last long, with you behind a desk. At least I can get out at the Farm sometimes. You should come down and muck out the stables on your days off. That will keep you fit."

"I can hoist some flour sacks at Redcake's. That will probably work."

"No doubt. My wife has unusually shapely arms due to all her labors, not that she would thank me for saying so."

"I can see from the gleam in your eye that you do not find this unattractive."

Hatbrook set down his book. "This chat wasn't why I invited you for dinner."

"Are you here alone?"

"Yes, just a quick trip to meet with my man of business, and to give you these." He went to the imposing desk in one corner and tapped his finger on a crate.

Judah peered in. Rose-colored notepaper in bundles, along with other letters, and a collection of blue notebooks. "You found Mother's papers?"

Hatbrook nodded. "In the attics. Beth and I spent half a day looking. She couldn't let it go."

His stomach growled, reminding him that he'd come for a meal, but he pushed his hunger aside. "Did you read them?"

"No. I saved the honor for you. If there is some answer there, I wanted you to find it."

Judah raised his eyebrows. "At least that way I won't have to tell you if it's bad."

His brother chuckled. "If you tell me we're related, at least that won't pose a problem."

"No, but would you feel the same about me if I was sired by a stable hand?"

"I'd be more concerned if you were sired by one of the Dickondells," Hatbrook said, naming an extremely fertile local family in their circle. "But your looks do appear to come mostly from our mother. No one would think we weren't full brothers, and I will never share your secret."

"You do understand that I need to know the truth?"

"No, not really. To keep your position in Society, you can never have a relationship with that person, regardless of who it is."

"I don't want a position in Society."

Hatbrook pulled a card from a drawer and tossed it at Judah. He caught it in the air and turned it over. "This is an invitation to a musical evening with a family named Courtnay next week. He's from Liverpool, made his money in manufacturing. Daughter is nineteen, I think, so they are entertaining in the hopes of marrying her off."

"You're trying to find me an heiress?"

"Why not? But my primary purpose in handing you that is to point out Society is useful in your search. This party will include Mother's circle." He hesitated. "Not the highest, of course. She wasn't well liked for reasons I never really understood until this year. But, among her lifelong acquaintances is where you are likely to find answers, if they are not in that box."

Judah glanced at the card. "You make an excellent point. Not about the heiress, but about my search. Hopefully I will find the answer before next Friday, but I shall accept the invitation."

"Good." Hatbrook clapped him on the shoulder. "Shall we dine?"

Chapter Six

Judah spent the next morning in his small study, drinking innumerable cups of tea while he poured over his mother's elegant handwriting. He had sorted the contents of the crate, putting the newest material at the bottom and tossing the material before 1860 onto the table at his elbow. His mother could have had a longstanding amour, but since he was born in late July of 1863, the beginning of the Season in 1860 might have answers for him.

He poured through an appointment book and a series of letters from various ladies, relatives long dead, Aunt Mary, even one drunken scrawl from the late marquess. Nothing appeared immediately relevant and he took a break to eat, attempting to stave off the headache blossoming behind his eyes.

Fending off tribesmen with sharp weapons was one thing, but spending hours reading about the banalities of card parties and ancient gossip tortured him.

After lunch and a medicinal shot of brandy, he took up the rose papers, which seemed to be first drafts of his mother's letters. Her love of that color must have started early. As he read her drafts, he remembered how young she had been then, about twenty-two when he was born. Surely her youth could provide the answer and excuse for her mistakes.

He found no mention of men, just amusements, tidbits about her baby son, much discussion about redecorating Hatbrook House in London. Then, part of a letter dated at the end of October intrigued him.

> *The P of W is lately returned from the United States and Canada, and he has such interesting things to say on the subject. Oh, I do wish I was a man and could have had such adventures, but instead I must dine on reflected glory. I had never been to Oxford before but the marquess's particular friend invited us to a house party nearby and HRH, back at his studies, came to a dinner.*

The Prince of Wales? Judah read the letter again, then set it aside and flipped through the rest of the drafts. Finding nothing more, he searched her appointment book. She had indeed been at a countess's house party at the end of October, 1860. Had he been conceived during an Oxford liaison?

It seemed unlikely. After all, his father had been present. But he'd always heard much tiptoeing was done at night at these parties, as the men and women sought companionship outside the marriage bed. His father would probably have sat at cards day and night, gambling away his inheritance. In this early year of their lives, they had still been young, glittering and wealthy, prize guests for almost any hostess. The Prince of Wales might have been enticed. His mother hadn't been so much older than him.

Was it possible? He laughed at himself. That would make him Queen Victoria's bastard grandson. Not bloody likely.

But still. He read the letter again, and wondered. Particularly when he found another letter in the stack, to the same friend, one his mother called Sally.

> *I do love curly hair on men. And full lips. As you know, Hatbrook has neither attribute. But the P of W? Both in abundance!*

This was dated a few days after the house party. Had she stayed in Oxford after her husband returned to London or Heathfield? A man might step out of the way if royalty wanted to woo his wife.

Not that he would ever let that happen to himself. If he married he wouldn't share.

He read late into the evening, ruining the household candle budget as the gaslighting in the study was poor, but he found no more obvious comments about the prince, though there were a couple of veiled references to men who might have been him. By early the next year, her letters were taken up with news of her pregnancy. He did notice the volume of correspondence had diminished by half, or at least only that much had survived. Was she already in disgrace?

As the last candle guttered, he leaned into the headrest of the armchair. At the very least, the idea of him having a father was obtainable. The Prince of Wales was alive. Now, if he could only find this friend of his mother's, Sally. She would know the truth.

He rubbed at his chest, feeling a knot of pain dissolving. He'd had trouble swallowing for months, ever since that strange deathbed confession had arrived at his station in India. But he'd found the key to his identity now. He simply needed to find the lock.

Hatbrook had insisted Judah call on his tailor, saying he must be kitted out properly for parties. Of course, his brother wanted him married off, his own happiness being so acute. He also worried about his younger brother's finances, but his manager salary covered the small house with no problem. It was meant to be the salary of a family man, albeit one who didn't need a current evening suit.

The next Friday night, his man, Lawrence, finished brushing down his new shawl-collared coat. Judah picked a thread from his low-cut, white piqué waistcoat. Neither had been in style when he went to India. He also had a new silk top hat, button shoes, and pale yellow gloves. Hatbrook had been right that he couldn't wear his old suit to fashionable functions. It was much too out of date, not to mention ill fitting.

"You look the proper gentleman, Captain," Lawrence said.

Judah nodded his thanks as he placed the new hat on his head. "Has the carriage arrived?"

"Yes, sir."

His destination was an upscale street in Mayfair, not too far from Hatbrook House. While he had no interest in Courtnay's daughter, he wanted to fit in well enough to ask questions about his mother. His brother had been down to Heathfield and was back again. He hoped it wasn't for the purpose of attending this party with him, but the carriage would take him to Hatbrook and they would arrive together.

"Tell me about Courtnay's daughter," Judah said to his brother, as the carriage rattled along the graveled streets.

"She's not for you," Hatbrook said.

Judah rested his elbow against the wall and put his hand to his chin. "Then why did you mention her at all last week?"

"She's an eligible heiress, but her father insists on her residing in Liverpool after her marriage." He pronounced the name of the city with great distaste.

"She agrees to that?"

"She is entirely under her father's thumb. Last year, she was quite in love with an earl's younger son, but the father said no because he had no money. Perfectly decent fellow."

"Just someone like me. No property of his own."

He held up a finger. "Not your drive. No army, no position. But he has found another bride; wedding coming up when the Season gets going again."

Judah grinned. "At least he had a focus."

Hatbrook's hand closed into a fist. "Indeed. And what about you? To be blunt, where has all your army pay and estate allowance gone? I realize I could not afford to be generous when I first inherited, but I did send what I could. I never understood you to have a gambling habit like Father and you claimed to live simply. It wasn't until you came to the house in that appalling old evening suit that I realized how poor you really were."

"Invested," Judah said bluntly, not offended, because he too remembered how their house and property had fallen apart as their father gambled everything away. "If the ship ever gets here, I will be in funds."

"Ship?" Hatbrook's gaze sharpened.

"Yes. I invested in a cargo of emeralds, rubies, and sapphires. Watched them load myself. Funded by other gentlemen officers and Lord Burnham."

"Ah, formed a syndicate, did you?"

He was flattered by his brother's keen interest. "The profit should be enough to purchase property and set up a household properly. I could reinvest, of course, if it all goes off well."

"Bit of a gamble." Hatbrook rubbed at his chin.

Judah didn't like having to defend himself, and if this was anyone but his brother, he would not. "Everyone involved is reliable. The ship captain, a man called Howard, is well thought of, and the ship is sound. It's not faro."

"Of course not, and I've never heard anything negative about Lord Burnham. Don't think he's in Town yet."

"It's early still."

"And yet the middle of September," Hatbrook mused. "This year has been the happiest of my life, but it has flown by so fast it is hard to grasp any small piece of it."

Judah smiled. "I hope the memories will fly back in old age. That is supposed to happen. The good memories become clear again, so we can bore our grandchildren with them."

Hatbrook's lips thinned. "Our parents did not live to be old."

"Worried about that, are you? I only have half the worry."

"And no sign of my medical complaints, either. No, you did well in that regard and Alys will keep me going."

Judah leaned forward. "If I am interpreting Mother's letters correctly, my father may still be alive."

Hatbrook scrubbed his lips with his finger. "Oh? The mystery is solved so soon?"

"If I am right it is a delicate situation. But at least I would know. Do you remember Mother's friend Sally? I never found more to her name than that, but she appears to have been her most faithful correspondent in our early years."

Hatbrook stared at the carriage ceiling, then shook his head. "No. Maybe she was someone Mother quarreled with later. Or she died."

"She is my goal tonight. I will talk to Mother's old cronies and see if I can identify Sally." They had joined the queue of carriages waiting to disembark in front of Courtnay's house by then. "Why doesn't he look for a husband for his daughter in Liverpool?"

"I'm not certain, since he doesn't seem insistent on a title. What he's after is something of a mystery."

"What was his connection to Mother?"

"Simply that they were of an age, and his guests are likely to be Mother's kind of second-tier Society. Those who mostly live in London year-round."

"Too poor for country houses?"

"Or they rent them out, or they are falling down. Or very disgraced, like Earl Gerrick." Hatbrook's normally impassive face showed disgust.

"And all his Cross kin?" Judah couldn't help interjecting.

"And Lord and Lady Mews. Everyone mixed up in that decadent circle. A lesser version of the Marlborough House set."

Hatbrook's mention of Marlborough House, the home of the Prince of Wales, perked Judah's ears. "I suppose Mother was rather decadent in her youth."

"She would have fit perfectly into the end of the last century, one assumes, but such behavior was rather frowned upon in the high Victoria and Albert years."

"The Prince of Wales is about the same age as Mother and her friends. Were they part of that set, before they became, well, a lesser version?"

"I can't imagine they had the funds by the time the prince was married and embraced his present lifestyle. Prince Albert was still alive when you were born, you know."

Did Hatbrook understand where his private thoughts and the correspondence had led him? He wanted to protect this dream of his. "I must say I've never understood her disgrace. Surely the marquess was the source of all the family pains."

Hatbrook pressed his lips together, the only sign the topic discomforted him. "Whatever happened, it was before I can really remember. She wasn't very nice, you know, not to anyone."

"But she was a marchioness."

"Not to anyone," Hatbrook repeated. "I realize now that she was very ill after Father died, but if she'd been that unpleasant in her early years, before I really knew her, she probably made enemies. Without money to spend, no one would have cared to cultivate her."

"Sad."

"Yes, very. Society is hungry. You must have something to offer. Charm, money, beauty, connections . . . something."

"What do you think I have to offer?"

Hatbrook smiled wickedly. "Beauty? The promise of fabled gems?"

"Connections," Judah interjected.

"I do not think your connections are much to barter upon," Hatbrook disagreed.

"Yet here you are escorting me to a party of Liverpudlians and aging roués."

"Quite."

The carriage jerked to a stop and a few moments later a footman opened the door. Judah slapped his hat back on his head as soon as he exited, following Hatbrook up the steps. He felt like an actor entering the stage for the first time, as this was his first taste of Society.

After running the gauntlet of servants, they entered a grand drawing room. Wild seascapes decorated the walls and the ceiling was painted with mythological scenes. When Judah saw the crowd, he felt for a moment like Sir Alexander Burnes, facing the mob in Kabul. He had expected a small gathering, given the month and unfashionable, if presumably wealthy, crowd. For a moment, he focused on the carpet, which was covered with fantastical flowers in unusual colors.

Hatbrook patted him on the shoulder as a tall, broad, graying man approached. Their host?

"My lord, I am so pleased you accepted our invitation. May I presume this is Lord Judah?"

"Indeed, this is my brother, Captain Shield," Hatbrook said smoothly, shaking the proffered hand. "He has made London his home just this past six weeks or so."

"It is a pleasure," Courtnay said, offering his hand to Judah. "I hope we will see much more of you around Town. The entertainment is sparse now but you will find yourself with a plethora of amusements soon."

Judah smiled thinly. "I am a working man, and that keeps me amused."

"A man must have his work," Courtnay agreed. "No matter what is fashionable. I myself am in dye manufacturing. Are you managing your brother's interests?"

"No, his wife's," he said. "Redcake's, to be exact."

"Ah, an excellent establishment. I believe we have a cake from them tonight. My daughter arranged that."

"I shall have to take a look."

"I will find her for you," Courtnay said readily.

Judah felt that he might not be found wanting, despite being a second son of no fortune. "Most kind."

As Courtnay walked away, Judah held up his hand to his brother. "I can feel your smirk from here."

"He must want a man with a work ethic for his daughter."

"Or the brother of a marquess is better than the son of an earl."

"There is that," Hatbrook allowed, glancing around. "Ah, Lady Mews."

A middle-aged lady with large feathers poking from her hair turned to them. "Why, my lord. I thought you would cut me."

"Did I not respond to your letter of condolence?"

She tilted her head, presumably to display her fine neck. Or the magnificent emerald necklace clasped around her throat. "Yes, you did. I am remembering New Year's, I suppose. I assumed I would be in disgrace still."

"You really shouldn't play with boys, my lady."

She smiled. "Manfred Cross is hardly a boy."

Judah's attention perked at the mention of a Cross. He supposed Manfred must be one of the scandalous ones.

Hatbrook sighed. "I want to make my brother known to you, Lady Mews. This is Captain Shield."

Judah inclined his head, as did she.

"It is hard to believe that I've never seen you, given that I was such close friends with your dear mama."

"I had a rusticated childhood."

Lady Mews perused his person blatantly, her gaze capturing the up-to-date apparel. "As did your sister. But I understand she will be presented soon?"

"That is true."

She smiled, exposing excellent teeth. "I do look forward to making her acquaintance."

Judah took a step toward her. "Speaking of acquaintances, we have been going through Mother's papers."

"Oh?" Lady Mews's hand fluttered to her white throat. She played with the shortest of her three ropes of pearls, dangling below the emerald necklace.

"Yes. We cannot remember one of the dear friends of her youth. Did you know Mother's friend Sally?"

Lady Mews twirled her finger in her second rope of pearls. "You know, Captain Shield, I was several years younger than your dear mama. I don't believe I met her until the midsixties."

He believed her. She didn't look past forty. "The correspondence I've seen was earlier."

"Then I am afraid I cannot help you." She patted his arm, her fingers lingering on his sleeve.

Courtnay approached, with a corpulent young lady dressed in an overabundance of lace and corsetry, such that her breasts were put on display as if in a sample case. Judah's first thought was she should be prevented from eating the cake, lest her dress explode from her body. His second was a man could suffocate in that bosom. His third was his brother must be very happily married indeed, for when he glanced over, he realized his brother's gaze had never drifted below the young lady's neck.

Lady Mews, on the other hand, seemed fascinated by the sight. Her hand drifted to her own torso, shaped upon the most delicate feminine lines. Judah thought she'd never been beautiful, or even pretty, but her form might have been exceptional once.

"My lord, Captain Shield, may I present my daughter, Miss Victoria Courtnay?" Courtnay said, tugging her forward.

"Hello, dear," Lady Mews said. "Such a pleasure to see you so blooming."

Judah wasn't sure what to make of that comment, but he inclined his head as the girl curtsied. Hatbrook cleared his throat in an irritating manner.

"Your father said you might show me the cake you ordered from Redcake's. I am most interested in it."

"Why, Captain Shield?"

He appreciated her bold manner. "I manage the establishment."

Her large gray eyes brightened instantly. "You work around those lovely cakes every day?"

"I do indeed."

She clasped her hands together, her dance card waving as it hung from her wrist.

"Perhaps I could claim a dance as well?"

She stared at him a moment, shrewd eyes so like her father's assessing his potential, then peered at her card as if she needed to wear spectacles. "I believe I have a waltz available."

"Excellent," he said grandly. "Pencil me in."

She scribbled his name down with the attached writing instrument. He was concerned to see the available waltz was one of the last ones. It would be a long evening.

"Will you be dancing a great deal, Captain Shield?" she asked.

"You are the first lady I have offered for," he assured her. "But I see you have been much in demand."

"It is my party."

"Of course." He glanced at her father. "Is this a good time to see the cake? Or does the dancing start soon? I have not been at all in Society. This is my first evening out."

Miss Courtnay's mouth rounded. "You are a debutant!" She laughed heartily.

While her deeper voice did not have the soothing, bell-like tone of Miss Cross's, nonetheless her laugh was a pleasant feminine noise. In truth, he thought she might be a rather likeable girl.

"Yes, there is time to see the cake," said Courtnay indulgently. "But do not take too long, dear. As you say, this is your party."

His daughter patted his cheek and looked expectantly at Judah. He held out his arm and she took it, then strolled along beside him, breathing heavily.

"Will you be staying here through the rest of the year?" he asked. "I understand the fogs are appalling."

She smiled at him. "My father is becoming very interested in politics, so yes, we stay while Parliament is in session."

"Does he plan to stand for a seat?"

"No, he is far too engaged in his business for that. But there is legislation that affects it, so we came in early so he could take meetings."

"I see." They walked out of the drawing room and into a smaller salon, then an anteroom, and then into a sitting room.

"Here is the cake," she said, pointing to the wall farthest from the fire. "I thought the ladies could withdraw here."

"Forgive my curiosity, but why is it important to have a cake in the ladies' withdrawing room?" He moved to the cake, which had been decorated in frosting dyed a shade of apricot. Over that were innumerable layers of white frosting lace. The confection reminded him somewhat of Miss Courtnay's dress.

"It's something pretty to look at. A conversation piece."

"It is certainly that." He placed his hands behind his back and strolled around the cake, noting a couple of small imperfections in the lacework on the backside. Someone had been astute enough to hide them.

"I especially ordered the cake topper," she said, pointing to the top of the third tier.

"Who is it?" A lumpy gum-paste creature sat on a chair.

"Queen Victoria, my namesake," she dimpled.

"Ah, very clever." They needed to change purveyors of gum-paste work.

"Oh!" came a voice from the doorway.

Judah glanced over his shoulder and saw Magdalene Cross enter the room. Her dress was so plain that even he thought it might be more suitable as a dinner dress than an evening gown, but at least the green fabric had no obvious repairs. The animation of her sharp-featured face lent her grace and beauty, however.

"I am very sorry to interrupt. I was told a cake was here." Her glance at Judah was nervous.

"Miss Courtnay, have you been introduced to Miss Cross?" Judah asked.

She pasted on a hostess smile. "Yes, of course, Miss Cross. Do you have a particular fascination with cakes? Or are you simply hungry?" Her gaze raked Miss Cross's slim form.

"I understood it was a particularly pretty cake," Miss Cross stammered.

"Would you like me to show Miss Cross the particular details?" Judah asked. "I know I am keeping you from your guests."

She inclined her head graciously. "I will see you for our waltz."

He bowed. "I cannot wait."

Miss Cross had her hands clasped tightly together at her waist as her gaze followed Miss Courtnay out of the room. She was a little wild-eyed when she turned back to Judah. "I thought you would give me away."

"Of course not. I think more quickly than that."

Her clasped hands moved to her lips. "I did want to see how it turned out. What do you think?"

He could see how anxious she was and could not criticize. "It's very well done, from the front at least. Did you work on it?"

"I assisted. Just the odd details. Nothing I can call my own."

"But you are decorating more than baking, now?"

"Assisting."

He frowned. "I shall speak to Betsy again. What if she leaves Redcake's? Where would we be then if you are not trained?"

"Do you think she is leaving?"

He noticed that the thought relaxed her. "I have no reason to think so, but Ewan Hales warned me that young girls of marriageable age often do, so we always need to be hiring."

She twirled around the cake, her bustle twitching as she walked. He felt his tight evening pants press against him, as an urgent wave of lust took control of his groin.

When they walked to Redcake's in the morning, he made certain to walk next to her, so that he couldn't catch sight of her movements. Otherwise he would spend all morning in an uncomfortable state of turgidity. One that had no release. It was maddening, the hold this girl's hips had on him.

Perhaps it was just the bustle. The sooner it went out of fashion, the better.

"Did you say something?" she looked at him expectantly.

"No." Had he sighed or moaned? Perhaps.

"I can see some small issues with the lacework in back," Miss Cross said.

He was pleased. "I saw that too."

"Unfortunately, the marchioness was the master cake decorator. Miss Popham has less than a year's experience. I wonder if you should search for someone at another bakery and hire them away. After all, I might marry too, some day."

With hips like hers, someone was bound to offer for her, dowry or no. "I expect you are correct."

"I should return to the party," she said. "It's not proper for us to be in here alone."

"May I have a dance?" he inquired impulsively. "I see you have a card."

She glanced at her wrist and held it up to him. He stepped dangerously closer, until he could smell the delicate scent of violet. But underneath that, he thought he sensed the earthier odors of dried fruit, powdery flour, and baking. His erection stirred again, to the point of readiness. How did she have such power over him?

He put his hand to his collar. "I'll take a polka," he rasped.

She fumbled for her pencil. "Are you certain? I have two waltzes free."

He shifted his stance. "No, a rollicking polka. Military man, you know. I like to move."

Her little sharp teeth massaged her lower lip as she wrote his name in. "That's the second dance of the night."

"I shall look for you," he promised. "Now, do you want to leave first, or shall I?"

"Miss Courtnay knows we're here."

"Good point." He leaned forward, forgetting his purpose for being here that night entirely, and swept his hand around the base of her neck, tilting her head up to his. When would they have another moment of privacy?

Her eyes were huge, but they drifted shut as his mouth met hers. Her breath seemed to sear his lips as he tasted her. His other arm wrapped around her waist and he pulled her close. The soft, thin fabric of her dress allowed some body heat to escape and her back warmed his icy fingers. All his blood seemed to have moved south. His free hand found her jaw, stroked the fine skin.

She moaned, so he let his fingers continue to dance over her skin, drifting downward. His index finger brushed her clavicle, then the delectable expanse of flesh the evening dress left uncovered. She tilted her head, so his lips trailed down the side of her neck. Her body shifted restlessly, creating an inch between them, just enough for his fingers to slide over the rounded top of one breast. No protest resounded, so he dipped inside her bodice, learning the contours of her. When he found her pearled nipple, she gasped and pulled away. He moved his fingers north and pulled her mouth to his again. She kissed like a wanton, his touch having aroused her despite the protest.

How he wished he could pull up her skirts and have her right there, if current fashions allowed. Perhaps it was best that her clothing confined so.

She moaned against his mouth, relaxing again. He touched her lower lip with his tongue. The tip of her tongue touched his, but when he tried to suckle it she pulled away and covered her mouth with a trembling hand.

"Have you been drinking? You know how improper this is."

"You could tell I have not," Judah said. "You tasted my breath."

Her eyes were unfocused as she glanced around. "We spend too much time in each other's company."

"Twenty minutes five days a week is not too much time, especially on a public street."

She moved her hands to her cheeks. "I am so confused. You are my employer. You are not courting me."

"I am your friend, I hope."

A throat cleared behind them. Judah turned and saw Hatbrook in the doorway. What had he seen?

"I found another friend of Mother's. One who did know her from the time of her marriage," he said, looking at Miss Cross with impassive disdain.

"You should go," Miss Cross said quickly. "This sounds important."

He inclined his head and followed his brother out of the room, too aroused to think clearly.

Chapter Seven

Judah expected Hatbrook to lead him into the drawing room, where presumably the lady waited for them, but instead he turned sharply and opened a closed door that led into a dimly lit library. His brother paced in front of the fireplace for a moment, then turned to him.

"Really, Judah. Magdalene Cross?"

"We had a moment of insanity."

Hatbrook's gaze raked his body. "A moment of lust."

Judah stared at a small metal statue of a pug. "Something about her pulls me in."

"Lust," Hatbrook repeated. "With a Scandalous Cross. I assure you it is a common affliction among a certain class of Society."

"A lower class, I presume?"

"Don't make this about your parentage, brother," Hatbrook growled. "But stay away from that girl."

"Why?"

"She is a confidante of Lady Bricker," Hatbrook said. "A cousin. That woman is poison. As we speak, Alys is in Heathfield, caring for her sister, who is having a most difficult time. Alys should be enjoying her own expectations, not worrying about her sister's life."

"Lady Bricker did not impregnate Matilda Redcake," Judah said coldly.

"No," Hatbrook said after a pause. "But they are a licentious family of gossips. Their indecent way of life sent Miss Redcake down a dark path."

He wondered if Hatbrook's life had been completely without taint, or if he was moving into the paterfamilias role. "You are, perhaps, the only member of our family that is better. Our parents fit that profile—or I should say your parents—and I like the Crosses that I've met."

"What about Beth?"

Judah shrugged. "Not out of the schoolroom. Who knows what she will become? We are not speaking of children."

"Very well." Hatbrook showed his teeth. "What about this? I know Miss Cross is employed at Redcake's. Do you think it appropriate to dally with someone there?"

"She is hoping to find a husband, not a long-term career."

Hatbrook put his hands on his hips. "Planning to be that husband, are you?"

"Certainly not." He said the words without thinking.

"So you are dallying with an avowed husband hunter, and think you can escape the noose when you kiss her like that?"

Judah mirrored his brother's position. "You think I cannot evade one woman's wiles?"

Hatbrook gave him a patronizing eye roll. "A private tête-à-tête with Courtnay's daughter is one thing. She's an heiress. But Magdalene Cross is nothing. She will not bring money, she will not bring position."

"I'm not looking for a wife. I'm looking for my father."

"Then why are you kissing young girls? If you have to kiss someone, make it a less complicated choice."

"I cannot afford a mistress right now, even if I wanted one."

"Judging from the way your trousers are fitting, I'd say you need one," Hatbrook said frankly. "I know we have never been close due to circumstance, but I want to be your friend, Judah, as well as your older brother. Do not make this mistake. There will be consequences."

"Would you please introduce me to Mother's friend?" Judah asked. "I have had quite enough of this brotherly chat."

Hatbrook's knuckles cracked as he made a fist, but then he relaxed his hand.

"You cannot make me over in your image," Judah said. "We have not lived the same life. I'm not educated, I'm not civilized."

"You are intelligent. You are an Englishman of good breeding. You will learn the rules of fashion soon enough. For instance, like our mother before, there are plenty of married ladies in bad circumstances, or comfortable widows available to a handsome man without the need to be supported. Stay away from anyone looking for a husband and there will be no trouble."

"I take your point." To be like most men, even the Prince of Wales, who had many mistresses. He wondered if any of the Cross women were among them.

Hatbrook led him back into the drawing room, then introduced him to Mrs. Owen, a plump matron dressed in a sea green gown much too young for her. Judah thought her, if anything, older than Mother would have been if she were still alive.

"I'd know those earlobes anywhere," the lady cried. "Or at least the lack of them. It so upset your poor mama that she couldn't wear ear bobs."

"Thankfully it is not fashion for men to do so," Judah said wryly.

"Quite, quite. How have you boys been coping with your loss?" Mrs. Owen inquired. "And poor Lady Elizabeth, she must feel quite alone in the world. Though of course you have your dear wife, my lord. And there is an aunt as well, I believe?"

"Aunt Mary," Judah agreed. "They are all in Sussex."

"Your sister must be delaying her presentation at court due to your poor dear mama's passing," Mrs. Owen said.

"Yes, but it will take place before the end of the year. Mrs. Owen, I am trying to locate a dear friend of Mother's youth. Do you remember a Sally?"

"I have known many Sallys," Mrs. Owen said. "But in connection to your mother?"

"Yes, a correspondent of hers during the early days of her marriage," Judah said.

Mrs. Owen thought for a moment. "You must mean her godmother. They were very close, but she was lame, and they rarely saw each other. She stayed in Brighton for her health, she said, very unfashionable by then, of course. Queen Victoria detested the place."

"But she was an older lady who remembered when King George was there?"

"Exactly," Mrs. Owen beamed. "Her parents were intimates of the King when he was the regent."

"Is she still living?"

"No, I am afraid not, Captain Shield. As I said, she was an older lady, and not in the best health. She's been gone, oh, fifteen years now."

"Did my mother have any other true intimates in those years? Before I was born?" Judah fought desperation.

Her forehead creased. "I'm sure there were many. She was a vivacious lady."

"She socialized with a set that had Oxford connections," Judah said, pressing hard. "Did you go to house parties there in eighteen-sixty? That seemed to be a special highlight of her young life."

"Oh my, no. My children are all quite an age with you and your brother. Of course, none of the oldest survived, poor things."

"I am very sorry."

"It was long ago. But I was too occupied in those years to leave London for parties. My late husband was a Member of Parliament, you see."

"I thought you would like some punch, Mother," said a young lady, dressed in a delicate gown of pale yellow, rather like the color of his gloves.

"Thank you, Bathsheba, dear. May I present my daughter to you, my lord?"

"Happy to make your acquaintance," Hatbrook said.

She curtsied as Mrs. Owen introduced them. By the end of the conversation, he was engaged for a waltz with the young lady, still young enough to be on the marriage market but too old to have much hope.

Hatbrook walked him around the room for a while after that, hunting for other likely friends of their mother, but no one remembered the fateful house party, especially when he couldn't explain why he cared about it. He would have liked to ask direct questions about the Prince of Wales, but didn't want to sound like an idiot.

Eventually, it was time for his polka with Miss Cross. Thankfully, the exuberant nature of the dance kept them from speaking very much, though, quite un-Scandalous Cross-like, she blushed nearly every time she looked at him. How unfortunate she wasn't a widow. They talked politely of the things one must at parties. Her brother, her ailing sister-in-law, whether Judah had heard any more news about Mark. He promised to let her know immediately if he did. Then, the dance was over, and as he immediately had to take Miss Owen waltzing, he said his good-byes until Monday at Trafalgar Square.

Magdalene had spent the week since the Courtnay's ball caring for her rapidly sinking sister-in-law. She was scarcely able to find enthusiasm for cake decorating, though her salary now paid for Nancy's companion as well as the apothecary bills. The doctor said there was no hope for Nancy, and indeed, she was rarely awake anymore.

The only thing Magdalene truly looked forward to was her walk with Judah from Nelson's Column to Redcake's. However, the weather was changing now, and this was the first time it had rained really heavily. She wondered if Judah would simply take a cab to work, since he had the means. As her shoes squelched through another puddle and she discovered a new hole between her sole and the old leather, she knew she couldn't blame him.

Even so, she saw him talking to Eddy, holding his umbrella over both their heads as he waited for her. Forgetting her shoe, she quickened her pace. Three feet from him, she tripped over a stone and windmilled her arms as she tried to maintain her balance. Her parasol dropped as she started to topple, then, in an instant, an arm covered in damp wool caught her around the waist. She was flung headfirst into a wet, hard chest. Slowly, she found equilibrium again and got her feet back underneath her. She stared into Judah's tiger eyes. The morning had been dreary, but now it turned delicious.

But he was not in the mood for amour.

"Are you well?" he asked, holding her. "You have deep circles under your eyes."

Surely a gentleman should find some compliment to offer a distressed lady, rather than find a fault.

He must have seen something in her expression. "No doubt the consequences of a great attention to your work."

She relaxed against his warmth, heedless of the public place, until she saw her parasol turn like a top as it was caught by a gust of wind. "My parasol," she gasped. She couldn't lose it and be forced to buy another. Her money needed to go to Nancy's care.

Judah gave her a puzzled look, then went after it, the wind no match for his long legs. He swooped down on the silly thing and shook the rain from it, before putting it back in her hand. It dripped onto her shoes.

"You look like the wind could pick you up and send you away," he observed. "Are we working you too hard? Are you returned to cake-making again?"

"No, I've been working on icing," she assured him, then had a moment of inspiration. "Would you like to learn how to frost a cake?"

"Really?" he asked, amused.

"Betsy has a holiday today. It is her eighteenth birthday."

"You don't say." He lifted his umbrella above them and she folded her own. It would be rather useless until the inside dried.

She felt daring. "I could use another pair of hands. Thankfully the world has not yet descended on London. We have another week or so before the general return, but that doesn't mean there isn't a great deal to do."

"I am sure of that. I can spare a little time. It's a good idea to know all aspects of an enterprise when you are managing it." He took her arm and guided her across the Square.

She hurried next to him, her usual strides no match for his. "I saw you in the bakery last week. Were you learning the baker's trade?"

"No. One of the ovens is misfiring again."

He released her arm so they could skirt a puddle. "I suppose you will be calling in Mr. Noble?"

"Why do you ask?"

She edged closer to him again, after her shoulder caught a droplet of rain. "It is simply that he invented the mechanisms. He assured me he was the only man who understood them."

"He may be right about that. Do you know he has a horseless carriage?"

"I have heard rumors."

"A most unconventional fellow."

Very handsome too, and pleasant, though he smelled of mechanical things. "That is not always such a bad thing."

"It depends." He glanced past the spines of his umbrella. "This will be my first autumn in London."

"It is a season to be endured," she said. Though the enduring was easier when you had a congenial morning companion. "But the tea-room is doing a brisk business."

"There is a cheerful thought," he declared. When they reached the back door, he asked, "When shall I come to you?"

"In an hour? That will give me time to check our order book and set out supplies."

"Excellent." He helped her with her damp outerwear.

He had successfully sheltered them both under his large black umbrella during the remainder of their walk, though she was soaked through anyway, thanks to her thin coat and escaping parasol. "You are most chivalrous."

She saw Ralph Popham glowering at them down the corridor and hurried off, wondering what had upset him. She was a few minutes early so it wasn't that.

Betsy had trained her to treat various cakes differently. Almond paste topped wedding cakes. Buttercream went between sliced small cakes. Either could be covered in fondant or royal icing, depending on the customer and look. Then one moved on to decorating with frosting, colored or white, gum paste, and cut dried fruits, among other items.

She had mastered none of these things, or even worked with many of them, but it all took time. She knew Betsy was no master after applying herself most of this year to her apprenticeship.

An hour later she had made up a bowl of their basic white royal icing, using the stove in an alcove off the bakery. Usually, a man was assigned to make their pastes, frostings, and fondants, and he delivered the assigned quantity to the Fancy each day, but Betsy had insisted she learn how to make everything in case of supply issues. Since Magdalene couldn't find their supply of royal icing this morning, Betsy had made an excellent point.

She supposed basic knowledge was never a waste, but she was nervous about the coming Season and being unprepared for her primary duty of decoration. But seeing as this was only the end of her third week, she couldn't expect too much of herself. In fact, this was the first time she had been alone at the stove, or in the Fancy.

Really, the work was too much for one person. Betsy said it

would soon be too much for two and they would need at least two more sets of hands in the Fancy. She had fretted a great deal, saying that Alys had expected to be here through the autumn season. Irene, one of the cakies, had assisted Alys in the spring, and would be assigned here for the duration, and Tom would take over the actual cake baking, but Betsy still hoped Alys would appear. Based on gossip she had overheard though, Magdalene knew this to be impossible. Between her own expectations and the unfortunate circumstance of her sister, Alys would not be leaving Sussex any time soon.

Magdalene took four round turntables from the cupboards and placed them on the table, then four matching christening cakes on cardboard, which they had topped with their second best almond paste flavored with strawberry, and left to dry. Making cakes was at least a three-day process because of the need to cool and harden them in stages.

She was going over the order book when a knock came on the door. Captain Shield opened it and put his head in. She noticed, now that he'd taken his hat off, that his hair had grown a bit long and displayed a natural curl he probably hated but she found endearing.

"What are we doing today?"

"Christening cakes. I need eight of them for this afternoon." She turned back to the cupboard and pulled out another four turntables, ignoring the fast rate of her heartbeats. He was a necessary second set of hands. But at the thought of his hands, she remembered how he had caressed her breast at the party. She grabbed the edge of the cupboard, and forced herself to think only of cake.

"You need cakes."

"Yes, the ones I need are in that cupboard." She pointed, and Judah found the correct cakes and brought them over. "We covered them in almond paste yesterday. Now it is time to frost. Then I'll pipe the child's name on each one and decorate with dried strawberries."

"We do a brisk business in these?"

"Yes. Like wedding cakes, the christening line is very popular." She pulled two frosting knives from the drawer. "Now, Captain, the trick to frosting with royal icing is all in how you hold the knife."

"I shall watch you do one."

"Very well." She did well with the top and sides, but matching them with a clean edge was still a challenge. Her fingers were steady on the knife, though. She'd become used to being observed by a far more critical eye than Captain Shield's.

"Admirable," he declared, when she'd finished smoothing the first cake.

"Are you ready to give it a try?"

He took off his coat, exposing a burgundy waistcoat and snowy linen. Without comment, she handed him a large apron, but he didn't only don it, he rolled up his sleeves, showing corded forearms dusted with dark hairs. She felt a little faint as she noted the thick, masculine wrists, how his shirt molded his arms, all the way up to muscular shoulders that seemed to dwarf the apron. The working men at Redcake's were fit specimens, but Judah was a head taller than most of them, clean-shaven instead of mustached, with the thick muscles of a warrior. He didn't smell of flour and butter, but sandalwood and lemon. She wondered that cakies didn't swoon in the corridor when he walked by. Had the temperature raised ten degrees in the past few minutes?

"It is hot in here today, is it not?" she asked, fanning herself with an order sheet.

"A trifle warm," he agreed, taking up a knife. "Now, as to angles?" He scooped up a glob of frosting and dropped it on top of the cake.

"That's too much," she said, scooping about half of it with her knife and placing it atop the third cake. "You don't want to tear the cake. You did place it correctly, though."

"Now we smooth out to the edge."

He slapped the spatula down and pressed the frosting.

"Glide it," she suggested. "Like you are ice skating."

"I've never skated," he said, amused.

She didn't know what else to do. Her palms tingled. "With your permission?"

He nodded, and she placed her fingers over his, showing him the proper motion.

"Back and forth. See, gently push the frosting out to the edges." She turned the stand with her free hand, trying to keep her eyes open, when she wanted to close them to focus entirely on his decadent scent, the heat of his hand under hers. But she couldn't help noticing how burnished his skin was after years in the Indian sun, such a contrast to her pale color. The tendons and veins on the back of his browned hand showed in high relief as they moved the knife back and forth.

He was breathing a little harder now, as she was herself. "Let's clean the knife," she said. "A warm knife frosts better."

He dipped it into the bowl of hot water she had set out.

"Now, let's frost the sides." She placed her hand back on his again after he put more frosting on the cake. Her legs felt wobbly and an alarming heat had spread down her chest from her breasts to her belly to the top of her thighs. She had never swooned in her life and wasn't about to succumb now.

"Excellent. We need to smooth everything. The first step is to clean the knife again, and place it on the seam around the edges."

"Now what?" His voice was terse, and his hip brushed hers.

She inhaled sharply. "Leave the knife where it is and turn the stand."

He followed instructions.

"See? Now we have a clean edge." She wiped the stand with her apron to remove a stray blob of frosting.

"A good first effort?"

"Oh yes," she assured him. "Much better than my first."

"I don't imagine Betsy guided your knife." His tiger gaze captured her gaze.

She licked her lips when words didn't come. Her gaze drifted downward. Without his coat on she could see a decided bulge in his trousers. Being a Cross girl, she knew what that meant. She had excited him, or at least cake decorating had. His chest rose and fell with great emphasis, as if he was involved in some kind of athletic activity. She wondered if he imagined some kind of activity with her, something that involved his masculine parts and the hot, wet heat between her legs.

"I wish I had a husband," she whispered.

"What?" he nearly shouted, so completely had she shocked him.

She put her hand to her temple, wishing she had not glanced at his trousers. "I do not know what I meant to say. Oh, it is hot in here."

"Why, what . . ." He tried and failed to form a complete sentence.

"I love my position," she said quickly. "Have I taught you well enough, Captain? I should finish and get these up to Mr. Popham."

"Yes, quite," he said, his tiger eyes glittering.

She noted his trousers fit more loosely now. What a ninny she was. She understood what she meant, that a husband could relieve the tight stress her body felt in his proximity, but she could have said nothing more designed to cool his ardor. Was that not for the best?

She was his employee, not a marriage prospect. If she made an overture she could lose her position. He held all the power, and from the quick way he was discarding his apron and tidying his clothing, covering all that masculine glory with his jacket, she knew he wasn't intrigued, but horrified.

"I apologize for my outburst."

"No, I understand. You would not have to do this labor in an overheated room if you had a husband to support you. I am sorry you continue to do uncongenial work. Betsy will be back on tomorrow and I will continue to emphasize that you are here to decorate, not do all the foundational tasks."

She nodded, crushed by his speech. "I do not mean for you to think I dislike frosting. But I did have to make it myself. It wasn't delivered as it should have been."

"With Betsy gone there must have been some misunderstanding. I shall look into it."

"No, not necessary. If it happens again, we shall speak to Mr. Melville."

He nodded. "Then, good day to you, Miss Cross. Since you do not come in again until Monday, I shall see you at the Column that morning."

"Thank you, sir." She hadn't even finished speaking her three words before he was out the door.

Leaning against the table, she pushed fringe out of her eyes and attempted to tuck it behind her ears. Her heart beat like a marching band and her stays felt much too tight. She must learn to control her tongue. And unfeminine lustful urges.

Over the next week, Nancy continued to sink, rarely waking from her stupor and refusing to take anything but a little beef tea or water. The weather change had not helped either, as a pleasant September became dreary, foggy, pestilent October.

On the first Monday in October, Magdalene dashed into Nancy's room to kiss her good-bye before leaving for Trafalgar Square. The drizzle outside was persistent and she was only looking forward to the part of the walk where she was sheltered by Captain Shield's umbrella and warmed by his large, furnacelike body next to hers.

Mrs. Gortimer glanced up with a sad smile. "Her breathing has changed. It won't be long now."

Candles were lit around the mean little room because so little light came in from the window. Nancy looked like a wax effigy. Her chest didn't seem to rise under the quilt and Magdalene could hear rattling.

"I will fetch George."

Hetty was walking up the hallway in her ponderous way, holding George's tea tray. Magdalene snatched it.

"Run to Nelson's Column and tell Captain Shield that I can't come in today," she ordered.

"Is it Mrs. Cross?"

"Yes."

Hetty nodded and turned to descend the steps. Magdalene, now an expert with trays, balanced the tea with one hand and opened the door with the other. She set it down on the bedside table and pulled open the curtain.

George stirred under his blankets and mumbled something. She leaned over his ear.

"Wake up!"

She scarcely missed being hit in the face as he sat up, sputtering.

"Who?"

"It's me, George."

He blinked. "Maggie? What is it?" He scrubbed at his face.

She saw the moment he caught her expression. "Her suffering is almost over, dear."

"Can you get me my clothes?"

She handed him what was draped over the back of the chair, then went back to Nancy's room to pray for her suffering to end. When George arrived, Mrs. Gortimer went to fetch the children. Even Manfred came in. The entire family was together when Nancy stopped breathing, just when the rain finally stopped and weak rays of light entered the room, making candles unnecessary.

Chapter Eight

Judah's first impulse had been to go to the Cross home when Hetty met him at Nelson's Column that morning with the sad news, but instead he thanked her and, when he arrived at work, sent around a note telling Magdalene that her position would be waiting when she was able to return. In return, he'd received a note thanking him and the information that funeral services would be on Friday.

He worked late the first half of the week, strangely disquieted by the lonely walks to work in the morning. Missing Magdalene's smiles and friendly chatter had been unexpected. She had become his favorite companion and without her he felt set adrift in this large city.

Hatbrook had offered to arrange a membership for Judah at his club, but he couldn't afford the fees quite yet, thanks to his investment in new winter clothing and bed linens, which he had not needed in India. This left him only at home and at Redcake's. The day before the funeral, he took a half day and went to the Bethnal Green Museum, where the National Portrait Gallery was temporarily installed.

The brick building was not convenient to Londoners, nor were the exhibits at all interesting, other than the portraits. He did wonder how they would survive a building with an iron and glass roof. Would they not fade, and what would happen if the glass broke? He found many portraits of royals and examined them all closely for a match to his face, but no image of the Prince of Wales was evident.

When he spotted a guard, he inquired.

"No one is included in the collection until ten years after their death, except the Queen," the man said.

"How disappointing. I particularly wanted to see the royal family."

"Did you know the Prince and Princess of Wales opened the museum back in eighteen-seventy-two? I believe we have a commemorative photograph of the event downstairs."

How fortuitous. "You don't say. Thank you." He went to the first level and hunted until he found a framed image of the prince and princess surrounded by other people. When he examined it, he discovered a man with wavy brown hair and a full beard, a somewhat portly fellow. Because of the beard, it was difficult to ascertain the shape of his face.

Frustrated, he went back and stared at the portrait of the late prince consort, but with so many images of him scattered about, proof of the Queen's unending devotion, he scarcely needed to do that. As the sky above the glass roof began to darken, he left the building and took a cab back to his home, stewing in irritation the entire way.

The next day was Nancy Cross's funeral. The ladies of the family did not attend the church service as was often the case, but afterward a crowd gathered at the home of Earl Gerrick, who was Magdalene's uncle. Judah knew his brother would not approve of him going to the childhood home of the infamous Lady Bricker, but this was a funeral, after all.

He was pleased to see a portion of Society had turned out to say good-bye to Mrs. Cross, though she had not been much a part of it in recent years, once George's parents had died, leaving large debts.

"Lord Judah, is it?" A gruff man in a black suit walked up to him, a glass of port in his hand.

"Captain Shield." Judah nodded at him.

"I'm Gerrick, know your brother. A very direct fellow."

"Yes," he agreed. "I am sorry for your family's loss. I am friendly with Mrs. Cross's immediate family."

"I heard you served with Mark. I am glad to see you have not let your brother's prejudice against us color your feelings."

"My association predates any action of your daughter, my lord," Judah said.

The earl chuckled. "What a merry mess that has been. She has been writing me weekly, begging to be allowed back to London for the Season. I cannot see any harm in it, with Matilda Redcake down in Sussex, though I'm surprised Hatbrook allows his wife's relatives on his property."

"I only have the vaguest notion of the circumstances as I was in India or traveling until late summer."

"Well, it's a bloody disaster," the earl said frankly. "I don't envy Hatbrook or his wife, for that matter. And I am sorry for what small part my daughter played. I believe she has learned her lesson."

Judah suspected his brother would not trust that to be true. "My brother has been up to Town for a visit, and my sister is coming soon to be presented, but I do not know the rest of the family's plans. I do not think they will want to see your daughter."

"No. We'll just have to make sure they do not attend the same parties." The earl clapped Judah's shoulder. "But you, Captain Shield, are always welcome. As is your family too, of course. We shall not make the feud go both directions, eh?"

"Thank you."

"Do you know my second son, the Honorable Geoffrey Cander? Just a bit younger than you. Did you go to school together?"

"No, I was educated at home. I never came to London."

"No? Let me introduce you. A young man needs his friends and Geoffrey can be a good friend to you."

Judah doubted that, if Lady Bricker was any representation of friendship, but he allowed himself to be introduced to the young man, who seemed a lively sort. He was able to say a few words to George Cross, the widower, and caught Miss Cross's eye once, though she was surrounded at all times by female relatives.

Eventually, he felt he had done his duty by the Crosses. He went home and he wrote a long letter to Mark Cross, detailing the occasion and health of his relatives. When he sat back from his desk, though, he realized he had nowhere to direct it.

He set the letter aside, but on Tuesday, when he walked into his office, shivering from the first snow of the season, he found Gawain Redcake waiting for him. Judah knew he might find his answer.

"You must be a very early riser, Sergeant," he said, hiding his own yawn behind his glove. Without Miss Cross to meet him, he only had Eddy Jackson's jokes to wake him up in the morning, but the newsboy had seemed withdrawn. Increasing numbers of transients in Trafalgar Square were changing the mood of the place, making it uneasy. "The tearoom becomes quite busy in foul weather. Come for a cuppa?"

"As I import my own special blend of tea mixed with eye-strengthening herbs, that would hardly make sense."

Judah glanced at the small table to the side of the armchair where he sat. "Yet I see a plate with crumbs."

"I may have filched an almond pastry," the sergeant said. "I apologize for borrowing your office, but I was waiting to see you."

"Sadly, I do not think you are here to offer your professional services."

"Why, having trouble?"

Judah went to his desk. "Only the shocking ramp-up that I'm told we must have for the Season. All these additional staff and ingredients are a huge expense."

"A lot of people come to Town along with the politicians. Redcake's is in fashion, so yes, I expect it's all needed. Have you compared the estimates to last year?" He limped to the ledgers on the corner of the desk and perused one.

Judah poked through a stack of papers. "They are about ten percent above last year, but I am assured that the Jubilee functions account for it."

He nodded. "You can count on Mr. Hales if you have questions. He has an interest in the daughter of the financial manager here, so always seems to have the relevant information at his fingertips."

Judah found another sheet. "Overall business has been up seven percent this year, not ten."

"Even during the spring Season?"

"Yes."

Sergeant Redcake steepled his fingers. "I can see your concern, then, Captain Shield. I would hold everyone to seven percent until they can prove differently."

Judah nodded. "A man after my own thoughts. I will see what profit the rest of the year brings."

Ewan Hales entered, carrying a tray with a teapot, cups, and an assortment of small cakes. "I thought you might like this, sir, given the beastly fog, and these cakes are going to be introduced next week if you approve them."

Sergeant Redcake raised an eyebrow. "How did I manage to be so fortunate as to stop by today?"

Judah laughed and produced a knife from the desk. He cut each cake into three parts. "So tell me, Hales, how did you manage to find a lady friend among the accountants? I should have thought the cakies were pretty enough for any man."

Hales patted his stomach. "I'd rather have money than pastry. It's not as if food is hard to come by here."

"Well said," Judah agreed. "I take your point." He separated the pieces onto three plates and handed them out, then sat back.

The telephone rang shrilly in the outer office. The marchioness had it installed when Hatbrook put them in at Hatbrook House and Farm, but Judah still didn't like the sound. Hales excused himself, taking his plate, while Sergeant Redcake took a slip of paper and pencil and started making notes.

"Not to your liking?" Judah inquired as he poured himself a steaming cup of the brew, leaving it dark so as not to adulterate his tasting session.

"I do not like blue-dyed food, unless it is blueberry flavored or some such. Dyes are often toxic."

"What is the flavor?" Judah eyed the cake and took a small bite. "Just vanilla? No, maybe a bit of cardamom."

"Exactly. Just because it might taste a bit exotic is no reason to poison people. Put a bit of fruit or nut on it. Makes it look more expensive that way anyhow."

Judah reached for a slip of paper and made his own note to inquire into the dye. "I met a dye man recently. Courtnay, from Liverpool."

"He's in clothing dye, not food. Redcake's has always prided itself on clean food, suitable for fine ladies and children. Something to keep in mind."

"Sound advice," he agreed. "Now, what do you think of this pink number?"

"Fruit dye," Redcake said. "So that's all right. But say, I was here to tell you more about Mark Cross."

Judah licked cream off his lips. "This cake is very good. Flavored with coffee."

"I shall try it next."

"So, Lieutenant Cross?"

"Yes. My man Khan ran across some more news in India."

"I am happy to pass along anything you hear. The family would no doubt be pleased to receive you, except they suffered a death last week."

"I'm sorry to hear that."

"I wrote Mark Cross a letter of condolence but then wasn't sure where to send it."

Redcake limped back to the armchair by the fire. "I'll put it in my next packet for Khan, if you like. I'm sure he can get it to Jaipur."

"Thank you. So Cross is still with that trader?" Judah took the other armchair, still holding his teacup, and stretched his damp shoes to the fire.

"Apparently. Though it might be getting a bit sticky."

"Why do you say that?"

Redcake stroked his chin. "First, Khan said he'd heard that Lieutenant Cross was trading in moonstones."

"For the trader?"

"That was the thing—no. I thought the family had no money."

"Maybe he had army pay. He couldn't have spent it all on clothing and he didn't gamble or have more than the obvious vice."

"Anything is possible. At any rate, he made a deal to sell them to a friend of Khan's who is a jewel trader. Then, when he came back to the shop, he had two black eyes and an arm in a sling."

"What happened?"

Redcake shrugged. "I have no idea. The trader beat him because he stole the stones? Some rough trade? A fight?"

"Your friend didn't inquire?"

"Nothing else about it was in the letter."

Judah swallowed the rest of the coffee cream cake. "Not sure if this is anything I should be reporting to his family."

"I see your point. But if he sent some other word to them, this might put things in context."

"Pooling information."

"Exactly. That's what we're doing about Theodore Bliven, between myself and your brother."

Judah bit the insides of his cheeks, not quite sure what to say about the sergeant's sister's wayward lover. "I understand the lady is having a difficult time of it."

"My sister Matilda is enjoying the worst of luck," Redcake agreed. "My sister Rose, well, she fell out with your brother from the start. She's at the manor for now, keeping house for Father while Mother helps Matilda in Heathfield."

"Our families are quite mixed in with each other. But come, it is a bad time of year to be melancholy, what with the weather."

Redcake narrowed his eyes. "Accusing me of moodiness, Captain?" His slitted eyes pulled his brows close over his prominent nose, giving the man a look of sheer villainy.

Judah held up his hands, laughing. "Never."

One side of Gawain's mouth tilted up. "I did always think you were a good one, despite being a toff."

"Now our roles have reversed somewhat."

"I may have more money than you, but we're both businessmen and that gives us a great deal in common. I'll stand for you at my club, if you'd like. The word in Society is that you haven't claimed a place anywhere."

"I've thought about the Travellers Club. I know the waiting list is long, so by the time they contact me my ship should be in."

"Ship?"

"I invested in gems. I don't intend to be without funds forever."

"Funny that our lieutenant had a similar thought. But then you were friends."

"Lots of good stones in India. But no one beat me over mine. Let us hope they arrive and then I can speak to you about your club."

"It's nothing fancy. We have rooms for now, rather than an entire house to ourselves. No accommodations." Redcake shifted in his chair. "You can afford it on your salary here."

Judah scratched at his cheek. "Then it might be just the thing. A club for men of business mentality?"

"Importers, local tradesmen. You know, Courtnay is a member, though I think he has one or two other memberships. Why don't you come for dinner some night this week? I am here until Friday."

"You are certain they would want me?"

"You fit right in as manager of Redcake's, but as a marquess's brother, you shall be an utter coup. I would imagine the board will elect you in that very night."

They both stood, shook hands, scheduled an appointment for Thursday night. Judah never thought he would find enduring friendship with a sergeant, but life had taken him strange places this past year.

He held up a finger and hunted in his desk for the letter to Lieutenant Cross. "For your Khan."

Redcake took it and tucked it into his coat. "I will send it along."

The next day Judah called at the Cross home. The news from Redcake might not be worth passing along, but he wanted to check on Miss Cross.

He found George and Miss Cross much altered from the cheerful duo of his last visit. Dressed in black, the lady looked glum. Even her hair had lost its sheen. The shabby house's vitality had fled as well. The children were still at the nursery at Earl Gerrick's home so that the house could be thoroughly cleaned, an activity that had not taken place in some months thanks to Mrs. Cross's illness.

"She ran this home as neatly as you please," George told him earnestly, setting down a black-rimmed teacup. The contents had been openly doctored with a flask. "I wish you could have known her before our life became all about doctors, medicines, and treatments."

Miss Cross patted her brother's hand. "She was truly the best of women."

"At least now"—George hiccuped—"we won't need your salary anymore to pay for Mrs. Gortimer and you can run the house. I know you learned a great deal from Nancy."

Judah watched Miss Cross's eyelids lift as she heard this bit of news. He could tell George's plan had not been discussed.

"Dear George," she said, patting his hand again. "You know you cannot depend on me. I might marry."

"You might, you might," he said mournfully.

With a glance at Judah, she said, "I think the best plan is to keep my salary and hire a housekeeper. That way you'll have someone trained if I do leave."

"We cannot afford a housekeeper," he cried. "That is for a greater home than this."

"Then at least someone to do the heavy work," Miss Cross said. "Hetty is quite competent if she doesn't have to do everything herself. Then there might be money left for school fees for at least one of the boys, once we've paid the doctor bills."

"Well," he sighed, with a sidelong glance at Judah. "It is true that Cross ladies should not go unmarried. Our blood runs too hot, you know."

"Really, brother," Miss Cross said, her cheeks flushing. "I simply meant that I am still young and might have a household of my own one day. And you might remarry in time. I know dear Nancy wished it."

"I'm sure Captain Shield does not want to hear of our domestic trials."

"Captain Shield may find them quite interesting, in fact," she replied. "Since he has so recently come to London and set up his own household."

"That is true," George agreed. "Have you found satisfactory servants, Captain? I have never had a bachelor establishment, at least until now."

"I am not home very much," Judah confessed. "But the house is warm and clean."

"Make sure they are not robbing you," George said, emptying his teacup and filling it again with his flask. "The maid we had before Hetty was a dreadful thief."

Judah set down his teacup. "Employees are necessary but can be troublesome, I give you that. However, I came to speak of troublesome relatives, not of staff."

Miss Cross pulled her shawl more tightly about her shoulders. "Do you have word of Mark?"

"I do. Apparently he's been trading in gems, so he might be building his fortune. But, I've also heard he sustained minor injuries."

"How?" said Miss Cross as George barked, "What?"

"Nothing serious. Some kind of arm injury. I considered not sharing the information as you've had so much trouble already, but if it were my brother I'd want to know any insignificant detail."

"Quite," Magdalene said.

"I took the liberty of sending him a letter. I assume you've done the same."

Her fingers laced over her heart. "We wrote him in care of the army as usual, but I don't suppose that will get to him now."

"It is hard to say," Judah agreed. "I sent mine through a different channel. Perhaps one or both of the letters will reach him."

"I've dreamed of opening the door one day and finding him on my doorstep, restored to us," George said.

"It may happen," Judah said. "How about Manfred? Is he in residence presently?"

George pulled out his flask. "Took himself off to Brighton directly after the funeral. Went to stay with some friends there. Seemed odd with the Season beginning."

"He can cast off mourning in the south," Miss Cross said, a decided edge in her tone.

"Youth," George said, touching his black armband. "He does not understand what we have lost."

"Captain, I should tell you that I think it will take me a little longer before I can return to work. We have much to do here before the children can come home."

He nodded. "Take as much time as you need."

"I thought another week, past this one. I absolutely plan to see you in the Square on the twenty-fourth of the month."

"I shall tell Betsy."

"Have Irene and Tom started to work in the Fancy?"

"On Monday, I believe."

She licked her lips. He couldn't help remembering their kisses. He shifted in his chair.

"Should I return sooner?"

"Of course not. You need to settle the house for the children. And hire the new servant you mentioned."

Miss Cross gave him a grateful smile.

George turned his gaze to Judah as if he had not been paying any attention to the conversation. "We are planning to pick up the children on Monday next, Captain Shield. I wonder if you'd do us the honor of dining at our uncle's home that night. Our family feels so strongly about the connection with you."

Judah wondered if the earl was befriending him in the hopes of winning back Hatbrook's regard, securing his sister's hand in marriage to his second son, the Honorable Geoffrey Cander, perhaps, or his heir, Viscount Napsea. All this talk of marriage made him a bit nervous. He liked the girl, but she was an employee, after all.

However, he'd absolutely like to talk to some of the family, to hear the gossip about the Prince of Wales. "I would be pleased to accept."

"Jolly good," George said with a burst of enthusiasm. "I shall not keep you any longer."

"Thank you for relaying the information about our brother," Miss Cross said. Her gaze met his.

He thought she meant to convey some message, but wasn't sure what it was. At least he would see her again soon.

On Friday evening, Judah was sitting in front of his fire when he heard a thumping at the door. As he set down his papers, his valet appeared.

"The Marquess of Hatbrook and Lady Elizabeth Shield are here to see you," he announced.

Judah jumped to his feet. "They are? I was expecting a summons to appear at Hatbrook House." Without instructing his valet, he rushed into the front hall.

Beth was all dimpled grin as she rushed into his arms. "I knew you'd be happy to see us!"

"Of course I am." He set her at arm's length and admired her fashionable black gown. "Aren't you all grown up? But you could have sent me a note. I'd have come to Belgravia."

"I wanted to see your cozy nest and understand why you would choose bachelor digs rather than stay at the mansion." She glanced around the hall. "I do not know what I expected. Dancing girls? Purple velvet fainting couches and mysterious smoke drifting through the doors?"

"You're confusing me with some ladies' novel, I expect," he said. "Penny, take the coats, if you will."

His housemaid came into the hall and took the outerwear. Judah ordered tea and took them into the parlor.

Beth glanced around her, proclaiming everything full of charm. "Do you play?" she asked, pointing to the hired piano.

"No. The furnishings came with the house. You can try the instrument for me and see if it is any good." He turned to light the fire.

Beth sat on the bench and lifted the keyboard cover. The familiar sound of a Mozart piece assaulted Judah's ears with flat keys. He hoped his fire would be more successful than the music. His only callers before now were George and Manfred Cross a time or two when the weather had been much warmer.

"Stop that racket," Hatbrook said, laughing. "A piano tuner must be called immediately."

"I agree," Judah said. "On my list."

"Are you going to purchase your own furnishings?" Hatbrook asked, settling himself in an armchair.

"I haven't thought to do so," Judah admitted. "Seems like the duty of a wife, and I have no thought to marry."

"You should."

"Bah. I do not know what I have to offer a wife. My paternity—"

"Is irrelevant," said Hatbrook. "You are my brother and that is good enough for most any woman, excepting a royal."

Judah held back a smile. What would his brother say to his suspicions about his parentage? The parlor door opened and he looked up, hoping to see a decent presentation of tea and cakes, but instead, it was his valet again.

"Mr. Gawain Redcake to see you, Captain. Are you at home?"

"Yes, of course."

The sergeant stepped into the small room a moment later, followed by the tea.

"You'll have to tell me if the tea is any good, Beth," he told his sister, who frowned at the piano as she tried each key. "I haven't hosted a lady yet."

"Ah, but we have a connoisseur," Hatbrook said, nodding in return to Sergeant Redcake. "The importer himself has arrived."

"How are you, Hatbrook?" the sergeant asked, shaking hands.

"Very well, Gawain. Have you come to sort my brother out about Redcake's?"

The sergeant bowed to Beth, who smiled at him before returning to her keys. He stumped to the sofa. "Not at all. I came to offer my congratulations if you want them."

"Good news?" Judah asked. "Beth, shouldn't you pour the tea?"

She left the piano and took a chair next to Hatbrook. Judah noticed the sergeant watching her pour with an air of complete concentration.

"Sergeant?" he prodded.

"You should call me Gawain," said the man absently. "We are related by marriage now."

"I shall in future. What news?"

"Ah, that. As I expected, you were voted into the Euphonious Commerce Society yesterday. Are you going to become a member?"

"You've chosen a club without consulting me?" Hatbrook asked. "You know I could find you a place in one of mine."

"This is a club for businessmen," Judah said. "I fit right in."

"I see." Hatbrook's face was impassive as he thanked Beth for his tea and slice of bread and butter.

"Where do you live, Gawain?" Beth asked.

"At the family home in Bristol," he said, smiling at her.

Judah had never thought Gawain the type to smile, not since their acquaintance had been refreshed. His wounds had served to make him taciturn. But now he saw a toothy smile, a certain geniality of manner. Could Gawain have feelings for Beth?

Chapter Nine

Judah wondered how his brother would feel if Gawain, his wife's twin, asked for their sister's hand. Gawain was rich, true, but Beth had an acceptable dowry for her station. There could be no doubt that she'd be marrying beneath her if she accepted him. Gawain, the son of a manufacturer, made no pretense of being a gentleman.

Hatbrook's forehead creased, his gaze moving from Gawain to Beth to him. Judah had his answer. Hatbrook would not be pleased at the match. Gawain, insensible to the marquess's irritation, enticed Beth to share her favorite piano pieces.

"I am sorry I cannot play you anything," she said. "Judah's instrument is in no condition for that. But you have heard me play before, I think."

"No, I have not had that pleasure," he said, leaning forward.

Hatbrook cleared his throat. "Alys is learning to play," he announced.

"Speaking of my sister," Gawain said, turning to Judah, "I wonder if I might trouble you and your brother for a private word?"

Beth pouted prettily, but before she could speak Gawain bowed his head in her direction. "I would not abandon such a charming lady, but the matter is a delicate one that requires speed."

"I understand, of course," she said.

Judah stood. “We shall leave you to the tea and go into the study for a moment.”

Hatbrook rose and the two men followed Judah up the creaking stairs to a spare room he had designated as his study.

“This is a cozy nook,” Hatbrook said, glancing around. “It must be a wonder to engage in creature comforts after so many years in India.”

Someone who had never been to India could not imagine the place properly. His brother’s guilt that he had been so far away from home was evident in letters he’d sent over the years. He had always wished Judah could have had a private income and a place in Society, seeming to forget Judah had entered the army long before Hatbrook’s father died. What else could he have done with no money and no education?

Judah invited them to sit and took his favorite tattered armchair. “A drink?” he offered, pointing to the decanter next to his chair. Upon both men refusing, he said, “This is the room I would refurbish first. As you can see, I simply appropriated bits of furniture from other rooms.”

Gawain sat on a faded red fainting couch and Hatbrook took a straight-backed chair.

“Now, what is this about?” Hatbrook asked, still a little cold.

“Theodore Bliven,” Gawain replied. “The seducer himself.”

Hatbrook rubbed at his temples as if the name brought on an instant headache.

“Have you located him?” Judah asked.

“Is he wed to that woman he claimed to be engaged to?” Hatbrook asked at the same time.

“Unwed and yes, he’s in Madras.”

“Should I go after him?” Gawain leaned forward, almost as if he wanted to perform a service for Hatbrook.

“For what purpose? To drag him back to marry Matilda?” Hatbrook said.

“If he isn’t married, why not?”

“I cannot imagine it would be a successful marriage. He’d probably live off her funds.”

“You cannot see the average marriage through the lens of your own happy union," Gawain said. "Would not any husband for my sister be better than none?"

"You cannot go to India and be back before the child is born," Hatbrook said. "You cannot even reach India in time."

Gawain leaned back on the couch and used his arms to lift his bad leg onto it. "You are right, of course. I just wish I could do something. If he'd just gone to Scotland or somewhere like that, you'd have wanted me to go after him."

"If he was in Scotland, he would know what has transpired by now," Hatbrook told him. "As he insisted he was seduced, he may continue to feel an ungentlemanly lack of interest in the outcome."

"You speak of my sister, my lord," Gawain said.

"She is also my wife's sister," Hatbrook returned. "And a resident in my home. I cannot see any reason to pursue this subject further this evening. Beth is downstairs with no one to entertain her." He stood.

Judah followed suit, with the sure knowledge that Gawain was deeply hurt by Hatbrook's dismissal. Different classes had different expectations about behavior. Such misunderstandings were the outcome of unequal families coming together.

Judah stared across Earl Gerrick's table very late Monday evening, wishing he had declined the invitation. The ton's hours were the opposite of a working man's. Miss Cross, seated next to him, still appeared quite fresh, though rather pale in her mourning gown, but she had not returned to work. One more week until they resumed their morning walks.

She caught his eye and he smiled at her. Her chin ducked down, as if for a moment she hadn't recognized him, just seen him as some gentleman, but then she smiled back. He wondered what the countess had meant by seating them next to each other. Were they aware of the professional relationship? Or did they suspect him of some other interest in a hot-blooded Cross?

Society understood you did not have to marry a Scandalous Cross. You might, of course, but that ran you the risk of being cuckolded. Across the table, for instance, was the case in point—Lady Amelia March, the earl's sister, who had been the Prince of Wales's mistress at one time. He had learned that from the Cross brothers.

He regarded the lady, still rather slim and pretty though she must be nearly his mother's age. Lady March, who had married a baronet after her affair had come to a close, turned from her dinner partner on the right to the man at her left, her gaze raking Judah's as she did so.

He inclined his head, hoping to somehow convey the message that he'd like a word with her. Her slight smile indicated she understood him, though they were strangers.

An hour later, they were enjoying an intermission between an indifferent singer and an underfed poet, the evening's entertainment, when Lady March came up to Miss Cross, who was at Judah's side.

Her bustle twitched as she settled herself in front of her niece. "You must introduce me to this handsome young man, though of course I knew his mother well."

"Please, Aunt, may I present Captain Shield," Miss Cross said, then completed the formalities.

"I understand you have been speaking to your mother's old friends," Lady March said. "I believe I can count myself among them."

"Then I am doubly happy to make your acquaintance, Lady March," he said, bowing slightly.

"I also have been led to understand you all but recoil when called 'Lord Judah' these days," she said, her shrewd gaze considering him.

"I am proud of my military title," he said.

"Oh, I do not think that is the reason." Her lips tilted upward in a private kind of smile. "I am guessing you have learned something about your mother."

Miss Cross frowned and glanced at him. Judah felt torn, desperate to learn what the lady knew, but not sure he wanted Miss Cross mixed up in his business. Still, given that her family were notorious gossips, she would find out eventually.

"I understand you were a close friend of the Prince of Wales," he said baldly.

Lady March nodded.

"My mother? Was she also a close friend of His Royal Highness?"

Her eyebrows rose and she smiled openly this time, delightedly. "My dear boy! Is that what is troubling you? Why dear Bertie didn't even have close friends, as you say, until after you were born. No, I'm quite sure of that."

Judah's next breath stuck in his chest. He held himself rigid. "You don't say."

"Oh, I do. His mother did her best to marry him off right after Irish Nellie got her claws into him. I ought to know as I was next." She tittered. "How very indiscreet I'm being, but you know it was a very long time ago."

"The wine was a bit strong," Miss Cross murmured, taking her aunt's arm. "Why don't we sit in the anteroom? I'm sure it is much cooler there."

Judah was left to stare at their backs as the two women walked away. He could not help but note that Miss Cross had her aunt's charming walk. What about Miss Cross? Was she as pure as she seemed?

She might have thought they had too much wine at dinner but he rather felt he'd had not nearly enough.

Magdalene helped her aunt sit down and found her a glass of lemonade. "What was that about?" she asked.

"I believe Captain Shield has discovered he was not the late marquess's blood son," Aunt Amelia said.

"Oh. How dreadful." She seated herself next to her aunt on the settee. "Do you really think so?"

"I am very sure of it. What young man, when faced with the truth about his parent, would not at least hope he was the son of a member of the royal family? But no, I am sure that is not the case."

She couldn't help asking, "Then who do you think was his father?"

The older lady shrugged, a movement as graceful as any dancer's. "I have no idea who he was, just who he was not. The prince held nothing from me when he was mine. We were terribly young then."

"Did he love you?"

"I'm sure he did in his way. He was a bit backward and naive. All long ago."

"And best forgotten?"

"Not at all. My memories are precious to me, and I harmed no one. I never had children who might be embarrassed."

"Unlike Lady Hatbrook."

"Quite. This is unfortunate. I hope his brother is standing by him."

"As much as the captain allows." Magdalene found she was gripping her skirts. "He is my friend, a very good friend to me, and to George. If you don't mind I'd like to go to him."

Aunt Amelia nodded graciously and Magdalene took her leave, swiftly walking back into the music room, but she could not find the captain. Had he left the party? She went into the corridor, opening doors because she was certain he would not have gone into the cold night, but didn't spot him until she had reached the front hall.

He was speaking to a footman and she suspected he was asking that his coat and hat be fetched. She increased her speed and was breathless by the time she reached him.

She put her hand on his arm and drew him into an alcove. "Surely you cannot be leaving."

His face was very stern. "I must be at Redcake's early."

"You only go there so early because of me," she said. "I know you used to leave later until you were concerned for my safety."

He said nothing, only put his hand over hers where it rested on his opposite arm. "Miss Cross."

"Yes?" Without thinking, she went on her tiptoes, the better to see his face in the dim light. He was so very tall.

He bent his head to hers. "Now you know the truth about me, that I am a bastard, and yet you still come for me," he murmured.

Before she could respond, his mouth found hers, hot and demanding. His body remained still, an inch from hers except where their hands met, but his lips, how they plundered, stealing her senses as thoroughly as they stole her breath.

The blood rushed from her brain, leaving her with nothing but a craving for the taste of him, the pressure of his mouth, the faint taste of wine on his tongue as it dipped into hers. Her free hand tangled itself in his lapels, slipped lower than it should until her fingers danced along his low-cut waistcoat. She felt the hard ridges of muscle under his shirt and her mouth opened further in a hot rush of pleasure at his strength.

His tongue took full possession, tangling with hers. She felt his hand in her hair, heard the small clatter of pins hitting the floor. Her breasts tingled where they made contact with his chest, her nipples tightening into hard peaks desperate for further sensation.

Giving in to the moment, she arched her neck. More pins fell and she felt a lock of her thick hair brush her cheek. The sensation shocked her into sense.

Her hand moved back up his chest and she pushed at him, stepping away. "Captain! We cannot keep doing this if I am going to be employed by you!"

"No?"

She could see his breathing was ragged, forced herself to keep her gaze on his face, not drift lower down and see if he was hot and bothered, like she was, below his waistcoat. "I cannot possibly work for a man who kisses me."

"I am not your direct supervisor, nor indeed the owner of the establishment," he countered.

"You are still in authority over me." She pushed at her hair, knowing there would be no hiding what she'd been up to if anyone saw her.

"I am not demanding you kiss me as a part of your position." He knelt before her.

"Captain Shield!" What was he going to do? Propose? Her heart skipped a beat and she took a deep, involuntary breath as black spots danced before her eyes.

He grinned then, the expression so alluring that she felt moisture dampen her thighs. Heavens, but he was a rake. And she, a Scandalous Cross who could fall so easily.

Her spine straightened and her nose lifted, even as her knees quavered and her female parts hummed with expectation. She clasped her hands in front of her breasts.

He picked up the pins that lay on the floor and handed them to her. "I will see you at Nelson's Column next Monday, Miss Cross," he said.

Footsteps sounded on the marble floor behind them and a footman called for the captain.

"I am off to bed," the captain said. Then after a pause, he continued, "Alone, unfortunately."

With that, he turned away, striding confidently like the military man he was, but with just a hint of boyish swagger that she, disgustedly, recognized from her brother, Manfred, when he was pleased with one of his conquests.

She was no conquest to be swaggered about, and tomorrow, she resolved, no matter how impertinent, she would tell him so. How could he leave her so wanting . . . so . . . disappointed and empty? Continuing on like this would be unbearable.

Magdalene persuaded George the boys would be better behaved if they had some of Redcake's petits fours, and that they weren't too dear since she received a discount now. Early the next afternoon she had dodged omnibuses, carriages, and carts in the rain to go there. When she went up the steps to the offices in her wet, dragging mourning skirts, she felt like an interloper, an outsider, and hated the feeling. She wanted to be back here, not sitting at home staring at the walls. Nancy's things had all been sorted, given to servants or friends, or removed to the rag basket when necessary. The children would be home tomorrow.

Ewan Hales wiped his hand down his pomaded hair when she entered, then stood. "I am sorry for your loss, Miss Cross."

"I—I didn't know you knew who I was," she stammered, somehow thinking she'd have only seen Captain Shield in here.

"I know all the employees," he said with a proprietary air.

"That's very, er, thorough of you." After a pause, she asked, "Is the captain in?"

His gaze took in her dripping skirts. She checked to make sure the dye wasn't coming off and staining the floor. It wasn't.

"I will see," he said, bustling off importantly in trousers that were just a bit too tight.

He had nice legs, she decided, but the obsequiousness was a bit much.

Mr. Hales appeared at the captain's door and held it open for her. "He is in."

She nodded her thanks as she ventured into the inner sanctum.

"You can close the door, Hales," the captain said, standing up from his desk.

She saw a sheath of papers, a faded rose ribbon discarded to one side, on his desk. It looked like correspondence, not Redcake's business.

"Rose was your mother's signature color, was it not?" she asked.

"Indeed." He came forward. "Hales should have taken your cloak and hat."

"Oh." She fumbled with the ribbon of her hat and undid the clasp of her cloak.

His fingers brushed her shoulders as he helped her remove the threadbare wool. Her shoulders tingled, or perhaps she was merely shivering from the damp.

"This little stove is very warming," he said, inviting her to a corner of the room behind the desk. He put his hands forward, demonstrating. "Though I like the fireplace too."

"So this is what makes it so cozy up here," she said, coming to stand next to him.

"That and the kitchens, I expect. How could any part of a bakery really be cold, unless it's specifically an ice room?"

"Yes, I expect the oven in the Fancy keeps it toasty in there, but that might not be the best thing for delicate frosting work."

"Alys told me that, as in all things, there must be a happy medium in the temperature."

"Of course. Did Mr. Lewis Noble design this stove? It seems so clean."

The captain nodded. "I think he made some slight alterations. One finds he used Redcake's as something of an inventor's playground."

"It's very nice. I wish I had one for my bedchamber at home." She blushed, realizing what she had said. Maybe her attraction for him was in their way, not his attraction to her.

"If you can, change your sleeping arrangements to a room over the kitchen. I find that is the best approach."

She touched her hair, found the back of her neck damp from ringlets that had caught the fog if not the rain. "Captain, you shouldn't speak to me of sleeping arrangements."

"You mentioned your bed first."

She felt herself pulled into that tiger gaze of his, until it seemed there was nothing in the room but him. They must have both lifted their hands at the same time for, when she looked down, she realized they were touching.

She jerked back, wild for something else to discuss, something that would allow her to ignore the trembles in her knees and the dampness that had traitorously seeped between her legs yet again.

"That is your mother's signature, is it not?" she asked, peering at the letters on the desk.

"I suppose, now that you know my shameful secret, you might as well see what I am doing," he muttered.

"You are hardly the only son of the ton who does not really belong to his family," Magdalene said. "Why, sometimes, it even happens on purpose, when a man cannot father a child."

"That was hardly the case here. Of my siblings, I am the only one in question."

"Marriages go through many stages," she said. "Your parents must have grown apart, then reconciled."

"Or my mother was merely unlucky," he countered.

"Does she reveal anything in her correspondence?" Her fingers itched to take it up herself, even though she knew she couldn't share the gossip uncovered.

"I thought it revealed an indiscretion with the prince, but I must be wrong."

"You might be correct next time, if you are quite certain your mother strayed."

"Told me so herself."

His glance caught hers again, sending her off balance. She clutched the edge of the desk. "I just came to say hello before I picked up some small treats for the children."

"You do not want to look at the letters?" he asked.

"Do you want me to?" She wasn't sure if she could remain close to him without something happening, but if nothing else, he was her friend and she wanted to support him.

"I do. But I need to meet with Melville downstairs in a minute. If you like, I could have tea sent up and you could read through them."

"For a little while," she said, not sure if she was happy or irritated that he didn't mean for this to be a shared activity.

"Excellent. I shall call on you tonight to see if you have discovered any avenues for me to pursue."

She nodded. "George will be happy to see you. He becomes very morose outside of company. For now, it is a good thing he is teaching the boys."

"Do you think we should find a position here for him?" the captain asked.

She was startled by the idea. "I do not know. What would he do here?"

"It is a question for another occasion," he said.

"Yes, of course." Her fingers stroked the old ribbon.

He nodded to her. "I must go."

She watched him leave, fighting the urge to call him back and tell him he must stop kissing her, but they had managed a private conversation without it happening again. He had proven he didn't find her completely irresistible.

The thought was not as comforting as she might have hoped.

Judah could have nodded off in the comfortable chair in the Cross's parlor that evening, as George had little to say. He was in his cups and hiccupped when he spoke more than a few words. Miss Cross stared daggers at George, clearly wanting a private word with Judah, but until the housemaid called for her brother, due to some detail regarding the boys' room, she had kept her conversation to polite inanities.

"The boys return home tomorrow," Miss Cross said, as her brother stood. "They have broken enough of the earl's vases as to be unwelcome for the rest of the year."

"Not even for Christmas?" Judah asked.

"Perhaps for Christmas," George allowed. "I will return in a moment."

As soon as uneven footsteps were heard on the stairs, Miss Cross jumped up and sat on the frayed ottoman by Judah's feet. "I read over the letters."

"Did you come up with any theories?" He liked this image of a neat woman sitting at his feet by the fire. It implied a cozy domesticity.

"I wish I could say I had, Captain, but it seems your search is at an end if this is all you have to go on. Your mother traveled frequently, so her acquaintance was large. What did her final letter to you say exactly?"

"That I was not the marquess's son, and she was sorry for her lack of propriety in her youth. She wished she had been a better mother and asked my forgiveness."

"Did you offer it to her?"

"To her memory, you mean? By the time the letter came she was already gone, though I did not know it for months."

"Yes." She leaned in.

He bent his head toward her, smelling violets and mothballs. Her mourning gown must have been tucked away from some previous loss. "You'll have to detach the white collar and cuffs from your cakie uniform, I suppose," he said. "I shall see if we have any in black for you to wear."

"Focus, Captain."

He sighed. "I was very angry with her. I do not know where I fit in anymore. I cannot really go out in Society. I am a fraud. I could be a stable boy's son for all I know."

"It doesn't seem likely. I imagine you are the son of some other member of your mother's close circle. An earl, at least." She toyed with the fringe on the ottoman to keep herself from touching him.

"Have you ever met anyone I especially look like? You are far more familiar with the families than I am."

"I've never seen anyone with your eyes," she said. "But family characteristics often skip a generation. It is only when you look at portraits that you see a resemblance."

"I looked at a photograph of the Prince of Wales," Judah admitted. "But I expect Lady March would know the truth. I have given up on that idea."

"Your father does not have to have been a prince, but he is assuredly distinguished. I do not think you should trouble yourself. You are a fine gentleman. I have enjoyed our conversations greatly these past months. You are sensible and competent, more than one can say about many elevated personages."

Her praise warmed him far more than the insufficient fire. "Thank you for the compliments."

"You are very welcome." She sighed. "I look forward to talking about more than housecleaning, when I return next week. Even Betsy's gossip about the amours of the bakers seems fascinating to me now."

"I cannot imagine not working, myself. The idle life of house parties, one after another, does not appeal. My brother and I have that much in common. Though I would like to hunt. I miss that. Excellent hunting in India."

She folded her hands into her lap. "Do you have tiger heads on the walls in your home?"

"No. I shot to get rid of them, not to decorate with them. Tigers are killers, both of men and cattle, so they need to be contained."

"Elephants?"

"No. I hunted for a reason, for food or to contain pests. But sometimes we hunted from elephants."

She tilted her head up to his. "How exotic it sounds."

"Yes. We shot all the big cats, like panthers, that could wreak havoc on villages. There was some talk of containing them with poison, but I prefer a solitary battle of man over beast." His fingers itched to take her hands in his, but they were not courting.

"Would you like to grouse shoot? I know game birds are not the same as tigers, but I am certain my aunt would invite you to her estate in Derbyshire. The shooting goes until December, I believe."

"Not this year, too much to do, but maybe next." They were interrupted by the reappearance of George, who seemed not to notice where Miss Cross was seated. Judah smelled liquor as George tossed himself into a chair.

"Early day tomorrow," Judah said, rising. "I had best take my leave."

"I do not know how you do it," George said, rubbing the heel of his shoe on the carpet. "I find far too much to do in life than to lower myself to working. I am planning to start a beetle collection with the boys."

"Fascinating," Judah murmured. "Thank you for a pleasant evening." He would not be offering George Cross a position, that was certain.

Chapter Ten

The next day, Judah was called downstairs by Lewis Noble, who had arrived as contracted to do routine maintenance. But instead of a consultation on some broken piece of machinery, he found the men circled around one of the long tables, Noble at the head. He presided over a hand crank, which turned a frosting knife against a cake on an attached turntable.

"No gas or coal needed for this model, Captain Shield," Noble said, catching sight of him. "But it should save time."

"I thought frosting cakes was an art."

"Most art can be brought to heel by science," Noble said, lifting a lever that placed the frosting knife at an angle that allowed it to smooth out the edge of the cake where the side frosting met the top.

One of the men clapped. Another of the bakers elbowed him.

" 'ands don't 'ave to be steady no more," the clapper said. "The job will be done right regardless."

"Doesn't mean you can come to work drunk," said Alfred Melville, sharply.

"What do you think, Melville? Is the contraption a time saver?" Judah asked.

Melville shrugged. "It might work for the factories, but I don't think we need it here. The shilling cakes come from Bristol, you know."

Judah clapped his hands. "The demonstration is over. Return to your work."

Melville nodded at him approvingly. Judah walked over to the machine and scratched his chin as he looked it over.

"I thought it might help in the Fancy, so your ladies can focus on the detail work," Noble said.

"Has Betsy seen it?"

He detached the frosting knife and tossed it into a sink, then fit his machine into a box. "Yes. She was out here for a minute before she had to return to work. Run ragged, she is."

"Her assistant had a death in the family."

"It sounds like she's been gone a long time."

"She'll be back Monday. Now, what is your price? I'll see if her ladyship is interested in the expenditure." Had everyone seen Miss Cross's leave as excessive? That was the problem with trying to treat her as a lady instead of as an employee. He didn't want to damage his credibility or hers, but it was too late to consult one of the managers now.

Noble named a figure that seemed quite reasonable. "Just three lever changes and the cranking, and the cake is done. I estimate it cuts frosting time by two-thirds."

"Impressive. I will let you know." He went back upstairs and found his brother waiting for him next to the fireplace in his office.

Hatbrook lifted a teacup in his direction.

"I must have been in the basement for longer than I thought, if you had time to arrive and cadge a cup of tea."

"Hales is most efficient." His brother yawned and set down the cup.

Judah seated himself and poured fresh tea for them both. "I've noticed. What brings you by?"

"Town bores me," Hatbrook admitted. "But I promised to stay with Beth until her court presentation in a couple of weeks."

"Shouldn't you be closeted with your man of business?"

"Not every second of every day. I thought I could persuade you to come to Brooks's tonight for dinner."

Judah felt an instinctive recoil. "I've heard their dinner is nothing to thrill the palate."

"The conversation is far more elevated than that silly club of Gawain's. Are you so desperate for companions that you joined a tradesman's club?" Hatbrook's tone was snappish.

"There are many members of great wealth and erudition, including Courtnay, whose daughter you find appropriate to be my wife," Judah said, stung. "What do you have against Gawain Redcake?"

Hatbrook tapped his foot. "He has ideas above himself."

Judah stirred sugar into his tea. "You mean Beth. I agree she is too young and sheltered for someone who has lived Gawain's life, but after all, you did marry the man's twin."

Hatbrook's chin rose. "My wife may not have been raised to be a lady, exactly, but she didn't spend years in the army either."

"Well, I did, and I like him," Judah said, then felt the need to add, "For myself, not for Beth. Besides, my new club took me now, and Brooks's would probably not have an opening for a mere brother of a marquess for years."

His brother's tone softened. "You can come as my guest."

"You are rarely in London, Hatbrook. I live here now, and I want to make my own way, as much as is practical. You must allow me my own society."

He rolled his eyes. "Like the Crosses? You seem very cozy with them."

"Not to spite you, brother. I have had no dealings with Lady Bricker, only the others."

"You hardly seem of the temperament to run with Mother's crowd."

"To meet them is to gain access to their children, who are my age," Judah said. "Are the Honorable Geoffrey Cander and the like not appropriate as companions?"

Hatbrook drank off his tea and slammed down his teacup. "Not for the manager of Redcake's. You don't have time for the gambling and other activities they indulge in."

"I just had an invitation this morning for grouse shooting," Judah said, changing the subject. "I do not know if it was solicited or not."

"Where?"

"Lady March's estate in Derbyshire."

"She likes young men," Hatbrook said. "Beware."

A chuckle escaped Judah before he could contain it. "She seemed rather maternal to me."

"That's how she hooks the motherless young men," Hatbrook said darkly. "You should have seen her a decade ago, before she became maternal. Then it was all gypsylike allure and whispers of sexual misdoings."

"Nothing wrong with the occasional misdoings among friends," Judah said. "But I assure you my desires do not lean toward Lady March."

"Keep in mind that your brother associates with the royal family and others of that ilk." The chin went up again.

The marchioness's pregnancy seemed to be turning Hatbrook into a holier-than-thou, head of the family sort. "I will do my best not to disgrace you, Hatbrook." His brother's marriage had not set the bar as high as he seemed to think.

"I should think you will not have the time, if you continue to work."

"I'm sure working men can be disgraceful, even in their limited free time. But speaking of time, Lewis Noble is here with his new frosting machine. He seems to think the Fancy is just the place for his tool. Would you ask your wife if she wants me to indulge in the expenditure?"

"You cannot take the decision upon yourself?"

He named the sum. "It is beyond what she set for me to spend."

Hatbrook stared absently at the teapot. "Yes, that does seem high. But I understand the Fancy needs all the help it can get during the Season."

"I know. Shall I write Alys a note?"

"No, I shall ask myself when we return. Beth had all her fittings so we can return to Heathfield for a few days. I do not like being away from Alys for so long."

"Will she come to London at all?"

"For the court presentation."

"I look forward to seeing her again." He glanced at his desk to see how high his box of papers was.

Hatbrook leaned forward. "I realize we have become near strangers, Judah. But I would like us to be easy with each other."

They were not off to a good start. "Not only are we near strangers, we are not equals, either."

"I don't accept that. You have no idea how different I am than the usual marquess."

Judah had no heart to rebuff his brother. "I have some idea, given your choice of wife. But a man who is proud of his royal associations is as different from me as milk to cake." Only a fool would not wince at that statement, given he'd been hopeful of a blood connection to the royalties so very recently, but he'd said it, and had to watch as his brother stiffened.

"I will not lose you," Hatbrook said.

"I think you would lose me in a heartbeat, if I associated with Lady Bricker."

"Do not assume even that. I am sheltering one of Alys's sisters at times, and she did us a grave disservice early this year. Her behavior appalls me, yet I did not dismiss her from my household."

"You are most tolerant." But even if Hatbrook wasn't, who would criticize him?

"I will be, for the sake of family."

"For your sake then, and not just Beth's, I will try to fit in as best I can. But I must make my own way. The very name 'Shield' gives me a sense of disquiet and you must allow for that."

"I understand Mother set you adrift. But you are not so very unusual." Hatbrook smiled wryly. "Do you know there are even rumors about the Queen's parentage?"

Judah chuckled. "Not very loud ones, I assume."

"Of course not, but be heartened by that."

"I doubt it gives Her Majesty any pleasure, any more than it gives me. I cannot explain the sensation of uncertain parentage to one who has no doubts. Yet, I assure you it is not a constant burden upon my shoulders."

"No, you are too active." Hatbrook clapped his thighs. "And I should leave you to it and get to my own vast collection of papers. Do you know, we are thinking of putting in more fruit and starting a line of Hatbrook Farm jams?"

"I'm sure your wife will direct me to stock them if they come up to snuff."

"Yes. She still has Redcake's as her end game at all times. Not surprisingly, since this establishment is hers."

"Do you think she would ever sell it to me? When I have the funds?"

"No," Hatbrook said. "I don't think she would."

"I can't blame her, of course."

"Perhaps you can set up a jewelry emporium or some such. You must have quite a fortune in that ship."

"Some things that are very popular here sell for almost nothing in India. At any rate, I am well settled for now. I shan't think about leaving until I am bored."

"Fair enough. Will you come for dinner before we depart?"

Judah nodded and they took their leave. He was sorry to lose the notion of buying Redcake's for himself. He'd grown very fond of the place.

" 'appy to see you, miss," Eddy Jackson said, handing Captain Shield his paper. "I 'ear yer sister died. So sorry."

"Thank you," Magdalene said, smoothing her tight new collar with her glove. Had the captain been chatting about her?

He tossed Eddy a penny and gave the lad a wink, then tucked her under his umbrella without ever touching her. Her arm and waist tingled where he might have rested a hand if he'd wanted to.

"I hope you don't mind my saying it is pleasant to walk to Redcake's with you again, Miss Cross."

Magdalene smiled, pleased Captain Shield had missed her. "I am glad to be returning, and thank you for sending over the black collars and cuffs."

"I assumed you would not want to don white again until nearly spring."

"Exactly, Captain. You are very thoughtful."

"My pleasure. Everything is much the same in the bakery, though increasingly busy. I have made one change to your department."

"Oh? The additional staff, you mean?"

"No. With the marchioness's approval, I have purchased a new contraption from Mr. Noble. A froster that is meant to save precious minutes."

She had spent so much effort perfecting her frosting skills, and now there would be a machine to do it? For a moment, she felt kinship to the Luddites of long ago. Was she to be put out of work as quickly as she returned to it?

"I think it will help the operation. You will have more time to focus on the intricate work. Betsy assures me there is a great deal of it."

But not so much when fashionable Society was not in Town. Still, they were in the busy time now and she couldn't borrow trouble. Enough was present at home, with the boys not at all themselves, and George drinking himself into a stupor each night after they'd gone to bed. Of course, he insisted on imbibing expensive claret, which they could not afford in the quantities he drank. The household was becoming one she could hardly tolerate. If George continued in this vein, the boys would need to be sent away to school.

"I'm sure," she said, when Judah looked at her, "that it is an excellent contraption."

"The demonstration made it look easy enough. He should have it for us in a week or two."

"Is it very large? We'll have to find a place for it."

"I've arranged all that with Betsy. You don't need to worry your artist's soul with any of that." He angled his umbrella to better protect them from the rain.

"I see myself as rather practical," she ventured. If only he knew the concerns that filled her thoughts.

When she saw his quizzical glance, she flushed. How could he not see her as practical, a Society woman with employment? Most women would focus on their embroidery or causes and not worry about money, but she did, very much.

"Can you not be practical and artistic?"

"Oh yes, I suppose so, but it is a difficult combination."

The corner of his mouth tilted. "Ah, so you declare yourself to be a difficult woman?"

She wished for a fan to tap him with, but she didn't even have a newspaper. "Is my society so painful? You have just said it is a pleasure."

"I am not in your company all day. Perhaps you are impossible at noon, for instance, or appalling at six. Or unmentionable in the wee hours."

She sniffed. "Wouldn't you like to know?"

When she saw his secret smile, she realized she had all but propositioned him, and from someone in her family, a man might take the proposition seriously. Why did she have to be so different from the lot of them?

"A few days away from you and I've become a hoyden," she said. "Please forgive me."

"I like you in all your moods, Miss Cross," he said gallantly. "And here is the loading dock."

He held open the door for her, then folded his umbrella and placed it in the stand just inside the door. They tried hard to keep the floors dry since falls could mean the destruction of expensive goods. Then he followed her downstairs.

"Walking me to the Fancy door, Captain?"

"I promised to consult with Mr. Melville first thing this morning," he said.

"How is the busy season going?"

"Busily." His teeth flashed at her as he opened the door at the bottom of the step.

"I thought I heard your voice, Captain!" Betsy Popham stood just to the right, a flirtatious grin on her plump, pretty face. She brushed her substantial bosom against his arm as she went to the steps.

"What are you up to?" The captain stared at a rolling table covered in boxes.

"My father needed a few special orders early. Lady Burnham's maid arrived sooner than expected to pick up her decorated cakes."

He gestured to the table. "Why aren't you using the elevator?"

"The bakers have it."

He grunted. "Right. We'll help you."

She batted her eyes. "I'd appreciate it very much if you do, sir, but Magdalene is needed to finish another special order."

Magdalene set her jaw. Betsy had never called her by her Christian name. What an insult that she'd use it in front of Captain Shield, as if she was some lowly subordinate. "Why, Betsy, I am so sorry you've been overwhelmed. I shall rush forthwith." She lifted her head and, after a nod to him, walked toward the Fancy with a stately gait. Two could play this game. Betsy must be jealous of their morning walks, but surely the girl didn't think Captain Shield, brother of a marquess, would be interested in the likes of *her*.

Unless she wanted to be his mistress. The thought gave her pause just as she reached the Fancy door. Betsy would lose her position if she had a child, but she probably thought the captain would support the child until its majority, and her too. She'd need to keep a close eye on Betsy's flirtation.

* * *

The next morning Judah walked up to Nelson's Column, glad to see the end of the rain for now, but he wasn't happy to see the state of his favorite newsboy. That the sun poked through the clouds now and then only illuminated the condition of Eddy Jackson's face. He'd lost his cap again, and one arm of his jacket had been torn away from the shoulder. Judah noted a black eye, bruises on the young knuckles, and the way Eddy ran his tongue over his teeth indicated concern for a loose incisor.

Nonetheless, his smile was bright. "Paper for you, guv?"

"In another fight?" Judah said.

Eddy shrugged, but not without a wince of pain. "Knock, knock?"

Judah rolled his eyes. "Who is there?"

"Boo."

Judah knew what was coming, but he appreciated the boy's pluck. "Boo who?"

"Do not cry, guv, it's only a joke."

"Your face isn't a joke, Eddy, particularly if you were hit hard enough to loosen teeth. Now I see your lip is cut and you've a mark on your jaw. Can't you avoid these bruisers?"

"I live with 'em, guv."

"Your father?"

"No, I 'aven't one of those, nor a mam either, but I've got a roof over me 'ead, and food to eat."

"Did these friends of yours steal your hat?"

Eddy touched his head. "Lost it somewhere, I expect."

"Right." Judah dug in his pocket, found three shillings. "Mind that you do not lose the money."

"Ah, guv, you don't need to pay for another."

"It's bad enough that you have to be out in bad weather. I won't have my personal newsboy looking disreputable. Mind you sew up that jacket." A shabby man brushed by him. Judah clapped his hand against his pocket, thinking the man might have seen the money and come to rob him, but the man stopped a couple of feet away at a milkwoman, a yoke over her shoulders holding her cans as an advertisement to passersby.

Eddy grinned and tossed him a paper as Miss Cross arrived. "Yes, guv."

"Oh, Eddy, your face!" she cried.

Judah put a hand on her shoulder. "The lad is fine, and you are running late this morning, madam. Shall we go?"

She nodded at Eddy and walked beside Judah briskly as they left the Square. "Who did that to him?" she asked as they left Eddy's earshot.

"Someone he lives with, apparently. I believe he's an orphan."

"Oh, dear. I wish there was something we could do for him."

"Keep buying his papers is the best thing. Money gives a man options, and a lad too."

"Yes, you are right about that."

"Why were you late this morning?" He pulled her around a puddle.

"George didn't come down at the usual time this morning, so I had to help give the boys their breakfast. It won't happen again."

"Is George ill?"

He noted that she hesitated before answering. "I think the boys should go away to school. The earl wrote a lovely note that came home with them, offering to pay their way at St. George's School in Ascot."

"That is a generous offer."

"Yes. It will position them well in life if he is willing to pay for their education. They will need to do some kind of work. The trust income won't be enough for them to go on as my brother has."

"I am glad your nephews have an opportunity presented to them. Do you think George will accept?"

"I do not think he has even read the note yet."

"He must be very ill."

Miss Cross poked at her eye as if an eyelash had fallen into it. He took her elbow in order to cross the street safely, as she was not paying attention.

"He is ill, yes."

"You are under a great deal of strain," he observed.

"I can still do my work." She moved away and he let go of her elbow.

"I didn't mean to suggest you could not. Is there anything I can do? Speak to George?"

"He has not even read the note," she repeated.

"When he does, if he is hesitant, I could speak to him, to show where no education leads a man."

"Where does it lead?" she inquired.

Judah pointed at himself. "To the army. I would imagine, when a man has lost his wife, his children become even more dear to him. He won't want his sons serving far away, years going by between meetings. If they need to work, then get them education. Perhaps they can go into politics or some such."

"You should not put yourself down, Captain. You have done very well for yourself."

"I am very pleased with my accomplishments, but I don't think your brother would want my life for his children." His laugh was harsh. "Even my own brother does not want it for me."

"We are not the regular sort of people, you and I, content to do the things our well-meaning relatives have planned for us."

"No." He guided Miss Cross through the back door and nodded his good-bye, unable to discuss the matter further. It wasn't until he was seated at the chair behind his desk that he felt like he could breathe again. How did it hurt boys to be effectively without a father? He knew it well, could see what it was doing to Eddy Jackson, a lad with all the brightness and cheer you could wish, but no future to speak of. He suspected George Cross was simply staying drunk. Was this a habitual problem or merely a temporary situation created by the loss of his wife? He would not dare to prod in the man's personal life, but Miss Cross, as an employee, was under his protection, and if she worried about her nephews, so did he.

He had done quite well for himself, despite being all but fatherless, but he knew himself to be unusually lucky in his friends. And his brother. What would he be doing with himself now, if not for Redcake's?

It troubled him that his gem ship had not yet arrived. He had expected to hear news at any moment over the last week. A call on the captain's wife, who lived somewhere in London, might be in order. He made a note to look up the address when he arrived home, and send her a letter with his respects.

Eddy looked even more disreputable the next morning. He'd fixed his jacket with white thread, which showed against the fabric like sutures in a savage's skin. While he had purchased a new cap, which sat jauntily on his head, his bruises had turned purple.

Judah felt a raindrop on the back of his hand just as Miss Cross raced across the Square, clearly determined not to be late again. He and Eddy exchanged nods and he moved toward Miss Cross.

"Just a moment," she gasped. "I wanted to give this to Eddy."

"Of course."

She went past him, holding out a little bundle. "Here, Eddy. We roasted potatoes this morning, and I thought you might like one in each pocket to keep warm."

His smile was infectious. "Oh, thank you, miss. I do not mind if I do."

She opened her cloth and he popped out the potatoes, then dropped one into each pocket.

"Lovely and warm, miss. Thank you. I shall 'ave an 'ot lunch too."

"You are welcome." She hesitated, then trotted back to Judah.

"That was nicely done."

"I wanted to do something for him," she whispered. "I think about my brother in India, how he was injured, and wonder if anyone cared for him."

"Your brother is a grown man."

"I know, but wounded people tug at my heart."

She had hesitated at the word "wounded" but he didn't know why. He wanted to pursue the subject, but she glanced at the sky and a fat raindrop dropped on her nose for her trouble.

"Where is your umbrella?" she asked.

"The sky looked fine twenty minutes ago."

"You must always have one with you in London," she scolded. "This makes it very clear you never resided here until now."

The rain fell harder and they sped up, trying to duck under awnings as much as possible as they made their way through Regent Street. Miss Cross's shawl was soon wet, and her black bonnet dripped dye down her cheeks.

"This is too much," Judah said, after five minutes. They happened to be passing by a woman's clothing shop. He took her elbow and sent her through the door. Despite the early hour it was open, probably because of the strain of keeping deliveries up at this time of year.

A shopgirl took one look at them and her expression went from pinched frown to pleasant smile. "Can I help you, sir?"

He stared at a display. "I want that coat, and can you tell me if the bonnet above it is for sale?"

The salesgirl walked over and picked up the items. "I will sell it to you."

Miss Cross frowned. "Those are women's clothes, Captain."

"You aren't dressed warmly enough."

"I have a cloak."

"I've seen it and it isn't good winter wool. This is. And you can't possibly wear that bonnet you have on anymore."

She wiped at her face. Her fingers came away black. "It is a coat meant for traveling."

The salesgirl tutted. "I will find you a cloth."

She sighed. "You do not need to buy me a coat and hat. Besides, they are both gray."

"You need to be practical, Miss Cross. I will not have you catching a chill. Look, you are shivering." Impatient, he yanked at her bonnet strings, untying them from her soft under-chin. His gloved fingers stroked her. He could feel the fine texture even through the leather. "You travel through the streets each morning, so do not speak to me of fashion."

"You have a soldier's attitude of practicality," she said.

The salesgirl brought the towel and Miss Cross cleaned her face, then the girl helped her put on the new bonnet before holding up the coat.

"Your friend is right. It is very warm. Not fashionable, but warm. You can dye it if you have to."

Magdalene took off her soaked shawl and let the girl drape the coat around her. Her smile told Judah she was finally warm. He checked her shoes but they looked sturdy enough for the weather, though the leather was worn. When was the last time anyone took care of her, this young woman who brought potatoes for newsboys and fretted over her nephews more than their own father did?

Judah paid for the garments and asked for Miss Cross's old things to be packaged and sent to her home address, then he took her arm and steered her out of the shop.

"We're going to be terribly late."

He turned her to him while they were still safely under the awning and checked the bow under her chin. "I will excuse you. Warm enough?"

She smiled. "Gloriously, and you know, all of this has put what I meant to tell you today quite out of my mind."

Chapter Eleven

"You meant to suggest I roast some potatoes for my own fingers?" Judah teased.

Miss Cross laughed as he led her back to the main thoroughfare so they could hurry their tardy way to Redcake's. "I should have thought to bring you a couple as well."

"Quite. What did you forget to tell me?"

"I wanted to suggest you contact Sir Cyril Kirkville."

"Do I know him?"

"Your mother certainly did. The family are notorious libertines of the kind a lady should not know about, but of course I am a Cross and therefore have had relatives mixed up with them."

"Ah. Are they gossips as well?"

"No, but they do like a public spectacle. Still, they know everyone, and if there was ever a person who might know the truth, it would be him."

"Any chance he is the one?"

"Anything is possible, but I expect he is a bit too young."

"I shall send him a note then."

"He should be in London, since he is active in politics."

"Excellent." When they arrived at the back door, they found Betsy lurking by. He sensed her disappointment when she saw Miss Cross was with him. Had Betsy wanted to yell at her for being late?

"You'll have to forgive us, Betsy. I insisted Miss Cross take part in an errand of mine. Inexcusable, I know."

"Will you always be walking together?" Betsy asked.

"We come the same way at the same time," he said blandly. "And of course I am a friend of the family."

Betsy glanced sidelong at Miss Cross. Could the girl see the bonnet was new? Probably. Women always seemed to know these things.

He patted Betsy on the shoulder and passed by. "Much to do this morning, ladies." He fairly leapt up the stairs, anxious to avoid feminine stares and get to his letter paper in order to dash off a note to Sir Cyril.

Magdalene arrived home that afternoon, basket under her arm, tucked with slices of cake that had crumbled into a less than spherical shape and therefore could not be sold to the public. She felt cozy and daring. The bonnet, with its tilted brim, was fashionable, and quite the nicest she'd ever had as an adult, and the coat had appeal.

"That looks like something a cowboy might wear," Manfred said when he opened the door for her. He was dressed to go out himself, but he raised his eyebrows hopefully when he saw her basket. "Still potatoes in there?"

"No. Cake." She brushed past him, feeling like a gunslinger in her long, swinging coat.

"I think I'll stay home for a bit. No need to rush out."

She couldn't help noticing that even with her smart bonnet and gunslinger coat, he was dressed far more expensively than she was. "Where were you going? Not to the Mews's home, I hope."

They had been out of town during the summer, but had returned a couple of weeks ago. Manfred and Lady Mews were close conspirators of a kind she tried not to think too much about, but that lent itself greatly to the legend of the Scandalous Crosses. Magdalene hoped she'd experienced her only personal scandal when she was ten years old, and it hadn't been the usual kind of Cross drama at all.

Manfred propelled her into the kitchen and pulled out a chair, then whisked the basket from under her arm and opened the napkin. "This looks like good cake."

"It was meant for a wedding cake, but it fell apart."

"To our benefit. Cup of tea?"

"Please."

She sighed and untied her bonnet ribbon. At least Manfred had a practical side, more so than George in a way. He could take care of himself, as she expected Captain Shield could. He knew how to get a stove going in the morning, knew how to heat water and make tea.

"Does Lady Mews buy your clothing?"

He sat next to her with a freshly filled teapot. "I thought we didn't discuss these things."

"I am afraid we are coming to a time when we must discuss unpleasant things in this household."

"You mean George's drinking? He hasn't been at it for long."

"But there are children in this household who need a stable influence."

"I could get money for a nursemaid."

"I think school is the answer. Do you know the earl has offered to pay to board them?"

He shook his head. "I'll miss the little blighters."

"So will I, but if George doesn't come to his senses soon—" She paused when she heard footsteps in the corridor.

Her eldest brother lurched into the room, his face red and his eyes unfocused. Did he have on anything under his dressing gown? She saw a flash of pale, bare calf and turned away with a shudder.

George leaned over her. She thought he was reaching for cake, but instead he picked up her new bonnet, the ribbons dangling in her thankfully empty teacup. His breath oozed wine into the air as he slurred, "Where'd this come from?"

"My old bonnet became too wet and the dye ran all over my face."

"This isn't proper mourning." He shook it at her.

"I only got it today."

"And the coat?" He pointed an unsteady finger at her, then staggered back a step as if moving his arm unbalanced him.

"Come and have a cuppa," Manfred suggested, pushing back a chair with his shoe.

"Who bought you that coat? You always say we are poor. I know you wouldn't spend money on yourself. You're too s-s-spinsterish," he stuttered.

Her heart rate increased. "I am not spinsterish. I'll have you know Captain Shield bought them for me, when both my bonnet and shawl soaked through in the rain this morning."

"Whore!" His arm swung through the air.

Her eyes crossed as his hand moved, then her head snapped back as his knuckles caught her cheek. She started to fall backward. Manfred leapt up, his chair crashing to the ground as he grabbed for her.

His teeth gritted. She saw he'd knocked over the teapot, and hot tea cascaded over the table, dripping onto his greatcoat. Thankfully he was still dressed for the outdoors.

She put her hand to her cheek, feeling the hot place where George had struck her. Tears welled in her eyes from the sheer sting of the blow. He had never hit her before. She felt the inside of her mouth with her tongue. Blood dripped, hot and coppery, where her teeth had sliced a gash into her flesh.

"You've made this house unsafe for both your children and sister," Manfred hissed at his brother. "Go back upstairs, now."

"You don't tell me what to do," he pouted, his lips trembling.

"Lock yourself in the boys' room with them, Magdalene," Manfred said. He seemed to have gained half a decade in maturity in the last minute. "I'm going to Uncle's."

She backed out of the room behind Manfred, wanting to take her basket of cakes upstairs for the boys, but not daring. George regarded them with narrowed eyes, his head moving side to side, snakelike, but he didn't move.

When she and Manfred were at the stairs, she whispered, "Will someone from Gerrick House come get them tonight?"

He pulled out his handkerchief. "Spit."

She complied and the cloth turned red.

He tucked it back into his pocket. "I'll make sure of it. Bar the door. Pack what you can for them. Don't trust the lock. He has all the keys, of course."

She nodded and dashed upstairs. It wasn't until she was inside, a chair thrust under the doorknob and the boys asking questions and pointing at her cheek, that she began to shake.

On Thursday evening, Judah sat on a plush sofa in a gaslit parlor in Mayfair, at the home of Sir Cyril. The man had returned an invitation by the next post. When the door opened, Judah stood, but it was only a footman with a tray.

He considered it, but one result of working at Redcake's was he was rarely hungry. Too much sampling of pastry, and he now was able to have a hot bowl of soup each day at noontime, thanks to the new menu. While he had a good walk each day, to and from Regent and Oxford streets, he would like to ride as well. He wondered if his purse would extend to that.

To that end, he noted a variety of paintings featuring horses on the walls. He stood and walked over to peruse them. "Sir Cyril must keep quite a stable."

"I come from a racing family, Captain Shield," said a rich voice. "Out of Newbury, though I met your parents at Ascot many years ago."

Judah turned and saw a man of middle years, comfortably paunched, with an exceptionally thick head of graying brown hair and a full beard. "Thank you for seeing me, Sir Cyril."

"By all means. I would be happy to thaw relations between your family and mine."

"I have recently come back to England and was unaware of any tension." Was he stepping on Hatbrook's toes yet again? He thought if he avoided the aristocracy he could keep free of Hatbrook's crowd, but of course politics was another place where his brother might be involved.

"Yes, of course. Your late father and I did not agree on a farm bill. Your brother and I disagree on various points as well."

"The late marquess was active in politics?"

"Sometimes," Sir Cyril said. "He was a man of moods and seasons."

"So you say. I did not know him well. Or my mother, for that matter."

"Your mother seemed to grow into motherhood. When your sister was born that was the first time I saw the domestic side of her. I often dangled Lady Elizabeth on my knee before I broke with your father politically."

"You must have been to Hatbrook Farm then."

"Oh, yes. My grandmother moved to Eastbourne in the early eighteen-sixties so I was in the neighborhood during school holidays and the like."

"What year? I cannot believe I never met you."

"I'm not sure of the exact year."

Judah regarded the man closely. Sir Cyril's eyes were a watery blue, nothing like his, but his frame was not so different, minus the paunch. Could this be his father?

"Do you have children?" he asked. "Perhaps I would remember them."

Sir Cyril coughed. "No, an injury, you understand."

"So sorry." He wondered when the injury had taken place, but the man had a mortified blush high on his cheeks and it would be ruinous to press further.

Sir Cyril sighed. "My lady would be here to greet you as well, but I am afraid she had a family engagement this evening."

"Some other time," Judah said politely.

"I believe you mentioned that Miss Cross told you I had been a family friend?"

"Yes."

"Are you close to her family?"

"Tolerably so."

Sir Cyril leaned over, knocking a teacup with his elbow. "Dreadful doings there yesterday. I understand the young Cross boys were sent haring across London to their uncle's house in little but their short jackets."

"I did not see Miss Cross today," Judah said, alarmed. "We often meet in the street, because we, er, live near each other." He had seen Hetty, however. Their housemaid had come with a note from Magdalene, begging off work for the day, with no explanation. Hetty had seemed rather upset, but he had thought it was because she was forced out in the rain. He'd planned to call after seeing Sir Cyril.

"Grief can do great damage to a household, and of course a man is never so civilized as when he has a kind wife."

"Do you think there is damage?" He tapped his shoe on the carpet, eager to leave.

"Well, George Cross has shut himself up in his house since his wife passed. Not so unusual under the circumstances, but since he was all but nursemaid to the boys, he usually goes out to the park with them. It is greatly remarked about among local governesses."

"I am sorry the family pain has become such a source of gossip. I did know the earl had offered to ease their way into his old school, despite the time of year. Perhaps the headmaster was only willing to hold the beds for a day or two."

Sir Cyril lifted a knowing eyebrow. "It is a good story to put out, at any rate. They do not have enough servants, or live in a good enough street, for too much of the truth to leave their doors. But, if you are an admirer of Miss Cross, you may want to take a close look at her situation."

"Do you have any immediate fear?"

"I know young Manfred Cross is often seen at a certain lady's card parties, and he was not there last night."

"No doubt sharing in the tender family leave-taking."

"Quite. Now, let's have a maid in to pour for us, and we shall discuss our friends and interests." Sir Cyril settled in for a long monologue.

Judah was captive for forty more minutes. Then, he had a cab driver go by Miss Cross's home, but the lights were all extinguished. "By Jove," he muttered. "I wish I knew what was going on inside that house." He tapped on the roof of the hansom so the driver would go on. If things were very bad, Hetty would have told him.

Resigning himself to not seeing Magdalene until the next day, he tossed and turned all night. Could Sir Cyril be his father? He wasn't sure if he even liked the man. His enjoyment of gossip reminded him of the cakies in his employ, all of them a flock of high-pitched, excited starlings. And Sir Cyril was a bit smug, though he did admire the man's size, rude good health, and head of hair. Compared to most Members of Parliament, he was a god among men.

It seemed to take double the usual time to shave and dress the next morning. He needed the strong cup of tea that would be waiting on his desk when he arrived at Redcake's.

Thankfully, he could see Miss Cross in her new coat and bonnet, now covered in black crepe, standing next to Eddy. He felt instantly relieved. What he didn't expect was their almost matching visages. The marks on her face were fresher than Eddy's. He swore. Reaching for her chin, he tilted her face into the light. "What did George do to you? That madman."

She pulled back. "Captain Shield! It was a misunderstanding about my outerwear. He thought I was being disrespectful about mourning."

"So he hit you? Is this how a man treats his sister? Where was Manfred?"

"Shhh," she soothed. "Manfred is fine. It is unspeakable to have this conversation."

"Pardon me for saying, miss, but there ain't no point to keepin' it private, leastways when you have a gentleman concerned," Eddy said, handing Judah his paper.

"I am your protector, Miss Cross," Judah said, inspired to his theme by Eddy's words. He tossed the lad a penny.

She blinked.

"As your employer," he explained. "You are in my care, and this is unsupportable."

She smiled faintly at Eddy and took Judah's sleeve, to pull him to the side of a fountain on the Square, where the noise of the water might make their conversation more private. "He is my brother."

"He isn't the head of your family. The earl is. Is he comfortable with your treatment? Do you know the news about your young nephews is all over Town? I had to hear it from Sir Cyril, of all people."

Her chin went up. "You saw him? Did he give you any answers?"

"I am not concerned with myself at this moment, but with you. Miss Cross, you cannot go on like this." He opened his umbrella to protect them from the drizzle that had just started misting the pavement.

"You do not live in my house," she said stiffly. "You cannot know what goes on in my private life. If someone had damaged my face at Redcake's, that would be very different. I allow you are my protector there."

Was she going to dismiss her pain, and the risk, so lightly? "Are we not friends, Miss Cross?"

"You claim to be my brother's friend, too."

"Then I shall go to him this instant," Judah said. "As soon as you are tucked into the Fancy, I shall take a hansom to your brother's door."

"That is rude and presumptuous. It was a momentary derangement, brought on by my wearing gray. It shall not happen again."

He regarded her still-gray coat until she flushed. "If you truly thought that, your nephews would not be gone."

"That was Manfred's plan."

"Did he witness this act of brutality?"

She looked down, then sighed. "Yes. It is as if he became a man overnight."

"So he is there providing protection whenever George is there?"

After a moment she shook her head. "George is always there. Manfred has his own company to keep."

"With Lady Mews."

"Do not gossip about my family, sir," she hissed.

Judah felt abashed and wondered if he were more like Sir Cyril that he realized. All those years he'd spent in the officer's mess where shop talk was not allowed at table had had its effect on his conversation. "Could you not go to your uncle's, too?"

"I can't leave George. He only eats what I hand to him. He is disconsolate."

"But he drinks."

"A great deal," she responded in a tired sort of way.

Judah scratched his chin. "Was it like this before his wife died?"

Her expression soured. "You'd never have known he cared about her until she became ill. He was not a very good husband, any more than most gentlemen."

"I wonder that you lived in his house."

"I never thought to consider anywhere else. Nancy kept the tone as high as she could, though circumstances diminished over time."

"You have been placed in a very difficult situation."

"I do not deny that. Nancy kept things calm as long as she could, and he certainly loves the boys, but he did not trouble himself much with family before he fell into debt."

"Were you able to get the boys' things to the earl, or to the school? From what Sir Cyril reported, they didn't have their trunks."

"George has insisted they'll be coming home as soon as his illness has passed. He doesn't want them to go to school."

Is "illness" what they are calling habitual drunkenness now? He had always smelled liquor on the man's breath when they met, but he had never seemed impaired. "That is terribly selfish of him."

"They are all that is left of Nancy, he says."

"He does no credit to her memory. The boys must go. Who shall reason with him?" Judah stared down a trinket seller who had moved toward them, a professional smile on his face.

"Who can reason with a man in his state of mind?" she countered.

"And he claims to be ill?"

"Yes. It is the drink, of course, and grief. He can call it whatever he wishes."

"Meanwhile the boys have only the clothes on their backs."

"It isn't as bad as that. I made bundles for them, nightshirts and so forth. Mostly they will wear their school uniforms."

"If George will not sign for them, can they go to school?"

"I believe they will trust the earl's word at the school. They are his great-nephews and no one would be surprised if he says their father is not well enough for paperwork."

Without considering his actions overmuch, he took her hand in his and squeezed. Their gloves squeaked coldly against each other, but she looked down with a tiny smile.

"I know you are my friend, Captain Shield. You have done so much for me."

"I would do more," he said on instinct. His hand moved from her glove to her hair, and he tucked a strand back into her bonnet. "You will need to repin, I think."

"Manfred had only so long to wait for me this morning. I didn't do a very good job."

"How can I make your situation more safe?"

"Keep employing me," she said. "Money makes a world of difference."

"Do you mean to set up your own establishment?"

"I do not know what my plans are. I hope my brother will resolve his grief and get hold of himself."

He wondered what might go wrong before that happened, if it ever did. "I think your uncle should have a chat with him."

"I'm sure he will when the boys are gone from Gerrick House."

"Do you have friends you can stay with?"

She shook her head. "My oldest friend lives in Yorkshire. Her father died young and she went to be a ladies' companion due to her family's changed circumstances. There is Lady Bricker, of course. I'm sure she would take me in."

"Also in Yorkshire."

"I am afraid so."

"What about Lady March?"

"She is back in Derbyshire."

"You could speak to your brother about Lady Mews. Perhaps you could stay in her household."

Her mouth fell open for a moment. "Good heavens. That is no place for a single woman."

"No? A pity. Your circle is very constrained, it appears."

"We are still invited to parties, but I have few intimates. Once Nancy became ill, we couldn't return calls. And I have a secret life now too. That would become evident to anyone I stayed with." She smiled ruefully.

"You could go to Hatbrook Farm, but that would mean leaving your position behind."

"I do not want to be dependent," she said. "I am not fragile or helpless."

"No, it is merely your home life that is the trouble. But we will think of something."

"Thank you for including me in the decision making about my own life," she said tartly.

"There's that lock of hair again." He tucked it back under her bonnet.

"We're going to be very late for work," she said.

"Just tell Betsy you were courting," he said. "She will understand."

Judah thought Betsy would understand, but Magdalene most certainly did not. Who was she to claim was courting her, particularly when he bussed her unbruised cheek a full block from Redcake's? If he was going to claim to be courting her, he could at least kiss her in front of the loading dock.

"Why did you do that?" she asked, putting her hand over the kiss.

"Because I'm worried about you, and felt you needed a sign of affection."

But then, peeking out from under the umbrella, she saw a trio of cakies trudging into work, their cloaks damp with rain. One of them had an expression of utter astonishment as she stared at them. She turned her head to the others and started speaking rapidly as they trotted through the rain.

Had Judah noticed them? With three cakies having seen the kiss, no matter how brotherly it had been, word would be all over Redcake's before it opened to the public.

"We are very late to work if cakies are on the streets. I'm always in the Fancy before the serving girls arrive."

Judah's expression was all innocence. "If they saw us together, all to the better. No one will think to ask about your cheek when they have me and kisses to gossip about."

He was wrong. "They will be terribly jealous and you'll have crying girls with their aprons over their heads at the end of every corridor."

He chuckled. "I do not think my powers are so great as that."

"A marquess's brother, and the manager of Redcake's? Oh, your power is great."

He smiled wolfishly.

"But truly, Captain Shield, speaking of your family. What did Sir Cyril say when he wasn't gossiping about my family?" She wanted to think of something other than herself.

"The timing was about correct, as you suspected. But I had the sense it was unlikely that he might be my parent. Not impossible. But how does one ask these things? I could not be blunt about my mother's behavior. It would ruin her reputation if he did not know."

"Even you do not like embarrassing your family. You see how it is for me?"

"I tend to think of your family as being perennially embarrassed."

"How dare you?" She wanted to cry. What a horrid thing for him to say.

"As is mine," he said hurriedly.

"Really, Captain Shield?" She injected all of the hauteur of her position in Society into her voice.

"My parents, in the past. And given the disaster with Matilda Redcake, now."

"Which your family blames upon mine."

"I should not truly think so. Lady Bricker is an easy scapegoat. I feel constantly irritated by my own situation and I do apologize for slurring your family."

"It was not kindly done." She sniffed.

"I quite agree. But here, we are standing on the street. We will both catch a chill if we remain." He tilted the umbrella toward the pavement.

"I wonder why you associate with me."

"We are both in distress," he said in a short tone that indicated he desired to close the subject.

She let the conversation end, appalled that it had ever started. How she wished she could rewind time a couple of days and never have accepted the coat and bonnet. However, George might very well have found some other occasion to attack. He was not in his right mind.

Chapter Twelve

Captain Shield did call at her home the next day, Saturday. Manfred received him. Magdalene had been at Gerrick House saying her good-byes before her nephews boarded the train to school with a tutor come from that establishment to fetch them. Thankfully, the earl had called Friday and persuaded George school was best for the boys. Magdalene had even been able to prepare more of their clothing and send it with the earl's servants. She knew Captain Shield and Manfred had engaged in indiscreet conversation regarding the situation, but since George had remained locked in his room during that visit, he had not been the wiser.

Now, she wondered if a calm household would help George, or if his inactivity would send him deeper into the bottle. She ordered a lower quality of claret from the wine merchant, assuming George wouldn't notice if he was drunk, and sent Hetty to buy a black coat from a secondhand stall. It would do for the streets, though it wasn't as warm or dashing as the gray coat. It was folded into the back of her wardrobe, ready to reappear when mourning ended.

On Monday morning, she buttoned herself into the coat, which fit very well over her modest cakie uniform, thanks to slight alterations she'd made to the sleeves the night before, and pinned a black wool shawl over her shoulders to make it warmer. Her new bonnet was the only item of apparel that made her feel like a lady.

Still, if she couldn't have everything, at least she had a handsome gentleman meeting her in the Square.

Eddy doffed his cap when she walked up to him. "New coat, miss?"

She twirled. "What do you think?"

"Serviceable, miss, if thin for London."

She noted Eddy had on a new coat himself, a bit large for his wiry frame. "Your coat looks nice and thick."

"One o' me regulars gave it to me, because his boy had grown too large for it," Eddy boasted. "Me customers are a loyal lot, and that's no joke."

"I can see that. You're a good boy, Eddy."

He puffed up his bantam chest. "I'm no boy. I takes care of meself."

"Of course. My error," she apologized, wondering if her nephews would have his bravado when they were a bit older. Of course they would. The school would mold them into British gentlemen and courage was one of the primary characteristics of the breed.

"How are you?"

Magdalene whirled around, her hand on her chest. "You startled me, Captain."

"The wind is up. Makes it hard to hear footsteps."

He had a muffler tucked around his chest and lower mouth, in addition to his heavy coat and lined hat.

"You poor man. The cold must make you suffer terribly."

"I am not accustomed to it," he admitted, giving Eddy a penny. "Walking will stir my blood."

Eddy gave him a friendly grin and tossed him the paper. "Stay warm, guv. This is only the beginning."

"By next winter I'll be so well acclimated that I'll be in a linen suit with no coat on." He grinned.

She shook her head. "As long as you bring your umbrella you can wear whatever you want." That gave her a pang. She had no intention of still being employed at Redcake's a year from now.

The captain tucked her under his umbrella as they set off, her mind churning. She had to find a suitable husband so she could escape George's roof. But how could she do that when she was in mourning? Even if she went to Society events, she couldn't dance, and she looked best on the dance floor. Her long body gained grace with movement. Certainly she wasn't her best on calls now, when she was tired from a long day's work, and besides, with Nancy gone, she had no one to take her.

Perhaps she needed to move in with Lady March, although she didn't go out much. Would the earl officially pardon Lady Bricker in time for next spring's Season? Then she could live with her, and try very hard to find a husband before summer. Yes, that was the best plan. Work on the earl to pardon Lillian.

"You are very deep today, Miss Cross."

"Just making plans," she said absently.

"I had a good visit with Manfred on Saturday. I was sorry to miss you."

"Yes?" she said, thinking how few men called. Didn't Manfred have any friends a little older and less debauched than he was? "Thank you for calling. I'm sure Manfred told you I was at Gerrick House."

"Yes. I am glad the earl was able to aid the boys."

"It has all worked out for the best," she said.

"Except you sacrificed your new coat."

"I made that choice to have peace," she told him. "It will do fine for these walks, and I can keep my bonnet."

"The crepe will stain it."

"I'm sure it will be out of style by the time my mourning ends. That is the way of things."

"Of course. You must be a slave to fashion."

Her smile felt sour. She certainly must be if she was to get a husband. Perhaps she could persuade the earl to offer a small dowry for her? All she had now was two hundred pounds from her mother.

With that kind of dowry, she'd be lucky to get a nice, respectable vicar, and what man of God would offer for a Scandalous Cross girl? A soldier couldn't afford her and a peer wouldn't want her. She didn't want to marry into the merchant class.

If she didn't act soon, before her looks faded, she could see a long descent into spinsterhood. She'd end up keeping house for Manfred, and he had no more money than she did.

In frustration, she increased her pace to a march, then realized her high stepping walk was sending tendrils of muddy water up her boots onto her skirts. She shuddered as the cold water soaked past her petticoats to her stockings.

"I have a question to put to you," Captain Shield said.

She had scarcely realized he was still there. "Yes? I apologize for woolgathering."

"You have had a most trying week, and here it is only Monday."

She laughed at his little joke. "At least my face is mended."

"Yes, I can scarcely see the bruise. Which brings me to my subject. You are aware that the marchioness worked the cake table at parties for a time, the best parties? She used the opportunity to share information about Redcake's and it often brought in new clients for wedding cakes and other special events."

"No, I did not know that."

"We have a fashionable wedding on Friday morning, with a cake table after the breakfast. I wondered if you would be willing to serve the cake. I know it's one you'll be completing this week, so it will be your handiwork."

"Who is in the bridal party?" she asked.

"The Earl of Fitzwalter's daughter and some American," he said. "I cannot recall the American's name."

"I couldn't possibly, Captain," she said. "I have met Lady Honoria many times. You would ruin me in Society if you sent me thus." How could he even ask? Didn't he realize how tenuous her hold was?

"Ah. I thought they weren't the most fashionable, because of marrying the American."

"I believe they are land rich and cash poor," she said tartly. "I hope you've settled their bill."

"I will check on that, but I assume the American father has funds."

She snorted. "He won't care about a London tradesman once he sets foot on the boat to America."

"You may be right. Are you certain?"

"Very much so. Lady Hatbrook was not in Society at the time she was serving cake, but I am. Decorating is one thing. We did have an arrangement." She folded her arms.

"Yes, of course. I apologize if I made you uncomfortable with my request."

"Not at all." She was happy to see the loading dock as it put an end to the conversation. However, Betsy was hovering by the loading dock once again.

"Ah, Miss Popham," the captain said, surprising Magdalene. "If you have a moment, I'd like a word in my office."

Her beady dark eyes lit up, like a bowl of tobacco being set on fire. "Yes, sir. Shall I follow you up?"

The captain closed his umbrella, pointing it into the alley so he didn't spray all of them with rain. "Very good." He nodded serenely at Magdalene and walked off, dratted Betsy trailing him like a fat puppy.

Magdalene sniffed and went down to the Fancy. Was he going to ask Betsy to be the server? She had no idea how to speak to the wealthy and powerful. It would be a disaster.

Later in the morning, she could no longer stand the cat-in-cream expression Betsy had been holding since she reappeared. "Why are you so pleased?" she asked, finishing a lacework tier for the wedding cake on the schedule before Lady Honoria's.

"I am just so pleased the captain saw fit to consult with me," Betsy said, affecting an accent she had not been born with.

"Oh?"

"Yes. He asked me who the most intelligent and genteel cakie was, for a Society wedding. They are going to serve at an earl's wedding breakfast."

"An earl's daughter?"

Betsy waved a plump hand, sticky with sugar from the dried fruits she'd been slicing. "I suppose you are right. I do not know if we've ever made a wedding cake for an actual earl's wedding."

"Who did you recommend?"

"Irene. She knows the Fancy and she's very pretty. Her voice is cultured because she worked in a shop for a time."

"A good choice," Magdalene said grudgingly, wondering why the captain hadn't asked her advice. Was he angry that she'd refused his request? He could not be surprised that she had.

Judah continued to be concerned about Miss Cross. She arrived late for their walk to Redcake's on Tuesday, her bruise showing again because she was so pale. Her boots were wet because she'd dashed across the Square too quickly to ignore the rain puddles. He knew she'd be damp for hours, even in the hot bakery.

"May I inquire if I have upset you in any way?" he asked, when she hadn't spoken for five minutes of their walk.

"Not at all, Captain. I did not have a restful night."

"It must be hard to have the boys gone."

Her lips pressed together before she spoke. "Yes, it is."

He knew from her pause that her trouble wasn't because of the boys. "Were your brothers distressing you last night?"

"Do not trouble yourself, Captain. I am in no danger."

"You may not be the best judge of that. Your love and concern may color your thoughts," he said, trying to keep his voice gentle.

"I am not a fool," she said in low, measured tones.

"You do not have the mien of one without troubles," he said.

"I am in no way incapacitated and will do excellent work today," she countered.

"That is not enough for me, Miss Cross. I am your friend."

She caught his gaze for a second. "I do know that. But you have your own tortures. Should you not focus your intellect on the search for your father, since it troubles you so?"

"I have reached a dead end," he said. "The letters can tell me no more. I have spoken to every old friend of my mother's in London."

"There are certainly more. In the spring many more of them will be in Town."

"You are right, of course. See? We can offer each other counsel."

She smiled faintly. This did not relieve him. He liked his pretty girls fresh and carefree, not worn down by life's tragedies.

Betsy Popham waited for them by the back door. When Judah had unbuttoned his coat, he took a quick look at his pocket watch, to see if they were late, but they had made it with a minute to spare. What did she want now?

"May I speak to you, Captain?" asked Betsy, her lips shining from the dart of her pink tongue over them.

He nodded. "Come upstairs, Miss Popham." He waved a hand at Miss Cross, who bore a look of resignation, and gestured Betsy up the stairs in front of him.

He could not avoid noticing how she made full use of her hips and skirts on the stairs. Despite the lack of a bustle in her uniform, her hips twitched and her skirts twirled. She had a voluptuous form, the kind old women said was made for babies and men said was made for, well, the same thing, really.

He was holding back a smile as they reached the top of the stairs. Hales was ready with his tea tray, exactly what he needed after such a damp walk. Judah opened his own office door and ushered in both of them.

After Hales set the tray on his desk, he ushered the man out. "I will be with you in a moment for the day's schedule."

"Shall I shut the door?"

Judah kept his best poker face but felt his male parts shrivel slightly in horror. "No, no. Leave it open."

"Such a lovely teapot you have, Captain," Betsy purred, running her finger along the forest green spout.

He thought the thing far too feminine, with the hand-painted daisies decorating the sides. "It is a sample from a line the marchioness considered selling."

"I am sorry she decided against it. I'd have been happy to purchase a cup and saucer and drink my tea out of them at home."

He had never noticed how she purred over her words, pursing her lips breathily at every opportunity.

"Shall I pour?"

"No, Miss Popham. Kindly state your business. I need to be about the day's work." He noted how very bright the whites of her eyes seemed around the very dark pupils.

"Of course, sir. I only wanted to say, well, you see, about the servers." She put her hand to her chest, between the lapels of her white collar. It seemed to make the shape of her breasts pop from her dress.

Judah swallowed hard. How could such proud, British breasts make him recoil? They seemed the breasts of some tracking beast, a tiger waiting to pounce. He glanced over his shoulder, making sure the door was open still. Should he have asked Hales to remain? He took a step toward the door.

"What about the servers?"

She moved toward him, still pushing out her chest. "If you need any more advice, sir. I've worked here since the day the doors opened, you know. I can give you a list of the more cultured girls, to serve at fashionable events."

"Redcake's is not opening a catering arm, Miss Popham. It is only those rare events with large cakes that ever require extra service."

"Now that we are serving eggs and soup, it might be something that we consider."

He watched, prey caught by a predator's eyes, as a tendril of her glossy hair loosed from a pin and framed her oval face fetchingly. Miss Popham, the picture of rude health, would be an enticement to most men, but he was not interested. He never should have let her in here.

"Thank you for your suggestion," he said with a crisp nod. "Can you write?"

She frowned, the first chip in her sensuous facade. "Yes, of course."

"Then feel free to send a note to Mr. Hales if you have any more ideas. We will take them under advisement."

Her lips rounded into an O. "I thought I could come directly to you." She stepped toward him again. "We had such a nice chat yesterday." Her hand fluttered. "Wasn't I helpful?"

"I am a busy man, Miss Popham. Does your father have time for chats?"

She shook her head woodenly.

He felt like a cad. Could he blame her for using the gifts God had seen fit to bestow? "Thank you for your time. If you could send in Mr. Hales?"

She bobbed a small curtsy as if she were servant to some grand dowager, and turned, her rigid spine and bowed head the very picture of wounded womanhood.

Judah took his first deep breath since the encounter had begun, and went to the fire, standing there until his shoes began to steam.

"Is something wrong with the tea?" Hales asked, coming into the room.

"No. Blasted damp outside. Just warming my boots."

Hales quickly poured him a cup and added cream. "There you go, sir. She's a rum one, eh?"

"On the prowl," Judah said indistinctly around his teacup.

"I do think she has hopes beyond her station."

"Who are we to say she cannot achieve them?" They shared a look of male appreciation. "But not with me."

"No, sir."

The way he said it made Judah think. "You fancy her, do you?"

"In the common way." His fingers twitched, as if desiring to demonstrate her abundant curves.

"No more talk about it," Judah said. "It is not appropriate in a ladies' establishment."

"You do know what the cakies say about you, though?" Hales said.

"What?"

"They say you make them balmy on the crumpet. Oh, yes. They are mad for you, Captain. Be careful, if you don't mind a word of advice."

Judah saluted with his teacup. "Thank you, Hales. Now, let us delay our own business no more." The less talk of cakies the better. He was young and had no mistress, after all.

Magdalene arrived home on Wednesday to find fat letters sent from Yorkshire, both from Cousin Lillian and her friend Constance. She threw off her things and went into the kitchen, hoping to find the kettle on and a quiet moment to read.

Hetty was there, and shoved a dishrag into her apron as she came forward. "Mr. Manfred ain't here, miss."

"And George is?"

They shared a glance, both knowing the days ran smoother when Manfred was in residence.

"Mr. Cross, 'e went down to the cellar and came up with four bottles of claret. When he saw the labels he was angry, miss, oh, very angry."

Because she'd bought a less expensive brand in order to afford her coat. "Did he smash them?" she asked. "Go and buy more?"

Hetty wrinkled her nose. "I don't think 'e's bathed in a week, miss, and the way 'e's been drinking, well, it fair makes a man smell bad."

"So he didn't leave."

"No. Shut himself in the boys' room with the bottles."

"Do we know where Manfred is?"

"At Lady Mews's, I expect."

Magdalene looked mournfully at her letters.

"Could be that he's sleeping off the bottles," Hetty said. "Maybe we'll have a quiet night around 'ere."

"If he's sleeping now, he'll be awake all night." They sighed simultaneously.

Magdalene sat at the kitchen table. "I don't know how to help him. All this grief for a woman he took so little notice of in life."

" 'e knows 'e done wrong," Hetty said wisely. "Can you get a vicar 'ere to talk sense into him?"

"This is London, not some country parish," she said. "I do not think so."

"You have relatives with money. Could he go to some country estate, where they can afford their wine?"

Hetty was being terribly impertinent, but then, they had banded together of late, two women in a dangerous house. "I will write my uncle and my aunt."

"I worry about meself," Hetty said.

She didn't think Hetty, over forty, gray, fat, and plodding, had much to worry about, but wisely made no remark. Violence was a possibility even if a sexual approach was highly unlikely. "Why don't you sleep in my room? We can make you a pallet by the fire."

"I'll disturb you when I rise to get the stove going and clean the grates."

"At least we will both have a few hours of comfort."

"Thank you, miss. Very kind of you. I was thinking I might have to leave this household."

Magdalene heard the threat loud and clear. "We will make sure that does not happen, Hetty."

The woman cleared her throat. "I expect you'd like to read your mail. Shall I light the fire in the parlor?"

"No, the kitchen is fine, if I'm not interrupting you."

"No, miss. I'll just make you a cuppa."

Hetty bustled around the stove as Magdalene opened the letter from her cousin and began reading.

> *Dear Maggie, I had a letter from Father that made me quite worried for you. Poor Nancy's death must have been hard enough for you without additional challenges. You must come and visit me, and by that, I mean, live here. Let Cousin George and Cousin Manfred have their bachelor establishment. Come to Harrogate. I have found you a husband! Yes, dear cousin, your spinster days are over. Do you remember the painting my father commissioned of all us girl cousins three years ago, after our presentation at court? Well, Sir Octavian Feathercote, a distant connection and friend of my lord husband,*

has seen it, and fallen madly in love with you! He is quite, quite eligible. A bit under forty, and a thousand a year! Please send your arrival date. We shall have you engaged before Christmas and married before Easter. Very best wishes, Lillian.

Magdalene tugged at her starched collar. She dashed into the parlor and found the somewhat tattered copy of *Debrett's Peerage and Baronetage* on the bookshelf. Yes, there was Sir Octavian, who was a baronet. She calculated quickly. He was her fifth cousin, once removed. Really, quite suitable. She could not expect to do better. The age difference was a minor concern, but surmountable, and she would be living near her cousin and her dear friend. She clutched the book to her chest and waltzed around the room.

Her imagination put a partner in her arms, rather than the book. When she searched the vision in her mind's eye, she discovered her thoughts had placed Captain Shield before her. Not unexpected. She had never seen a more handsome, well-built specimen of manhood. But he was no baronet, and he would not marry until he understood who he was. She could have a husband *now,* and escape this unhappy house.

What about her position? This was the busy season. She could not desert Betsy or the captain until Society departed for the country again. But that was only a month away. She could delay one month, to pack and say good-bye.

As soon as she read Constance's letter, she'd respond to Cousin Lillian. No, as soon as she read the letter, she would write a note to the earl, and make sure everything was as her cousin represented it. The earl would know if the match was sound.

She opened the book again, curious to know if Sir Octavian had living relatives. Then she shut it again. Her uncle would be the best source of information. Her *Debrett's* was at least half a decade old.

A smile dancing on her lips, she waltzed back into the kitchen with her cup of tea and letter from Constance. If only one tiny sour note didn't resound through her waltz. That tiny sour note being the tiger eyes and cardamom-scented kisses of Judah Shield.

Chapter Thirteen

The day before had been all about jumpy females. Miss Cross had been pale but for two bright circles of pink, high on her cheeks, though thankfully without new injuries. She had barely spoken on their walk, and every time Judah said anything she nearly hopped in alarm, then said she'd been woolgathering. Betsy had again been hovering by the employee entrance, but she'd put her sharp nose into the air when she saw him and latched both plump hands around Miss Cross's arm, dragging her into the building. Miss Cross had looked alarmed, but had not found it difficult to depart him without so much as a "good morning." He did not think she had been angry, merely utterly beset by some inner dialogue.

This morning, Miss Cross had been animated, speaking of London at this time of year as if it were an old friend soon departing. He was becoming overdependent on these walks. His house was so cold and empty, an utterly unlikeable change from the warmth and camaraderie of the officers' mess in India, or the sheer crammed-in humanity of the ship home. He had left too late in the year for a troop ship and had returned on a merchant vessel, but still, there had been English travelers. His club was a pleasant alternative to dinner alone, cards or chatter instead of a solitary newspaper or book at home, but in the end, he always returned to the quiet house.

"Have you been sleeping well?" he inquired, before they'd even left the Square. She could be a different girl entirely from the introspective one of the day before.

"Oh, not very."

"Your brother?"

"Manfred has a little cold. Every illness makes me jumpy, of course, so soon after Nancy's passing, but it is only a head cold."

"The sneezing is reverberating through the house?" he inquired.

"Oh, a little." She laughed.

"George is behaving himself," he stated.

"He has been staying in the boys' room, drinking himself into a stupor. Our maid is terrified of him but he has not caused any trouble."

She seemed almost lighthearted as she gave this report, but not sleeping was a serious matter. "Then what is troubling you? It cannot just be Manfred."

"Why not?" she asked, tossing her head so that the black ribbons of her bonnet fluffed through the air.

At that, he knew the conversation was done. She was not in a confiding mood. When they reached Redcake's, Betsy was not at the door. To make things more interesting, Ewan Hales was not at his post either. Ralph Popham, that august personage himself, brought in a plate of scones and a pot of tea, and told him he'd left Betsy sick at home with a cough and hot forehead, and that Mr. Hales's landlady had stopped by the back door with a note excusing him for the same reason. Popham handed Judah a note, which was indeed in Hales's handwriting, then stood at his elbow, fingers combing through his thinning locks.

Judah set down the note. "I understand Miss Cross's brother is ill as well. I hope we do not have a burst of influenza."

"This time of year is difficult," Popham allowed.

"What did the marchioness do when Hales was unwell?" He was used to Hales putting him through his paces each morning, but was unaware of how the man gathered his intelligence.

"Hales has never missed a day of work as long as I've known him," Popham said, shifting where he stood.

Judah interpreted this as desperation to get back to his own post. "I shall manage without him for the day, then. Any cakies missing?"

"Not a one. We stay very clean in the bakery."

"Of course. Very appreciative, and all that. I will do the rounds in a bit, as Hales must."

Popham inclined his head and quick-stepped out of the room, his head still bowed. Judah poured his tea and picked up a delicately scented scone, which had almond slivers neatly spaced across the top, along with a dusting of sugar. The bakery really was top notch.

Half an hour later he was through a pile of requisitions that Hales had placed on his desk late the previous afternoon, and had looked over paperwork on the man's own desk. There was surprisingly little, which led Judah to believe Hales picked it up rather than having it delivered.

He went downstairs to beard Popham in his own den. "Do you have any paperwork you would normally give to Hales?" he inquired.

Popham scratched his chin. "He goes through my reports and enters our sales and supplies information into his own system. Then he takes my reports to Accounting."

Judah thought, but he really had no idea what Hales's system was. He only saw the end result. Abashed by the realization that he was a manager who could not do his assistant's job, he thanked Popham and went back to Accounting, where he closeted himself with the manager there. He promised to send someone to Judah's office to figure out Hales's system and get the reports up to date.

Judah thanked him and walked through the rest of the operation, checking the basement and the tearoom, chatting with Simon Hellman about delivery schedules and Alfred Melville about the need to call in Lewis Noble again.

When he asked about staff, Melville said, "I'm not missing anyone, but you might have heard that Tom Mumford has left us to try his hand at performing."

Judah frowned. "Isn't he seconded to the Fancy?"

Melville nodded. "Expect they are hurting."

"You've sent them someone else?"

Melville shrugged. "No one has asked me."

Judah put his hands on his hips. "I assume Mumford had delicate hands, to manage those cakes. Find someone of equal skill and reassign them."

"But Miss Popham—"

"Is not in today," Judah interrupted. "Get someone for the Fancy, as soon as possible." Irritated, he turned away and stomped down the hall to the Fancy. Seeing as Miss Cross was even newer to the enterprise than he, he expected disaster awaiting him. He opened the door, and saw Miss Cross staring wide eyed at the big table in the room, which was loaded with a variety of cake toppers. "Come a cropper?" he asked.

She blinked, but didn't look up.

"Miss Cross?"

She started, and turned to him.

"Where is Irene?" he asked. "Isn't she still employed here? I heard Mr. Mumford has left us."

"No one told me," she said. "Or Irene. And please call me Magdalene inside Redcake's. It looks odd if you are going to call the cakies by their first names."

"I call Betsy Miss Popham."

"She is a department head," Miss Cross said primly.

"Not formally." *Heaven forbid.* "But I shall do as you request, Magdalene." The exotic name tripped from his lips, the syllables seeming to wake up his mouth, his tongue. His groin tightened painfully as he regarded her dishevelment. Even her hair was a bit wild, as if she'd pushed her hands through her usually tidy bun. Or a lover had.

"You are remarkably pretty, you know, Magdalene," he said, just having to use her name. "A most *pukka* beauty."

"I look just like my mother," she said absently. "She was never photographed but I do have a small portrait."

"As much as I'd like to discuss the family beauties, I think I had better be employed in helping you dig out of this mess."

"Irene is working on the cakes, you see," she said, "because of Tom missing. There are weddings next week for which no cakes have been baked."

Judah went to the slots where the orders were stored and started paging through them. It did appear Betsy had been on top of the workload, at least until recently. Perhaps the busy season had been more than the untried former cakie could handle. He remembered that his family was coming up from Heathfield next week for a final dress fitting for Beth and the usual business for Hatbrook. Alys could be consulted soon.

"There is a wedding this morning. Has that cake gone out?"

"Yesterday," she said. "We have two cakes to deliver for Monday."

"What about this christening cake for Sunday?" He showed her a sheet.

"That order just came in yesterday," she said after checking it over. "I haven't seen it."

"Do you have any suitable cakes?"

She showed him an empty cupboard. "Irene has the right kind in the oven. I shall have to come in tomorrow and decorate one for this."

"You don't work Saturdays."

"What if Betsy is out again? We must be practical."

"I appreciate your dedication, especially when I am sure you have parties to attend."

"No, still in mourning," she said. "I did think I might hear from Uncle today with an invitation, but of course I will not know until I arrive home."

"I wonder if you should reside with him, under his protection."

"Then I wouldn't be able to come here," she said. "That would be devastating to the operation today."

"Quite. What can I do?"

"See that receipt?" She pointed to an open notebook with a list of ingredients. "Could you make up the buttercream for me?"

"Absolutely." He couldn't think of any place else he needed to be.

As the morning wore on, Irene came in to take one set of cakes from the oven and add more. The room filled with the scent of freshly baked fruitcake. When Melville arrived, towing a baker's apprentice he swore could do the job, Irene took him for a tour of supplies, after wheedling use of another oven from the bakery.

All the while, he watched Magdalene laboring over an intricate lacework design on one of Monday's wedding cakes. Despite all of the commotion, her hands never faltered.

"Can you help me stack the tiers?" she asked. "It works better when there is someone to spot a bad aim."

"Of course." He had no difficulty keeping a deliberate eye on her slender arms while she lifted a tier after she had placed her dowels. She had developed some strength. He couldn't imagine the usual Society miss hoisting heavily decorated cakes about. Still, every movement she made was graceful.

He'd seen women at their work before, servants cleaning, washerwomen married to soldiers who did laundry for officers, mothers with their children. Grace had never been his first thought until now.

She picked up a smaller layer, using her hand and a spatula. "Is it correct?" she asked. "It doesn't feel quite right."

He stepped closer and peered over her shoulder. "You need to pull it a little toward you."

She picked up the cake again and pulled it a little closer. "Oh! I hit the lower level."

"How do you fix the dent?"

"With a towel." She took a piece of clean linen and massaged the damaged edge until it was unblemished.

"Amazing." He spotted for her as she placed the third and fourth layers. After that, she measured the cake and found a wooden rod of the correct size.

"How are you going to get that in?"

"With a hammer." She pulled a stepladder over to the table. "Would you like to do it?"

"Looks like fun." He climbed the stepladder and took the hammer and dowel from her hands.

"Down the middle," she instructed.

"Just like a tent." He put the sharp edge to the unblemished cake and hammered it home until he felt the base underneath the cake.

"Thank you. Now, buttercream down the hole." She handed him a spoon with a bit of frosting and a flat spatula.

"You haven't let me frost any cakes today," he mentioned, as he smoothed, careful with his handiwork.

"We can't frost cakes that aren't cool."

"I should come in tomorrow and help you." He handed her the spatula and stepped down.

"I hope Betsy will be here."

"I think it is best to assume she will not. But if she is here when we arrive, we will discuss the situation with her."

"At least we will have enough cakes."

"Let us hope the apprentice can do the job."

She stepped back to get a full view of the cake. "Betsy likes to stack before she decorates, but I like to focus on each layer individually. It does make the stacking a bit fraught, however."

"I do not see any damage."

"Nor I." They shared a triumphant grin.

While she minutely inspected her artistry, he found himself amazed by how little a Society miss she was. Here was someone who understood his desire to work, the need to take action rather than exist on the money someone else had provided. She was his female counterpart.

He had no sooner been struck by this when the door opened and Irene and the apprentice came in, to do their work of changing out cakes.

"We will run out of room soon," the cakie said cheerfully. "Where do we cool the rest of them?"

Magdalene's attention turned to them, and Judah murmured that he'd fetch them both some lunch, since Magdalene was going to stay much later than normal. He walked out of the Fancy bemused, wondering if she was the solution to his quiet home. He might never find his father, but the cure to loneliness might be much simpler.

Magdalene woke late on Sunday after her busy Saturday, surprised by the stillness of the house. George had gone twenty-four hours without drama, and had even slept in his own bed. Could the worst be over?

At breakfast, Manfred handed her a letter from their uncle. "It came yesterday."

"Thank you. I was hoping he would call, but a letter is good."

"Asking for more advice about George?"

"For me, actually. Cousin Lillian wrote me to say she'd found me a husband."

Manfred lifted his teacup to his lips. "In Yorkshire?"

"Yes. The usual distant relative. A fifth cousin."

"Go on then," Manfred said with a smirk, imitating the long vowels of Yorkshire. "Open it and tell us what his lordship says."

She glared at him and perused the letter. Her heart sank just a little, but really, what could she expect? The earl had married his young daughter to a man nearly fifty. The match for her would not be a perfect one either. "Sir Octavian is deemed suitable."

"A knight?"

"A baronet."

"Ancient?"

"Thirty-eight."

"Ancient," Manfred said to his oatmeal.

"I suppose he is old enough to be your father. And he is a father, to a ten-year-old boy. His wife died in childbirth with her second child, seven or eight years ago."

"He took a long time to remarry."

"He does live in Yorkshire."

Manfred smirked. "Are you going to accept him?"

"I think I must consider it very seriously, now that I have the earl's approval."

"What about your position?"

"Now that Uncle is paying for the boys' schooling, it is less necessary that I work."

"We don't have to feed them, either."

She made a face. "I'd rather feed them than pay for claret."

"I'd hate to see you go, but it is best," Manfred said.

"Thank you, Freddie. I cannot tell you how much I have valued your support recently. I will miss you too."

"You are going then?" Manfred's voice drained into a squawk. He coughed. "To Cousin Lillian's?"

"I think I will go for Christmas," she said. "Uncle says he will take the boys to his country seat for the holidays. You should go too."

"Yorkshire for Christmas?" He swallowed wrong and coughed, the remains of his cold rattling his chest.

She patted him on the back. "The train shouldn't be too bad. I might as well see the countryside at its harshest. Then it will seem very pleasant later."

"You have a friend there too?"

"Yes, Constance." She was surprised he remembered.

He shrugged. "You do send and receive letters to Yorkshire regularly."

"Should I tell Uncle you will join him for Christmas?"

"No. I have commitments here."

"Must you?" she whispered. "If I am to change my life, why do you not do the same?"

He glared. "You do not know everything, Magdalene."

"I do not wish to meddle in your affairs, only to see you happy."

"I am happy enough." He spooned a large bite of oatmeal into his mouth and chewed vigorously, far more so than hot cereal required.

Steps shuffled across the threadbare runner outside the parlor door, and George walked in on stocking-clad feet, though he did have on clean clothes. He dropped into his usual seat, eyes half closed. Magdalene poured him a cup of tea and took the cover off the oatmeal bowl.

"Dry toast, please," George said in a ragged approximation of his voice.

She pulled the rack toward him and put two slices on his plate. Manfred quirked the side of his mouth at her. She allowed herself to hope that things might get better for all three of them, and basked in a moment of nostalgia for the way things had been a year or two ago, with Nancy presiding over the teapot. Could they all find a measure of serenity again?

Judah did not walk to Trafalgar Square on Monday morning. Instead, he left early and went to Magdalene's house by hansom. He arrived a few minutes before he assumed she normally departed, fighting the brisk November wind when he opened the carriage door and stepped down. After telling the driver to wait, he walked up the step and knocked smartly at the door. Under his gloves, his hands felt slimy with perspiration. His collar felt much too tight. Nonetheless, he felt the rightness of the question he was going to pose. A marriage proposal, yes, to Miss Magdalene Cross.

He had not queried his brother, or mentioned his plans to Gawain, or really, even, thought about it that hard. Still, she had been there in his dreams these past three nights. He imagined her filling his rented house with feminine geegaws. With all his money having gone to the ship, he had not done any collecting in India, so she would have a blank canvas on which to paint a proper English family home.

Not only that, he would be rescuing her from an unpleasant home. As an earl's niece, she was a suitable choice for a marquess's brother. It would have been better to marry money, but he did not really plan to live as a gentleman, even when he was in funds. They both liked their positions. He also knew she would be a good mother, thanks to her concern about her nephews. Yes, a cozy domesticity would soon repair his life from these long, lonely nights. He also knew she found him attractive and his nights would transform into sensual idyll.

Magdalene even knew his secrets, yet still treated him with respect. He could imagine the scene now, as he offered his hand to her in marriage. Her pale face would be transformed by a maidenly smile and blush, her fingers trembling as they met his. And then, a tender kiss that would turn into something warmer.

Just after Christmas, a wedding. They could start the new year together. He would build a family of his own, a true family. His wife, children of his own blood. No fashionable Society shenanigans with bed-jumping, gambling, or other dissipation. Just a nice English family.

The Crosses' maid-of-all-work opened the door when he knocked, looking very confused when she recognized him.

"I thought we'd take a hansom instead of walking," he explained.

She peered outside. "Well, it ain't raining, but it's cold enough."

"Exactly." He pointed at his muffler.

"Ye came from India, didn't you? Must be hurtin' yer bones."

"Indeed."

Behind the maid, he saw Magdalene coming down the stairs, caught a flash of slim leg above her half boots as her skirt swirled. He waved at her.

"You had an early start this morning."

"I thought you deserved a treat after such long days Friday and Saturday." He couldn't take his eyes off her, though she hardly seemed to notice him as she covered her beautiful hair with her bonnet and her splendid form with the ill-fitting coat. He would cover her in silk and fur when his ship came in, and throw out the cheap clothing she'd been forced to wear. George Cross had a lot to answer for, dressing his beautiful sister this way.

He supposed all of Magdalene's hardships had preserved her for him. If she'd had money, she'd probably have been snapped up during her first Season, rather than looking forward to what was probably her fourth.

He would save her from all that, and the censure involved with being a Scandalous Cross, tucking her into the warmth of the home she would make for them.

"You are smiling like a saint," she observed.

"A saint?"

"It's a peaceful, heavenly kind of smile. I do not think I've ever seen you with that expression."

"Certainly not while frowning over frosting."

She laughed, the sound reminding him anew of holy bells. "I was not pleased with the idea of the mechanical frosters at first, but now I think they will be an excellent addition."

"Mr. Noble promised the first of them for midmonth." He cleared his throat. How had business crept into this conversation? He had better things to discuss. "You look lovely this morning, Magdalene."

She didn't look at him. "It's still Miss Cross outside the Fancy, Captain Shield."

"Right, yes, of course," he said quickly. She had been Magdalene in all his dreams.

"We should go so we are not late."

"I have a hansom waiting outside."

"Oh? Is the weather very bad?" She walked into the parlor and peered out the front window.

He followed. "No, I wanted a little time so I could ask you a question."

"What was that?"

"Could we sit for a minute?"

She turned back, her dark eyebrows raised quizzically. He sat on the settee and patted the seat next to him. She tilted her head in censure, given the inappropriate nature of the gesture, and took the armchair next to him.

"What is it? I hope you are not going to ask me to serve at a party again. Or has Betsy given her notice?"

"Heaven forbid. No, neither of those things."

"That is good, because I have something to discuss with you as well."

He swallowed. "Do you want to go first?"

"No, Captain Shield." She folded her hands in her lap. "I am all attention."

His heart was beating faster than it ever did before a skirmish with the mountain tribes of India. He would rather lead a company into battle with nothing but a rusty bayonet than say what he had come to say. But of course she would accept and that gave him strength.

"Miss Cross, Magdalene . . . I know I should have spoken to your brother first, but under the circumstances, I would like to ask if you would do me the honor of becoming my wife."

He reached for her hands but her gloves remained clasped, one over the other, on her lap.

"Captain," she exclaimed, blinking rapidly. "This is a surprise for a Monday morning."

His mouth had filled with saliva. He swallowed, wishing she had accepted his touch. She did not behave as he had imagined. "A happy one, I hope. I will speak to the earl if you think it proper."

"No, no." She shook her head. "That would not do at all."

What was her meaning? "We are so compatible," he told her. "You understand the joys of hard work, and you know how to live on very little. Your life will be easier with me. I keep two servants. I think I can afford another next year, a maid for you, or even a nursemaid."

Her mouth set firmly and he had the sense he was digging his own grave, but he couldn't stop speaking. "We are such good friends, you and I, and we both have felt the want of a warm, family home. I wish it for us both, a cozy domesticity."

She remained still, not gracefully bending toward him as he'd hoped. "I had thought you unready to wed, with the confusion of your parentage."

"I am tired of being alone in this world," he stated. "I have been ruled by my fears, but if my parentage is unknowable then I must move on. I am sorry I cannot truly offer a marquess as my father, but you and I, we live on Society's outskirts. I hope you think, as I do, that remaining on the outskirts is best, regardless of our income. We can forge something new for ourselves."

"I do not wish to," she said, unsmiling. "I like Society. I like pretty dresses and dancing and the opera. Flirtations and card games now and then."

"You do?" He could not understand the appeal of such pastimes.

"Yes, I do. Economizing is not a pleasure."

He pulled at his muffler. "But your home, it is not safe. I can provide better, possibly much better, in time."

"I do not mean to stay here." She shivered, too cold when he was too warm. "That is what I meant to tell you. I am going to leave Redcake's at the end of the year, and go to Harrogate. I believe I have a husband waiting for me there. A family connection. A baronet."

"You want a title." His heat turned to ice. He sat back in the settee, tucking his hands into his greatcoat pockets.

"I want the lifestyle I would have had if my brother and parents had been more circumspect," she said. "My birthright."

"I see."

"Also, you come from womanizing stock. I do not want a marriage like my brother's. I do not want to be an embarrassed wife."

He could not deny it. "And this baronet, he is the sort for you?"

"He was married before. His wife died. By all reports it was a good marriage."

"He is older?"

She hesitated. "Yes. I shall become a stepmama to one boy."

"Is the Society in Yorkshire good?" he asked, hearing the sarcastic tone in his voice.

"My cousin is there, and a dear friend. It is a spa town, not the desolate moors."

He was going down quickly, but he rallied one last attack. "Men in my regiment, they are known for being steady and reliable, and never giving up. I expect to have money soon, and I have connections. I could try Society, for your sake."

"You never lived in London. You do not fit into Society. You are a good man, Captain, a very good man, and I so appreciate everything you've done for me, but I have made other plans for my life." She paused for a moment. "To be honest, I am aware your family does not approve of mine, especially my cousin, Lady Bricker. I do not wish to be forced to take sides against my own family."

Each phrase tore a fresh wound through him. Could he deny the tension between their families? No. He cleared his throat, gathered himself up. He saw no point in abasing himself. The lady had made up her mind. "I had best get to Redcake's. Will you be joining me?"

"I have no intention of leaving until just after Christmas. I have not even told George of my plans."

He bit the inside of his lip until he tasted the rich pang of blood. "I take it the earl knows?"

"He approves, yes."

"Then I wish you happy." He opened the parlor door and held it out for her.

She swept in front of him, graceful in her sad coat and sensible shoes, but far more genteel than he could ever hope to be.

His charge had failed. He would not win the battle today.

She turned back to him, just before opening the front door. "I am sorry, Captain, and I do wish you well. It is just that I have different ideas for myself."

"I did not know," he said. "I want you safe above everything. Again, I wish you happy."

Chapter Fourteen

Magdalene had found it hard to breathe for the past thirty hours, ever since she had rejected the captain's marriage proposal. When the Marchioness of Hatbrook passed through the door of the Fancy on Tuesday, Magdalene's lungs seemed to stop working entirely. Her stays felt three sizes too small. Would Captain Shield have told his sister-in-law what happened? Her face flamed hot with embarrassment, but she forced herself to return to the lacework icing she was creating.

"Alys!" Betsy cried, and ran to give the marchioness a hug.

Magdalene watched, dumbfounded, as Lady Hatbrook hugged Betsy's round form. She might have thought they had not seen each other in years, rather than a matter of a few weeks.

"How is the baby? Are you feeling well?" Betsy asked.

"I am excellent. No more trouble in the morning." Lady Hatbrook made a face. "I do need to acquire a new wardrobe, however."

"Oh, I am happy for you," Betsy squealed. "I would not know yet, though, to look at you."

Lady Hatbrook saw Magdalene and gave her a nod. She returned it, her heart pounding.

"You are in Town for dress fittings, then?" Betsy prodded.

"Yes, Hatbrook's sister is being presented at court next month. I took the opportunity to have fittings for myself."

"You never cared for clothes."

Her hand went to the drapery at the front of her skirt. "No, but I do care for comfort, and I certainly don't want to refit my existing wardrobe. I am not such a fan of sewing."

"Don't you have a maid of your own now? I remember when you had to share with your sisters."

"Yes, but Matilda has been very ill. Her confinement is only a few weeks away and I have insisted all attention be on her."

"I see." Betsy nodded wisely. "You might as well take advantage of the shops here."

"And the modistes. But I did want to stop in and see how Redcake's was faring. Is it as busy as last year?"

"Yes," Betsy declared.

"You are recovered from your chill? Captain Shield said you had been ill last week."

Magdalene still wasn't sure about that. Betsy had no sign of a red nose or cough when she returned.

"I am very well, thank you."

"Good. There is no time for illness in this operation."

Magdalene hoped she had heard a threat in that sentence. The door opened and the apprentice baker bustled in with a tray of fruitcake, hot from the oven.

"Who is that?" Lady Hatbrook asked.

"Tom Mumford left to go on stage. This lad has taken over."

"Who else is helping?"

"Irene."

Lady Hatbrook looked inquiringly at the boy. "Very well. Why don't you fetch us a pot of tea and a few scones, Betsy, and we'll go over orders."

"Love to." Betsy watched imperiously as the lad deposited his cakes on a cooling rack and checked the oven in the alcove, then departed the room in his wake.

Magdalene tensed. She set down her icing bag.

"Captain Shield tells me you have resigned," Lady Hatbrook said, when the door closed behind them both.

So he had told her something. But everything? "Not until after Christmas."

"I see. I suppose you could not have expected to remain long." Her voice was disinterested.

"I wanted to marry," Magdalene said tentatively. "I think I shall, early next year."

"Will you be out of mourning by then?"

"As soon as the time has passed," Magdalene said, wondering if that would present a problem to the baronet.

"I hope in future the captain hires girls who plan a longer employment," Lady Hatbrook mused. She wandered around the room, looking at the cakes in various stages of completion. "I cannot fault his hiring for talent, though. You do have skill."

She stared at her icing bag, knowing now that the captain had not exposed her. "Thank you, my lady."

Betsy soon returned, pushing through the door with a tray laden with a large pot, four teacups, and a tier of scones and sandwiches.

"You do understand a lady in my condition," Lady Hatbrook said happily, pulling a stool up to the table.

Magdalene noticed that even though there were enough cups, none were poured for her or Irene, when she returned from the storeroom with containers of spices and dried fruit.

She and Irene began cutting up the fruit, but she couldn't help listening to the conversation.

"How is the captain as a manager?" Lady Hatbrook asked. "By this, I mean, how is he in comparison to the last manager we had? He has been here just a bit over three months."

"You let the last one go at three months," Betsy said, handing Lady Hatbrook a plate.

"Quite. Your opinion?"

Betsy's eyes met Magdalene's over her teacup. Magdalene looked hurriedly back at the fruit.

"He's a bit free with the ladies. Not like the other one. No hands on the girls, if you understand. But he is quite a flirt."

Magdalene's mouth dropped open. That was not true! Betsy had all but thrown herself at the man. She couldn't help interjecting. "I'd like to know what you consider flirting, Miss Betsy Popham."

"Every morning he's smiling, and asking how I'm doing, telling me to come to him if there's anything I need."

"That is because you greet him at the back door every morning," Magdalene said coldly. "Some might call that inappropriate as you should be at your post at that hour."

"What about you? Coming in the door with him every morning,

all huddled up under his umbrella like you're courtin'," Betsy shot back, losing her pretend gentility.

"Girls," Lady Hatbrook scolded. "Irene, your thoughts?"

"He's handsome," the cakie said. "Any girl without a fellow would be a fool not to make eyes at him."

"Who would you say is his favorite?"

Irene's eyes darted from Betsy, to Magdalene, to Lady Hatbrook. "I think he's nice to everyone. Mr. Hales does the rounds of the departments in the morning, and Captain Shield does the same in the afternoon."

"They treat the girls with equal respect?"

"The captain is much friendlier," Irene allowed. "But I've never seen him paying special favors."

"But nothing to discourage their fancies either?"

"Well, no," Irene said. "My goodness, it would take a lot for that. His eyes? Those broad shoulders? You know, my lady, being married to his brother. The Shield gentlemen, if you don't mind me saying, are best of breed."

Magdalene saw the marchioness's lips quirk.

"How good of you to compare them to livestock," said Lady Hatbrook, buttering a scone. "Is he too handsome to be let loose around unmarried ladies, do you think?"

"It is possible," Betsy said, imitating her accent again.

"How dare you?" Magdalene said, unable to control herself. "You'd cost a good man his position because he is handsome?"

"That's enough, Magdalene," Lady Hatbrook said. "I will not have a raised voice."

"I apologize, my lady. It is just that I feel the injustice of Miss Popham's statement very keenly."

"I am aware of that," Lady Hatbrook said. "However, there are other factors to consider. I am very glad to hear there has been no molestation of the girls. It has happened before and I promised myself to be vigilant."

"Soldiers have rough manners," Betsy said, with a smirk in Magdalene's direction.

Magdalene had little to lose, mentally packed for Yorkshire as she was. "Captain Shield is a gentleman, and an officer, no common soldier. He is the epitome of English manhood and that is why you have been making eyes at him."

"Magdalene!" Irene gasped.

"It is because he is not interested in you, Betsy, not at all, not in the slightest bit, that you are so sour," she continued.

Lady Hatbrook stood. "That is quite enough. You have curdled my tea, girls, and I was looking forward to that scone."

"I am sorry," Magdalene said. "I know Miss Popham is your friend, but Captain Shield is mine."

"A strong statement." Lady Hatbrook put one hand on her back.

She felt her lips tremble. "He bought me a coat and a bonnet, when mine were ruined. And he has done more, much more. He's as good a person as you could possibly imagine. You are married to his brother. Please don't let Miss Popham cost him his position. He likes it here."

"You are overset," Lady Hatbrook said. "I believe I should have had this conversation with each of you separately. But, Miss Cross, your loyalty speaks volumes." She stood slowly and left the room.

Had she listened? Magdalene, Betsy, and Irene stared at the door as it swung closed, then Betsy turned with fire in her eyes.

"How dare you," she hissed. "I'll have your position for this."

"I already gave my notice to the captain," Magdalene retorted. "I'm leaving just after Christmas."

Betsy's mouth dropped open. "After all the training I've given you?"

"I do not think you will be here much longer, either," Magdalene said. "You seem most eager to marry."

Betsy's plump face went purple. The door banged open and the apprentice slid in, a small tray in his hands. Irene dropped her knife and flew to the tray.

"Where are the rest of the cakes?"

The apprentice shrugged. "They burned, miss. I can't say as how it 'appened."

Irene threw up her hands in theatrical despair. "I needed those for a birthday cake! Now I'll have to beg something from Mr. Melville." She stormed out of the room.

Magdalene turned back to her lacework, ignoring Betsy. Though she did have to wonder why her comment upset the girl.

Upstairs, Judah saw his door open, and instead of his secretary, his sister-in-law popped her head in. He stood immediately. Did his family have to be in Town today, on the day after his greatest humiliation? He had not the heart to play the gallant brother just now.

"Alys." He forced a smile. "I did not know you were coming by today."

She lifted her arms, then lowered them again. He noted she had shed her outerwear already and wondered if she'd come right to his office.

"This is a very short visit, given Matilda's condition. I did want to see my friends, though."

No, she had been wandering the building. "Do you find everyone well?"

"I was a bit perturbed by a conversation I had in the Fancy, just now."

And there it was. *Bloody hell.* Judah gestured her to an armchair by the fire and took a chair opposite. "I expect it is tense down there. Betsy was out ill for two days, and Magdalene worked twelve hours or more extra as a result. Even I helped out."

"They are at each other's throats," Alys said succinctly.

He felt terribly guilty, knowing Magdalene had been working in an unsettled frame of mind, thanks to her plans. "I am sorry to hear that. Should I intervene? The scene was calm yesterday."

"I am afraid it was the subject of you that had them perturbed."

What had Magdalene said? "Really?"

"You must understand that management needs to set a certain tone, Judah. You cannot play favorites, or encourage any of the girls."

"Is that what you were told?"

"It is obvious Magdalene is considered the favorite, and Betsy wants to be. The fact that you bought Magdalene a coat and bonnet, and apparently spend a great deal of time with her, will not benefit you among a group of young, unmarried women. You cannot be seen to have favorites," she chided.

"Magdalene has given her notice," Judah said, surprised by the path this conversation was taking. "I have tried to curtail Betsy's interest in me, pointing out that I'm not her direct supervisor and that she does not belong in my office."

"Of course she doesn't," Alys agreed. "But Magdalene?"

"That is a different situation. She is like me, of gentle birth but limited funds. We are friendly with her family."

"We are not," Alys said. "Her cousin is Lady Bricker."

"I am friendly with her family, then," Judah said, "though not Lady Bricker of course, as she lives in Yorkshire now."

"I believe you should leave the hiring of lower staff to the supervisors of those departments," Alys said.

"I agree. But you left the Fancy without a supervisor."

Alys frowned. "When Magdalene Cross leaves her position, I strongly suggest no one replace her as your friend."

"It is unlikely I would make the same mistake again," he replied.

"No. It is hard for an unmarried man to work here, I believe. One is perpetually looking for a wife among the girls. Do you know, Betsy's father had his eye on me at one time? Mr. Hales too, quite possibly."

"I can imagine that. Ewan Hales may be courting Betsy now, though I had thought him situated elsewhere. I don't know about her father."

"You would do well to marry, Judah, if you wish to keep your position long term. You did tell me you liked it here. Marriage will make it easier. We do hate to think of you here, alone in London. Do you go out in Society much?"

"Hatbrook took me to one party. I am invited to a dinner at Earl Gerrick's at the end of this week, but you probably will not want to hear that."

"Anyone special for you?"

He sighed. "I had not planned to marry any time soon, Alys, but I did find myself proposing marriage only this week. The nights are long in London in the autumn."

She raised her eyebrows. "I wish you very happy. Who is the lady?"

Judah shook his head. "She did not say yes."

"No? Why ever not?" Her expression was half angered, half confused.

"The lady is Magdalene Cross," Judah said, his voice constricting in his throat. "I learned she has a better offer."

"Better than you? To hear her speak, you are a knight of old."

"Really?" He found this curious.

"She defended you to Betsy Popham quite stoutly when Betsy inferred that unmarried women were not safe around you."

He narrowed his eyes, but kept his voice calm. "As you say, they are not friends at the moment."

Alys's look had changed, from one of matronly judgment to sympathetic sisterhood. "I am very sorry. Do you love her?"

He put his hands on his knees and leaned forward, holding the weight of his upper body on his lower. "I thought she would be a good companion. I thought she was better off with me than in her brother's household. It seemed to make sense."

She shook her head. "A young lady wants to hear of love, not sense."

"As you say. She said no, after all." His chest ached.

She put her elbow on the arm of the chair and leaned her chin into her hand. "We are both tired, you and I. My sister Matilda is my burden, and Rose, who always has trouble with her lungs at this time of year. What is on your mind?"

"It is too soon to rid my thoughts of Magdalene," he said. "Her brother struck her not long ago. I'm afraid for her. I am glad she is going. It cannot be soon enough."

"The Scandalous Crosses," Alys said with a sad smile. "Magdalene is a fiery personality herself."

"I cannot offer her what she wants."

"What does she want?"

"Society. She is very proud of being part of it."

"You are as well born as she. Better, actually."

"You and I both know that isn't true," Judah said.

"I do not. After all, I am a tradesman's daughter. You are at least half gently born, through your mother."

"Legitimacy is everything," he said. "Unless you are a royal bastard, I suppose. But I am not."

"No one in this family will ever tell," Alys said. "You can hold your head high."

"No, I can't. I work for a living. I want to work for a living. I want to be what I am. I am perfectly content with myself. I thought Magdalene fit my life. She has other ideas about her place in the world. That is all." He wished to stand, to pace, to go outside, but he could not be rude to Hatbrook's wife. And his employer.

"Knowing what you want is at least half the battle," Alys said. "I understand from Hatbrook that you could marry Courtnay's daughter. Victoria, I think? Perhaps when you have reconciled yourself with your present disappointment you can revisit her."

"Thank you, sister," Judah said, an edge in his tone. "Have you picked out a wife for Gawain, too?"

"I do not believe he is in the market for a wife," she said.

"I do not want to marry." Was he telling a lie? At least Gawain had a mistress. He had wanted to find his father, not find a woman. Besides, Gawain had money to spend on a house and clothes for his mistress.

"Do not fool yourself. You do. And trust me, a good marriage is such a precious thing."

"I am sure it is."

"You can be sure," she returned. "I hope to see you for dinner at Hatbrook House tomorrow evening."

"I shall be there."

She stood and offered him her cheek to kiss. "Have faith, Judah. It will become easier in time. But I would not look for a wife inside this establishment."

He shuddered. "I have no intention of doing so."

It had been a couple of weeks since Judah had seen Eddy Jackson bear the wounds of recent battle, so he was disheartened to see the boy's bloodstained collar when he arrived for his newspaper that foggy, gray Wednesday. The weather suited his mood after the many disasters of the day before and he suspected the same for the newsboy. At least the blood on Eddy's collar was dry.

"New details about the Mitchelstown Massacre," the lad shouted, drawing the interest of a wild-eyed young man in checked trousers, who threw him a penny and received a paper.

Judah had considered going to Magdalene's home in a hansom, but he would not throw himself on that altar again. She might not want to see him today. He had thrashed the sheets from their place tucked under his mattress the night before, wondering why she had defended him so fervently if she didn't care for him.

"Where is Miss Cross?" Eddy asked with a cheery grin somewhat diminished by a split lip. "She is usually here before you."

Judah glanced around. Trafalgar Square seemed busier than usual. He saw a number of tangle-bearded men wandering the rain-darkened tarmacadam with flyers. Women too, in clothing so black and disheveled you'd have thought them birds caked with coal dust. Lifting his chin to one trio of men, he asked, "Who are they?"

"Agitators," Eddy said. "There's always fellows who are unhappy around here."

"Who was unhappy with you?" Judah asked, poking at Eddy's collar.

"Oh, that's not my blood, guv. I'm learning." He put up his fists in a pugilist's stance.

If the boy had any actual muscles on his skinny frame, Judah would eat his muffler. "I see you've kept your cap this time."

"He needs a muffler and new shoes," Magdalene said, coming up behind him. "I would give you some of my nephews' clothing, but they are smaller than you are."

Not so much smaller though. Eddy did not look like he ever got enough food.

"Good morning," he said to her.

With a nod in his direction, Magdalene reached into her pocket and pulled out a steaming cloth.

"Just one potato this morning, Eddy. I'm sorry. We need to do the marketing."

"Oh, thank you, miss. One potato is lovely." Eddy tucked it in his jacket pocket.

Judah handed him money for the paper, noticing Magdalene looked around uneasily. Because of him? No, he didn't think so. She seemed to be looking at a man with rectangles of wood covering his torso in front and in back, a human sign.

After Judah received his paper, he nodded to Eddy and took Magdalene's arm, since she seemed to be lost in thought. At least she didn't pull away. "What is wrong?" He heard the lilt of Irish voices raised in anger as they crossed the Square. "Do you recognize any of these people?"

"They are trouble," she said simply. "I wonder how safe Trafalgar Square is right now. I worry about Eddy. He's so small."

He felt the slim bones of her upper arm under cloth. She was small too, would be defenseless in many of the places he'd found himself over the last several years. "He's a tough street rat. He'll know where to burrow if necessary."

"I don't like it. You saw the flyers, didn't you? The Social Democratic Federation and the Irish National League have scheduled a rally here in the Square for Sunday. And Eddy sells papers here every day."

"Why are you so concerned about him? Missing your nephews?"

She rubbed at the back of her neck with her free hand as if it pained her. "I always worry about boys of that age."

"Why?"

She sighed. "The recklessness. When I was that age, I was quite wild. Climbing trees, running races. I was not a young lady."

He smiled. "I can believe that."

She loosened his grip by twisting gently, and then pulled her arm away, though she stayed close. He put up his umbrella to shield them from the misty rain, and in order to keep her close.

Without looking in his direction, she spoke. "One day, we played follow-the-leader. I was the leader. It had rained all morning, but stupidly, I took the other children, all boys, up an ancient rock wall. The stones were slimy and slippery. All the more fun, I thought. But we were making the climb a race as usual, and one of the boys was on a tall part of the wall, a good eight feet or so."

"He fell?"

"Yes. He hit his head on one of the fallen rocks. That is why he died, from hitting his head at the bottom of the wall."

He blew out a foggy breath. "I am sorry. That must have been terribly upsetting."

"I became a proper young lady overnight."

"And now?"

"I hate seeing boys put in harm's way," she said with a shrug. "There is trouble coming. Gatherings and demonstrations aren't allowed, you know, but they happen anyway."

"Why Trafalgar Square?"

"It is where the West End and East End meet, geographically, but there have been battles with the police recently all over the place."

"I've seen the papers, of course. I am glad I don't belong to one of the clubs that have been attacked by ruffians."

"A soldier not spoiling for battle?"

"I don't understand anything about the Irish question. Things seemed tidier in India. The Pathans attacked the villages and we fought back. A mad, warlike bunch of tribes. But here, the warlike types are all mixed up with the politicians. It's not for me."

"They are also agitating about unemployment and worker issues."

"Redcake's is an elite establishment. We hire good people and pay them very well. Best treatment of bakers in the city. We offer women respectable employment, no matter what Miss Betsy Popham wants to claim."

"Now I have your dander up." She smiled.

"I would terminate her instantly, if she wasn't friends with the marchioness," Judah said.

"I do not blame you. A woman scorned is a power unto herself."

"Thank you for standing up for me, Magdalene," Judah said, using her Christian name deliberately.

She didn't seem to notice. "You deserved no less. But you ought to have some concern for local politics. After all, the anarchists could come after what you hold dear next. You never know."

Chapter Fifteen

"Do you think it is possible anarchist violence could touch Redcake's?" Judah asked Alys that evening. Hatbrook had agreed when Alys suggested they forgo their male prerogative of brandy and cigars after dinner and go right to tea in the parlor, since Judah had to work the next day.

He suspected, however, that Hatbrook would dearly love a private chat. His brother had been staring at him with a mixture of irritation and ire all evening.

"I shouldn't think so," Alys said. "Everyone is well paid and we do not employ unskilled labor. Also, there are the iron gates that are locked each evening and bars over the windows in the alleyway."

"I walk through Trafalgar Square every morning. A huge demonstration is planned for Sunday."

"Why don't you come down to Heathfield for the weekend?" Hatbrook suggested. "You can lick your wounds there and stay out of the way of the police."

"Lick his wounds?" Beth asked from the piano. "What wounds? Judah?"

Gawain, seated at the end of one rose sofa, put his head theatrically into the crook of his elbow. Judah heard him mutter something like, "Women."

"Michael, I shared that with you in confidence," Alys said.

"Judah knows better," Hatbrook retorted. "Really. I cannot believe you proposed to a connection of Lady Bricker."

"My sister is far more culpable, along with Mr. Bliven. Really, darling, you hold on to your anger much longer than you should. Why does Lady Bricker taint Magdalene Cross?" Alys asked.

"They are very friendly," Hatbrook said. "You know they are. And she is Manfred Cross's sister. I have had cause to run into him, as well you know, last New Year's Eve."

"He is a child compared to the other parties who were involved," Alys said. "Really, Michael. That was nearly a year ago."

Judah glanced back and forth, back and forth, as they exchanged these remarks. He understood very little of it.

But Gawain stood, after a last sidelong glance at Beth. "I must go. Thank you for a pleasant evening."

"Gawain," Alys said. "What is wrong?"

"I would prefer never to hear the name 'Bliven' mentioned again. In this, I agree with Hatbrook."

"How much money did he take from you?" Alys asked. "I've always wondered."

Gawain glared at his sister. "Shield? Care to join me? I believe we had business at our club."

"Not me," Judah said equably. "My brother will not be able to rest until he has his consultation with me."

"Why would you want to marry anyway?" Gawain asked.

Judah could tell he planned to elaborate, but Alys was smirking at him.

"Yes, for you, it worked out very well indeed, but for us young men building our fortunes, marriage is a distraction."

"I did marry a slightly older man," Alys allowed.

"I need a brandy," Hatbrook muttered. "Beth, do you not need your rest?"

"This is as entertaining as a theatrical performance," Beth said brightly. "I am not going anywhere."

"I am sure this conversation is far too mature for your ears," he said.

"I would already be out if not for Mother's death," she said, fluffing her black skirts.

Gawain seemed riveted by the graceful movements of her hands.

"Nonetheless," Hatbrook said. "Why don't you play us a little something. Music would be very soothing."

Alys looked at Gawain. "Weren't you leaving?"

Gawain smirked at his sister. "Music would be nice."

Judah sank deeper into his chair. He could not imagine that Gawain would be allowed to court Beth. But this evening, Hatbrook's censure was focused on him.

"A Scandalous Cross?" Hatbrook muttered into his ear, joining him on the sofa.

"She has been the soul of propriety. In fact, she even shared with me the very event that molded her into a young lady, instead of an absolute hoyden."

"So no risk of a baby coming?"

Judah had turned away, but he jerked his head back around. "What?"

Hatbrook held up his hand, palm down. "If that was an issue, it would change the situation."

"No. I should not have thought it was polite to ask me that."

"We are brothers. I do not want secrets between us."

"At least not my secrets," Judah said. "I offered for her because I thought us compatible, but she has other ideas about her life."

"I am told her family intermarries," Hatbrook said. "In and out of a set of titles."

"I expect you are correct," Judah said. "I am sorry I became involved." As soon as he said it, he knew that was a lie. He had enjoyed becoming involved, and had been happy all day because she had still met him in the Square, despite the way she had opened his eyes to the anarchist threat.

"Are you still having dinner at Gerrick's house Friday?"

"I don't see why not. I need more friends than just Gawain."

Hatbrook sighed. "The Honorable Geoffrey Cander, again, Judah?"

He shrugged. "Why not Gerrick himself? Did you know he was a military man? Served in Egypt when he was young. He wasn't in line for the title then. An older brother who died, I think."

"At least the earl is a busier man than his sons," Hatbrook said. "I could tolerate a friendship with him. He seems reasonable. Quite ashamed of his daughter."

Judah almost covered his chuckle. "You must be having a tough time, down at the Farm with a houseful of expectant women and their relatives."

"Hell on earth," Hatbrook said in a low voice. "You have no idea. The conversations they have are appalling."

Judah didn't think it sounded too bad. A houseful of family. But perhaps a house full of in-laws was different than one's original family. He wouldn't want to live with George Cross. "I wish you luck."

"Thank you. Do not think you can escape the Farm at Christmas, no matter how many women or babies are in residence."

"Redcake's is open on Christmas," Judah said, feeling very satisfied with this.

"It shall have to do without you," Hatbrook said. "Upon my life, you will be there."

"I have responsibilities."

"Judah," Beth called, from her position next to Alys at the piano. "You had better come home for Christmas. It will ruin the holiday entirely if you do not."

Judah squinted into his sister's eyes. What a little manipulator she was. "I will think about it."

"Hmmm," Hatbrook said as Beth squealed in delight.

Judah patted his brother's knee. "I had better say good night. Good luck to you."

"I will take all the good wishes I can muster," Hatbrook returned.

Judah was astounded to discover the earl served no spirits when closeted with his male guests after dinner on Friday night. Geoffrey Cander dropped into the chair next to him with a sigh and handed Judah a cigar.

"Irritating, isn't this edict?"

Judah set the cigar down. The room was already blue with smoke. He didn't see a reason to add to it. "What?"

"This is Father's way of sending a message to Cousin George. Drunkenness will not be tolerated."

Judah looked down the table, to see the earl in deep discussion with George Cross. "Is it a family disease?"

"We have a large extended family. One or two in every generation seem to have trouble holding their liquor. Since you see Cousin Magdalene every day, and have seen Cousin George's handiwork, there is no point in keeping the truth behind closed doors."

"I will not be seeing her much longer."

"No. That family is dispersing. Strange how one quiet soul can hold a family together."

"I agree it is an interesting phenomenon. My sister seems to be holding my brother and me together."

"I didn't know you had a sister," Manfred Cross said, leaning across the table between two candelabra.

"She is about to be presented," Judah told him. "I'm sure you will see her at all the balls next year."

"Will you descend on Society then too?" Manfred asked with a grin.

"By Jove, I hope it isn't necessary," Judah growled. "Surely Hatbrook will be in Town."

"She will need a chaperone," Geoffrey Cander said.

"I'm not suitable. Maybe our aunt will come."

"Not Lady Hatbrook?"

"No. She will be presenting my brother with offspring about then."

"That is the difference with a small family versus a large one," Geoffrey Cander said. "Finding a likely chaperone is never a problem."

"You could marry," Manfred suggested. "Very quickly. Then she would have a chaperone."

Judah narrowed his eyes. Did Manfred know about his proposal to Magdalene? No, he seemed innocent of subterfuge. "Can one still run off to Gretna Green these days?"

"Not as easily. There is a residence requirement for marriage in Scotland now," Geoffrey Cander said. "Since before we were born, actually. You'd have to be able to hide with the chit for three weeks."

Judah laughed. "Why do you know that?"

"I did wonder," Manfred said, setting his cigar on an ashtray. He looked bilious green.

"You don't know the story?" Geoffrey Cander grinned. "I would not exist if not for Gretna Green. My great-grandparents March were married there, or rather, Coldstream, which was a similar destination back in the day."

"People still go to Scotland to marry."

"For the romance of the thing, and to marry young girls. Personally, I'd prefer to go somewhere warm. Maybe run off to Italy."

Judah laughed. "Planning a scandalous marriage?"

"As soon as I can find a racy young heiress to wed me," he said, smacking his lips.

"You don't need an heiress," Manfred said.

"I disagree, old boy. I have funds from my grandmother, but not enough to live in true style."

Manfred and Judah shared a glance. The Honorable Geoffrey Cander was very well insulated from the difficulties they faced.

The earl cleared his throat. "Shall we join the ladies?"

The men all stood with alacrity, the after-dinner hour not being as convivial without spirits. Judah had been seated too far away from Magdalene to speak to her, so he took the opportunity to sit with her on the piano bench, where she was working her way rather inexpertly through a Mozart piece.

"I am out of practice," she said, laughing. "Too much baking."

"At least I recognized the composer," Judah said. Her cheerfulness drew him despite her rejection. He'd have thought he would want to avoid her but the reality was quite the opposite.

"That is something. I did want to speak to you."

"Oh?" He straightened his waistcoat.

"I was at Nelson's Column before you this morning, and I tried to speak to Eddy about Sunday. I'm worried about the protestors. You know the police will be out, and they are saying the army is coming too."

"Did you make him promise to stay home?" He brushed a speck of ash from his coat.

"He would not promise. He laughed at me, Captain, and wondered why I thought a protest would be any less rough than where he lived."

A list of Eddy's injuries over the past months flipped through Judah's brain. "What do you want me to do? Take my sword, put on my old uniform, and stand guard?"

She smiled wanly. "Maybe?"

"Does he think the protestors will buy newspapers? Maybe we can persuade him to sell elsewhere."

She shook her head. "They are very territorial about their spots. To move would likely guarantee a beating."

He kept himself from touching her hand by ruffling through the sheath of scores and looking for easier music. "How about this then? I go to the Square, just as Eddy is getting there, and buy up his entire stock of papers. I'll insist he help me bring them to Redcake's. He'll have no reason to go back until Monday. He can spend the day in some less dangerous entertainment."

"That's a marvelous idea, Captain. Do it, please."

"Very well. Do you know when he reaches the Square?"

"About seven, I believe. After he has made deliveries to private customers."

He handed her a Bach piece that looked simple enough. "He works a long day. No wonder he is so thin."

She took it, seeming not to notice their fingers touching. But the feel of her skin sent a bolt of awareness to his groin. "Do you think he might like to train as a baker? I know that is a hard life, but he would be out of the elements."

"I rather thought him destined for the stage, with all his comedic routines and jokes." They shared a smile. How would he find any pleasure in his mornings with her gone? "I'm going to miss you terribly, you know."

She glanced up, as if afraid others in the room had heard, but with no mother, sister, or aunt present, who would censure? "That is a very kind sentiment, Captain. We have had some lovely mornings."

"At least you'll still be here for Christmas."

Manfred came toward them, loudly requesting a round of Beethoven to drown out the idiocies of his cousin. Judah chuckled and made his good-byes. Magdalene was not working the next day, but he was.

"Captain?"

Judah pushed himself up and rubbed his eyes as his valet put a candle on the bedside table. His valet yawned, then quickly covered his mouth. In the dark, Judah wouldn't have caught him if not for the man's gesture.

"We both sleep in on Sundays. I am sorry for the inconvenience, Lawrence."

His valet sneezed. "I am sorry, Captain. I did not wake early as planned. I think I have a fever. I slept badly."

"What time is it?"

"Nine a.m."

Half asleep, Judah couldn't remember what his plan had been. "That's all right, then. Plenty of time to intervene." Judah reached for the dressing gown at the foot of his bed.

"It is too bad the boy is too stubborn to stay away." Lawrence coughed.

"We do not know enough about his personal life to understand. Perhaps he is beaten if he doesn't come home with money each day."

"Very likely," the valet said with a sniff. "It is often said that the lower classes value a shilling over a life."

"Bring me my shaving water, will you? I'll have breakfast downstairs by the fire."

Judah dressed himself and reached for a case on top of his wardrobe. He loaded his gun, planning to tuck it into his greatcoat. Lawrence had opened the curtains. It looked a pleasant day for November. Though still dark, it wasn't raining or particularly windy.

The meeting of the Social Democratic Federation had been announced for two-thirty p.m., so he had plenty of time to find Eddy and buy the newspapers. He thought that after, they could have a friendly chat over tea and buns in his office, and discuss the boy's future.

Lawrence came back in and put a steaming bowl on his washstand.

"Thank you. I think you should go back to bed."

"I have many duties."

"I do not care. I am sure Penny does not want your illness any more than I do."

"Thank you, Captain. I shall stay in my room as much as possible."

"Thank you." He did not want the illness to spread through the household or Redcake's. After a large breakfast, he perused the papers he'd been too busy to read the day before, seeing that two thousand police and four hundred troops had been ordered in and around Trafalgar Square. This was a worse situation than he realized.

He heard a banging at his front door and sent Penny to open it.

Then he picked up his mail, finding a note from Alys in response to his thanking her for dinner the other night.

Penny came back into the warm kitchen. "I put her in the parlor, Captain. Miss Cross, that is."

He glanced at his pocket watch. It wasn't much after ten a.m. Had George been making trouble again? "Thank you, Penny."

A few moments later, he opened the door to the freezing parlor. Magdalene was looking at the embroidery on a pillow Beth had given him, still fully dressed in her outerwear.

"I'm sorry. I should have told her to bring you straight to the kitchen. I was not expecting callers today."

She set down the pillow. Her face was pale, but seemed unmarked by violence. "It is fine. I came because I am so worried about Eddy. Did you find him? Do you know there are five thousand police out? Cavalry men with swords? The streets are madness."

This was the bucolic England of his dreams? "You should have stayed at home. I was about to leave."

"Every time I fell asleep last night I remembered seeing that boy's blood on the rock next to the old stone wall. Do you know? I cannot remember his full name. We called him Jamie. That is all I recall. I can't let Eddy die too."

"You are not in charge of him, not even for a game of follow-the-leader, Magdalene." He took her by the arms and forced her to look at him. "He lives on those streets. He has worked in the Square, side by side with all the homeless who've been moving in as long as I've been here, and he's never run into serious trouble."

"How can you say that, with the beatings he's taken?"

"He says they are from home."

"I think he lives on the Square, Captain. I've been thinking about it. I will wager he lives there along with all the anarchists." She wrung her hands.

Judah shook his head. "He manages to keep enough money to buy his papers from day to day. I doubt he could do that if he was living rough."

Magdalene's look of assurance faltered. "I didn't think about that."

"Stay here, in the kitchen. Penny will take care of you. I'll walk over to your house and tell your brothers you are safe, then I'll go and find Eddy."

"I should go with you." She lifted her chin.

"No. Not with all those men about."

"Do not worry about speaking to my brothers. Neither of them is home."

"They aren't going to this protest, I hope?"

"No. Manfred caught a train this morning on some errand for Lady Mews and George went to the twins' school."

"To visit them or make them return?"

"Visit. My uncle has been working hard to restore my brother's good sense."

"That is good news, at least. I shall find my coat and then I will depart."

"I am coming with you. It is early yet. The protest is hours from now."

"I do not want to look out for you as well. Stay here so I don't worry, please."

"It isn't proper."

"Are you afraid the other man will not want you if you are in my house alone?"

She pressed her lips together. "There could be gossip. That I had another relationship."

"It would not be a lie. We've kissed, more than once. I am quite sure you enjoyed the experience."

She stared at the bare planks on the floor. He hadn't gone to the expenditure of rugs yet, save the one in his bedroom, and he'd brought that back from India.

"Am I such a bad choice of husband?"

"I was raised be a Society wife, not a tradesman's wife. I never thought to want anything else."

"Consider that your brother's profligacy has ruined you for anyone but a relative."

"It's not as if I'm going to marry Geoffrey Cander. The baronet is my fifth cousin. Scarcely a relative at all. And, at least, the baronet does not dislike my family."

"I can resolve the Lady Bricker situation. You cannot expect me to give up fighting for you." He gentled his tone.

She said nothing and he was gratified that she hadn't told him to stop fighting. He sensed a level of indecision still existed in her mind. Finding only one approach that made sense to him, he moved to her, put his fingers under her chin, and tilted her mouth to his.

He was gentle, at least that was his intention, but she met him with a cry almost like a sob. Her mouth opened under his, hot and welcoming. So, he plundered, licking her tongue until it tangled with his, the taste of his morning Assam mingling with her Darjeeling.

Then, he felt a pressure on his chest and realized she was pushing him away. When he forced his legs to obey and moved back, he saw tears were drifting down her cheeks. She wiped them away with a sniff.

"I will not be your problem for much longer. Please, go find Eddy."

"You've never been my problem, Magdalene. You are my delight."

"I am Miss Cross. We are not in the bakery." Her back stiffened and her chin came up.

How he loved her stubborn little chin and those rosy, kiss-swollen lips. How he loved *her*. What a moment to discover this truth, so inappropriate yet perfect, when he was about to stride onto a battlefield to save their friend.

He held back his smile and said, "I apologize, Miss Cross," with studied gravity. He opened the parlor door for her, then led her into his warm kitchen.

"Make Miss Cross a pot of tea, Penny, will you? And whatever else she needs. I'll be back soon."

"Be careful, Captain," Magdalene said. "I wish you'd let me come with you."

"I will be fine. I'm going in armed, just in case. But as you say, I have plenty of time."

His estimate of time diminished rapidly when he reached the street and started moving toward Trafalgar Square. Everywhere, he saw people gathering. Pushing his way through the area, he saw that a march was planned for every direction.

Eventually, he realized there was no easy entrance and he began paying attention to any boy about Eddy's size. He circled the Square, trying to avoid crossing the mass of humanity, then began to thread his way to Nelson's Column. Soon, he realized there was no way Eddy could be in his normal spot, as Life Guards were guarding the monument on horseback. A few feet away from them, he saw a policeman raise his nightstick and hit a screaming man. The crowd surged toward the monument. Someone threw a drum into the air and two men with sticks attempted to rush a mounted soldier.

As this one scene occurred, he saw better dressed men attempting to pull a cart toward a fountain, to use as a stage, perhaps.

Where would Eddy stand? Had he gone home, wherever that might be? Or to the news shop where he bought his daily supply? No, that was wrong; Eddy bought direct from the publisher. Where was that office? He glanced around frantically, confused by the fact that everyone here was white. Who was the enemy when you couldn't note them by their dark skin and tribal costume?

"Keep your swords in your scabbards!" he heard a subaltern yell from his position, as one of the mounted cavalry put his hand to his belt.

Judah walked over to the young officer and, steering clear of hooves, called up to him. "When you first came here, did you chase off a newsboy? He's here every morning."

"Not me," said the subaltern.

Judah circled the monument carefully and found a captain, then, after introducing himself, repeated his question.

"Yes, he was here," the captain said. "I told him to find another perch for the day. We're in for some nasty business. You should go."

"Did you see what direction he went?"

The officer shrugged. "That was hours ago."

Judah thanked him, then began to wander the Square. For now, it was actually quieter than the streets around, since the march had yet to begin. He found a newsboy and made his inquiry.

"Eddy stands at Nelson's Column," the youth said. He was about Eddy's age but looked less scruffy. Perhaps he still had a mother.

"I know, but he was chased off by the Life Guards. Any idea where he would be?"

"Check with the chestnut man who works the northeast corner," the newsboy advised. "Eddy sleeps in the same building as 'im."

Judah tossed him a shilling and went northeast, thrilled by this first crack in the mystery. Eddy didn't live in the Square after all.

He recognized the chestnut seller by the round pan, smelling of charcoal, in which he roasted the chestnuts.

"Apples," cried the street seller in an Italian accent. "Hot apples, chestnuts! Sixteen a penny!"

Next to the man was a hot potato seller, and she did a far brisker business, with a line of redheaded customers three deep. Judah remembered part of today's protest was about the Irish question. He went up to the Italian.

"Have you seen Eddy Jackson recently?"

"Eh?" The man pretended to be deaf.

Judah got the point quickly enough and gave him a penny for six uncooked apples. "Now, my man, Eddy Jackson? The newsboy?"

" 'e's at the Column."

"Not today he isn't. The cavalry is guarding it."

"Try down by the Strand. 'e said he'd go there if he couldn't get into the Square today."

"Are you responsible for him?" Judah asked.

"Not me. Old 'ighmark is our landlord."

"Is he a relative of Eddy Jackson's?"

"I don't think so. Eddy just came to 'is attention-like, as did the lot of us at one time or another, being the best in our trade."

Judah glanced at the busy potato woman. "I think you need to consider changing trades."

Now he was at the opposite end of the Square from where he needed to be. He dashed across as quickly as he could, aware that two-thirty was approaching. Enough people were present now that he could smell human sweat, along with horse dung and the smoky food smells of the vendors. The cart was in place for speakers and he could see banners being waved to the north. Clouds hung in the sky, promising precipitation. He picked up his speed to a fast trot, wishing he was on horseback.

Eventually, he muscled his way out of the Square and craned his neck in the direction of one street corner, then another. Thankfully he was a full head taller than many of the stunted protestors. How was he going to find one undersized newspaper boy?

Just then, he thought he heard Eddy's shout, but a phalanx of policemen passed toward him, sticks in hand. He swore and dashed in the direction of the shout, only to see a ragged boy holding a very familiar cap, running fast.

Stepping in the boy's path, he grabbed the cap out of his hand.

" 'ey! That's mine."

"No it isn't." He took the boy by the shirt. "Stealing right in front of the bobbies?"

The boy wrenched away, tearing his shirt. He stuck out his tongue at Judah and ran.

A group was forming in the street. Judah began to step through, threading his way across to the corner. Women let him pass, but then a huge man stepped in his way and grinned, showing blackened teeth, and not nearly enough of them. Judah tried to step around him to the left but the man danced sideways.

With a sigh, Judah made a fist and slammed it into the man's jaw. His eyes widened in surprise as he fell back a step. Judah feinted to the right and moved past him, shaking out his hand. His glove had absorbed a little of the blow.

Eventually, he made the street corner, to find Eddy, standing on a box, holding the *Times* high. As expected, the lad had no cap, and his lip was bleeding. His jacket had been half torn off his arm again, but he was still trying to earn his pennies.

Judah grabbed him. The lad winced as Judah pulled him down so he could speak into his ear. "I'll buy the rest of the day's papers. Come with me."

Eddy looked at him with surprise, no sign of a smile today. Judah tugged at him. "Come."

Eddy stepped carefully off his box, wobbling. On the other side, a boy ran by, grabbing a handful of papers, then moving off in the opposite direction.

"Oy!" Eddy shouted, but Judah kept a firm grip on him.

"I'll pay for them, Eddy."

Eddy looked at him, wild-eyed.

"You're done for the day," Judah repeated, overturning the box, then snatching the rest of Eddy's papers and loading them in. "Miss Cross wants you."

Eddy blinked. "That's different then. Her brother beat her again?"

Chapter Sixteen

Magdalene heard rustling on the other side of one of two kitchen doors.

"That's the tradesman's entrance," Penny commented. She sat at the other end of the table, calmly peeling potatoes, while Magdalene fretted. Penny seemed a severe sort, unlike her Hetty. She wondered if the servants mirrored their master's personalities.

Judah brought Eddy in through the back door, dropping a box of papers next to the stove. Magdalene cried out when she saw Eddy's bloody face. Judah appeared undamaged, at least. Penny ran for towels.

Eddy smiled at her as she rose and came to him. "Miss Cross!"

"Your jaw is bruising," Magdalene said, after she'd pulled him toward the gaslight and examined his face.

Eddy thrust his tongue into his cheek. "I think 'e loosed a few of my teeth."

"I saw you were limping. What happened?" Judah tossed Eddy's cap onto the table.

"Where'd you get that, guv?" Eddy snatched it and slapped it on his head.

"A little tosser ran off with it."

He shook his head admiringly. "I never thought to see it again."

Magdalene poured him a cup of tea from her cooling pot and added plenty of cream. "Sugar, Judah?"

"I don't keep it on the table, but here's a bowl of raisin buns from Redcake's that I'd been planning to eat at tea."

"Mind that lip," Magdalene said as Eddy wrapped his hands around the teacup. "Is it madness out there?"

"More and more," Judah said. "Little battles everywhere. People are going to die before the afternoon is over."

"How am I going to get home?" She hadn't thought this through.

"I sent a note to Hatbrook House, asking for the carriage just before dusk. Hopefully the streets will be clear by then and a fancy carriage will be left alone."

"Smart idea," she said, grateful she wouldn't be compromised by spending the night here. She didn't trust herself in a house at night with Judah, and the baronet might have second thoughts if he heard rumors about her.

"I met that Italian you live with," Judah said, sitting next to Eddy. "Who is this Highmark?"

Eddy inhaled a raisin bun in two bites. " 'e's the man what will beat me bloody if you don't give me the chink you promised for my papers."

"Looks like you were beaten pretty well already."

Eddy shrugged. "I didn't want to go into the Square today. I knew it'd be dangerous, and them without money would be taking the day, likely enough. Not the toffs like you who have a penny to spare."

Magdalene forgot her own problems when she heard this report. Someone had beat him because he didn't want to try to sell papers during a riot? She bit her lip hard to distract herself from tears.

"How would you like to live here, Eddy?" Judah asked.

Had she heard him right? A marquess's brother, adding a ragged newsboy to his household?

"Where's this?" Eddy asked.

"My house. I live here."

"Does Miss Cross live 'ere, too?"

Judah shook his head. "Unfortunately, no. She is leaving London."

Magdalene felt hot all over for a moment. He still wanted her, even though she had rejected him. Why couldn't he want the life she deserved, that they both did, as a part of fashionable Society?

"It's for the best," Eddy said. "In my experience, once a man starts 'ittin 'e's unlikely to stop."

"My brother has stopped drinking," she said defensively.

"For now," Eddy said, with an air of philosophy. "Don't trust 'im, miss, that's my advice."

She crossed her arms over her chest. Was Eddy right? Was it safe to stay until Christmas? Redcake's needed her, and she could use the travel money, but her home would be so dreary this year and maybe even as dangerous as Eddy's home was.

"Do you owe this Highmark any money?" Judah said.

"Yes, for the papers and my pallet and food."

"Does anyone ever escape his accounting?" Judah asked.

"Not unless they leave London," Eddy said. "And no one ever does."

"Does he get mail anywhere?"

"No. Least I don't think so."

"I'll take him what he claims you owe if you agree to live here," Judah said. "How much?"

The boy wiped his lip on a napkin, leaving a streak of blood, and started on another bun. "Four shillings would do it, but you don't want to go there, Captain. Don't let 'em see your face."

"The Italian has already seen me."

"Give 'im the money," Eddy cried, frustrated. " 'e's an 'onest sort for an Italian."

"It's probably close to a week's wages for the man," Magdalene said doubtfully.

"It's worth a try," Judah said. "But I won't go today. Tomorrow. I'll look for him on the way to work. Is he always in the same place?"

Eddy nodded and inhaled his third bun. "If I'm not 'ome tonight, I'll get a beating."

"Do you have anything of value there?" Judah asked.

"No."

"Then you shouldn't worry. Penny, could you dish up a bowl of soup for the lad, then figure out how we can kit out the second bedroom for him?"

Penny looked at him like he'd gone mad, but she ladled pea soup into a bowl and placed it in front of Eddy, then went down the hall, muttering. Magdalene had the same feeling. The second bedroom? For a newsboy. She liked Eddy very much, but in helping him, she'd thought vaguely of finding him work indoors, or even a charity school somewhere, not taking him in.

Hours passed before she had a minute alone with Judah. Eventually, the day had worn Eddy down, and they tucked him into a small bed in the second bedroom, then tiptoed down to the parlor. Judah lit the fire and Magdalene brought in the tray they'd readied.

"No raisin buns," Judah said mournfully.

"We'll get by with this shortbread Penny found."

"That's right." Judah grinned in a way that made him look not that much older than Eddy.

"It's very Christian of you to take Eddy in, but what are you going to do with him now?" Magdalene asked. "Give him a job at Redcake's?"

"I think he should stay out of the public eye for a time," Judah said. "He needs to heal."

Magdalene poured the tea, drinking in the sight of his broad shoulders and beautiful, strangely colored eyes. She knew she would see him in her dreams for the rest of her life, wherever circumstances took her.

"I shall hire him a tutor," Judah declared. "I know he can read; newsboys like to argue the politics of their own papers. A little more education and perhaps he can become a writer himself. That's how Dickens began his career."

She shook herself out of her sensual reverie. "You think he is going to become Dickens?"

Judah grinned. Oh, he was handsome. Her stomach seemed to drop into her knees and she knew she wouldn't be able to eat a bite of shortbread.

"He has intelligence and wit. I think he has a good future if he's educated properly."

"He won't be happy shut up here. He's used to the streets."

"It's not the path to a long life," Judah said. "He deserves better."

"But in your home? A bachelor establishment?"

"Since you refused me, you have no say in my establishment, Magdalene."

"Miss Cross," she corrected. "I know I do not. But you are bound to have clashes. This is not the life he was raised for."

Judah set his jaw. "I'll not have you claiming superiority of blood to someone like me, who does not know his own blood."

"I'm not," she started, but met his glare and subsided. Why couldn't he see that his parentage didn't matter? He was legally the son of the late Lord Hatbrook, and on his mother's side, the grandson of an earl. Far superior to wherever Eddy Jackson came from. With a name like that, he should be a prizefighter or some such. "I have his best interests in mind."

Penny came into the room. "The carriage is here, Captain."

"Just in time," Judah said. The light of battle had yet to leave his eyes.

"Please do not think ill of me. I cannot express how relieved I am that he is safe," she said.

He took her hand. She hadn't noticed how cold she was, with the fire barely lit, but his palms were both toasty warm against hers.

"I know. You took a risk this morning coming here, one I'd have preferred you not take. I understand what happened to you as a young girl has weighed heavily on your conscience, but I do believe you have paid your karmic debt at last. Eddy will live because of you."

"Karmic debt?"

"It is an Oriental philosophy. You have done a good deed to offset a bad one, or so the Hindoos say."

She didn't really understand, so she said, "I will get my coat and bonnet and be on my way."

He took her hand. "Still friends? I will see you tomorrow?"

"Will it be safe to go on the Square?"

"I will take a cab to your house."

She hesitated, and he said, "No proposal this time. You have made your position clear."

"I am so very fond of you, Captain Shield. I am honored. Perhaps if I had not received what amounts to an offer sanctioned by my family first, I might have answered differently."

He licked his bottom lip, his eyelashes dusting his lower lashes. "It makes no difference. A no is a no."

"You are very logical today."

"I apologize."

She knew she had made a terrible mess of their friendship and had no idea what to say, so she forced a smile and went out of the parlor, then ran down the hall to the kitchen, as if she could escape her conflicting emotions.

Despite the chaos on the streets, she found a pile of mail on the hallway table when she entered her house. As she removed her coat and hat, she noted all was silent inside, though she could still hear the distant noise of people outside. She had been very grateful to travel home in a closed carriage with footmen to guard her.

Her house, though quiet, did not smell clean, like a place with adequate servants. A hint of dust, a hint of unwashed body, the fish Hetty must have cooked today, drifted unappetizingly through the house and puddled in the hallway next to the front stairs. The huge gap under the kitchen door let out the food smells, but they could not afford to replace it.

Too tired for a conversation or tea, she lit a candle stub and took her letters upstairs. A loud snore emanated from George's room. All was darkness under Manfred's door. He had moved down from the attic to the room Nancy had stayed in during her illness, and must not have returned from his secret errand.

Magdalene unlocked her door and put her candle on her dressing/writing table, a scratched and battered affair. Upstairs their furnishings were a poor lot, but like many families, they saved their best for the public rooms while the private only had tattered cast-offs. Soon, she would leave poverty behind for the life of the moneyed class. Even leaving London did not seem such a trial on a day like this. Surely Harrogate was free of anarchists and rioters.

She lit her fire and exchanged her boots for slippers, then sat with her letters before changing for bed. After she'd finished reading, she wished she'd saved the missive from Lady Bricker for morning. Now she was being instructed to go to the home of Lady Varney, her friend Constance's employer, rather than Lady Bricker's own home. Why? Was she being offered employment instead of a husband?

Either way, she thought it was time to leave. She needed to escape her brother's home, the employment she enjoyed far too much for a girl on the marriage mart, the man who made her tingle and yearn, even as he steadily made one decision after another that lowered him on the social ladder.

She had to admit though, even the furnishings of his second bedroom were nicer than anything George possessed. Though Judah's house had no feminine touches, she suspected he lived better than they did, and his clothes were nicer too. He had two servants. It was at least as clean as hers had been when Nancy had been alive and they had kept house together.

She shook her head. Harrogate, that was her release. Not Judah. *Please,* she prayed. *Let the baronet have something of Judah's charm, intelligence, and good looks. All of it is far too much to ask, but please, something.*

"How are your plans for Yorkshire coming along?" Judah asked as he sat next to her in the hansom the next morning. Asking was like reopening a wound, but he couldn't help picking at it.

"I had a letter from my cousin and I scratched out a reply this morning for Hetty to post."

He noted she was biting her lip, instead of the hot apple he'd given her. Little puffs of cold air emitted from her lips with each breath and she was pale again. "All is in order?"

"Mmmm," she said, not really responding.

"Did I do something to anger you?" After her level of engagement yesterday, he'd expected more questions and concerns.

Her blue eyes caught a flash from the lanterns. "No, of course not. How is Eddy?"

"Chafing at the bit. He wants to be out selling papers, not stuck inside a cozy home having a peaceful morning of buns and tea." He took a bite of his apple, and enjoyed the heat of it.

"You'll have to pay that Italian today."

"It is already done," Judah said, pointing to their apples. "I went to the Square first."

She took a small bite. "I hope he gives that horrible man his money."

"He seemed very concerned about Eddy. I think he will do the right thing."

The bite of apple seemed to go down the wrong way, for Magdalene started coughing. Judah put his hand on her back, alarmed, but the coughing subsided. "You are nervous this morning, Magdalene. Usually you are the steady sort."

"Yesterday did try my nerves on many levels," she admitted. "And that is Miss Cross."

He laughed and stroked her back. "I do not think I could see you as Miss Cross anymore."

"Soon enough you will refer to me as Lady Feathercote," she said. He detected the hint of snarl in her voice and preferred it to nerves.

"What a name," he said lightly, to disguise his hurt. "I much prefer Cross or even better, Magdalene Shield."

The carriage rattled into the brick alley and bounced to a stop before she could speak. Judah unlatched the door and held it for her. She lifted her nose into the air and walked in the door in front of him, punishing him for his cheek.

"Off you go, cake wallah," he said. Thumping came from the office staircase.

She turned to him, but before he could speak, Ewan Hales had appeared in front of them, after a mad dash that included leaping down stairs, if Judah was any judge. He had never seen the man excited.

"What is it, Mr. Hales?" Judah asked. Had influenza struck Redcake's? Or anarchists?

Magdalene stepped around the secretary and disappeared down the steps.

"There's a man here to see you, Captain, from the docks!"

Judah's hands tingled in anticipation and relief. "Did he mention a ship?"

Hales nodded enthusiastically. "He did. Your ship!"

Judah grinned, suspecting he revealed every single one of his teeth. He dashed up the stairs, Hales's pounding steps following him. "Fetch tea, Hales, and some cakes."

The anteroom was empty, but in his office he saw a man standing in the pose of a sea officer, legs spread wide to steady himself against the roll of the sea, hands clasped behind his back to keep from bumping anything on a crowded ship. Judah recognized the imposingly tall form, the black-as-midnight hair, far too long for fashion.

"Captain Howard," he exclaimed.

The man turned, and Judah was reminded anew by the mythical stature of the man. He must be nearly seven feet tall and dressed in the style of some seventy years ago, tight breeches and tall boots. His boots would cover the entire leg of most women.

Judah had to admit the old-fashioned style revealed the admirable physique of the man and hoped Hales had got him up to the office before the cakies spotted him. They'd find him a common sort once they spotted Howard.

"I would imagine, by your appearance, that the *Fleetfoot* has docked."

"Our fortunes are made," the captain agreed. "We had some trouble with pirates in the Arabian Sea, and then weather difficulties around the Cape, which slowed us down. Had to stop along the Ivory Coast for repairs twice."

"Is your ship salvageable?"

"Yes. The benefit of your merchandise being so long at sea is your lordly partner made arrangements to sell the goods. He is already at the dock with a variety of middlemen. You should have your funds before the holidays."

Judah felt like he did after battle, a combination of exhaustion and exhilaration, unsure if he should go to a church and fall to his knees, or make love to a woman until he collapsed on top of her. "That is good news."

Captain Howard pulled a small pouch from his belt and tossed it to Judah. "Each partner receives one of these. You can sell them or have them set for your woman."

Judah opened the pouch and let the gleaming blue stones fall into his palm. "Sapphires."

"Enough for a parure."

The stones matched Magdalene's eyes. A pity. Maybe they matched Beth's as well? No, she probably had all their mother's jewels. His stones would best be saved for his future wife, but she seemed far off in the future. His heart wanted no one but Magdalene.

When Hales arrived with the tray, they sat and discussed the voyage in more detail.

An hour later, they shook hands, and Judah said, "Thank you, Captain. I am certain you have much to do."

"One more partner to visit," the giant agreed.

Judah promised to visit the docks for a tour that afternoon. Hales came in the moment Howard left, too excited to knock. He exclaimed over the stones. When Hales had left, Judah went down the stairs to put his pouch into the safe in Accounting.

Dash it all, he could bring Magdalene up and show her the stones. Would they sway her from her Feathercote? At least they would show her he was far from poor. He dropped the stones into his pocket and turned to go downstairs to the Fancy.

Would a token like these prove his love to her? He could compromise a little on lifestyle, now that he had the funds. Go to Society parties sometimes, purchase a fine home. He could afford to dress her properly, far more finely than she dressed now. His gamble had paid off, or rather, his investment. He couldn't wait to write to Hatbrook.

When he reached the main floor, he was about to cross the hall to the steps to the basement, when he heard arguing voices just outside the employee door into the bakery. He needed to intervene immediately. The voices were loud enough that customers might be able to hear.

A woman started crying. Concerned, he sped up. He recognized Betsy Popham, wiping her eyes on her apron. In front of her was her father. Was this a family dispute?

"You knew she wasn't to work the counter," Ralph Popham was saying. "Were you trying to force her out?"

"I didn't think, honest!"

"Now you've ruined a nice young lady's reputation, and lost Captain Shield a good employee to boot, during a busy season. He ought to sack you!"

"Now, now," Judah said. "What is all this fuss?"

"Captain," Popham said, clearly relieved to see him.

Betsy gave a loud theatrical cry and flung herself into Judah's arms. Horrified, he pushed her back at arm's length. "Get ahold of your nerves, Miss Popham. This is no place for the vapors."

She sniffled, suddenly much quieter. Judah didn't want to try to make sense of her, so he looked to Popham for information.

"Please explain yourself," Judah said.

"Miss Cross has left her employment," Popham said, running his hands through his thinning hair. "It is all my daughter's fault, I am afraid. I came in late this morning because I was visiting with Sir Bartley about some factory supply issues for the bakery. We were shorthanded."

"What does this have to do with Miss Cross?" he demanded.

"Betsy insisted the young lady come up here to fill in. They both worked at the counter for an hour. I was gone, and two of the girls have the influenza."

He barely heard the dreaded word. "Then what happened?"

"Lady somebody-or-other recognized Miss Cross and made quite a to-do. She couldn't decide which was more scandalous, Miss Cross working while she was in mourning for her sister-in-law, or her working when she was on the Society marriage mart. Said she'd have her struck from every guest list she had access to."

"Bloody hell," Judah said. This was Magdalene's worst nightmare come to life.

"Miss Cross was very polite," Popham assured him. "I came in just as the confrontation was ending. She told her ladyship she was leaving London in a few days to be married, then when the woman had gone, Miss Cross took off her apron and walked out the back door, without even going downstairs for her coat or reticule."

"In November? It is near freezing out."

"Yes, Captain."

Betsy sniffed loudly, but Judah had no time for her. "Make do in the bakery, Mr. Popham. Betsy, get back downstairs. You will have to accomplish twice as much in the time you have or I'll have your position for this."

"I need another set of hands," she whined.

"With this influenza, there are none available," said Popham.

"Could you help?" Betsy gushed. "You helped Magdalene."

Judah gave her his deadliest stare, one he usually reserved for Pathans and cheating merchants. "I will help by asking Mr. Melville to hire a replacement. But now, I'm going to spend my day trying to find a young woman wandering the streets without a coat or money. Now, go get me her things and look sharp."

Betsy fled. Popham shook his head. Before he could open his mouth again, Judah pointed him back to his station, then he went upstairs for his coat.

It took him several minutes to reconnect with Betsy and get Magdalene's possessions, then he went out the front door for a hansom, hoping that by retracing her usual path home, he could overtake her. But that fifteen minutes had given her wings. When he reached her home, Hetty opened the door.

"Is Miss Cross here?" he asked.

"Miss Cross isn't in," Hetty said in a formal tone.

"In to me, you mean? But she is safely indoors?"

Hetty frowned. "You picked her up just this morning, Captain, to go to work. Did you lose her?"

"I'm afraid so," Judah said grimly. "Any idea where she might have gone without a coat?"

The maid shivered. "In this weather? I don't rightly know. Into a shop, maybe."

Judah's muffler suddenly felt far too tight. He handed Hetty Magdalene's coat, bonnet, and reticule. "Do you think she might have gone to her uncle's?"

"We're much closer to Redcake's than the earl's house."

"A good point."

"Do you want to come in for a cup of tea? I'm sure Mr. George would receive you."

"No, I need to find his sister. Please tell him to look for her as well, if he is able." Judah went back down the step and asked the driver to take him to Adelaide Street, with the idea of enlisting Eddy's help.

When he entered his house, all was silent in the front rooms. He went into the kitchen to see if Penny knew where Eddy was, and he found the lad sitting at the table with Magdalene.

"You came here?" Judah said, his hands shaking with relief. "I went to your house but no one had seen you."

"I wanted to say good-bye to Eddy," she said, looking very self-possessed for a woman who'd just left her employment and been embarrassed to the point of losing her social position.

"What about me?" Judah asked.

"I was going to write you a note."

"You left your possessions in the Fancy," he said, feeling a fool.

She ignored his remark. "Penny was kind enough to make me tea and oatcakes."

Not trusting the evidence of his eyes, he went to her and touched her hand. "You are icy."

"I have not been here long. Perhaps twenty minutes."

"She was a fair wreck when she come in," Eddy said.

"I told Lawrence to go back to his room for fear she'd pick up his influenza," Penny interjected.

"I thought he was better." Judah frowned, suddenly remembering the illness had struck at Redcake's as well.

"He still has a cough," Penny said, her hand to her breast. "Poor man."

Judah scented the horror of a budding interservant romance, but chose to ignore it for now. "And a hot brick? Does she have one at her feet?"

"I am very close to the fire, and there is bread in the oven, and cakes on the stove," Magdalene said. "I'm much warmer already. I shall go in a minute."

"No," Judah said. "No, you will not. I will send a note back to your brother's house. I have a cab waiting."

"I can go instead of a note," she said calmly. "I need to pack."

"Do not," Judah said. "Please. The morning has been topsy-turvy."

She smiled kindly. "It is better this way. If I stay, there will be nothing but gossip, and I shall have to deal with Betsy Popham. I might very well slap her if I have to see her again. She literally pushed me in front of the countess, when I could have remained at the far end of the counter, quite usefully restocking the case."

"What was a countess doing buying her own pastries?" Judah asked, knowing he'd lost any power over her.

"It is the fashion now, à la Lady Hatbrook, for aristocratic ladies not so wealthy as to have their own pastry chef. It is like picking out your own fabric for your modiste."

"That is good for Redcake's, I suppose."

"But not for me," Magdalene said, the first tart tone creeping into her voice. "Thank you for holding the carriage."

She stood and offered Judah her hand. He stared into her eyes. "Please do not go to Yorkshire. I will fire Betsy, even if it means losing her father too."

"It is best for me, Captain. Please wish me happy."

Then, before Judah could formulate any other remark, she was gone. He hadn't even shown her the sapphires. As he stared at the table where her teacup still steamed, he knew he'd never be able to look at the stones without thinking of her eyes. They might as well be at the bottom of the Indian Ocean for all the good they would do him.

Chapter Seventeen

On Wednesday, after an exchange of telegrams, Magdalene left for King's Cross Station. The roads were icy. She huddled in her secondhand coat, trying to stay warm in the hired cab while slipping back and forth on the seat. She had paid for her ticket with the remainder of her Redcake's pay. Captain Shield had delivered it to her house the previous night and, while she hadn't refused to see him, she had declined to converse, telling him she had much to do and there was nothing left to be said. He had drawn himself up into a military line and left without any further attempt to woo her, the picture of a wounded but proud suitor. George had scarcely seemed to comprehend what was afoot, and Manfred had been busy placating their maid, who had threatened to leave again. It had not been much of a leave-taking.

As the train sped north toward Yorkshire, Magdalene settled back and watched the scenery change from urban to rural and back again while the hours passed. Her sense of geography was uncertain. She knew there were Yorkshire Dales as well as Yorkshire Moors, but would it be dark before she arrived that far north?

As she ate her cooling potatoes, she forced herself to think of the future, not the past. Sir Octavian, not Captain Shield. A life in the spa town of Harrogate, rather than the one she'd imagined for herself as a girl, in London Society, or the life she could have taken for herself and chose not to, that of a prosperous tradesman's wife with good family connections. She imagined motherhood versus stepmotherhood and decided it would be much the same if she loved the child. After all, had not her nephews been as dear to her as any child of her own might have been? She was not yet twenty-two, and would fill Sir Octavian's nursery with children of her own. They might even visit London sometimes.

What little sun the cloudy sky allowed sank, and night overtook the landscape. While she had never fallen asleep during the long day's journey, she was yawning by the time she disembarked, and was caught with mouth open by none other than her dear friend Constance, there to greet her on the platform.

"I cannot believe you are here!" Constance cried as they ran to each other's arms.

Magdalene pulled back, taking a look at Constance's silvery white hair, her coat that was of finer quality than her own mourning attire. "You look well. Such a young lady. It has been a good three years since I have set eyes on you."

"It has been an age," Constance agreed. She linked her arm with Magdalene's and took her to Lady Varney's carriage, then called to the driver to fetch Magdalene's trunk. "So nice of Lady Varney to send her carriage. You must be exhausted."

"Yes, but exhilarated too. I am starting a new life."

Constance plopped into the plush green seat next to her. "It is exciting."

"Do you know why I am to come to Lady Varney's instead of my cousin's home?"

Constance patted her hand. "The answer could not be simpler. Lady Varney is Sir Octavian's great-aunt. I believe she is not related to you, except by marriage."

Magdalene rubbed her gritty eyes, not sure this made sense. "Sir Octavian wanted me to meet his great-aunt?"

"He has put his marriage in her hands."

Magdalene didn't like the sound of that. "So Lady Varney is to determine if I am worthy of the baronet?"

"Yes. I have assured her you are the best of souls, so do not concern yourself."

"Does her side of the family marry relations like mine does?" Magdalene wondered. "It is not arranged marriage exactly. We have usually met our spouses at some point during the years."

Constance squeezed. "Sir Octavian has a son, you understand, and he wants to make sure you would be a fit mother."

She was stung. "Does he not know I've had my nephews to care for?"

"Yes, of course, dear, but who is there to speak on your behalf, with your dear Nancy dead? However, you need not worry. Earl Gerrick is for the match and Lady Varney sets great store in earls."

"And who is she, I wonder?"

"Her husband was knighted some twenty years ago. I believe he was an earl's great-grandson."

"I see. My birth should be good enough for her."

"Oh, certainly." Constance fell back a little as the carriage began to move.

Magdalene pressed her feet hard into the floor to keep herself upright. "I wonder that you did not try to marry Sir Octavian yourself."

"I had hoped to return to London someday," Constance admitted. "I am not independent here and I do not wish to be whispered about."

Magdalene put her head on her friend's shoulder. "I hope we both get all the things we wish. We certainly have had enough trials to deserve them." The thought of Captain Shield flashed through her mind, but she forced it out again.

"Now, I may never want to return. Not if you are here." Constance found her hand and patted it.

"I suppose it is a happy coincidence that you are living with the baronet's great-aunt. We will see each other often."

They chatted happily until the carriage came to a stop in front of a four-story multicolored brick mansion near the center of town.

"Lady Varney likes to take the waters, so she had to live closer to town. Before her husband's death they lived on a country estate a few miles from here."

"It appears to be a very pleasant establishment." Magdalene liked the look of the neatly trimmed hedges. Snow dusted the patch of grass, but the path was dry.

"Yes. It is near all of the amusements. Lady Varney does not consider herself well enough to go out every day, but in excellent weather we will go to the shops in Montpellier Parade. There is a wonderful toffee shop across the street from a very fashionable hotel. London Society does visit here."

Magdalene hoped the countess who had seen her at Redcake's never made the trip north.

A footman opened the carriage door and helped them both down. Magdalene followed her friend into the house, whispering a fervent prayer that she had done the right thing in coming here.

With Magdalene gone, Judah threw himself into the improvement of Eddy during each moment he had free from his work. He had instructed Lawrence not to let the boy out of his sight, and had asked Hatbrook's butler to find him a live-in tutor as swiftly as possible.

Meanwhile, he was busy with the disposition of the cargo from his ship, negotiating with Captain Howard and the other partners for the purchase prices. By the time the tutor arrived, a couple of weeks after Eddy had taken ownership of his second bedroom, the cargo had all been sold. They had benefited from the great popularity of fancy sapphires. The cache of stones purchased from a group of native hunters, along with the other cargo the partners had accumulated over a couple of years, had earned them millions of pounds, more than Judah had ever dreamed. He never needed to work another day of his life, if he invested carefully. But even this triumph dimmed before his failure with Magdalene. Had she become formally engaged? Could she even be married by now?

"Mr. Farmer is here, Captain," Penny said, appearing at the door of his study.

Judah was about to give up the room to Mr. Farmer, for a bedroom and classroom. He patted the mantelpiece one last time and took his book to his room before going downstairs. Now, he would need a man of business, and a new, larger home. A butler, perhaps. If Magdalene ever came to London again, she would be shocked by his aristocratic lifestyle. He wondered what kind of funds her baronet had.

Eddy was already in the front hallway, staring daggers at Mr. Farmer's thin face. "Who's this, then?" he demanded. "Taking on boarders?"

"Eddy, this is your tutor, Mr. Farmer. He will be living with us, and taking on the responsibility of your education."

"Education? Me? What do I want that for?" the boy cried.

"You must think of your future." Judah smiled at the boy, who had cleaned up most presentably. Under Lawrence's patient eye, even Eddy's language had improved dramatically in the past weeks. Eddy was being educated without even realizing it.

"I'm just resting up 'ere. You know, for the winter, like. Once me arm is better, I'll be back at my post."

"You should think of a proper future, Mr. Jackson," said Mr. Farmer, in an earnest tone. "I understand you like the newspapers excessively. Someday you could own a paper of your own, if you apply yourself."

Eddy sneered. "I'm a hands-on sort, not a thinker."

"You are a salesman, is what you are," Judah said. "You aren't selling me on being ignorant. I had a tutor myself growing up. I never went to school. Don't you want a nice house someday, a good position, and a family? If you stay on the streets, even working respectably like you are, something bad is bound to happen."

"It weren't the streets that hurt me, guv." Eddy glared.

Judah met his gaze with equal heat. "Well then, stay here and have a tutor."

"Can't I stay here and work? I could pay you. Just let me get back. I'll get my old job back. I haven't been gone long," Eddy coaxed.

"You will like your studies," Mr. Farmer said. "I understand you like to read."

"In English," Eddy snarled. "About politics and fights and gossip. Not Latin or Greek or all that other nonsense. I have no time for that."

"You do not want a classical education," Mr. Farmer said thoughtfully. "What about a natural education? We could study the sciences."

"Wot sciences?" The boy's face screwed up suspiciously, but Judah could see the tutor had captured his interest.

"Biology and botany," said Mr. Farmer. "Those are particular interests of mine. History should interest you, because of the politics. And there are many wars."

Eddy rubbed his nose. "I'm not interested in dead people."

"Recent history then," Mr. Farmer said. "Current events."

"And no Latin?"

"There will have to be some Latin," Judah said. "Because of the classifications. But you don't have to learn it well enough to speak it."

Eddy kicked the lowest stair. "I suppose I can give it a try."

"Why don't we show Mr. Farmer up to his room?" Judah suggested.

" 'e isn't sleeping in my room," Eddy growled.

"No, the study has been transformed into Mr. Farmer's realm," Judah said.

"You love your study," Eddy said, surprised.

"We shall use the parlor more often." He pointed the boy upstairs and Lawrence came to help them with the tutor's possessions. One thing was clear. Now that he could afford a larger home he needed one as soon as possible. He had already promised Penny he would bring someone in to help her with the heavy work, since he did not want to turn Eddy into a servant. He was more of a godson.

Another week passed, full of clashes between Eddy and the entire household. He was happy to go out with Mr. Farmer, looking on such flora and fauna they could find in London in November, purchasing books and visiting museums, but hated every moment he was at his desk in the tutor's room. He disappeared once for half a day, but showed up for tea.

The first Monday in December was Beth's day. She was to be presented to the Queen at St. James Palace. A many hour process, they would go by carriage to Westminster, then wait in the Gallery until being admitted to the drawing room where Queen Victoria awaited. Thankfully, being the daughter and sister of a marquess would speed up the events since the girls were presented in order of precedence.

Hatbrook had placed Judah in charge of Aunt Mary's well-being, while he managed Beth and his wife, so Judah had no ability to escape the events.

Hours into the long day, they stood in the Picture Gallery, a long room full of large royal portraits and not nearly enough fireplaces. Beth fussed with the feathers in her hair and Alys kept a sharp eye on her sister-in-law's train. Aunt Mary had been allowed to sit in one of the plush, built-in seats along the wall, quite close to the small fireplace.

Beth looked very different out of mourning, younger and a bit fragile, especially dressed in white. Her hair, untouched by sun at this time of year, seemed a darker shade than usual. He thought she had dared to put some sort of cosmetic on her lips, for they were stained red. She looked nothing like either of her parents as he remembered them, though she did look like Hatbrook.

He stared down the long room at all the other families with their daughters. His brother had made the rounds, talking to his counterparts, but Judah stayed close to his aunt and wondered. Was his father in the room? With that came a burst of shame. If he knew his parentage, would that have made a difference to Magdalene? If he was secure in his blue blood, would she have said yes?

A footman called for Lady Elizabeth Shield. Judah helped Aunt Mary to her feet, and walked with her to the door of the drawing room, where Queen Victoria and some of her family waited. No Prince of Wales, though. Through the door, he could see the great, glittering chandelier in the center of the room, but once again, only a small fireplace. Those who said the Queen liked a chilly room were not exaggerating.

He watched through one of the doorways as Beth made her first curtsy and was kissed on the forehead by the Queen, a privilege of her rank. A round of curtsies showed his sister's grace to the other royalties, then with one final curtsy to the Queen, she backed slowly out of the room, her train draped gracefully over her arm.

Judah glanced over and saw Alys, her eyes shining, as Beth executed flawlessly.

"A footman had to help me with my train," Alys confided. "I was not nearly so graceful in the spring when I was presented."

Aunt Mary took his arm when she reached the door, leaning heavily upon it. Now, he saw she was showing her age.

"Are you leaving London soon?" Judah inquired.

"In a couple of days. Everyone is away from Town at this time of year, so there is no need to attend parties. Are you returning to Heathfield with us?"

"No. I am very busy at Redcake's."

"I understand from Hatbrook that you have come into a fortune." Aunt Mary's eyes were shrewd under drooping eyelids. "Why are you still working there?"

"I like it and I need to keep occupied."

Aunt Mary patted his hand. "You have had some heartbreak, I expect. That is when young folk like to stay busy."

"I expect you are right."

"You will forget the girl when the next pretty face comes along."

"I hope you are right."

When the family party clustered together, he saw Beth's skin was goose-pimpled around the chest and arms. Her low-cut, short-sleeve gown was highly inappropriate for the season. Was the Queen attempting to kill off the brightest flowers of the aristocracy?

"Where is your cloak?" he asked.

"In the carriage," Beth said. "I could not bring it in."

"There is no reason to stay?"

"Do you want to mingle?" Hatbrook asked Beth.

She shook her head. "I will meet everyone in the spring, when it is warmer."

Judah tucked Aunt Mary tightly against his body to warm her, then followed the party outside to the carriages. Somehow, in the general tumult, he ended up alone in a carriage with his brother.

"I might have another lead for you," Hatbrook said, leaning back with an exhausted air and picking up a ham sandwich from a hamper.

"Tell me more," Judah said, reaching for a sandwich of his own.

"I might have a line on a servant who was with our family when you were born," he said. "When you come down at Christmas you can interview him."

"That is weeks from now. Can't I send him a letter?"

"It might not be the sort of thing you want to hear about in a letter," Hatbrook cautioned.

Judah narrowed his eyes. "You know something."

Hatbrook swallowed. "You need to hear it from this person. I do not know any details as of yet."

"Do your best to get them," Judah said. "I'll write a note for you to take back, if you don't mind."

"Of course not." Hatbrook sighed, and turned the conversation to the even less pleasant subject of Magdalene's departure and Judah's future marital plans.

After an age, they arrived at Hatbrook House, where they stayed up late into the night, Beth reliving her triumph, comparing notes with Alys about her presentation.

Gawain glowered from a corner most of the evening, though he did manage to stay close to Beth. Judah eventually interested his friend in a game of chess, once he'd written his letter imploring information from Hatbrook's contact, and it was after midnight before he departed for home. His walk to Redcake's in the morning was made triply dreary by the weather, no Magdalene, and no Eddy.

As usual, he'd heard the start of the day's arguments between Eddy and Mr. Farmer before he'd managed to leave his bedchamber. It took numerous strong cups of tea to get him through breakfast. He could not wait to put up his feet by the cozy fireplace in his office and read the newspapers. Hales met him at the door, however, ruining his plans by announcing a caller instead of handing him a tea tray.

Sir Octavian Feathercote was a couple of inches shorter than the average man. Still, Magdalene suspected he could have been called a pocket Adonis in his youth, for he was quite handsome considering he was closer to forty than thirty-five. His son was a charming imp of ten years and promised to have his father's masculine beauty in a few years.

They were a pleasant duo, though somewhat morbid on the subject of the late Lady Feathercote. Still, an obsession with the dead had been a feature of Society for Magdalene's lifetime. One had to be nearly Sir Octavian's age to remember a time when death had not been so celebrated in England.

Every day, Sir Octavian and his son walked to Lady Varney's home from their own mansion a few doors down. Magdalene might have enjoyed their company if not for the stultifying presence of Lady Varney. She, a couple of decades older than her nephew, could speak of nothing but her vapors and weaknesses. Magdalene suspected these were due to the lady eating almost nothing, while consuming too much whisky in her tea. She claimed it cleared her lung congestion.

Sir Octavian was excessively attentive to his aunt. She might have expected he was waiting to inherit a fortune, but if he needed one, he could find a wife with money, and the fact that he was interested in Magdalene meant this was not his object.

The upstairs maid assigned to Magdalene during her stay came into her room, where she was straightening her work box, and thinking longingly of cake ices and dyes rather than embroidery silks.

"Sir Octavian is downstairs for you," reported the maid.

"It is much too early for his call," she said, turning away from a clump of mixed orange and red silks. Lady Varney had given her the materials to embroider a bird for a pillow. Sir Octavian always came promptly at four, after his son's lessons were complete for the day.

"He has come alone," the maid said, dimpling. "And Lady Varney is not in the room."

Thank heavens. Magdalene instantly dropped a veil over that thought, but she was so bored. How had she not considered how she would miss the bustle of London? The excitement of Redcake's? The hurly-burly of her family home? Even with her nephews gone, Manfred still added a degree of liveliness. She even missed Hetty, who had in truth been her closest companion for months before Redcake's had entered her life.

She had expected the society of her cousin, but Lillian had been largely absent during these few weeks. Constance had whispered that her cousin was troubled by nausea. From this Magdalene had deduced that Lillian had conceived an heir for her viscount.

Constance herself was forever being sent on one errand or another and she wondered if Lady Varney was keeping her admittedly lovely friend far away from her nephew. If there was a tale to be told, Constance was not sharing it.

"Do you think we ought to dress you in your afternoon dress?" the housemaid asked.

Magdalene stared down at herself. She had inexplicably brought along her cakie uniform, and had been wearing it during the mornings that she spent alone. Her true mourning garments were few in number. "Yes, of course. How silly of me to forget."

Quickly, the maid set out the gown while Magdalene divested herself of her simple dress, then helped with tightening her corset and doing up the buttons on the back.

Fifteen minutes later, Magdalene entered the morning parlor, dressed quite the same as Sir Octavian always saw her.

"I have brought you a token," he announced, handing her a small box.

"Sir Octavian," Magdalene said, surprised. She sat down on the sofa in front of the fire, next to the high-backed armchair where he had placed himself. How irregular to offer her a gift, but she did not want to discourage her suitor. She opened the box to find a pair of black onyx earrings. Set in rose gold, a circle of teardrop-shaped stones surrounded a round stone.

They would not compliment her coloring in the least, but she recognized both their fashionable style and the appropriateness of the stones, given that she was in mourning.

"Thank you," she said. "I shall wear them at dinner tonight."

"I hope you will invite me to the meal, with my great-aunt's permission, of course."

"I am sure she would approve," Magdalene said, startled by the request. Why was he suggesting she had any power over dinner guests?

"As your betrothed," Sir Octavian said smoothly. Then he colored. "No, no, I have been presumptuous."

Magdalene put her hand over her heart. The moment had come. An eligible proposal. Yet, she felt nothing so much as exhaustion. Captain Shield's proposal had made her want to run, but this proposal made her want to hide under her bedclothes. If only she could switch the two men.

No, she could not see Captain Shield here in Harrogate. If he was this kind of man, he'd live at Hatbrook Farm with his family. He craved the hurly-burly of London just as much as she did.

"Sir Octavian?" It came out as a croak.

His hands fluttered. "Oh my dear, you must feel faint. I insist, take a day or two to think about it. I know it is an enormous step for a maiden to take. My dear Lady Feathercote took two months to make her decision. You are not such a delicate flower as she, nor so youthful, but nonetheless, though my cousin the earl assures me you are more than willing, I insist you think prayerfully on the matter. Cedric and I will not grace my great-aunt's door this afternoon. I shall attend on you in two days." He stood and bowed stiffly, then walked out of the room in a manner that suggested he wanted to run.

In that moment, she liked him better than before. He had surprised himself, she supposed, by his embarrassment. She suspected he had only proposed twice in his life and, given his propensity to maudlin thoughts, it no doubt overwhelmed him to remember the first happy occasion.

She stared at the unsatisfactory earrings. Was accepting the baronet nothing more than a prelude to a twilight kind of life? Could she ever be as important to him as his first wife had been?

"I was not sure if you would want to see him," Hales said, a nervous edge to his voice.

Judah noticed a reddened spot just above the man's collar. A bite of some kind? Then the mystery cleared. Hales had a love bite on his neck. He wondered which lady had created the mark.

"But since he is Miss Cross's brother," Hales continued.

Judah forgot about the mystery of Ewan Hales's neck. "Manfred or George?"

"George, sir."

"How very odd."

"Would you like your tray, sir?"

"When Cross goes."

Judah pushed open his office door and found George, thinner than before his wife died, and showing every one of the half decade of years he had on Judah, but dressed very soberly and correctly in dark clothing, with a black armband.

"Hello, Cross," he said, as the man scrambled to his feet. Judah offered his hand, then moved to the fireplace. Invariably, he had damp shoes and trouser bottoms after his trudge into Redcake's.

"Did you not take a cab? Beastly weather, what?" George followed him to the fireplace.

"I prefer to take the exercise. What brings you out so early in the morning?"

"I need your advice." He flung himself into Judah's favorite chair.

Had Magdalene announced her engagement? What would George Cross have to ask of him? A question of whether any of her former co-workers should be shipped to Yorkshire for the nuptials? Half-digested oatmeal churned in his stomach. "What about?"

"You may be aware that I have had some difficult times in the two months since my wife passed."

"Yes," Judah said, turning regretfully from the fire.

"Magdalene, I believe, has not forgiven me, nor should she, for my unspeakable behavior in my immediate grief."

He silently agreed. "How does this concern me?"

"She has not written to me since she left London."

Judah gripped the edge of the mantel. "She did reach Harrogate safely?"

George waved away his concern. "Oh yes. She wrote Manfred. And Lady March. And the earl."

Only now did Judah feel how strongly his heart was beating. "I am very glad to hear that."

"I did write her once, but she did not respond. I am concerned that she might have burned the letter unread, or something of that sort, since I begged a response and did not receive one."

"I have not written her, nor do I believe she was angry with me when she departed, so I cannot offer a similar tale. She had her back pay and I had no reason for further dealings with her as of some three weeks ago." Did he want money?

"Very good," George said. "I expected nothing less. But here is the problem I put to you. Lady March does not reside in London and the earl and his family are away, given the time of year. I have very little money to live on. I have realized only this past week how much Magdalene's wages here propped up my small household."

"Are you asking for employment?" Judah interjected, wanting to get to the point.

"No. I am asking your advice. Manfred is very ill, very ill indeed. Magdalene does not know. If I write her, you see, she will most likely not open the letter and there is no one else to write her. I wonder if you could, since you were her employer. She might assume it is Redcake's business. I feel she should know, especially since there is not much money for the doctor. I am so excessively grateful to Magdalene for paying Nancy's bills or the doctor would not come at all."

Judah's thoughts sharpened. "Is Manfred alone now?"

"No, our dear friend Mrs. Gortimer is with him, and she has not even asked for a salary. I could not leave him alone while I came here. It is that serious. Would you write Magdalene and ask her to come home?"

Chapter Eighteen

Judah inhaled. "Are you afraid Manfred's illness is mortal?"

George Cross's Adam's apple bobbed in his thin neck as he swallowed. "Manfred's fever is very high."

"Could you send Magdalene a telegram?"

"I have not the coin. If you could see your way to lend me a few pounds, old man? For expenses?"

"I will do one better. I will send the telegram and go to Harrogate to fetch her," Judah said, feeling buoyant. "She should be with her family and a telegram is too brief to adequately convey the situation. I shall merely state she must prepare to return, and then arrive with the news."

George put his hands to his cheeks. "That would be most excellent, sir."

"It will be the work of twenty-four hours or so. Send word to my office if there is any change with your brother's health," Judah said. He hesitated to give the man money, remembering Magdalene's complaints about George and expensive claret. "I will leave you now, in order to catch the afternoon train."

George bowed. "I cannot thank you enough."

Judah turned, squelching a little in his wet shoes, and went to instruct Hales to send the telegram and remove George from his office. He would send Simon Hellman to his house, to instruct his valet to pack a valise, and then meet him at King's Cross Station.

Two hours later, Judah was on the train going north. The weather had continued to be brutally cold and every time they reached an incline in altitude, he saw more snow on the ground. Snow on the tracks slowed the train and it was late into the evening when he arrived at the train station, in a part of England he'd never been to. His mood stayed positive, though he did wonder at how Manfred did. Should he have given George money?

He'd brought very little luggage, just a valise with a change of clothing and a selection of paperwork Hatbrook's man of business had provided, with suggested houses to purchase and investments to make. When he saw a porter, he detained him long enough to acquire the direction to Lord Bricker's home, which thankfully was not far distant. He hired a hansom and was at the house before the moon was any higher in the sky.

All the windows were dark there despite the relatively early hour. He knocked on the door, and eventually a butler answered.

"I am Captain Shield, come to accompany Magdalene Cross home," he announced.

"Ah, yes, sir. I gave Lady Bricker your telegram since Miss Cross is not in residence."

"She is not? Did she leave for London already?"

"No, sir. She has never been here."

Judah frowned. "What do you mean? She came to Harrogate weeks ago."

"Yes, sir, but she is in residence elsewhere."

"I would like to see Lady Bricker as soon as possible." Leave it to the dratted woman to complicate things as much as possible.

"Her ladyship is not available to callers at this hour."

He gritted his teeth, the long day of inactivity starting to catch up to him. "It is a family emergency. One of her relatives is near death."

"I see." The butler stepped aside. "Please come in."

He was led to a parlor where the fire was lit. Ten minutes later a tea tray was brought, and twenty minutes after that Lady Bricker arrived, dressed in a simple gown and looking very pale.

"You are unwell," Judah said, taking her hand as she offered it.

He could see little resemblance between this wan, plump young lady and Magdalene. "I am so sorry to disturb you."

"I understand you are here on urgent business. My butler said the telegram that arrived announced a family emergency, but it was addressed to my cousin so I sent it to Lady Varney's home with a footman this afternoon."

"Miss Cross is at this Lady Varney's home?"

"Yes. She is the great-aunt and confidante of Sir Octavian Feathercote."

He couldn't care less. "I apologize for disturbing you, but I must see Miss Cross. I promised her brother I would return her to London."

"Who is ill, Lord Judah?"

"Captain Shield," he corrected. "It is her brother, Manfred. George Cross told me that Manfred's fever is dangerously high."

"Has a doctor been to see him?"

"Yes."

"Then it is unlikely to be the imaginings of a drunkard," Lady Bricker murmured. "Hopefully my cousin read the telegram. For now, I have instructed the housekeeper to air a guest room for you."

"I need to go to Lady Varney's." He wanted to ask if Magdalene had become engaged. It was not a polite question, but this was Lady Bricker, after all.

"Not tonight. It is too late. It is snowing heavily, and there is no train until morning. I shall instruct the housekeeper to send a footman at the crack of dawn, and have Miss Cross delivered here before the morning train."

"She will want the news."

"As she can do nothing tonight, it is best to leave her in ignorance, I think. After all, she has already received the message to pack. I am sorry I am not good company." She went even paler, and covered her mouth.

Judah leapt to his feet and shoved his empty plate under her chin. When she grabbed it, he ran for the bellpull. He hovered over her shoulder while she retched, daring to spread a cloth napkin over her gown when it was needed.

A maid rushed into the room, and seeing what was transpiring, said, "I'll fetch a basin, my lord."

Soon, the housekeeper arrived, and a footman. The soiled articles were cleared away and Lady Bricker was helped to her feet.

"I am so sorry I took you from your bed," Judah called, regretful that he had learned no details about Magdalene.

"I am like this all the time," she said mournfully. "You can see why my cousin could not stay here."

A few minutes later, the housekeeper returned and led Judah to a bedroom overlooking the front door. He peered out the window as a maid ran a warming pan over his sheets. The snow was coming down hard. He could see there really was nothing to do but go to bed. Insisting a footman go out in that weather to deliver a note would accomplish nothing.

As a soldier, he had trained himself to have an internal clock and he woke at about six, to a cold, pitch black room. He changed into his spare clothing and packed his few belongings, then looked out the window. It had not kept snowing all night. While there was snow on the ground, it was hardly blizzard conditions.

He took his valise in hand and went downstairs. A footman saw him and directed him into the dining room.

"I am sorry, my lord," the housekeeper said, coming in. "We do not keep early hours in this household, but I shall bring you eggs, toast, and tea right away."

"Has a footman gone to Lady Varney's home?"

"Yes, half an hour ago. He was to suggest they send Miss Cross and a maid in a carriage here, then you could go to the train station together."

"When do you think they will come?"

"In an hour, I believe."

Judah ate his breakfast, then was allowed into the library where he passed the time looking at the viscount's collection. He had a goodly amount of volumes about the natural history of this part of the country, but little else. So, he settled himself with the papers until he heard bustling and voices in the hall.

He opened the door and stepped out. Magdalene stood there, dressed in her same shabby black coat and crepe-covered bonnet. He thought she'd lost a little weight, and she had circles under her eyes, but she was still the most beautiful sight he'd ever set his eyes upon.

Blood drained from her cold-stung cheeks when she saw him. "Captain Shield! What is the meaning of this?"

"It is Manfred. George sent me for you. Will you come?" He held his breath, wondering if she would turn him down in favor of staying here in her new surroundings. Given the weather, she had every reason to refuse to travel.

Her gloved hands went to her mouth. "Manfred? What has happened?"

"A high fever. Mrs. Gortimer has been caring for him, I believe, and a doctor."

"Is he at risk?" she whispered.

"George believed so. I said I would come."

Her hands shook as they lowered to her waist. "You should be at Redcake's. And since you are not, I must infer the seriousness of the matter."

"I have not seen Manfred myself," he admitted.

"Nor should you, or you could infect half the ladies in London through the tea shop," she declared. "Are you ready to leave? We should go to the station immediately. It is slow going out there."

A footman brought his coat and other possessions and they were back out the door into the black winter morning within a couple of minutes. They reached the train station with acceptable speed, but at that point all seemed to slow to a pre-coming-of-the-railway level. The snow started again, keeping the skies leaden and the tracks dangerous.

Magdalene woke as the train jerked to a stop. She glanced around, blinking, only half aware of where she was. "Are we in London yet?" She reached out a hand and brushed Captain Shield's knee, then snatched it back.

After insisting the maid return to Lady Varney's home since she was developing an illness that Magdalene could not afford to have, she had put herself at the captain's mercy. But, any fantasy she might have had, that he'd come to whisk her away, to seduce her from the life she was so close to accepting, had vanished since he'd scarcely said a word to her.

"We have only been on the train for four hours."

"Oh. Where does that put us? Leicester?"

"We have only made it to Doncaster. I just saw the sign."

"Doncaster? But that is less than fifty miles or so from Harrogate."

"Quite." The captain's voice was clipped. "We have been traveling at a snail's pace due to the snow."

A conductor opened the door of the compartment. "I am afraid there is too much snow on the tracks to continue, ladies and gentlemen. We are only a five-minute walk from Doncaster proper. I would suggest you look for accommodations in town."

"There is too much snow for the train, but you expect us to walk to town?" Captain Shield asked. "What about the women?"

"The truly heavy snows are about ten miles south of here. I do not think you should have trouble walking to town. But I would not dally." His speech was lent charm by his Yorkshire accent, but the words were no less alarming for the charm.

"Should we hire a carriage?" Magdalene asked. "I need to get to Manfred."

"Better to wait for the train," the captain said. "We've days to travel by carriage and only hours by rail. Come, let us find an inn before all the rooms are full."

She took his arm, feeling the muscles bunch, even under the thick wool of his greatcoat. He still had his valise, but she only had her reticule. The stationmaster promised all the baggage would be kept under lock and key. They hurried along with the crowd. Many dashed into the first inn they came across.

"Let us keep going," Judah suggested, passing by the inn. Next came a row of shops. One caught Magdalene's eye.

"Wait," she said, tugging on his arm. "Can we go into the telegraph office and send a telegram to George? I do not want them to worry and he can send word back to us in care of the office."

"Very well," he said, allowing her to pull him into the building.

Quickly, she wrote out a note and Captain Shield gave it to the operator and paid for it. Within five minutes, she also had directions to all the inns in town, which she thought was adequate recompense for the stop.

"Let us go to the inn two streets over. That is least likely to be overrun by the passengers." She took his arm again and they moved as quickly as possible through the steadily drifting snow.

Unfortunately, street traffic was heavy and when they entered the inn they discovered it was full.

"I am Lord Judah Shield," the captain said.

Magdalene jerked her head in his direction. He was using his aristocratic title instead of his military one? He must be worried.

"And this is my wife."

Magdalene froze. No, he wasn't stubbornly declaring ownership despite her rejection of him; he was trying to give her higher status in order to find her a bed for the night.

"I am truly sorry, my lord. The only accommodations we have are stalls in the stable. Ideal for a bachelor of low birth, but certainly not you or your wife."

"Any suggestions for us? We are stranded by the train and I would imagine the other two inns are full by now."

"There is a boarding house behind us, my lord. We share the alley. I would try there, or Mrs. Miller's house on that same street. She is a widow who takes in the occasional boarder as well."

"Thank you." Captain Shield tugged Magdalene's arm and pulled her out of the lobby.

She was mortified. "We shouldn't have stopped. I'm so sorry."

"Do not trouble yourself. It is completely understandable that your brother would be paramount in your thoughts."

"You have gone to so much trouble for us. Why, Captain Shield?"

"Call me Judah," he said, pulling her closely against his body as they crossed the alley and walked through a snowy side yard. "We are husband and wife in Doncaster."

Little did he know he'd rescued her from having to give Sir Octavian her answer this morning. The mere thought of the word "wife" was enough to give her a megrim. Why wasn't she excited to receive the proposal? She would be Lady Feathercote, a high-ranking member of local Society.

Perhaps it was because she knew she would never outrank Lady Varney, or Lady Bricker, two extremely strong personalities. It had never troubled her before to not be at the top, as long as she was a part of Society, but at least as a Scandalous Cross she had stood apart, part of a tribe with a very specific identity, rather than a colorless younger member of a local family.

"Here we are," Judah said, pointing to the sign in the window of a large house.

They were turned away here too, all the rooms having been filled. They walked down the block, feet leaving tracks in the snow.

"This will be Mrs. Miller's," Judah said.

The house looked very small. "We may end up sleeping at the train station," Magdalene said. Her voice sounded hollow in the snow-dampened air.

"Chin up," Judah said, tugging her up the steps. He tapped the door knocker on the plate and a couple of minutes later, the door opened to show a robust lady in her late fifties.

"Mrs. Miller?" Judah asked. "The innkeeper at the Doncaster Arms said you might have a room. I am Lord Judah Shield and my wife and I have been stranded by the weather."

"Is that all the luggage you have?"

"The rest is at the station."

She clucked. "Come in, then. I do have a small room with a double bed. Not what you quality are used to, but I'm sure young people like you can make do for a night or two."

Magdalene turned to Judah. He caught her look of horror and raised an eyebrow, then squeezed her shoulder. The warning was obvious. *Say nothing or we'll be sleeping at the station.*

"You are most kind," Judah said.

"I expected guests what with the weather today, so the room is ready. Would you like to dine first? I have some fresh bread and stew. Normally I would not offer food this early in the day, you understand, but I am sure it has been a trying day for you both."

"Thank you," Magdalene said. "But I think I would rather go to our room."

Judah's expression remained distant as Mrs. Miller expressed surprise. "Oh dear, my lady, you must be soaked through. Come upstairs then. I hope your husband has a change of clothes for you in that bag."

Of course, he had nothing of the kind, but not five minutes later she and her false husband were ensconced in a room in the back of the house. Mrs. Miller had the fire going, though she assured them that this was the warmest room of the house, because it was over the kitchen.

"I'll have to charge extra for the coal, of course. We do not usually have fires in the bedrooms, but on a day like today it seems necessary."

"You are too kind," Judah said, pressing shillings into the lady's hand and gently maneuvering her to the door.

"We are lucky there is a fireplace," Magdalene said, a little faint at the idea of being alone with him in a bedroom. She had certainly joined the ranks of the Scandalous Cross women today.

"You're shivering," Judah said, pulling the one armchair in the room directly in front of the fire.

"I don't have anything to change into." Nor was there a screen she could change behind if she had anything.

"You can wear my nightshirt," he said. "Take your shoes and stockings off. We can get those dry easily enough."

"Captain! You are talking about my garments."

"Judah," he corrected. "You cannot afford to become ill. You will be nursing your brother soon."

"We should go back to the telegraph desk," she said. "My brother may have written back."

"He told me he had no money for telegrams," Judah countered.

"Manfred always has a few shillings to spare," she said. "Unless George has found it and spent it on claret."

"He was sober when he came to Redcake's. But I didn't give him any money, mindful of what you've said."

"You keep being forced into my family's business. I am sorry for that."

"I love you," he said, kneeling at the side of the armchair. "I have not stopped loving you, even though you rejected me and left me."

"Oh, Judah," she whispered. Why wouldn't he let her go? Why couldn't she do the same? She should have accepted Lord Octavian's proposal instantly.

"Are you engaged to the baronet?" he asked.

She dropped her head into her hand and rubbed her forehead. "No."

He made a noise, but she couldn't quite interpret it. She squeaked though, when she found his hands above her knees, expertly removing her garters and rolling down her stockings. No man had ever touched her thighs. Her flesh heated where his fingers landed.

"Your shoes are soaked," he said, working at the stiff leather. "And your legs are like ice blocks."

"Kindly do not discuss my limbs," she said, wishing his hands were on her thighs again. She felt like a damsel in distress with a knight worshipping at her feet.

"Then let us discuss the baronet. Has he not come up to snuff, or have you rejected him?"

She gritted her teeth as he pulled her wet stockings off her feet, then began to massage her toes. Should she push him away or run? Or stay . . . ? But the feelings his touch provoked could bring about madness. She could feel the sensations evoked traveling up her cold calves. As each stroke of his fingers warmed her, it sent sparks of heat into places they had no business going. Her belly, her breasts, even between her legs. Even her lips felt puffy and hot. No unmarried woman should be put in this position. She was not made of stern stuff where he was concerned.

"Magdalene?"

"Neither," she said. "He proposed, but kindly gave me time to think it over. Then you came, before my deadline."

"Deadline. What a romantic way to consider a proposal." His warm hands closed around her heels.

She pulled her feet away. "They are quite warm now. You must be soaked."

"Good point." He sat on the floor and calmly removed his own shoes and socks, then put both sets of footwear and stockings on the screen in front of the fire. His toes were long and elegant, but pale with cold.

"Your lower attire is soaked as well," she remarked, amazed by her own daring. She should not have looked.

"I'll take off my trousers if you take off your petticoat and dress. They are equally damp."

Before she could think up a reply, there was a knock at the door. Mrs. Miller came in, balancing a tea tray.

"I thought you might like this," she said cheerfully, setting it down on the trunk at the foot of the small bed.

Magdalene tucked her feet into her dress as Judah jumped up to shield her. "Thank you, Mrs. Miller. I believe my wife would like to rest now."

Mrs. Miller looked her over, as if to assess if she had a reason to be tired. Magdalene let her hands creep over her flat belly. If it gave them some privacy it was worth the deception.

"Of course," said the lady knowingly. "Dinner will be at seven.

We gather in the parlor for a scripture reading at a quarter to the hour."

"Excellent," Judah said, rubbing his hands together.

Magdalene stared at the teapot while he moved the woman out of the room.

"No lock," Judah reported. "I would wish for a spare chair to hook under the doorknob."

"She will not interrupt us again. She thinks I am with child," Magdalene told him.

Judah shook his head. "We are getting ahead of ourselves. Now, as to your engagement. Are you going to accept? Were you going to accept?"

"It matters little now. I cannot respond to him by letter or telegram. It shall have to wait until Manfred is recovered."

"What about me? Is it too brazen for me to suggest that, if you had no feelings for me, you might have found it easier to accept the man with alacrity?"

"Pour me a cup of tea, will you?" Magdalene asked.

"If it gives you time to think." His voice dropped into a seductive register.

She shivered, listening to the sound of the tea and cream being poured into a cup. Such quiet, domestic sounds. Outside the room it was silent, as if they were cast on a mighty ocean all by themselves. The stillness pressed in on her, just like her slimy cold garments. In that moment, she could take it no more, and began to unbutton the front of her dress. He took a flask from his pocket and doctored her tea.

She'd worn her cakie uniform, which was easy to remove, but when it was off, she still felt covered in slime. So next, she pulled off her flannel petticoat. Not good enough. The linen one was next, until nothing covered her lower limbs but her combinations.

She heard an exhalation and when she looked up, the teacup in Judah's hand was wavering dangerously. A step brought her to him, her hand under the teacup to steady it, but it was too late. The cup tipped and half of the contents cascaded over her corset cover.

Judah swore, pungent military words. She drank the rest of the cup down, taking the warmth into her belly while he dabbed at her chest with the tea towel. How she appreciated that he didn't flutter and move away as the baronet would have. It made her daring.

"I am tired of being cold," she announced, and unbuttoned her corset cover. Judah moved behind her and helped her with her corset. She dashed into bed, still in her combinations. "Do not join me while a stitch of damp clothing is on."

He stood there, damp garments hanging from his fingers. "You want me to join you?"

"How else are we to get warm?" Her teeth chattered. "You know my feet are like ice and the rest of me is not much better."

With an unreadable expression, Judah set her clothes over the chair by the fire, then began to disrobe. Men's clothing did not obscure the body to the extent women's did, but she still reveled in each moment a new part of him was revealed. The muscular calf, the strong shoulder, the tight buttock.

"You are removing everything?" All of a sudden she second-guessed herself. How far was she willing to go?

"My dear girl, I am wet all over. The baggage, damp with snow, pressed against me as I walked, as did your coat." He walked toward her.

She did not mean to let her gaze drift lower, but it did. "Oh my," she squeaked, when she saw his manhood, jutting arrogantly forward through a nest of dark curls. She wanted to curl her fingers around it, taste it. How scandalous.

The bed sank as he climbed in. They could not avoid touching each other on the narrow mattress, but it was what she'd wanted, why she'd dared him to join her. For warmth, for one taste of scandal. She reached out her hand, inviting him closer.

"Why, Magdalene?"

"I am cold?"

He stared at her. She could see doubt in his features, and resolve. "You are nothing like a Society miss. You are too strong, too daring. I know you want to be that perfect marriage mart candidate, but I admire you so for what you truly are."

"My character defects have not prevented me from receiving two excellent proposals," she said, distracted by the way he put his arm around her.

"I hope mine was one of them." His lips came down on hers then, before she could think of a response.

Could she be dreaming? Because she was quite sure she had dreamed this every night for months. Her fingers pressed into the hard muscle on his marble-cold torso. Flat disks jutted against her palms, his nipples. When she ran her nails over them, he groaned into her mouth, thrust his tongue against hers. Every inch of her body pressed against his, pliant, like an ice sculpture melting into a warm, living Scandalous Cross woman. They warmed together.

Why had she fought her ruin for so long? This was paradise. Judah's lips left hers and she would have protested, except that they slid across her cheek and down her neck, to her collarbone. Only one garment remained between her skin and his, and it seemed as if he kissed it off. One moment, his fingers were whispering along the linen, and the next she felt absurdly hot flesh against her body. She had thought she was leaning on her elbow, sitting half up, but no, she was on her back and Judah was *everywhere*.

He moved too quickly for her to find time to protest. His hands cupped and molded her breasts, then drifted down to her waist while his mouth took over. She arched her back in response to the way his tongue raked hot streaks of pleasure from her nipples, but then his hands were on her thighs. Yes, her upper thighs. He circled her legs, coaxing them apart while she was still rattled, boneless, from the way his mouth caressed the undersides of her breasts.

Then, his fingers found the curls between her legs, but before she could react, his mouth was at the seam of her private place, hotly caressing the damp flesh open. She was a Cross girl, she knew about the pearl hidden underneath the hood there, but Judah could find it too.

She cried out, then put her forearm against her mouth and bit into her own flesh, trying to be quiet while his tongue did things she could only have imagined in her darkest, most erotic dreams. Writhing, she used her other hand to direct his head, trying to find the perfect place for his lips and tongue.

Perfection eluded her until she pulled back her legs, resting her feet on his shoulders. Distantly, she realized her toes were no longer cold. He had heated every small place on her body. But then, she forgot her body as it seized in delight, throwing her consciousness outside herself in a nimbus of stars. All because of Judah. Her head fell back and her chest heaved when she returned to earth. A few moments later, she blinked her eyes open to find Judah over her, staring down with tenderness in his eyes.

"You liked that?"

"I was born to experience that." Her tongue felt thick in her mouth. "I want all of it, Judah. I want all of you."

"Are you certain?"

"Cross women learn their bodies. I won't conceive your child today."

He nodded, a lock of hair falling over his forehead. She brushed it away and kissed him there.

"Just love me, Judah. We've both been waiting so long."

She could feel the tension in his shoulders as he settled himself over her body. When his hot manhood nestled between her legs, a glaze came over his eyes. He was already lost to pleasure and he wasn't even inside her. She ran her fingers down his back, his flank, then found the hard length of him. He groaned as she found her center with him and positioned the tip of him there.

Then, she found his hips with her fingers. His buttocks tightened and he thrust forward, opening her like a flower. She arched into him, moving past the pain that marked her first time, but couldn't quite stop a cry from piercing her lips.

Judah stopped moving, staring down at her. "You are a virgin?"

Chapter Nineteen

"I was two seconds ago," she panted. "Why are you stopping?" She felt a delicious edge of the cataclysmic glory she'd experienced with his mouth on her pearl, and wanted the sensation again.

"But you seemed so knowing. You wanted me so fervently."

She was panting. "Just because my mother explained the process to me, does not mean I indulged."

He began to roll off her, but she clutched his back. "Don't stop!"

"Magdalene, we shouldn't be doing this. You don't love me." His eyes were desperate.

"I never said that."

"You refused to marry me."

She kissed his neck. "We don't want the same things. But that doesn't mean I don't want you."

"How can you accept the proposal of the baronet when you might have my child in your belly?"

"I told you." She gently danced her fingers down his back, cupped his buttocks. "There are only a few days a month a woman can conceive. This isn't one of them."

He sighed. She could feel his chest move against hers. "I don't understand your family at all."

"You do not have to. You only need to understand me." She slid her legs up his, then crossed them around his back. "Love me, Judah, please."

"I can't stop," he groaned, pulling her hands from him and sliding his fingers in between hers. He began to move then, long luxurious strokes inside her that seemed to simultaneously tear her apart and knit her together again.

"Judah," she whispered. "I adore you." She lifted her legs into the air, feeling the angle of their joining change and deepen. Sore, stretched, amazed, she couldn't decide how this all felt. She only knew she had been missing something indescribable.

"Love me," he commanded. "Tell me you love me."

"I do."

"Tell me." He thrust so deeply that she cried out.

She tried to pull her hand away from his, but he would not let go. His gaze, intense with exertion, found hers.

"Tell me."

"I love you," she whispered.

His mouth descended on hers. The deep, drugging kisses, stronger than any opiate, took command of her senses. She could do nothing but embrace him and let the passion take over. When he cried out, moving against her with intense depth and speed, she lost control of herself again, her entire being spiraling into a wave of pleasure.

Then, it was only them, warm and cozy in the tiny bed, falling asleep after a long, draining day.

They spent the long day and night together, in a lover's wordless happy haze, napping and making love. It was only when Judah sat beside Magdalene the next day on the train that he realized they had said little. He'd been too overwhelmed by the sights and scents of her strong, slim, feminine body to talk, still unbelieving that she'd given herself to him when she planned to marry another.

Now, they could not converse. The train was crammed full of people who had been stranded by the storm. He'd had to stand while she sat. When they arrived in London, it was even worse. No cabs could be found, and they had a dangerous trek through the snow on foot. By then, Magdalene was tense with worry for Manfred. No telegram had arrived at the small Doncaster telegraph office before they'd left.

At her brother's house, Magdalene let herself inside.

"I should come with you," Judah said. "I might be able to run for the doctor or do some other errand."

"Hetty is here, and George," she said. "Come tomorrow."

"Magdalene." He hated the pleading in his voice. Why was it necessary when she had said she loved him? Yet he had the distinct sensation that nothing had been resolved between them.

"Come tomorrow," she repeated. "I do not want you ill."

He frowned as she shut the door without so much as a kiss goodbye. She did not behave as he expected a woman in love would, but they had been two days without news of Manfred. Also, he had no reason to think she did love him. She'd only said so in the throes of passion. As he regained the street, he remembered his other responsibilities. Eddy and Redcake's. Surely they deserved his attention too, especially when he'd abandoned them so precipitously.

He walked home, balancing carefully on the snow-covered icy streets, forcing himself to pay attention to his feet, rather than to worries about Magdalene or memories of their night together.

At the door, Lawrence met him, looking exhausted.

"Have you slept since I left?" Judah asked.

"I could ask the same, Captain."

"It was a long journey through bad weather. What is your reason?"

"Did you know the lad has nightmares? He has woken us up at least thrice a night since you've been gone."

Judah frowned. "I never heard anything when I was here."

"Strange, isn't it? But he isn't bamming."

"A larger house will allow at least some of us to sleep. I have some residences to look at when I have time." He heard a clattering on the steps and Eddy appeared, looking a little wild-eyed but otherwise less injured than when Judah had left.

"Is Miss Cross's brother recovered?" Eddy asked.

"I do not know," Judah said, handing Lawrence his things. "But I delivered her to her brother's door. I shall call tomorrow."

"I do not like Mr. Farmer," Eddy said next.

"Think of him as a customer you must please," Judah advised. "Now, if you do not mind, I would like a bath. Lawrence, can you bring me hot water?"

"Yes, Captain." Lawrence went down the hall.

"I'm not a scholar," Eddy said. "I want to work with my hands."

"You haven't been here long," Judah told him. "Give this a chance."

Eddy frowned. "I could sell papers again."

"You don't need to work. For a boy in your position, this new life should be a dream come true."

"I never dreamed of it." He crossed his arms.

Judah stopped, trying to warm his feet. "Speaking of dreams, why are you having nightmares?"

Eddy shrugged. "Not 'appy, I suppose."

Judah scrubbed his face with his hands. "I have a great deal to do today. We shall continue this discussion another time." He climbed the stairs, ready to do his valet's job and lay out clothing, all the quicker to check on Redcake's.

After an afternoon hunched over papers in his office, he came home to an acrimonious dinner at his table, followed by a busy Saturday morning at Redcake's. With a little over two weeks to go to Christmas, the upper classes were gone from London but everyone else was ready to celebrate. Early in the afternoon though, he broke himself away to call at the Cross home.

Magdalene was napping in a chair next to Manfred when Hetty appeared at the door.

"Captain Shield is downstairs," the maid reported.

"Can George see him?" She yawned and stretched, half-asleep. Seeing the captain in a weakened, exhausted state made her fear she would say something she shouldn't, reveal some private part of herself. That was, if she had any privacy remaining, given their night together.

"I think he has a touch of the fever himself now. He's asleep."

Magdalene groaned. They all needed to be well or her nephews would be shipped to her uncle's country home for the holidays rather than to London. She stood slowly and walked to the basin and poured in a little water so she could clean her face and her hands.

On the way downstairs she looked at herself. Her dress was old, but at least she'd changed it that morning. Besides, Judah liked her disheveled. He appreciated an active and occupied woman, rather than a perfect Society miss. Maybe she was incapable of being the woman she had expected to be. Certainly she had been bored at Lady Varney's home.

When she saw Judah in the parlor, sitting in an armchair, his head back and eyes closed, the picture of exhaustion, she wanted to crawl into his lap and curl up against him. If not for Manfred, she would wish them back in Doncaster. Quietly, she closed the parlor door and tiptoed up to him.

His eyes opened and a lazy smile brightened his face. "Maggie."

She blushed. He had called her that for the first time in Doncaster. "Hello, Judah."

He stood and moved to a sofa, then patted the space next to him. His tiger eyes seemed to steal the light from the gas sconces and they glowed with intensity.

She felt a moment's unease. Would he pounce? "Hetty will be here soon with tea."

"I told her not to bother."

"Oh." She sat next to him and arranged her skirt, then folded her hands primly in her lap. Would he demand a kiss?

Judah inclined his head. When he glanced up again she saw he now wore a civil mask and it was as if the hunger she had sensed in him had departed. "How is Manfred? I stayed away as long as I could, but I must know. You might have sent a note."

She had considered it, but as she had stared down at the paper, did not know what to write. "I am sorry. I should have done so. I know you have been worried too."

He patted her shoulder, his big hands awkward on her, in a way they had not been when they were naked together. "I know you have been too busy to think of me."

She shivered at the memory of their bodies entwined. "On the contrary. It has been a challenge to think of anything else."

His lips twitched. "I feel quite the same way, occupied as I have been with my household and Redcake's. I did have news waiting for me. The marchioness has become an aunt, courtesy of her sister Matilda, who is recovering. But how is Manfred?"

She took a deep breath of his exotic scent, remembering how it had stayed on her flesh for a full day after she had come home. "Manfred is well enough. His fever was very high for six hours after I arrived. Hetty said he had some kind of seizure, but he has been awake a little and his fever is all but gone."

"He seems in his right mind?" He folded his hands over his knee, quite deliberately.

She thought he'd considered putting his hands elsewhere. "Yes, and he can move his appendages. George is becoming ill now."

"It is very contagious then. Should you be here?"

"I rarely become ill. My brothers were always more susceptible."

"Make sure you eat and sleep," he advised. "It makes a great deal of difference, I've always noticed."

She smiled at the advice. "I will, Auntie Judah."

He laughed. "I gave Hetty a basket of Redcake's treats. I even liberated some scotch trifle that is the specialty at the holidays." He reached for her hand and pressed it between his two palms. "I will not keep you away from your brothers. I know this is not the time to discuss our future. Please consider it though. I will call again soon."

He stood. His look upon her was serious and loving all at once. She felt the warm glow of his concern for her. It didn't diminish as he left the room.

She sat for a moment in the cold parlor. He had been respectful. He had brought a gift. She appreciated that, given that she'd all but declared herself a loose woman. What kind of future did he have in mind? Did he still want to marry her? Could she be happy with him?

She dropped her head into her hands. His kindness left her with more questions than answers.

Sunday passed in a haze of nursing her brothers. Judah did not return, nor could she have expected him to. On Monday, she found letters from Harrogate in the morning's post.

One note was from Cousin Lillian, expressing exasperation that she'd left and inquiring as to whether the baronet had made any declaration of intent. Lady Varney had penned a stiff note of concern for her family. And Constance had written as well, with tremendous news.

Magdalene, I know other concerns are paramount to you at this time, but I wanted you to have this bit of pleasant news. I shall not have to stay in Yorkshire forever! My great-uncle has passed away. I knew him as a child, but he has been shut away for years and I had all but forgotten him. He left me a bequest! I will not have to work any longer. No Season for me, but perhaps I can find an excellent sort of gentleman.

Like Judah. He was exactly the sort of man who would do very well for Constance. Good breeding, a good position, someone who might appreciate a wife with a private income but didn't need it, and would certainly not look down at her for being mostly alone in the world and not wealthy.

Yes, a man like him would do very well, but not him. She wanted Judah for herself. It seemed nothing could change that, not even a proposal from a titled gentleman. The question was, would Judah give her a second chance? It seemed more likely that he would want her as a mistress, now that she'd shown herself to be of low morals. No man in Society ever thought he had to propose to a Cross girl just because he'd enjoyed her favors. Being a Cross girl meant you were compromised from birth.

She stared into the tea leaves at the bottom of her cup, wishing she could read them to get some hint of her future. Of course, this would work better if she believed in fortune-telling. With a shake of the head, she pushed back her chair, ready to leave the warm kitchen to tend her brothers.

Hetty rushed in. "There is a boy here to see you."

"A boy?" Magdalene followed the maid into the hall, to find Eddy Jackson waiting inside the door. "Eddy! How did you find me?"

"The captain's valet knew your direction."

"Are you here for a chat?" She wondered why he had come. Had Judah become ill?

He took her proffered hand. "I came to say good-bye."

"Good-bye? Is the captain taking you to Heathfield for Christmas?"

"I don't know where that is," Eddy said, jamming his hands into his coat pockets. His wrists did not appear to be as bony as they had, nor his neck as thin. "I've found a job away from this part of Town."

She noticed his Cockney speech had been smoothed out in the past few weeks. This new tutor was performing his job well. She suspected his visit here was a cry for help, rather than a real good-bye. "Are you running away from the captain's house? Come into the kitchen. I think we still have some raisin buns left."

"Take your coat off first," Hetty said impatiently. "It's dripping."

Eddy pulled off his heavy coat and cap, both new. Magdalene knew Judah had cared for the boy with as much coin as he might have spent on a son of his own. She led him into the kitchen and poured him a cup of tea while Hetty slapped buns onto a plate and put them in front of him.

Magdalene suspected the maid had hoped to toast them for her own tea. "How is the captain? He called two days ago."

"I haven't seen him since breakfast. He went to Redcake's." Eddy inhaled the bun as if he'd had no breakfast.

"You have been working on your speech. I believe your vocabulary has improved."

"That tutor 'as me reading these books. Long books."

"You are used to short newspaper articles," Magdalene agreed. "But do you really want to go back and work in the cold? Perhaps you should stay until spring, at least. You are well fed and clothed."

"I don't want the captain to get attached to me, like," Eddy said. "I 'ave me a 'eart. 'e's a sad fellow, and I don't want to 'urt 'im more."

"Why is he sad?"

Eddy shrugged. "Maybe because 'e's all alone in a big city? Because 'is mother died? I don't know."

Maybe because the woman he loved rejected him. "I never thought him sad."

"You don't have to live with 'im. 'e's very reserved. 'ardly laughs at me jokes anymore."

Poor man. "It might be kinder to stay for a bit. You don't want your benefactor in the depths of melancholia."

"It's quiet and boring in 'is 'ouse!" Eddy pushed back his chair. "I like a bit of action and noise about. I like doing things with me 'ands. I can't even whittle because Penny doesn't like the shavings about."

A banging on the front door commenced. Hetty rushed into the hallway and was soon back with Captain Shield, followed by Lewis Noble.

Magdalene could not keep the smile from radiating across her face. Eddy, on the other hand, went into a slump, staring down at the table.

"Mr. Farmer came to me, saying this young man had given his tutor the slip." Judah frowned down at Eddy.

"You shouldn't 'ave left work, guv. You're busy," Eddy mumbled.

"I was concerned," Judah said. "Mr. Noble brought me in his steam car since he had just pulled up at the loading dock at Redcake's. It was a fast ride. Have you been here all this time?"

"Only for a few minutes," Magdalene said.

"I went around to the shops, to see if I could get a job. I start next week at a shop, fetching and delivering their paper subscriptions." Eddy puffed out his bantam chest.

"That does not sound like a step forward," the captain said. "Why would you want to do that?"

"He wants a more active life," Magdalene said. "He claims not to be made for quiet scholarship."

"Why don't you stay with me?" Lewis Noble suggested with a glance at Judah. "I could use another set of hands in my machine shop."

"I want to give the lad an education," Judah said. "He is an intelligent, likeable boy."

"The captain treats him like a son," Magdalene said. But she felt Eddy was far too independent, and had been on his own far too long, to want to be a son.

"I just need a bed and an interesting job," Eddy said. "I would happily work in a machine shop."

"Don't you want to learn mathematics, Eddy?" Judah asked. "And history and politics?"

"I don't need education for education's sake," Eddy said. "I can learn all that I want from the papers."

Lewis put his hand on the boy's shoulder. "I can teach him the math he needs for machinery. There is a great deal to learn. It is not a job one can do without any training."

"Are you offering him an apprenticeship of sorts?" Judah asked.

Lewis nodded. "There is a little room off the shop he can sleep in. I'll pay for his food and clothing, plus a bit of pocket money if he proves himself useful."

"At least he'll be indoors," Magdalene said, wishing Judah didn't look so troubled. He obviously wanted the boy to stay with him. He was a protector, a good honorable man who wanted to care for anyone he took under his wing. Like her. He had liked her so he offered her a job, then had fallen in love with her so he offered her marriage. She had thought, like Eddy, that the life he envisioned was not the one she wanted. But now, she could see what Eddy was throwing away and she wished he would not.

Judah cleared his throat. "You will always have a home with me if you need it, Eddy. But I must say Mr. Noble has excellent skills and unique inventions."

Magdalene was touched by his willingness to let Eddy go, despite his feelings. He was a good man.

"We will still be friends?" Eddy said, pushing back from the table and walking over to Judah. "And you'll give Mr. Farmer a reference? 'e's not a bad'un, just isn't for me."

"Of course," Judah said.

"Why don't I take him home to pack?" Lewis suggested. "You had half a dozen crises brewing when you left."

"I want to break the news to Mr. Farmer myself," Judah said. "Do you think you can take Eddy to your shop now, and I'll send his things over tonight?"

"Of course," Lewis said. "Do you want to ride in a steam-powered carriage, my boy?"

Eddy grinned. "Yes, guv, I do."

Judah inclined his head to Magdalene. "I apologize for disturbing your morning. How is Manfred?"

"He is sleeping comfortably. His fever is gone completely, but George has a touch of it now. He slept on a pallet next to Manfred's bed all those nights I was gone, so he was bound to feel the effects of the illness himself."

"I sincerely hope you do not succumb as well," Judah said. "May I call on you tomorrow evening to check on you?"

"You need to come back today," Eddy said. "I ate all of 'er raisin buns."

"Tonight then," Judah said. "With a hamper from the bakery."

She nodded quickly, wondering if he would pose his question to her again. The idea of a proposal from him now excited her, while the one from the baronet had filled her with dread. A fashionable life was all very well, but she'd rather have a busy life in the upper tradesman classes with a man who loved her, than a lonely life in high Society with a near stranger. Judah cared for the happiness of those he loved. She could not doubt it.

Chapter Twenty

Mondays were usually busy days, but Judah had not calculated in the added complications of a defected ward, terminating the employment of a tutor, packing and delivering belongings, and calling on a lover with a hamper of raisin buns. So it was with some trepidation that he sat down to his dinner before he left home to deliver the belongings and buns.

"Your post, Captain," said Penny, dropping a pile of envelopes next to his plate.

Normally, he would read them in front of the fire after he supped, discarding all the invitations that came despite his unsociability in the fall. But still the invitations came, and more besides, as the men from his club added him to their social world. He saw one from Lord and Lady Mews that he would normally discard, but that was Magdalene's social circle. The invitation was for a pre-Christmas gathering. For the sake of seeing her he would accept.

Next he found a letter posted from Heathfield. When he opened it, he recognized his brother's confident scrawl.

> *Judah, I know the question of your birth has continued to trouble you. I would rather withhold this communication from the former servant I contacted for you, as it does no credit to any of the involved parties, including*

> *you, me, and our sister, but I understand you will be happier knowing. Be assured of our love and devotion. In fact, after reading this letter, I do hope you will reconsider using your title for the family's sake, and for the sake of your future wife, whether you link yourself to the Cross family, the Courtnay family, or someone as yet unnoticed.*

Judah stared down at the folded papers Hatbrook had included. He could see through the top page to large, blotchy letters. Tears perhaps? Or a hand unused to a pen? Taking a moment to prepare himself, he stepped to his bar table, which had been moved into the parlor. Slowly, he poured a finger of Drambuie into a glass, savoring the uncertainty of the last moment before he discovered who his father had been. He stared into the fire and sipped the drink. Then, he returned to his chair and the letter.

> *Dear Lord Judah, I do not know if you remember me, but I am John Dewey, who was the underbutler at Hatbrook Farm when you were a lad. The marquess has been visiting those of us former servants who retired in Sussex, inquiring into your parents' lives. The matter is a delicate one, but he gave me your note, and assures me you do desire this information that I set before you.*
>
> *My lady, your mother, was sorely mistreated by your father, who was absent for long periods of time once his nursery began to fill. She leaned heavily on Robert Harmony, who was my superior and the butler to the family, as well as a distant cousin to the Shields. I believe they had an intimate connection. Two of the reasons I believe I am correct are this: After you were born, Mr. Harmony held his position for one more year. When the marquess made his appearance on the estate, the first one since your birth, he and the butler had a loud altercation, after which Mr. Harmony was turned out without a reference. This is not the way any family treats an esteemed, well-liked, and efficient higher servant, so something untoward must have occurred between him and the marquess. Shortly after, your mother was terribly ill and kept*

to her rooms for weeks. I believe she suffered the loss of another child, perhaps because of her husband's bodily mistreatment of her.

Judah put down the letter, sickened by the story. Had the late marquess beaten his mother when he discovered the truth? He could not focus on that terrible thought for long. His blood heated with interest about this Mr. Harmony and his fate after leaving the Farm.

That is the first proof I offer, Lord Judah. The second is this: I had never seen eyes so unusual as Mr. Harmony's, until I saw them in your own face. Tiger eyes, I believe the maids called them, for the striations of amber and brown were as pretty as the gemstone that carries that name. This is not a proof, but he shared your interest in military matters as well. Mr. Harmony joined the army after he was let go. He was ultimately sent to Ireland, where he died in 1870. A relatively young man, but there was illness in the camp. I believe he is buried there.

I do hope you forgive the impertinence of this communication, but if it is any comfort to you, I remember one more thing. You loved to crawl along the checkerboard pattern in the front hall, and when you learned to stand you would often hold on to the table in the front hall. It was there you took your first halting steps, and it was Mr. Harmony who held your hand. It was he to whom you walked. I witnessed the moment myself. Unfortunately, so did the marquess, coming in from a shoot, and I believe that was Mr. Harmony's undoing. Your servant, John Dewey.

Judah set the letter down and drained his glass. After a moment, he chuckled aloud. Having read this astonishing communication, his brother wished him to become Lord Judah Shield again? He should be plain Judah Harmony. Yet, all involved were dead, the mystery was solved, and his brother wanted no chink in the family armor. At least Robert Harmony had been a relation. His brother's heir would arrive in the spring, his sister had just made her debut, and his brother knew he contemplated marriage. The fact that he didn't make a complaint of his affection for Magdalene was a statement in itself. He could have her with nary a word of mistreatment by Hatbrook if he stepped into line.

And Magdalene? She would say yes far more easily to Lord Judah than Captain Shield. He knew this for a truth. But had he been Captain Shield too long to make the switch in her eyes?

The clock downstairs told him it was seven p.m., and he still had to make his calls. He opened the parlor door and yelled down the hall for Lawrence to order him a hansom and load in the baggage.

An hour later he had delivered Eddy's box and a Christmas cake to Lewis Noble. Mindful of the time, he had refused a slice of the cake and returned to the hansom, promising he would visit again later in the week. At eight p.m., the hansom came to a stop in front of the Cross home. Though heavy curtains protected the ground floor, he could see lights on the first floor. Magdalene must still be expecting him.

He climbed the steps, to which clung tiny particles of sand in the hopes of forestalling ice, and knocked. Hetty peered out a few minutes later.

Judah held up his hamper. "Raisin bun delivery."

Hetty took the hamper from his hand. "Thank you very much, I'm sure. Good evening to you, Captain." She began to close the door.

He heard footsteps on the stairs behind the maid.

"Hetty! Is that Captain Shield? Invite him in, please."

Hetty shrugged. "You didn't say you wanted to come in. I'll fetch a tea tray."

Magdalene's cheeks were pink. "I assumed you wanted to call. Was I wrong?"

"No," Judah assured her. "I have something to show you."

"Oh? I have a fire lit in the parlor."

"Thank you." He took off his coat and hat and handed them to her.

After she had placed them on pegs, she opened the parlor door and walked in. He followed, enjoying the movement of her hips, though he did wonder why she wore her cakie uniform instead of a more fashionable garment.

She blushed when she turned and saw him staring at her, then looked down. "Oh, you've caught me wearing this again. It is so comfortable for nursing."

"I believe my brother found it difficult to persuade his wife to give up her uniform," Judah said.

"Yes, they are such practical dresses. Well, I shall not bore you with garment concerns. What did you want to show me?" She sat on a sofa.

Her expression seemed so welcoming, with none of the reserve she had exhibited on his two previous visits. While he knew showing her the letter might finally end their relationship for good, she had offered him the ultimate intimacy and even for a Scandalous Cross girl, that had to mean something.

Without making a pretense of polite behavior, he sat down next to her on the sofa. "I want you to know that I have decided to resume my courtesy title and leave my military one behind."

"Oh?" She folded her hands and placed them in her lap.

"Yes. My brother thinks it would be best, and I believe it would make him happy, despite everything."

"Everything? I did not know you had a quarrel."

"We did not. But we are trying to support each other's happiness." He pulled the letter his brother had sent from his jacket. "Before I trouble you with this, I should ask what your intentions are regarding Yorkshire and the baronet."

"It has become very clear to me that I prefer London," she said, staring at her hands.

"And the baronet?"

"I saw him every day for more than two weeks, and did not feel I knew him at all. I confess I am more excited by the return to London of my friend, Constance Lively, than by the thought of a marriage with the baronet."

"I am sorry you went to all that trouble."

"Was I foolish to go?" she asked.

He wanted to say yes, but she had to pursue what she thought was best for herself. Just as he had when he had persisted in wanting to know his true parentage, whether or not it hurt his family. They had both been on a quest of sorts and neither had found anything that made them happy.

"At least you learned a truth about yourself."

She smiled. "Yes, I did. It is good to know what it takes to make one happy."

He handed her the letter. "This cannot be said to make me happy on most any level, but it is a truth."

"It is good the writing is large, or I would not be able to read it without additional light," she remarked, opening the pages.

She read in silence for several minutes. Hetty came in with the tray, but they both ignored it. Magdalene shook her head several times. Judah resisted the urge to pace and simply watched her read.

When she was done, tears stood in her eyes. "What a touching scene. I am so glad you had a little time with him, even though you do not remember. I am sure it comforted him."

"If he loved me, wouldn't he have remained in the area?"

"Your father might have threatened him, and he probably couldn't have found work. Maybe he didn't realize the army would send him away."

"Or he wanted to go. The person I feel most sorry for is my mother."

"Yes, you might have had a full-blood sibling."

"Probably not without scandal. As it was they kept the secret inside the family for their entire lives."

"I wish your mother had never told you," she said, handing the papers back.

He folded them back into his coat. "Since people obviously knew, it might have been kinder that she did reveal it to me. I could have run into this Mr. Dewey at any time, or one of those maids. It was better to find out in India, even if it put me into a rage at the time."

"You do have unusually beautiful eyes," she said. "So someone might have remarked on them. But I cannot imagine you in a rage. You seem so even tempered."

He bowed his head at the compliment. But then, when he heard the rest of her statement, he looked up again. "I contain my emotions well. No one ever cared about them, so I kept it all inside."

"I care," Magdalene said.

"Yet you trampled on my feelings, when you refused my suit."

"Not without a care," she demurred. "I was so focused on my plans for myself. I am sorry I hurt you. A good man like you does not deserve to be ill used."

"Then you agree I am ill-used?"

She hesitated. "As am I. You did not renew your suit after certain recent events took place."

He cleared his throat. "Am I to understand you would wish it to be renewed?"

She turned to him, pulling her interlaced fingers to her bosom, but she didn't speak.

"I see," he said, his heart breaking. "I wish it was otherwise, but I do respect your desires. Perhaps you are hoping to return to your position at Redcake's? I can promise you would be welcome there, and there would be no trouble about your brief departure."

"I want you," she whispered. "I do not know how to say it without sounding an utter and complete wanton."

With hope returning, he said the first thing that popped into his mind. "I like you as an utter and complete wanton."

She blushed. "I know."

"You want to go on as we did in Doncaster?" he asked carefully. "In your brother's house?"

"No, in yours!"

"I cannot have a mistress in residence."

She gestured to him. "You could if she was your wife. Perhaps a wife who decorated cakes at Redcake's during the busy season?"

He grinned. "Then you will marry me?" Was she sneaking glances at his trousers?

"Can we be utterly scandalous in private, as scandalous as we are proper in public?"

"For a Scandalous Cross, I doubt anything could be more likely."

"I shall do my best to be a proper tradesman's wife. And ensure that your family approves of me."

"And a Society wife," Judah said. "Fully accepted by my brother. Do you know, I already sent a note accepting my first engagement as Lord Judah? To Lady Mews, for next week."

"Is this the life you want? Truly?" Her eyes widened.

"My scandal is private, and my scandalous life will be private, and I see no harm showing off my beautiful wife in the latest fashion from time to time. As long as I have the energy to get up for work in the morning."

She laughed. "There will not be a party that will prevent you from getting up in the morning." In her light stays and cakie dress, it was all too easy to come up on her knees, and deposit herself on Judah's lap.

"Ah, Lady Scandalous," he said, wrapping his arms around her. "What a way to spend a cold winter evening."

"And morning. I resolve to make you late every delicious morning."

He kissed her brow, then her upturned mouth, before placing his lips on a path farther south.

"We should lock the door," she murmured, letting her head drop to his shoulder, and her fingers drift down his chest.

"There is always a little risk when you're scandalous," he said, putting his fingers to the first button at her throat.

She only smiled as he unbuttoned her dress, then captured her arms behind her in the fabric. Laughter came as he loosed her stays and pulled up her chemise, teasing her belly with his tongue. Then laughter turned to sighs as his teasing went lower. He slipped a hand in the opening of her drawers, then when she moved against his hand, he pulled the fabric down and cast it off.

Then, she was on her knees, helping him unbutton his own clothing and free his jutting erection. She took it in her warm fingers and guided him to that hot, moist depth between her legs.

"You are a scandal," he whispered, as he thrust home.

"I am at peace with that." Her arms entwined around his back.

"Mmmm, so am I." He thrust again, enjoying the luxury of her satiny smooth legs rubbing sensuously up and down his calves. Underneath her, he could feel the springs and coarse fabric of the sofa and he rolled, pulling her on top of him so that he would take the brunt of the old furnishing.

He could not wait until he had her like this in the spacious yet snug house he would buy for her. What fun it would be to share the truth of his wealth with her. Yet, it hardly bore consideration, because this moment, on a threadbare sofa in her brother's home, was perfect in and of itself.

Magdalene gasped as the changed position sent him deeper into her channel, then tossed her head back in delight as her body began to learn the special pleasures of controlling speed and depth.

He had found his way home, not just in London, as he'd expected, as a returning soldier hungry for Mother England, but in this newly scandalous lady's warm arms. Not for him would be the tragic marriage of the late Marquess and Marchioness of Hatbrook, or the lonely end of Robert Harmony. His mother had done him a great favor by telling him the truth. She had set him free to find his own path.

His discovery? The journey, and it had been a long one, led to Magdalene. A journey home always would.

Also available!

credit: Syneca Featherstone

About the Author

Heather Hiestand was born in Illinois but her family migrated west before she started school. Since then she has claimed Washington State as home, except for a few years in California. She wrote her first story at age seven and went on to major in creative writing at the University of Washington. Her first published fiction was a mystery short story, but since then it has been all about the many flavors of romance. Heather's first published romance short story was set in the Victorian period and she continues to return, fascinated by the rapid changes of the nineteenth century. The author of many novels, novellas, and short stories, she has achieved bestseller status on Amazon's Romance Anthologies list and on Amazon UK's Romance Short Stories list. The first Redcakes novel, *The Marquess of Cake*, appeared on the Historical Romance Bestseller lists at Amazon and Barnes & Noble. With her husband and son, she makes her home in a small town and supposedly works out of her tiny office, though she mostly writes in her easy chair in the living room.

For more information, visit Heather's Web site at www.heatherhiestand.com. Heather loves to hear from readers! Her email is heather@heatherhiestand.com.

www.ingramcontent.com/pod-product-compliance
Lightning Source LLC
LaVergne TN
LVHW091038080826
845145LV00002B/540

* 9 7 8 1 6 0 1 8 3 1 3 8 5 *